CALLSIGN WHISKEY

LA CLARKE

BALBOA.
PRESS
A DIVISION OF HAY HOUSE

Balboa Press books may be ordered through booksellers or by contacting:

Balboa Press
A Division of Hay House
1663 Liberty Drive
Bloomington, IN 47403
www.balboapress.com
1 (877) 407-4847

Because of the dynamic nature of the Internet, any web addresses or links contained in this book may have changed since publication and may no longer be valid. The views expressed in this work are solely those of the author and do not necessarily reflect the views of the publisher, and the publisher hereby disclaims any responsibility for them.

The author of this book does not dispense medical advice or prescribe the use of any technique as a form of treatment for physical, emotional, or medical problems without the advice of a physician, either directly or indirectly. The intent of the author is only to offer information of a general nature to help you in your quest for emotional and spiritual well-being. In the event you use any of the information in this book for yourself, which is your constitutional right, the author and the publisher assume no responsibility for your actions.

Any people depicted in stock imagery provided by Thinkstock are models, and such images are being used for illustrative purposes only.
Certain stock imagery © Thinkstock.

Printed in the United States of America.

ISBN: 978-1-4525-9168-1 (sc)
ISBN: 978-1-4525-9170-4 (hc)
ISBN: 978-1-4525-9169-8 (e)

Library of Congress Control Number: 2014901983

Balboa Press rev. date: 02/24/2014

*For Rob and Daddy, who taught me truth,
courage and humility*

GLOSSARY

AGC	–	Adjutant General Corps providing all administrative support across the Army
Artillery	–	The Royal Artillery responsible for all large weapons and guns providing artillery support to Infantry and those deployed further forward facing any threat. Nicknamed Gunners
Basher	–	Camouflage poncho suspended across the shell scrape as both cover and disguise.
Bergens	–	Heavy duty rucksacks
Callsign	–	Allocated name and number as a unique identifier on radio
Capbadge	–	Insignia on a beret that indicates the Regiment or Corps. Capbadge is shorthand for the Unit in which serving personnel belong.
Cam cream	–	Camouflage cream smeared on face to reduce visibility.
Casevac Rep	–	Casualty Evacuation Report
CAT A	–	Category Alpha, the most serious injury category, life threatening, requiring immediate treatment.
CAT 1	–	Most serious injury in triage requiring immediate priority
CAT 2	–	Serious injury requiring urgent attention
CAT 3	–	Walking wounded

CLP	-	Combat Logistic Patrols, convoys taking supplies to any location, with personnel providing on board armed protection.
CO	-	Commanding Officer, usually a Lieutenant Colonel in charge of a Battalion
Company Sergeant Major (CSM)	-	Most Senior Warrant Officer within a formed Unit
CNO	-	Casualty Notification Officer, the first representative from an injured personnel's Unit to inform next of kin.
CVO	-	Casualty Visitation Officer, takes over from the CNO as the liaison Officer who guides families through an injury or death.
Det	-	Detachment
DFAC	-	Dining Facility
DS	-	Directing Staff
ETA	-	Estimated Time of Arrival
ETS	-	Educational Training Staff, the Educational arm of the AGC
Ex	-	Exercise, a Training programme outdoors, where troops train in manoeuvres and skills
Final Exercise	-	The last most demanding Exercise of the Commissioning course, that needs to be passed to commission.
FOB	-	Forward Operating Base. A larger HQ outpost that provides support and direction to troops
FORM Cycle	-	Force Operations and Readiness Mechanism, a 4 phase approach to sustainability of Army Units readiness for operations, incorporating high readiness, training deployment and recuperation elements.
G1	-	Category that indicates welfare and administrative support in the Army

GPMG	-	General Purpose Machine Gun
Harbour	-	Collective resting area for a group of troops
HERRICK	-	Operational title for UK Forces in Afghanistan
H-Hr	-	The specific hour at which any Operation commences, also called Zero hour
IED	-	Improvised Explosive Device
Int	-	Intelligence
ISAF	-	International Security Assistance Force
ISTAR	-	Intelligence Surveillance Target Acquisition Reconnaissance
INT CORPS	-	Intelligence Corps, provide classified intelligence support to all Commanding Elements on any threat to GB or Allied Forces. Nicknamed Green Slime
J2	-	Intelligence on Operations
JNCO	-	Junior Non Commissioned Officer, a soldier in the rank above private holding the first rank of command beneath Sergeant (and are therefore not saluted)
KAF	-	Kandahar Airfield
Medevac	-	Medical Evacuation process.
Medical Discharge	-	Released from the Army owing to a medical condition preventing full physical fitness required for active service.
MERT	-	Medical Emergency Reaction Team
MIA	-	Missing In Action
Nav Ex	-	Orienteering Exercise specifically to test map reading
ND	-	Negligent Discharge, a round accidently fired which is a punishable offence in the Forces
Norwegian	-	Hot food and drink container

Nyrex	–	Waterproofed notebook, containing aide memories for tactics.
OMLT	–	Operational Mentor and Liaison Team. Group embedded with Afghan Forces to train and guide.
Ops Officer	–	Operations Officer who oversees activity/action on the ground
Opsec	–	Operational Security, procedures enforced to protect safety and contain information and reduce the physical signs of troops on the ground.
Patrol Base (PB)	–	Small outstation where teeth arm (infantry) are based to protect key terrain
Phys	–	Slang for Physical Training (PT)
PJHQ	–	Permanent Joint Headquarters, UK Head of Operations for all Military services globally.
Platoon	–	Band of soldiers, comprising 3 sections normally of 9-10 pax each.
POTL	–	Post Operational Tour Leave, leave/holiday that is given to serving personnel after a deployment, usually 4 weeks of recuperation
PVR	–	Premature Voluntary Release, resigning commission or as a soldier resigning from the Army.
Ranges	–	An outdoor shooting range
RPG	–	Rocket propelled grenades
RLC	–	Royal Logistic Corps, responsible for all of the Logistical support in the Army (post, food, rations, ammunition and any kit) nicknamed Loggies

RMP	–	Royal Military Police, responsible for enforcing Military Law within the Army, nicknamed Redcaps
Rumint	–	Rumour Intelligence
RV	–	Rendezvous Point
Sandhurst	–	Shorthand for The Royal Military Academy Sandhurst where Officers are trained in Military Leadership and after a 44 week course earn the Queen's Commission, they are therefore saluted by JNCOs and SNCOs in recognition of service to the Queen.
Shell scrape	–	Shallow ditch dug by soldiers to provide better camouflage and protection to sleep in.
SIB	–	Special Investigation Branch (of the RMP).
SIGNALS	–	The Royal Signals Corps responsible for all electronic or otherwise communications
SLAM	–	Single living accommodation modernisation
SNCO	–	Senior Non Commissioned Officer, a soldier Sergeant and above who has not been through Sandhurst and commissioned as an Officer, but still holds a Command rank (and are not therefore saluted)
SPS	–	Staff and Personnel Support Branch of the AGC providing Payroll and specialize administrative support, part of the AGC
Stag	–	Slang for being on sentry, or on guard watching for any threats
Staff	–	Shorthand for Staff Sergeant
Theatre	–	Term for any country where there is a UK Active Military presence.
Tour	–	A 6 -9 month deployment in an active Operational Theatre
U/S	–	Unserviceable

Warrant Officer	–	The next rank above SNCO, WO2 is Class 2 also called Sergeant Major and WO1 is Warrant Officer Class 1, the most senior rank for a soldier in the Army.
WatchKeeper	–	Radio Operator in the Operations HQ
Webbing	–	Slang for Soldiers combat equipment, either worn as a chest rig or more traditionally slung over shoulders and around the waist.
Y-Listed	–	Term for the rehabilitation or recovery element of the Army when any personnel are suspended from active duty to recover
Zap Number	–	Unique identifier number given to all personnel when they go into an Operational Theatre
OC	–	Officer Commanding
2iC	–	Second in Command
OiC	–	Officer in Command

1

THE RADIO CRACKLED, rendering the voice almost indecipherable, then loud, clear,

"Contact! Wait out!"

Banter stopped, the Ops room froze, faces etched with concentration and apprehension. Firefight, where? The Spring offensive by the Taleban had failed spectacularly to materialize. Instead ISAF forces and enemy alike had sweltered in the unyielding sun, heat sucking up moisture, drying the saliva in mouths. Both sides rendered exhausted by temperatures that could burn feet on metal, fry an egg on a land rover bonnet.

"Casevac rep."

The Watchkeeper flashed a look at the Ops Officer. Captain Sam Walton's eyes widened, cheeks hollowed by a diet of dust, coffee and cigarettes, an altogether more appealing option than the daily meals of sausage and beans. For the love of God who issued rations of sausage and beans in 50 degree heat anyway? Imperceptibly he nodded, the junior officer, fresh out of Sandhurst grabbed his pencil. As the Lieutenant he needed to capture this radio message, needed to get it right. First time.

"Call sign Romeo Romeo Charlie Patrol Base SANGHOLE..."

The where.

"0950zulu..."

The when.

"Zap number Whiskey10567290, Zap number Whiskey10567293."

The who.

Mouths dropped. Despite the spatter of GPMG, the whoosh of RPGs the Platoon Commander continued his report of an attack unphased. Whiskey meant a woman. It caught the attention. Whether that was wrong or right was beside the point. The point was there were only three women in that location.

Tom Fellows, the ISTAR lead snapped round, scanning Sam's face for the same realization. Eyes locked, Sam blinked, peering out to the heli pad adjacent to the sweaty Headquarters. The Whop, Whop, Whop, of propellers firing up; the Medical Emergency Reaction Team already on alert. The Ops team waited.

"Cat 1."

Sam felt the blood drain from his face. Tom made to speak, saw the hardening of Sam's jaw and stopped. The radio crackled again, irritated tutts permeating the air, frustration at the intermittent signal, annoyance at a distraction.

"Over?"

The young Platoon Commander waited for an answer. MERT were there first.

"Roger that Romeo Romeo Charlie. This is MERT wheels up in 1 minute. ETA at your location, figures zero five minutes. Over?"

"Roger that, out."

The heli's engine blasted hot dust into the Ops room, scattering papers and fag ash, moving around the fetid air, the stench of sweat, of stale coffee. The noise shook the corrimec's walls, rising to a crescendo, until it was above them and gone, leaving behind a small dust devil dancing a circle, collapsing in on itself, as if defeated by the heat.

Silence reigned. The Watchkeeper looked over at an ashen faced Sam. Something was wrong, they'd had these casreps before, why was the Ops Officer so still?

"Paul send the signal to PJHQ now. NOW!"

He strode out, throwing open the door, allowing a dust cloud to pile in, the heat to surge over them, and still no one said a word.

Paul swallowed hard. Christ wasn't CAT 1? Wasn't that multiple limb loss? He wished he'd paid more attention back in the Royal Academy, snoozed less, written more.

"Errm Tom?"

He saw how Tom had made to go out after Sam, how everyone seemed to be acting in slow motion. What the hell was going on?

"Paul? You happy with the signal?"

"I...I'm sorry Tom but CAT 1?"

Tom knew eyes were on him, that despite heads bowed, Senior Non Commissioned Officers, SNCOs and Junior Non Commissioned Officers, JNCOS alike, Sergeants and Lance Corporals, focused on the reports being fed in by every other call sign, all of whom would have heard the contact, all of whom would have heard the casualties, they were all listening for him to say what everyone was thinking.

"Cat 1. Most serious category of injury Paul. They've lost limbs. Life threatening. You need to get the signal to PJHQ now. It needs to hit their Units fast, compassionate chain needs to kick in so the CNO can get to the families. Clear?"

"Clear."

Paul began typing. The format engrained on his mind. CNO. Jesus. Some poor bastard back home was going to have the worst working day of his life shortly. As Casualty Notification Officer he would have to break the news every family dreaded, every soldier feared. He sped up his typing.

2

CAPTAIN DAN GREY was pouring himself a very large Glen Fiddich. He could not believe he was finally here, at Rachel's, two weeks leave, about to have the first alcoholic drink in 2 months. He was shattered, but so relieved to be finally out of uniform, in civvies, in the flat, not theirs, Rachel's, but hopefully soon, he'd move in too. He looked up, seeing her stirring ragu, long auburn hair twisted up casually, tendrils hanging loosely, framing the nape of her neck. Apron, wrapped tightly around her tiny waist. He smiled, felt the heavy knots of stress, exhaustion slowly loosen in his shoulders and he knew he was making the right decision. Slumping onto the sofa his mind drifted back to Lucas and the conversation in the Mess. Dan had been in a hurry, he wanted to avoid the M25 and Rachel had said supper would be on for 7 with the implication hanging in the air. Don't be late, not this time, not again.

"So, thank fuck that is over. I am gonna get so right royally hammered in London I cannot tell you."

Lucas had raked a hand through hair well overdue a wash. Their faces still stained with cam cream despite brillo-like scrubbing in showers. Flushed, Dan looked up from writing in the warning in/out book. He was going to be out of this bloody accommodation for a full fortnight. He couldn't remember the last time he'd had leave, the tempo had been relentless, and today Dan had realized unsustainable.

"You enjoy mate, I'm off."

"You all right Dan? Bit quiet?"

Dan's face creased in irritation,

"You serious Lucas? We've just been on fucking exercise for a month, eating bloody midges in the arse end of Scotland and that's after we got back from HellHole Helmand only 7 months ago. Post Op Tour Leave didn't happen because of manning shortages and I've let Rachel down so many times it's a bloody joke. There's supposed to be something called Harmony guidelines remember? The FORM cycle? Sound familiar? Y'know the principle of Train Deploy Rest Recover? Sound like something we are meant to implement with our guys? And we do, don't we? Every friggin' Officer here checks that their blokes and girls get leave, gets away, that their families are kept informed, that the Chain of Command has the detail they need. But what about us? Who the fuck has our backs? Because it sure as hell isn't our Chain of command, it isn't the Brigade Commander and it isn't bloody PJHQ. Nope, those fuckers are only interested in furthering their careers off the backs of poor bastards like us at the bottom of the food chain. I am fed-the fuck up with being treated like a bloody mushroom. Fed shit and kept in the dark, by people who probably don't even know what a PB is or have never set foot in a Forward Operating Base. This bloody war costs too much, this job is not a job- it's our lives. You can't have a life outside of the Army because the fucking Army demands your life IS the Army."

Dan paused, the tirade leaving his face red, brow furrowed with fatigue and fury. Lucas looked sheepish.

"Hey, I'm sorry, I..."

"No...,"

Dan shook his head, embarrassed. He was a private guy. He just needed to get home, he just needed to see Rachel, assuming she'd let him. Even that seemed in question now.

"...things are tense with Rachel. She's amazing, but even for her, the endless separation, the constant fastballs and letting her down. Well it's too much for anyone and it's turning the word relationship where we're concerned into a flipping joke. Do you know I've seen her 4 days and nights in the last 9 months? It's...well...I've had enough..."

The statement hung there between them, Lucas's mouth twitched, unsure.

"Are you saying? I mean are you...?"

"Going to Sign off? Yep. I want to talk to Rach about it, timings and all that. But come back from leave and our holiday, I'm taking her to Malta as a surprise for a week. Well once back it's me and PVR."

Premature Voluntary Release. Signing off, resigning your commission. Lucas was disappointed but not surprised. Their peer group were leaving in droves. The Op tempo was brutal and with more people leaving, there were less folk but the same amount of work and now Libya front had opened up and everyone was looking nervously at Syria...

"Mate, I'm, well I'm really sorry, but if it's what you want, then it's the Army's loss. Look I'm sorry, gotta get to the station. Say hi to Rach for me and I hope Malta Rocks. Geddit? Rocks."

Dan watched his friend walk away cackling at his own joke. It was ok for Lucas; he was single and happy to stay like that. He'd made it abundantly clear that he didn't want any ties, no commitment. In a way it was easier. He only had to think of him, no one to let down, no one to echo your frustration or to have to explain why no, he was the only Officer who could do it and he wasn't volunteering. Still, he loved Rachel, he wanted this to work. He'd joined the Military late and meeting Rach had been a small miracle in itself with both of their careers trying to scupper every chance. But make it they had, and whilst she had been astonishingly patient and resilient in the face of his unpredictability and frequent bad news, he knew that her increasingly long silences on the phone were an indicator that she was approaching the end of tether. He didn't want to get to that point.

He lifted the tumbler of amber nectar and wondered if the ragu could wait whilst he and Rach made up for lost time. Then his mobile rang. He slowly lowered his glass.

It wasn't his mobile. It wasn't Rachel's. It was the duty mobile. Rach turned to him grinning holding out a wooden spoon laden with sauce, her face a picture of delight that dissolved,

"Babe?"

He picked up the phone, snapping back the receiver,

"Duty Officer Captain Grey speaking...Right...Oh Right..."

Rachel watched as Dan rubbed the back of his head, the small bald patch a worry point for him. She didn't think he even noticed the habit, such a give away for bad news.

"Right...Ok? What? No just a minute..."

He looked up hurriedly at Rach. Rustling in some drawers she thrust a pencil in his hand and the back of a window-cleaning flier. She watched as he scribbled. It was an address in Cambridge, hours away and it was 7 o'clock at night. Couldn't this wait? What was so damned important? Rachel could feel her temper rising. Biting her lip she watched Dan's face. He wouldn't meet her eye.

"Yep, got it. Yep. Ok. Right. Bye."

He snapped the phone shut. The silence could have been an ocean between them.

Taking a deep breath, he looked at Rach, his eyes those of a broken man.

"I...I've got to go."

"No! No no no! I've had enough! What the hell?? Why?"

Dan wondered if Rach had even noticed she'd stamped her foot.

"For God's sake Dan I haven't seen you in bloody months? This is a joke! I've been patient, I've not pushed, but you've got to *see* someone to actually have a relationship with them!! What the hell is so special that can't wait until tomorrow?!"

It broke Dan's heart seeing her rage, he let her fury fly, took the verbal battering, because he felt he deserved every bitter accusation. He was letting her down. He also felt devastated as his plans for a surprise trip to Malta slipping away. £2,000 he wouldn't get back.

"Babe, please, someone... there's two females. They've been injured, seriously injured in Afghanistan. Both might not make it..."

He paused, his situation aside, this was as bad as it got. He could not believe this was happening.

"I have to go to Cambridge. I have to go now to tell the families, amazingly Unit Int has suggested they may even be together, so I need to check that is true, or I'll have to hunt around for another address which will waste time. There is a slim chance they'll get flown to Sellyoaks. In all likelihood they may not survive the flight, but the trauma surgery and capabilities in Theatre are amazing, better than anything in the UK. So if they stabilize them, well they need to be brought home, so they can say goodbye at least. I…I'm so sorry Rach, please believe me, I'm…"

His throat caught, tears springing. At every turn they were being stymied. Rachel sighed, throwing her arms around him.

"Oh babe, go, just go. It's only crumby ragu, it can wait, I can make it anytime. This is awful, awful. I wish you didn't have to break such God awful news, but whoever the families are, to have you knocking on their door, well I can't think of anyone else I'd rather have to tell me something so dire. I am so proud of you. Now go before I stop being so reasonable."

Dan grinned sheepishly at Rach, cupping her face,

"I love you y'know? Thank you…."

He hesitated, should he tell her? Should he say it now? Would it tempt fate? Sod it.

"Rach?"

He stared into her eyes as if driving the point home,

"I'm leaving the Army, signing off. You are too important to me, you matter more. So I'm going to resign. Just as soon as I've done this…"

Rach gasped, her face reward enough for Dan, her eyes shining with barely disguised delight.

"Really? I mean are you sure? I don't want to push you? You've got to do this for you."

God he was lucky.

"Yes Rach, for you, for us, for me…Now go and pack your bikini because as soon as this is over, we're off to Malta."

He faltered, pulling her down to sit with him, sinking into the creamy cushions, wishing he could relax here forever, wishing this would all go away.

"Rach, I've booked to take you away."

"Wha..?"

He smiled, stroking back a stray hair, using the nub of his thumb to rub off some rogue ragu on her nose.

"I want, wanted and still do, to show you I care, that I appreciate you waiting, tolerating all of this. It's my job that's hurting us and well, you've been amazing."

Rach lowered her eyes, blushing, but equally he was right, that knowing he realized that was important, because she'd begun to worry he didn't.

"So, I promise this is the last thing that will spoil our plans. I've got to go now, and at least you know it's for something properly serious. But as the CNO, I well, my role,"

He swallowed hard, feeling the first jabs of dread,

"Is to just break the news. Sorry, just sounds so callous, but y'know what I mean?"

Nodding emphatically Rach urged him on,

"So then I step back. The Army has learnt through painful practice that the first to break the news becomes the focus of the families' anger. So, as soon as possible I bow out and the CVO, Casualty Visitation Officer, well he takes the family through it all. Arguably that's much bloody harder, because you hold their hand through the whole horrific process, bad and good news alike, whilst I can just go, but at least the CVO isn't actively loathed on sight. So, this should take a day or two at max and then I'm back. Back here with you and if you'll let me, I'd like to sweep you off your feet."

Rach bit her lip, relief washing over her.

"Thank God babe, I…I wasn't sure if I could really take much more. I'm sorry…," she lowered her head again, "but I just don't think I'm cut out to be a military partner, it's just…you guys, what's asked…it's, well I'm just not up to it. I'm sorry."

Dan was surprised at the stab of disappointment that sliced through his stomach. Rach was right, he had to make this decision for him, not her but maybe latently he'd hoped? It was irrelevant now. The decision was made, this disappointment was a small price to pay, and the knowledge that he wouldn't have to sweat his arse off in some hovel in Afghanistan was an additional prize; whilst the family he was about to meet would have no such consolation.

"Look, I've got to go. Save me some ragu?"

He managed a smile raising Rach's spirits.

"Course, you drive safe babe and well, text me? Call if you can? Good…good luck Dan, I can't imagine what it will be like… But I think you're amazing."

Dan nodded thankfully, but thinking he wasn't amazing, the girls who'd been blown apart and whose families he was about to destroy, they were amazing.

3

CRAWLING THROUGH THE smart Cambridge suburbs, Dan cursed his satnav. It was pissing it down. The GPS had said the house was here on the right, or the right that was about 100 metres ago. Christ this was bad enough without getting bloody lost. Then he saw it, number 18. A rush of adrenaline made him desperate for the loo. Deep breaths, remember the training, the course that now seemed all too long ago and all too inadequate.

"Keep to the facts...,"

He heard the Warrant Officer's voice as if yesterday.

"Say only that which you know and Do. Not. Deviate. They will ask for all sorts of detail. You don't have it. Simple. That's the CVO's job. I'm sorry Gents, but you are bad cop here, good cop will come in and provide any developments. You as Casualty Notification Officer, CNO, will be the butt of their hatred. So make sure you are prepared. Don't go needing the toilet. The last thing you want to be asking is if you can have a piss when they want you out of their sight. Be prepared for violence, for shock, for hysteria, for behaviour that will be frankly bizarre. You will have just ruined their lives, so people do funny things. Be under no illusions ladies and gents, this is the worst job out there and it doesn't get any easier. If it did, there'd be something wrong with you..."

Turning the engine off, Dan watched the rain fleck the screen, orange glow of streetlamps giving the evening an eerie tinge. It felt sinister. Did they know? Did the families feel, sense something wrong, like a twin who intuitively feels the hurt of their sibling? Did the mothers have any idea? The brief said both parents were alive and living at this address. But Dan had been warned of variables. One of the casualties had two brothers and a sister. Anyone of whom could be home, Christ it was a Friday night they could have all popped round, who knew? Pulling at his sleeves nervously, Dan checked his watch, turning his mobile to silent. Didn't need a phone interrupting this. He tasted bile in his mouth.

Pushing open the car he was grateful for the spray of rain in his face. It woke him up, cleared his mind, sharpened his thoughts. He walked towards the house, blood roaring in his ears, pushing open the small wrought iron gate squeaking on rusty hinges. Dog barking, he hoped it wasn't vicious. What happened if it went for him sensing he was a threat to the pack? Get a grip.

He reached the front door, wooden with coloured pane glass. Surreally Dan admired it, made a nice change from the UPVC frontages that typified what he'd seen of military accommodation. They had taste. Focus. Licking his lips, his hand shaking, stomach cramping, he pressed the doorbell. The ringing echoed in the house, lights were on, he heard the dim sound of a TV. Voices, feet thumping downstairs, a youngish voice, damn one of the siblings,

"I'll get it!"

He saw them approach, for a second Dan contemplated turning, sprinting down the path. He clenched his fists.

Latch raised, the door opening, momentarily blinding him with hallway lights,

"Can I help you?"

She was tall, blond probably late thirties, pretty with blue trusting eyes and a smile on her face that made Dan's heart sink.

"My name is Captain Dan Grey, I was hoping to speak to Mr and Mrs..."

4

Seven Years Before

THE TRAINING EXERCISE had a nickname, Worst Encounter, because it was. During the next 5 days each male and female would face every discomfort that the Directing Staff could throw at them; the main one being sleep deprivation.

Wide eyed on the four tonners Cadets had fallen silent, each ruminating over the next week, what it would hold, was it as bad as the rumours? Wishing they'd somehow stockpiled sleep. All without exception hoping that the journey to Thetford would last forever. These were precious hours, they should really get their heads down, make the most of the calm before the storm, but adrenaline had different ideas and eyes met filled with anxiety, excitement, uncertainty.

It was the Intermediate term. The basics at the Royal Military Academy had been achieved. Civilian habits of lie-ins, playing X-box and self-interest had been drilled out of the trainee Officers. Survival lay in teamwork, helping each other, looking out for your brother and sister in arm. Fitness was critical, mental strength even more so, you never gave up, you just died trying.

Each Platoon had been hustled out of the vehicles. Quickly forming into familiar units, those already in command appointments fiddled with personal radios and were ushered off by staff to get their orders, leaving their 30 guys or girls, in a herring bone formation, down on one knee, bergens achingly heavy, rifles poised, faces focused. When the orders had come, they were no surprise. Trenches. They were to dig trenches, 3 of them, in their Sections. Half of the Section, roughly 4-6 blokes or girls would disperse outward, assuming the position of all round defence, the remaining elements would start the work of carving a rectangular hole from solid chalky ground. It was going to be back breaking work. It was meant to be.

Sophie chewed her gum, a straggle of chestnut coloured hair hung out from her helmet, tinged green from the camouflage cream raked over her face. Resigned to the next few days she was long past mental tantrums, that had been first term. Nothing phased her now, the ingenious ways to test them still surprised her, but she'd learned that screaming, kicking her kit, challenging the logic were ultimately pointless shenanigans, that achieved nothing but exhaust her. Right now she needed every ounce of energy. She also needed her friends. Head down, lips moving, muttering Welsh expletives, shifting on her knee, the dark auburn mass that was her hair threatening to break free from its tight bun was the easily identifiable Tracey. Percy was less obvious, motionless, head cocked, eyes trained on the horizon, the weight of her Bergen, balanced on a slim back, barely appearing to register just as the frustrated chuntering of her counterparts washed over her too. Sophie smiled softly; Percy was a focused wolf to Tracey's frustrated Labrador.

The allocation of areas with early excitement and competitive bravado colouring the breaking of the ground, had been replaced with restlessness and boredom which in turn became quiet steely resolve as each Cadet chipped away at the unforgiving ground, a steady exhaustion seeping into bones, like an invisible fog, weighing them down and eeking the strength from their muscles. The Directing Staff would emerge from the darkness, shadowy figures ominous, fingers in belts, berets expertly shaped. ColourSergeants, the very best in the Army looked on impassively as young would be Officers, men and women worked aching in the darkness.

It was pitch black, hand in front of your face and not see it kind of black, which made digging, using shovels or pick axes pretty dicey. Pulling out her lighter Sophie flicked her zippo immediately giving herself night blindness. The nicotine and flash of the scene in the trench was reward enough. Digging your own trench was no joke, but seeing Percy bent double, asleep on a shovel, whilst Tracey was slumped in the small step they'd dug into the side for sleep rotations, snoring noiselessly, head flung back, mouth wide open, was amusement badly needed.

Dragging heavily on her cigarette, Sophie dropped the pickaxe and lent against the muddy pit. 36 hours straight. Digging, pick axing, hauling chalk and gravel, they'd managed about a metre in depth, roughly two metres in length, which left a good half a metre to go down and over two metres still to push out. It seemed endless, felt pointless, which it was, unequivocally. They all knew that at the end of this hellish exercise, these holes would be efficiently filled back in with JCB style excavators, making their efforts look laughable and pouring salt into the gaping scars of futility.

Whilst the actual digging of trenches was agonizingly out of date, the process, the labour that went into it, was by far the most ruthlessly effective way to fatigue every muscle, robbing calories and leaving a grown man weeping like a baby for just a second, only one second of shuteye.

She sucked another drag, needing the nicotine. Her eyes reacclimatised, flicking a look at her watch. Green dial glowed 0212. Oh my God O'Clock and still a long way to go. Sighing, she scanned the area. Dim outlines peppered the space, heads bobbing up and down or if they hadn't progressed so quickly, the outline of backs bending too. The direction had been clear, they all needed to get this done before anyone got any real sleep, not the illicit handful of minutes that most teams were covertly snatching. Stubbing out the fag, Sophie pushed back hair that had long since escaped her unruly bun,

"Percy? Percy?"

"Wha…?"

Percy flung her head up groggy unsteady on her feet, shovel wobbling underneath her.

"Percy…?"

"Give Tracey a nudge. I'm hanging for some shut eye, and she's been sucking air for a good 20 minutes, which is 10 minutes more than we'd agreed."

Percy chuckled,

"Ooo we're all tired…"

Sophie rolled her eyes, feeling just a hint of rising hysteria. Lack of sleep. She'd seen a pink elephant before, just minding its own business trudging through the area, probably not a hallucination to share right now.

"Shut up and take this pick axe will you?"

Allowing the handle to fall towards Percy, Sophie shuffled to Tracey, then shaking her violently,

"Mate, wake up, you've had your time, get out of the snooze chair, you're up on pick axe."

Tracey groaned, resolutely keeping her eyes shut, bringing a hand up wiping the small spool of saliva dribbling down her cheek. Smacking her lips, she rubbed her eyes and using her helmet as a lever brought her head up.

"Ah bless ya mate for the loving wake up call, I was dreaming about shagging your boyfriend!"

Sophie pulled Tracey out of the sleeping snug and passed out within seconds.

Stretching loudly,

"God you guys have been blimin' slacking! You actually done anything? I swear this trench hasn't changed a bit in the last 20 minutes."

Tracey's Welsh drawl was endearing to Percy, for a moment she looked on as Tracey, bent double, patted the ground looking for Sophie's pick axe as if it were the most normal thing in the world. Unable to hold back her smile, she flicked it over with her foot.

"Here, catch. You sleep well?"

She pulled up the wooden handle, grunting at the weight.

"Ah, it was bliss, I was in bed, gorgeous king size at home, swallowed up by my huge duvet and wrapped around my beauti-ful boyfriend Bill. He was all warm, curled up next to me, just heavenly…"

Tracey drifted off. Bill was a civvy, Engineer in a firm whose name she always forgot because it was some obscure acronym, OBG?OLE?OPE? They were based in London as was Bill and although Tracey preferred her little escape in Cardiff, compact and bijous being more accurate, getting to London was easier from Sandhurst and meant they'd been able to steal weekends away together when Tracey had had rare time off training. More often than not the theme for those weekends would be sleep, Tracey bone crushingly tired, something about which Bill was losing patience... But she didn't want to think about that now, not now, not when she was this tired and she'd had such a nice dream.

"Do want a cigarette? Breakfast of champions?"

Percy held out a packet of Marlboro lights, the packet ghostlike in the dark. Smoking. Percy had never thought she would smoke. Blonde, from the Cotswolds, she'd grown up around horses, fields and all things hearty, slices of bacon, with warm hot toast slathered with butter would have been followed by feeding the horses, mucking out and cantering around her family's farm. She would be up early with her father, who'd sit quietly at the table, the thinnest slivers of light just cresting the horizon, their dog, Bernie curled around his feet itching to get out and bring in the sheep, to hurtle around the yard and hound that pesky goose that thought it owned the place.

Percy loved that time and knew that it was because of that lifestyle she didn't find the physicality of this training hard, unlike others. It was just the shouting, the endless orders, the hurry up and wait. She wasn't work shy but God how she hated being told what to do. She lit her cigarette, offered the lighter to Tracey, shaking her head ruefully at what a wildly inappropriate career the military was for someone who liked to be their own boss. She looked up at the star strewn sky and thanked God that it was mild. At least it was dry.

Tracey blew smoke rings, vaguely refreshed. A laughably short sleep had raised her spirits.

"So what do you reckon? Do you think we're all gonna get this done in time?"

Percy flicked ash onto the ground outside the trench, leaning against the muddy wall, savouring the pause.

"Hmmm, suspect, judging from other people's efforts we are marginally ahead, which whilst nice for us, is overall a bit depressing, because…"

"We're gonna have to do double the work. Damn."

Tracey rolled her eyes at the team ethos. Ok ok it was all about cohesion, but some of this Platoon seriously dragged everyone else down, and doing the same thing twice was knackering not to mention bloody boring. She ground her cigarette into the mud savagely,

"You chosen your capbadge?"

The perennial decision they all had to make, who would they join in the Army?

"I cannot believe that we are nearly at the end? Y'know? Seems like yesterday we walked up those steps clutching ironing boards not knowing the difference between a ColourSergeant or a Captain."

Percy's teeth glinted in the moonlight, grinning embarrassed,

"Well I didn't."

"S'alright," snorted Tracey, "I was still saluting Corporals at the start of this term."

They laughed, felt good.

"One more term, three more months, final interviews then, well, I think I'm gonna go for the RLC."

"The Loggies?!"

Tracey sputtered in the darkness, hurling the pickaxe downwards, breaking huge sods of chalk and soil.

"The Royal Logistic Corps who cart around food, post and blankets? You want to be a Truck commander or a Postie chief?"

Percy shook her head, sighing,

"It's not like that any more."

She heaped a pile of mud onto her shovel, throwing it over her shoulder in a practiced motion, that whilst had impressive results judging by the mound behind their trench, had left her right clavicle and waist cripplingly sore from the twist and throw. She gritted her teeth, thought of breakfast bacon, thought of her dog Bernie.

"The Loggies are at the front mate. In Afghan if you are in the Loggies as an Officer, you WILL come under contact on those CLPs."

"Combat Logistic Patrols? Those convoys? Seriously? I didn't realize they were targeted that much? You don't hear that much about it."

"That's because it's pretty much par for the course."

Percy wiped back mud caked hair, pulling her T-shirt away from sweaty skin. God she stank.

"The convoys are about 5-10km long. They're essential, getting from Patrol Bases to Forward Operating Bases. If you don't get to that PB or that FOB they ain't getting any food, post or supplies. Shit bust. So personally I think *that* is pretty important. Ok so it's not the Int Corps or the Gunners with their big'old Artillery or the Signals with their gadgetry. But y'know what? I'm not really interested in some suped up radio, or some intelligence that is so secret I can't pass it on to the guys on the ground who need it. Nope,"

She flicked back another hair and got a stray piece of dirt in her mouth for the effort, spitting out stale coffee and mud.

"I'd rather be on the coal face, making a difference I can physically see. Not stuck in some tent or in the strategic ivory tower."

"What about you?" Percy propped herself up for a breather,

"Well,"

Tracey grunted, flinging the pickaxe up, silhouetted dramatically like some horror film, before she plunged downwards into the base of the trench, a gaping hole appearing in front of her,

"I totally take your point about wanting to make a difference, about seeing stuff that you've affected. So, I've narrowed it down to the AGC either the SPS or the RMP and I'm still toying with the ETS."

"Really?" Percy mused in the dark, surprised.

"So, you want to be either," counting them out on filthy hands barely visible in the dark,

"Part of the Staff and Personnel Support Branch aka a pen pusher? OR a member of the lovely Royal Military Police, so dobbing in on

19

your own, orrr a part of the mighty Educational and Training staff aka a teacher?"

Percy chuckled, teasing,

"Why join the Army? You could have got a job with the Civil Service!"

"Ah sod off Percy," Tracey's Welsh accent deepening in irritation.

"Everyone needs to be educated, you'd be leading through example."

"In a classroom."

"Yes, in a classroom, but equally, people do join to get qualified."

"Warfare not welfare." Intoned Percy. She didn't really believe it, but it was part of the banter, poking each other, prodding, teasing.

"Yeah well in that warfare, you need to get paid don't you? I tell you, you may call the SPS,"

"The Special Pen Service."

"Just admin, but I tell you everyone's pretty quick to complain when you don't get your allowances or your pay gets cocked up eh? Especially Op bonuses."

"Ahh meh…" Tracey had a point. "But monkeys mate? Explain that?"

"The Military Police my little ignorant farming friend,"

Percy stuck out her tongue,

"Are crucial to ensure that people don't think that just because they are in the Army they are above the law, military and civilian. You gotta remember, Percy, we get all kinds joining. Soldiers come from all over and some ain't that nice and need a bit of reminding that they are in a fighting machine that demands adherence to rules and the chain of command. If we don't have cohesion, the whole uniformity of the Army falls apart? Right?"

Percy nodded amused in the dark, Tracey was right and it was this very uniformity that she was railing against internally. She just had to believe what their ColourSergeant said was true, that the real Army wasn't like this. Constant early starts, endless marches, being so exhausted you could fall asleep anywhere. The real Army couldn't be like this surely? It wouldn't be sustainable?

"What do you think about Sophie?"

Tracey paused, she chuckled at how Sophie was wedged into the small mud seat. At 5'10" she was taller than Tracey already lofty at 5'9". Her head was propped up by the edge of the trench, hair sticking up in tufts, crusty with mud, mouth half open, snoring softly. If exhaustion needed a picture, Sophie would be it.

"Ahh Sophie? Well,"

Tracey grunted as she caught a particularly stubborn piece of gravel and chalk under the pick axe, levering it she kicked away the mound of mud,

"Come on Perce, it's obvious isn't it?"

Percy shoveled up Tracey's mud, hurled it behind, pausing to rub her aching back,

"She doesn't really talk about it that much, Y'know? Always wonder what she's thinking actually. It's not that she's quiet, we both know that…"

Tracey snorted, thinking of how Sophie was constantly chivvying them on, motivating like some American self-help guru.

"Just she doesn't really talk about, well, her?"

"Hmm, meuh, I guess, but I think it makes it all the more obvious who she's going for?"

Percy slung her spade down and reached for her water canteen. It was barely visible in the dark, even with the slice of moon that had emerged behind clouds that kept the night muggy. Percy was used to remembering where she'd put things, too many Exercises patting the area around her furiously looking for kit or her rifle had made her almost pathological in putting things in the same place. The Army was making her borderline OCD. Taking a hefty swig she offered it to Tracey,

"Thanks, tell you what we're gonna need a water run…where's the Platoon Sergeant? Isn't Hathaway under scrutiny for this one?"

Liz Hathaway, always late, confused and uninformed. In some that might be endearing, in abrupt, cocky Liz it was irritating.

"Do you think Liz will care about water runs? She'll be filling her own canteen and taking a nap, with half an eye open for the DS, then she'll be cutting about, all professionalism…"

Tracey frowned, "Bloody DS watcher. Anyways, you still not got it?"

Percy grinned, mentally listing all the Regiments and Corps that would allow women for a start. Sophie found the sessions on voice procedure and radio agonizingly boring, doodling and snoozing through most of the classes. Memorizing ranges and weapon capabilities was something she found easy but still disliked, so it was unlikely she'd be seduced by the Gunners. She was as merciless as Percy about the AGC…so?

"Ahh, tip top super super secret, of course! God I'm an idiot! Int Corps! Can tell why I'd be no good, can't even work out who'd join them!"

"Well done Sherlock."

Percy bowed,

"Guys…?"

Startled gasps,

"Bloody hell Hathaway, scared the fuck out of me!"

"Yeah well, it's because I cut about tactically which is something your chat isn't. Keep it down."

Percy flushed with irritation.

"Sorry Liz, are the DS about? Worried you'll get back termed because your fellow Officer cadets aren't doing what you want?"

Liz grimaced, Percy, Tracey and Sophie. She hated them with their fitness, jokes and popularity. How they made this all look so easy, like a walk in the park, when Liz was terrified that the DS would come over any minute and catch her sleeping. She felt sick from fatigue, had no idea what she should be doing and knew that not having a clue this close to commissioning was getting harder and harder to hide and if she didn't Pass off the Square, if she didn't walk up those steps an Officer, carrying the Queen's commission what the hell would she do? Tescoes? She shook her head, pushing down her terror, focusing her anger on Percy instead,

"Persephone, I want you to do a water run for each Section and for fuck's sake wake up Sophie before the ColourSergeant sees her snoring. Can't believe you're sleeping, so unprofessional…"

Then she was gone slipping off into the night, wishing she had a torch and was back home in Hungerford, in bed with a book and her cat Jester.

Heaving herself out of the trench, realizing as she hooked her legs up over the edge that they'd made a lot of progress, Percy reached down,

"Someone is feeling the pressure, chuck us your canteen, I'll go and do a bit of a recce and check out how everyone is doing."

Glancing at her watch, a cheap Casio from *Watches R Us* in Camberley saw it was 0230. Time to wake Sophie anyway, irrespective of what Liz said, Soph had had quite a long snooze and frankly they needed the power machine's digging prowess.

"C'mon wake Soph will you? Let's smash this trench and go and help the others."

Trace handed her's and Soph's canteen,

"Your chat stinks anyway Perce, could do with some more refined conversation."

Snorting, Percy jogged off in the dark, looking out for large holes.

5

"SOPHIE…SOPHIE…?"

Sophie groaned, "One more minute,"

"Soph, come on you're on stag."

Stag? What was Tracey talking about they were digging trenches, groggy Sophie reached up to stretch and hit material. What the…?

Suddenly awake she looked around, startled, it was light, hot, intensely hot and she was sleeping in a shell scrape under a basher. There were no trenches, no Percy and why was Tracey calling her anyway?

"Sophie for God's sake, you've been asleep for bloody ages, it's your turn to be on point and, because I'm such a legend I've even made you a hot chocolate."

Hooking her head around the waterproof over hang, held up by two bungee cords connected to a spindly tree, she saw ground that was sandy and gravelley, no mud, no chalk. Rubbing her neck, she relaxed, laughing softly, looking up at Tracey,

"You will not believe this," taking the hot drink,

"I've only been dreaming about Exercise Worst Encounter. Y'know the trench digging sleep deprivation one?"

Tracey crouched on her haunches, her face a mix of green cam cream and light tan, she wasn't wearing the normal green combats but desert fatigues. It was the Final Exercise. They were in Cyprus.

"You. Are. Such. A. Loser. Dreaming of training when you are asleep. Me? I was fantasizing about Bill, Brad Pitt and frankly not enough whipped cream in the end…" She looked off in the distance wistfully.

Soph sputtered her drink.

"Gross mate, having my breakfast here. You got a fag? Then I'll get my ass on Sentry. How things going anyway? We any closer to knowing what the Final attack plan is? Any rumint on command appointments?"

Tracey shock her head, shuffling in to the shade, handing Sophie a lit cigarette, helping herself to another, quietly smug at having packed so many. At least they were lighter to carry than haribo.

"Hathaway is up for Platoon Commander…"

Sipping, pausing to whistle slowly,

"Really? God that girl is hanging by a thread, bet she is bricking it."

"Well if she wasn't such a bitch perhaps we'd all help her a bit more. Serves you right if all you're interested in is kissing DS arse, even they are gonna get tired of that kind of attitude. Plus not exactly going to work in downtown Helmand if you haven't got a clue what you're doing or how to even write a set of orders eh?"

Deployment. The word on everyone's lips. The blokes talked about it with bravado, brash about how they were gonna kick some terry Taleban ass. Tour was what they all trained for, but still, it was daunting. Whilst confident in her fitness, her knowledge and tactics, to be out there, to be on the edge, people looking to you to make the decision, to get it right. Soph swallowed hot chocolate, grateful for the sweetness, enjoying the bitter rasp of nicotein in contrast.

"Where's Percy? She was in my dream too you know…."

Tracey feigned disgust,

"She's off with Hardy doing patrol orders for the section. They're being super keen making a little model as well. Frankly I don't know why they're bothering, they've got nothing to prove. Just gotta keep your head down, stay unbroken…"

Their ex-platoon member, Heather Donington had broken. A really good laugh, knew what she was doing, jumped out of a four tonner, landed in a ditch and broke her back. Y-listed, aka the rehab platoon, which was beautifully optimistic since most likely she'd be medically discharged and all within weeks of commissioning, so close you could touch it but for Heather it was game over. Could have been any of them.

Soph tossed her cigarette into the bush, shuffled out of her sleeping bag and pulled on her combat shirt, glancing at her watch, 0715. Tracey was acting like she'd been up for hours, probably because she had been.

"Thanks for breakfast. How did you sleep?" Soph smeared cam cream on an already streaked face, scraping her hair back into a tighter bun, the chestnut now more lank than highlighted.

Draining her orange juice, sickly sweet mix of powder and warm water, Tracey was beyond being bothered by things like tepid liquid.

"Oh y'know, on and off, bloody mozzies, kept thinking of Bill…"

Dreams were one thing, reality another. Their reality was far from comforting. Sophie's hand on her shoulder.

"He'll come through, he's got to understand you're not choosing to be away from him. You're in training and it's nearly over…"

"We're nearly over more like, said he's had enough of me cancelling at the last minute. That there is apparently, I quote, lots of London totty who'd appreciate a catch like him… thought that was very understanding."

Soph suppressed her irritation. She thought Bill was a self-satisfied knob, who worshipped money and drink, snorting coke like a pig at a trough. She couldn't understand what Tracey saw in him and his doped up mates, but it was easy for her, she wasn't caught in the emotional drama. If they were all finding relationships tough now, when they hadn't even commissioned, what would it be like on Tour? Or in Barracks where time wasn't your own, when you could be sent off on a fastball tasking and you had to go because it was your job, your duty, your life?

"Right, show me my arcs and where the enemy are, can't have them crawling up on us when I'm on stag eh?"

Tracey smiled. She knew what Soph thought, knew Soph was right, but Bill was like an addiction and she couldn't quite shake the habit.

Scooping up their rifles, they wandered through the harbour, gaggles of bedraggled girls littering the area in various stages of undress. Some cleaning weapons gossiping, others peering over maps, pairs heating up rations, or catching up on sleep. It was the lull before the battle, no one knew when they'd next eat or sleep, so you did the most of both while you could.

They passed Hardy and Percy deep in conversation, bent over nyrexes, scribbling furiously, pointing sporadically at bits of twig and ribbon, discussing routes, timings, distances.

"Hey Hardy, how goes it?"

Stella Hardy looked up, hair a wild frizz of red, face pale with a smattering of freckles, smeared with dust and cam cream. She grinned cheerfully, in her element. She was a bladerunner, recognized as the likely contender for the honour of best cadet bestowed by the attending Sovereign at the parade. There was a running joke it would curse you into a career of ignominy, as many the shining Officer had disappeared into the ranks and floundered in the reality of military life. After all training was practice, the real thing was harder to predict.

"Ah y'know, just cooking up a storm. Percy here is doing all the work."

"Hey stop with the false modesty, Stella by name Stella by nature. How's you two? Anyone seen the Platoon Commander?"

Tracey snorted, "You mean 'Liz let me know when the war is over' Hathaway?"

"The very same."

"Yeah well, we just passed her and Sal Saunders who looked thoroughly depressed to be sat in the same shell scrape. Mind you anyone would be depressed lugging that World War 2 piece of kit around, weighs a flipping ton."

They all nodded wearily, each having suffered the discomfort of carrying the radio on top of their own kit. Its additional 5 or 6 kilos was back breaking when added to bergens, webbing, ammunition and rifles, reducing some of the platoon to silent tears of agony.

"Still, judging by my rough ideas we've got about 2 days to push. 48 hours left of humping and dumping and then home free."

They bathed hopefully in the thought.

Making the most of the delay, Soph crouched next to Hardy ignoring Tracey's frowns,

"So Hardy, never asked, who have you been accepted by? Final interviews were emotional for the INT CORPS, what about you?"

The last round of interviews for Regiments and Corps had taken place before the Final Exercise allowing each cadet the pride of carrying with them the beret of their soon to be Unit. The end of the Exercise would be celebrated with a glass of something bubbly and being able to don your beret, worn legitimately for the first time as a bona fide Officer in your chosen branch of the Army.

"REME."

"No way? Grease monkey? Didn't know you liked tinkering with tanks and Lannies?"

Hardy grinned sheepishly. "Degree in Engineering, Royal Electrical Mechanical Engineers was the natural fit. Pretty chuffed they said they'd have me."

"Ah bless you," Sophie nudged her teasing, "…have you? Who wouldn't Stella? You're a hot commodity, they'd be mad to say no!"

"Yeah, well, it's nice to have it formal. Still got to get through this though. You happy with the orders?"

Conversation closed, Tracey dragged Soph up to the edge of the line of trees delineating where their harbour finished and potentially the enemy lay, in theory anyway. They all knew the Gurkhas were snacking on kit kats somewhere being briefed by the real Platoon Commanders and Directing Staff on the plan for the Final attack. Tracey shivered.

6

Sophie pulled hard at her Bergen strap, hoiking it up to take the strain off her back. She itched to flick some sleep out of her eye but knew that cam cream, ground in dirt and mucky fingernails was an experience she didn't want to repeat. Sighing, she pulled on her combat jacket. A fitful night sleep had left her irritable.

The location for the harbour had been hopelessly ambitious. Difficult for an experienced Officer, it was way beyond the capabilities of a cadet who was under pressure and under scrutiny from Directing Staff. Selecting a pine forest admittedly created outstanding cover, but was hellishly dense and purgatorial to execute the formulaic insertion procedure. Whilst the platoon had pulled together for their own benefit, teeth were gritted and curses muttered as eyes got gouged and branches savagely clawed indiscriminately as they dug out shell scrapes and allocated sentry positions at the point of the raggedy triangle. Despite the hideous location, Soph was used to the SOP or Standard Operating Procedure that was setting up camp. Nonetheless the process of unpacking tactically after the best part of a three hour insertion march had left the platoon exhausted. She'd been so tired she hadn't even heated her sausage and beans ration pack. Instead, staring unblinking out in the woods, shoveling dirty forkfuls. Licking her fork clean and slipping it into her combat jacket, saving the biscuit fruit in her pocket for breakfast. Then like a zombie, folding the used ration pack into a square, sliding it into the zip compartment on the top of her Bergen, and exhausted sliding to sleep in the shared shell scrape with Tracey snoring beside her, who'd been too knackered to eat.

In the morning however the harbour was electric; figures moving in the dark, whispers of direction, where was kit? Had anyone seen someone's rifle? Can you help with my Bergen? Who's that? Who's on point? It was quiet chaos. Pine forest as a harbour meant the area was even darker by night, each in the platoon reaching out like a weary blind man grasping the Bergen or belt of the person in front, ensuring the line held, no man or woman left behind. If it wasn't so daunting, Sophie would have found it funny. As it was she swallowed a feeling of vague panic at not being able to see where she was going, peering frustrated into the darkness,

"Tracey you there?"

She could hear grunting, scrabbling round,

"Can't find my fucking rifle...ahhh, where are you?"

Sophie reached out, hoping they'd brush each other's fingers, orientate themselves.

"Oh for fuck's sake, had enough of this..."

There was a burst of red light as Tracey flicked on her headlamp, spotting Sophie but garnering a chorus of hisses,

"Opsec! Lights off!"

"Oh fuck off!"

Soph grinned in the darkness holding onto Tracey's hand.

"Come on mate, mind the..."

Oomph.

"...tree."

Tracey's helmet connected with branches.

"This is bloody madness. I am carrying a small house on my back, so much ammo I'm a walking Range package, I have no idea where I am going, and I'm being eaten alive by mozzies."

They laughed softly, then a crunching of pine needles. It was Hardy, she'd been appointed Platoon Sergeant at the last minute, with the Directing Staff reluctantly registering that if everything were left to Hathaway to handle, this platoon would be floundering around in the dark for days, literally and metaphorically. Everyone could tell Hardy was exhausted, crushed at having to step up again so late in the Exercise despite her relentless enthusiasm, she was digging deep to find the energy to focus after her own command appointment. She'd been the Company Commander in the Higher HQ, thrashed with endless orders, tested heavily by the DS as they decided who'd get the sacred Sword. Hardy had done her bit. She could do without having to save Hathaway from drowning in a sea of incompetence. Even for someone as instinctively competent and sympathetic as her, she had to admit that there was little she could do to salvage the diabolical set of orders Hathaway had delivered, or coordinate the carnage that was a platoon more confused after Liz issued direction than before. God how she wished she could be soaking in a hot bath, rubbing arnica on to bruises, Sandra cooking their favourite ratatouille, singing along badly to Kylie. Come on Hardy, just two more days, less than 48 hours.

"Tracey? Sophie?"

"Yep?"

"Need you out on the main line, take my belt, its bedlam in here no one can see a bloody thing, so change of plan, we're going to line up in herring bone outside the forestry block rather than in it. That way we get a bit of light from the moon."

Tracey and Soph resisted finishing Hardy's sentence, that it had been Hathaway's idea to adopt a complicated line up in an achingly dense pitch black forestry block.

Smacking her hand against the tree and some spindly shoots, Soph found Hardy's webbing, holding on with Tracey still clutched to her belt, they hobbled forward, heads bowed, helmets clipping braches and saplings, the blind following the almost blind.

Finally they were out.

"Thank God."

Tracey stood up eyes adjusting to the precious extra light, taking a deep breath. She could see most of the platoon now, on one knee, concertina style behind each other.

"Right, I've got to go and get everyone else. Aiming to move out in about 5 minutes. Ok?"

Hardy vanished leaving Soph convinced she had x-ray vision.

"That girl is a machine."

"I know."

Tracey rubbed the base of her back, already aching from being bent double, the weight of ammo and her rifle. She winced, easing her ankle in a circular motion. She'd gone over on it with a misplaced boot on a tree root. Almost screamed out with the pain, instead grasping Soph's belt so tight she thought she'd snap the webbing yolk. It throbbed angrily against her tightly laced boots.

Soph walked forward, slipping down on one knee behind the last man in the row,

"Who's that?" voice hoarse, already feeling dehydrated,

"Hey it's Percy. That was interesting."

"You're telling me," Tracey sank down behind Sophie at a 45 degree angle, each member of the platoon staggered down the line allowing for greater protection of arcs, more tactically sound. Although that was more a reflection of the platoon's innate learning rather than any inspired direction from their Platoon Commander.

"Nearly broke my flipping ankle."

Percy shook her head, licking her lips, using her shoulder to shift the mouth piece of her personal radio away from her cheek. Things were not going well. Rumour had come down the line they were late. Late was not good.

"How we doing?"

Percy twisted to face Soph,

"We might not make H Hour."

"Hmm, that's not ideal."

H hour. The key timing everyone had to be lined up, ready to attack at the line of departure. Missing H Hour was like the Groom turning up late to his own wedding. Or the Pope saying he didn't fancy going to Mass that day. It didn't happen.

"Christ! Bet Liz is having a fit!"

"She's been in tears most of the move out of the harbor. Sorry but that is just pathetic."

Percy shook her head, embarrassed by the histrionics; gave the female platoon a bad name.

They fell quiet, distracted by their own discomfort. Kneeling preferable to standing for long periods with your Bergen, but it still had its own unique agony. Bergens would tug at shoulders, causing a dull ache that became gradual torture between the shoulder blades. Until eventually it felt like someone was slowly sinking a sharp knife into your back, the Bergen obstructing any efforts to alleviate this slow agony. Sweat would slide down cammed up cheeks, a stray droplet into the eye would sting like shampoo, impossible to rub because of cammed hands clutching rifles. The whole experience was purgatorial, tolerated in silence, each a silent mantra shared by all of 'hurry up, hurry up'.

Four more bundled up behind Tracey and Soph. Then finally Hardy was running up the file. Whispers stopped, everyone poised, itching to get on with things. The sooner they were at the line of departure the sooner they could dump their bergens.

As the file in front of her moved off Soph couldn't help but think this was it. They were literally hours away from being real Officers. No more pretend, no more Officer cadet, it would be Second Lieutenant Jefferson, commissioned into the Int Corps, sent who knows where, but she'd be in charge, she'd be the one calling the shots, at least knowing what was going on, no more being led in the dark like tonight. She licked her lips, frowning at the taste of cam cream, wishing she'd drunk more water.

The evening was balmy; the moon had decided to show more of itself allowing each to calmly follow the footsteps of the person in front. They were spaced out, focused. Then news came down the line,

They'd caught up with the rest of the Company, they'd caught up with the blokes.

Tracey rolled her eyes with relief,

"Fucking well done Hardy."

Soph glanced to the side of those in front; the troop extended a long way now they were tagged onto the back of the blokes. The Company comprising three platoons made it the best part of 100 people, heads bowed, bergens, heavy, feet sore, shoulders aching. The question on everyone's lips where was the Bergen drop?

"Down!"

Soph nearly walked into Percy who dropped onto one knee,
"What the…?"

Crouched, giving up on tactical poise, Soph leaned against the road verge, ignoring thistles and nettles, grateful she could rest her Bergen against something, ease the weight for a second. She cradled her rifle, fumbled for the biscuit fruit she'd saved from her combat jacket. Munching in silence, waiting. Bit like a garibaldi this biscuit she thought, used to quite like those.

She heard Percy whistle a slow disbelieving note, turning, taking half a biscuit from Soph,

"You are not going to believe this?"

"Wha'?" Sophie munched,

"Well, looks like the navigator has got us lost."

"Oh you are kidding me, who the hell is that? How badly?"

"Company Commander is Tim Grey…"

"Can't be him."

Soph liked Tim, he was pretty brusque, but said it how it was and he was no slouch with a map.

"Who's the CSM?"

Percy swallowed, reaching round for her canteen, jostling her Bergen up to reach under the pouch at the base of her back,

"Could you pull out my canteen? Help yourself?"

Soph took a swig, passed it to Percy,

"I think," Percy wiping her mouth, cleaning a swathe of green from her lips and chin,

"It's Ben Kitson."

"We are so screwed."

Slipping Percy's canteen back in her pouch, snapping the tab closed with a click.

"Ben is a complete knob? I thought it was supposed to be the crème de la crème at this point? Y'know? No more fucking about, just get the job done. How can they put that muppet up front now?"

Percy sniggered,

"You mean Ben's inability to navigate himself to the loo? He's managed to keep it schtum. Each time there's been a Nav Ex or any

Command appointment, he's always got either Dom French or Joel Fixsome to be his check nav. They think he's a legend because he's a boxer, so the tragic little trio have managed to watch his back. Until now."

"Oh bloody hell, I'm knackered, I can do without having to walk an extra couple of kay because Ben knobber hasn't got a clue what he's doing. God, don't envy him though, Tim will be tearing a strip off him!"

They fell silent thinking of 6'4" of Tim Grey bearing down on you. Tim was another gunning for bladerunner, he wouldn't appreciate Ben scuppering his chances. Soph winced.

Whoosh! The sky illuminated a pale green,

"Down, take cover!"

Another schumulie burst upwards, its flare turning the sky a pale pink. Everyone hugged the ground, the explosion of light exposing any uncamouflaged silhouette. Adrenaline coursed through veins, everyone in the Company barely breathing, not wanting to be the one who gave away the position, not this close. The sky slowly returned to its star speckled black, leaving Soph and others rubbing their eyes, the flash causing night blindness, taking a second to readjust to the darkness.

"Bloody hell that scared the crap out of me!"

Percy looked round, eye whites wide in the dark.

Soph giggled uneasily, "We really need to move or the Gurkhas are gonna ambush us and I for one do not want to be running for cover under fire carrying this sodding weight on my back."

Bergen drop, Bergen drop? Where was it?

"Ready to move." Percy passed on the whispered order.

They marched along the chalky road for another hour, each interminable minute grinding into the next. Soph could see individuals in front, pausing, leaning forward, alleviating the strain on their backs, a second of relief before they jogged on. Soph was parched, her lips cracked, aching for a cigarette, grumpy in the knowledge that Opsec prohibited anything that could betray their position, the glow of a fag, the spool of smoke drifting in the air. Her skin itchy from prickly heat, she'd forgotten to take off her t-shirt under her combat shirt, now coated with dried sweat it rubbed against her chest, chaffing salt into dry skin. In a vague attempt at distraction she swung her rifle rhythmically, placing one boot in front of the other in time with her weapon. Left, right, left right.

It was ridiculous, she'd been here before, lined up for attacks in pouring rain, heavy snow, slipped and slid on ice to make it to check points to get there on time. Tonight though, she was tired, just wanted this whole game to be over. Playing at soldiers had been going on for the best part of a year. Seeing friends fall at the wayside, injured, broken, trudging out of the lines in the Academy to be rehabilitated or walk away from Military life. Whittling them down until 29 had become 23, barely enough to scrape the 3 sections and a headquarters that comprised a platoon.

Left, right, left, right. Kicking stones, watching them skitter away. Tracey thought of a week's time. They'd be home. This would all be a distant memory. Her bed would be there, soft and alluring, her room clean, tidy, duvet inviting. When rifles were cleaned, kit stacked away, the focus would be the parade and all things ceremonial, polishing, perfecting pleats and shirts. So nearly there, so nearly up those steps and then on and into the Red Caps, she was going to be the Royal Military Police and she could not wait to put on that famous red hat. The interview had been a grilling,

"So Tracey, why is it you feel drawn to the Royal Military Police?"

The General had drawn out his vowels making her feel like a pleb. Already intimidated as she sat before the highest-ranking Officers in the Royal Military Police. The surroundings only served to emphasise the ceremony of the occasion. Sat in deep leather chairs in one of the prestige rooms of Old College, the sense of tradition was almost palpable. These men and the lack of women hadn't been lost on Tracey, these men would decide if Tracey was up to the arbitrarily requisite standard of the Corps She'd pulled herself upright, stretching every inch of her 5'9",

"Well Sir, I feel that cohesion of the Force is crucial to its fighting power. I see us as acting as a Force multiplier, by ensuring that any issues within the Army of a criminal nature are dealt with fairly, swiftly and efficiently. It thereby removes the burden on both the ranks and Officers to address conduct that is diverting precious resources away from training and the Main Effort."

Tracey had been pleased with the answer, she'd drafted it close to a dozen times, practicing, rehearsing, tweaking, reading it in front of the mirror. Judging by the hush in the room, the girl from the valley had impressed.

She smiled as she trekked on in the dark, the flush of pride enough to help ignore the pain of her swollen ankle.

Percy's feet were in rag. Blister on the left foot on the inner arch, blister on her little toe on her right foot, and another blister on the back of her heel, slicing skin that had slapped in the breeze in the harbour. Tutting, her face creased with pain, trying not to think of the raw skin being cheese grated by her issue socks. She'd abandoned putting on tape after the last Exercise when it had rubbed off and just ground against raw skin, drawing blood and making even the Medic cringe when he peeled back her sock.

"Christ Miss you really need to square your foot admin away, this is like taping mince."

If Percy had looked closer she would have seen the glint of admiration in his eye; that same Medic who'd patched her up and returned to his Unit eulogizing about the female Officer cadet who insisted on pulling boots back on bleeding blisters. He talked about her for a week, but Percy never knew this. Percy who had been more intent on helping her mates, on making sure no one knew she was in so much pain she could cry a river. Percy who was trudging along now thinking of having her highlights done, of Bernie channeling sheep for her dad back on the farm, of making it into her beloved Loggies.

When Percy had walked out of the interview, into the echoey corridors of Old College, the cold paved stones making her heels clickety clack. She'd looked around for any other candidates and when sure no one was looking, done a spontaneous jig, flailing arms around in the air, a good impression of the twist and shake, pausing breathless, punching the air triumphantly. Then collecting herself, glancing around, she'd pulled straight her charcoal suit jacket, newly purchased for the occasion, and walked back to New College, oblivious to the ColourSergeant who'd grinned and watched her celebrations.

Footsteps, panting, it was Ben Kitson and he was bollocking Hardy.

"You fucking girls are slowing us down. We need to make the next RV in 15 minutes."

"Piss off Ben," Hardy had no patience for Ben and his ineptitude,

"Where the hell is the Bergen drop? Everyone has been tabbing for 2 hours with full bloody kit. Where the hell have you planned the kit drop so people can bomb up magazines and prep rifles? Or did you forget that in your little ging gang gooley?"

Percy kept her head down, though not before Sophie walked into her, straining to see the row.

"Sorry, blimin heck, rock on Hardy."

All three strained to listen in, all hoping Ben was going to give a grid reference, talk about some four tonner stop, they were all hanging.

"Fuck off Hardy, I'm the CSM and I'll bloody tell you when you can drop your bloody kit. Now man up you fucking lessie, and get your girls to get on with it. Bunch of bloody women."

Sniffing disgustedly he trotted back up, but not before Soph glimpsed a face etched in pain.

Percy swallowed her disappointment, ignoring the throb of her feet, focusing on just moving forward. And they did. For another 3 hours. Tears rolling down Percy's face in silence, her feet wet from blood.

7

EXHAUST FUMES FLOODED the air and Sophie could have screamed in delight. The company trekked into the staging area. Watching DS grimaced. Officer Cadet Kitson had royally cocked up, and not a member of Directing Staff had missed it. 3 hours of extra marching with full kit had each of them remembering their own Sandhurst days. Softening their chivvying, even ColourSergeants were less aggressive.

Platoons slumped in corners, dropping kit like boulders, collapsing gratefully to the ground, heads hanging, supping on water canteens like hungry infants. Cigarette smoke drifted across each group, there was no chatter, just drawn faces, staring haggard at the ground. Ben Kitson at that point was the most universally hated cadet ever to have walked Cypriot soil. He would never forget this moment for his entire military career, assuming he even had one after this.

Percy slung her Bergen down next to Soph and Tracey, all three silent with fatigue. Percy wondered if she should see a Medic. Tracy rubbed her ankle, swollen to twice its size. Thundering feet startled them as they watched 6 Platoon go cantering past.

The Advance party. Their role was to mark out the path to the line of departure. A pain staking process, it ensured the security of the rest of the force. As a consequence it was tediously time consuming and slow in its progress. The platoon would edge forward, leaving sylooms, like the glow sticks waved at festivals, as fluorescent bread crumbs to guide the inserting platoons to the central assembly areas and then onto their respective holding points on the hypothetical line of departure, beyond which the enemy lay. It took time and precision and was supposed to be one of the more dangerous roles for any platoon. Most of the cadets just found it turgidly boring and complicated to execute, more than a few of the other cadets sighed with relief that they hadn't been tasked with the job.

"Poor fuckers," Tracy muttered, looking up at Sophie wearily,

"Yeah well at least they'll have a chance to snooze, sorry did I mean stag on when they've marked the route in."

They nodded, conscious that time was moving on. Sal Saunders dragged her Bergen past them,

"Guys, the Bergen drop for our platoon's over here, Hardy wants everyone to bundle up kit and line them over here. Thank God eh?"

"Hey Saunders, how are things at the front, how's Hathaway actually doing? Is Green ok?"

Saunders shook her head,

"It was a bloody nightmare. Hardy was check navving most of the way for the entire company after Kitson cocked it up. She's like the walking dead she's so exhausted, but she was the one that noticed Ben had taken us the wrong way..." Sal paused, her face strained,

"...She pointed out to Ben that we were way off mark 2 hours ago but..."

She left it hanging, accusation heavy in the air, needless hardship that could have been avoided.

"...as for Green, that girl is a total hero. I don't know about you guys but I was in bits with my own kit. I don't know how she managed with that bloody radio as well. I offered to take it but she said she'd got into a rhythm and well, we were all convinced we'd be here a lot sooner."

Nodding in agreement, faces drawn with respect, they followed Saunders with their Bergens. It had been epic so far, and the battle hadn't even begun.

8

"MAKE READY!"

The sound of rifles being cocked echoed along the line. On the crest of the horizon, ribbons of yellow and orange streamed across the sky as live rounds came down the range. Dawn attack and Sophie was utterly freezing. They'd crawled on their belt buckles along the path of sylooms into position. She could hear Percy on her left. Something was wrong with her; her face was sheet white underneath what was now a thin sheen of cam cream. Normally she'd be gabbling under her breath, whispering excitedly about chucking their issue grenades. This morning she was monosyllabic, more strained than Soph had seen her before, taking long steady breaths, controlled, icily tunnel visioned. Tracey meanwhile was pumped and chewing gum like some speed freak to her right; the smack of Wrigley's delivering a welcome burst of mint into the air.

Whooosh! A schumulie shot up into the air, its illumination dented by the burgeoning sun, but the signal was clear and as one, all platoons rose charging into the attack. There was no denying it, no matter how exhausted anyone was, this bit was a rush; adrenaline firing through tired systems, blood racing, fire and manoeuvring forward, rounds spraying ahead, sprinting, hearts in mouths, breath coming in bursts. Tracey hit the ground hard, "Umph!"

She fired ahead, eye trained on her ironsight, rounds aimed, her finger squeezing then releasing the trigger in a practiced motion, smoke bombs obliterating her view, the smell of phosphorous bitter in her throat.

41

"Up, Up!"

She heard Soph screaming to left, gotta keep in line with her, adrenaline causing her heart to thud against her chest so powerfully she thought it would burst right through her body armour. They powered forward, in the corner of her eye she could see Percy, was she hobbling? Didn't matter now,

"Down! Enemy front, 100 metres fire at will!"

Tracey hit the ground, hip connecting with a stray rock,

"Ahh fuck!"

She clambered forward, pain shooting through her leg, firing her rifle until the chamber clammed, frozen,

"Stoppage!"

Fumbling in her ammo pouch, she swept off the trapped magazine, shook free the stuck round, slammed in another pumping rounds down the range.

"Hold your fire! Hold your fire!"

Bewildered Sophie around, was that Hathaway? Hold our fire? What the hell was going on? Tracer ripped through the sky, general purpose machine gun fire rattling in the distance, now was not the time to lose momentum.

For God's sake Liz, don't make us look stupid.

Sophie wheeled round looking for Percy or Tracey in amongst the fog,

"Trace? Trace?"

Puffing and panting through the white screen, Tracey flopped beside her.

"This. Is. A. Total. Cluster."

Soph felt relief flood over her. The one thing she hated about these assaults, was not knowing who was who, who was in your platoon, where you were meant to be running. It just turned into a total disorientating melee, with it being more often luck rather than design that got her to the right place. The number of times she'd stumbled over to another camouflaged figure only to discover not only were they not in the female platoon but she was entirely in the wrong place as they'd look at her laughing and point to some distant point on the horizon that was supposed to be her point of attack. The Final Exercise was not a good time to get lost.

"Liz has apparently lost both her bearings and any semblance of balls, heard Hardy, who I have NEVER heard shout at anyone, including Kitson when he was a cock earlier on in the tab out there. Did you hear him?? Is now currently screaming at Liz to get a bloody move on because her bottling it has slowed the attack. I think I heard on the radio that 7 platoon are having to hold their position before they take the first building in the village, because we were supposed to be up there acting as a reserve. Plus Hardy was not alone, Academy Adjutant pitched up just as she was calling Liz a loser or something like that."

Soph couldn't help but laugh shaking her head, had to be bad for Hardy to lose it.

"Talking of bad, have you seen Percy? She looked in a really poor way; she normally loves the attack. She went really quiet on me."

"That's because my feet are quite literally in bits."

Both turned to see Percy hobbling into view, abandoning all efforts at tactical she sank down beside them.

"This attack has gone to ratshit. Liz has lost it, think I just saw her sobbing to the Academy Sergeant Major about how much she hates the Army."

"Classic!"

Trace shook her head in wonder.

"She's been pulled off the appointment, Hardy's been stepped up, poor Saunders was in the wrong place at the wrong time, so she's now Platoon Sergeant. Should get this show on the road at least. Did I tell you my feet are actually bleeding?"

But before they could provide sympathy or plasters, Saunders was on them,

"Get down guys, ready to move? Move!"

They bolted, all up in unison, firing in front of them, slowly spotting the famous village where 7 Platoon waited for them. Soph was dimly aware of Saunders behind her, was that Green in her wake? How was she managing to move at that speed carrying a radio? God that girl must be shattered. Had to focus, look ahead,

"Down!"

Panting, Percy narrowed her eyes, peering through her iron sight, looking for any trace of 7 Platoon, all thoughts of blisters a throbbing pain at the back of her mind. Her feet were a mess, they'd take weeks to recover, but for now she'd just remembered her stash of painkillers tucked away weeks ago in her webbing ammo pouch and managed to squeeze some saliva into her mouth allowing her to neck enough Voltarol to float across the area,

"Show me the enemy, c'mon Gurkha boys, where's you hiding?"

"Enemy! Left, 50 metres, rapid fire!"

Tracey blatted off 5 rounds of automatic,

"Stoppage! Bloody hell!"

She struggled for her ammo pouch, Saunders hammering more rounds towards the Gurkhas who were pitched up as a pair behind a walled escarpment.

"Saunders! Saunders!" Sal snapped her head round, ears pricked,

"What? Green? I'm here!"

Green came jogging over,

"CSM is trying to reach you, wants to know where the hell the platoon is, I think Hardy's been caught up in some fake Medevac serial about 200 metres behind us."

"Oh bugger."

She chewed her lip, torn, she didn't want to cause any more delay, the longer this dragged out the longer the attack would last and she couldn't remember the last time she'd had a drink. She was do dehydrated she'd pee ash.

"Saunders!"

She looked up to see Tracey kneeling beside her,

"Look couldn't help but over hear, whole platoon caught in some blimin' casevac serial? Look, tell the blokes we're here, which technically we are. Soph and I will destroy that Gurkha position and then we can act as reserve. Mate, c'mon, it'll be fine, we've got the Pers-onator."

Saunders realized that Percy was knelt behind Tracey grinning maniacally, Christ she looked like she was on drugs. There was no time, and no other options.

"Ok, go for it, Green and I will give you three covering fire. On my count, one two threeeeee…!"

Soph and Tracey pelted forward, Percy acting as a second pair, "Down!"

Percy hit the deck, watching as Soph and Tracey raced to the Gurkha position, she flicked her rifle onto automatic, staring down the ironsight, chugging bullets at the enemy, dimly aware of someone shouting, until she realized it was her roaring,

"Die you fuckers!"

Tracey and Soph sprinted together, a force of nature,

"Throw the grenade! Grenade!"

Trace pulled the pin, flung the small green explosive ball, both hitting the dusty gravel,

Boom! The blank explosion kicked up rubble, springing back up they followed through on their assault, months of training honing their instincts, weapons on automatic, finishing the position, obliterating the enemy, overwhelming power.

They both screamed, gasping, leaping into the Gurkhas dig out, greeted with their grins and hands held akimbo. For a comedic moment they all stared at each other, until Soph lowered her weapon, and lent exhausted against the wall. The Gurkhas nodded at them, voicing Nepali words of approval and patting the girls who had just hypothetically killed them on the back.

Trace peered up over the wall,

"Position clear Sal, position clear!"

Saunders grabbed the receiver off Green,

"Hello Charlie 7 this is Charlie 3, we are in position over…"

"For God's sake bloody radio! Work for a change already!"

Exchanging doubtful frowns Green and Saunders listened for a response,

"Roger that Charlie 3. Out."

The next thing they heard was an almighty boom.

"Looks like 7 platoon are taking the building…"

"And those glory seekers will not want to use the reserve, fucking well done Sal, you did it."

Saunders grinned,

"No to be fair, they did it…" and she looked over to where Soph, Trace and Percy were propped up, munching kitkats with the enemy.

9

THE MARTINI WAS perfect, the olive injecting a silky salty flavour that set off the dryness of the vermouth to perfection. Soph curled her tongue around the green little fruit, sucking off the skin, swilling the stone around her mouth, plucking it out and slipping it on her neatly folded napkin. She'd arrived early deliberately, just for this little moment of indulgence. Sipping her aperitif, she gazed peacefully around the room, enjoying the space. Loch Fyne had been a good choice. It was airy, not too busy, the smell of fish sweet in the air. Pulling up the strap of her dress, Soph felt oddly incongruous in the floaty number she'd bought the day before from Ted Baker. Whilst it was hot and her dress appropriate, she felt strangely exposed, not used to showing flesh, not used, she had to admit, to looking so feminine. Her hair was swept up in a rough and ready chignon, and she'd even slipped on some bejeweled espadrilles from Claire's accessories.

"Quite the girly."

Soph looked up her face a picture of delight,

"You read my mind."

She reached up to give Percy a hug.

"Mind you, you don't scrub up too bad yourself! You look like something out of The Lady. Introducing Persephone 'position taker' Percy, lead of the light Brigade."

Smiling sheepishly she slipped onto a chair. Her hair was loosely plaited, streaks of blonde a long cry from the mud caked mess that had been her thatch on Exercise Worst Encounter. She was wearing denim shorts and most of the blokes in the restaurant had noticed the muscular lines of her thighs, wrought taut from hours of trekking, marching and labouring. They made a striking pair.

Antoine, the waiter who'd won the toss to serve their table, swept over, sucking in his stomach and wishing he'd bothered with aftershave when he'd splashed his face this morning.

"Ermm, can I have, what are you having? Or finishing rather?"

"Dry Martini, lush."

"Urgh, can I have a gin and tonic and do you want another one of those?"

"Oh go on, though it'll have to be my last. I've turned into a real lightweight."

Percy stared at her friend. It had been a week. A week since commissioning and she still felt like she was floating on air. What was stranger was how she felt a little lost without her friends. They'd lived and breathed sleep deprivation, physical exhaustion, found things to laugh about when circumstances demanded otherwise. It was hard not to miss them.

"All right my lovelies!"

They both wheeled around to see Trace striding towards them. Long dark hair loose, flying out behind her, maxi dress making the most of every inch of her 5'9", her eyes a sharper green than ever, giving her the look of a cat sashaying towards them. For a moment the restaurant seemed to go still, taking the measure of these three impressive women so oblivious to their surroundings, radiating fitness and focus.

"Tracey Tracey! You're late and you call yourself an Officer!"

Ensconced with drinks and hunks of warm ciabatta, Trace sat back, throwing her hair out of the way, big silver hoop earrings capturing the light.

"I cannot believe it's all over. I mean seriously girls? Best part of a year of our lives and bang, it's finished. Don't get me wrong," holding her hands up defensively,

"I'm not saying I miss the place, but it's weird eh? Still can't get used to waking up in Cardiff, in *my* bed, in the morning as opposed to shock o'clock, y'know?"

Perce and Soph both noticed the absence of Bill and both thought better of raising it. If Trace wanted to talk she would. Bloke was an idiot anyway.

"Still can't get over that last attack and what happened to Hathaway, what a shocker."

They fell silent for a moment, dipping bread into olive oil, remembering Hathaway packing her stuff back in the lines, emptying her room, her face pale, contorted with disbelief.

"7 days away from commissioning and back termed. I couldn't do it, I would leave."

"Really?"

Soph cocked an eyebrow, interested,

"Seriously? Just think about it, she was rubbish. She totally screwed up that last attack, and that was with Hardy virtually dictating what to do."

Hardy who'd marched proudly up to the King of Jordan, lowered her blade in salute, taken hold of the Sword of Honour and turned to the right marching back to her platoon, all grinning in silent applause, the crowds voicing their approval, cheering her success.

"I know,"

Percy looked up questioningly as she took the last piece of bread and slathered it with oil.

"It's just to have to go through those last couple of months again. I mean I know its seniors and you're not on Exercise as much as Inters, but Christ, still what a slog and you still have to do those bloody endurance competitions, and go through all that drill and preparation for the final Ex."

"Rumour has it too…"

Trace interjected, draining the last of her Pinot Grigio, catching Antoine's eye who was there like a shot with a refill.

"…that the Final Ex is not going to be in Cyprus next intake, but Otter burn instead."

Soph sputtered her martini in disbelief, chuckling appalled,

"Ah, that is a shocker! She'll be eating midges for breakfast and tabbing up hills the size of bloody Snowdon!"

Antoine hovered, quietly wounded that he'd barely been noticed, when most hen do's were begging for his service. He coughed, interrupting their banter to take orders, expecting the standard small salads and low calorie options, instead stunned by requests for extra mayo, heavy on the sauce and an extra portion of chips. He walked away staggered, wondering how those three could eat so much and yet look so lithe. Bulimics he muttered to himself, shame.

"But my point is that its only 2 months and then you are still home free and it's not like First term when you don't have a clue? At least she'll know what to expect and have a pretty fundamental level of fitness to carry her through.

"Anyway, sod Hathaway, what have you two been up to?"

They each regaled stories of decadent drinking, lengthy lie ins and laughed when they confessed that for each, hair appointments had taken priority. When the food arrived, conversation died focusing on the task in hand. Savouring the fresh silvery swordfish, light batter, tasty lobster. It made a nice change from rations and food at Sandhurst and only a week out meant they still appreciated the contrast.

Stuffed, plates scraped clean, picking at the chips in the middle, they mused over their futures, the conversation taking a turn for the serious.

"So, you looking forward to Belfast? Palace isn't it? Holywood?"

Soph nodded, the flip flap of her stomach a private message of apprehension.

"Yep, Platoon Commander to a bunch of Irish blokes. S'gonna be interesting."

"Why?"

"Why what Percy?"

They all nodded at Antoine about coffees, minutes later stirring lattes and filters, dropping in squares of sugar, dollops of cream.

"Why do you have to go and do a Platoon Commander attachment?"

Soph stirred her latte, sipping at the hot drink, savouring the bitter caffeine. Folding a stray chestnut hair behind her ear, the telltale sign of nerves as she picked at her thumbnail not lost on her friends.

"The INT CORPS usually works at Brigade and above. So as young Officer we don't get to do what we've been trained for at Sandhurst, i.e. command a platoon. Yes you'll get a large section of juniors and a Warrant Officer, but not the 30 odd blokes and girls you guys will have or well, you'll have Perce, not sure how it works with the Monkeys."

Tracey rolled her eyes.

"Nope, just like Perce ignoramus. Gotta platoon of about 30 guys, I'm going to Gutesloh after phase 2 training. 102 Logistic Brigade are out there and I join the Provost branch and prep with them for their next HERRICK, though I'm not sure when they're deploying. What about you Perce? Where the Loggies sending you?"

"Well," Percy sucking on an after dinner choccie, blue eyes suddenly serious "I think we go to Aldershot…"

"What Deepcut? Isn't that?"

Perce sighed,

"Soph, it's not like that any more, the whole bullying thing. Deepcut has cleaned up its act, there's none of this institutionalized harassment, bullying and all that crap. I'm not saying it's perfect, I've just heard that the powers that be came down heavily on all that; seriously bad PR if nothing else. Anyway, I'll be doing the Officer training. Think we're on Exercise a lot."

Soph groaned, sipping her coffee.

"Urgh, you can keep that, I'm looking forward to my comfortable barracks and patrolling the streets of Belfast. My days of digging shell scrapes and bollocks like that better be over!"

Tracey couldn't help but snort,

"Never over, even for the Int Corps? Depends on who you support doesn't it? Which formation? You could be out with a Brigade doing trench digging with the best of them, pouring rain, lukewarm brews. Nooo thank you. RMP, we've got our comfy cars."

The rivalry over capbadge was alive and well and as they bantered, their animation drew intrigued looks, their vivacity and humour attractive, compelling. Conversation quietening, Soph turned to Trace,

"Look, I wasn't going to ask but, the Commissioning Ball, everything that happened, I mean, are you…?"

Trace's eyes darkened, head dropping, wrapping a piece of hair around her finger, looking unexpectedly vulnerable making Soph wished she'd left it alone, ignoring Percy's protective frowns.

"Disaster wasn't it?"

Bill had been less than ecstatic about the timing of her commissioning. "Thursday? Seriously? I've got a big deal with the Japs coming over, we need to talk technical drawings and the fuel providers they want. Not to mention the complexities of their plans…."

As Bill rattled on Trace was pained by his lack of support, or celebration at her achievement. Yes there had been champagne and flowers and a rapturous welcome home, but that's because his buddies were with him and she'd been something, someone, to show off. He wasn't pleased for her, he was proud of himself to be *with* her. She could feel the curtains dropping from her eyes and she didn't want to see what was so agonizingly apparent.

"Babe, it's a huge occasion. The King of Jordan will be there and there's the Ball afterwards?"

At the mention of both royalty and booze, Bill's hesitation evaporated, asking how many friends he could bring and what time did it all kick off? Eyes glazing over when she talked through the details of the parade and re-engaging when she outlined the plan for the Ball. Her stomach had churned with anxiety.

"And Babe, it's a long day, you, you might want to pace yourself."

Bill's eyes had blazed with accusation,

"What are you saying Tracey? That I might get pissed? Might embarrass you? That what you implying?"

As she reassured him, she had wondered not for the first time how her achievement had become about him.

She looked up at her friends; their faces pained, Soph's eyes narrowed in anger, Percy a picture of compassion,

"So like clockwork he was pissed at three…."

Bill had weaved over to her, she aghast at how drunk he was; mortified in front of parents who'd only met him once.

"Bayyyyby, you looked amassshing…"

Tracey's parents had slipped past, eyes to the floor, giving Tracey some privacy, her Father's quiet cough slicing through her.

"Bill, I told you it would be a long day, *please*, you have to sober up, the Ball goes on well into the night, and I want you to be sober enough to pull the covering off the pips on my Mess Dress. Please don't ruin this for me."

Stiff with offence, Bill had become belligerent and brash, and whilst her parents ordered cream teas waiting for the daughter of whom they were so proud, Trace found herself begging her boyfriend not to ignore her, and could he perhaps drink the teeniest bit of water?

"Bloody hell mate! What a cock!" Soph couldn't hide her horror. "Please tell me your brothers clocked him?"

Tracey's brothers had pleaded with her to take him outside,

"Let us just have a quiet chat with him Trace…"

Trace had known they were seething, knew that neither Chris nor Mark liked Bill and would delight in filling him in, but equally they respected this was her day so resisted the urge to knock him out in the middle of the hotel lobby.

Playing with his ears at supper that evening like some dire party trick moving them upwards and downwards, sending texts and glaring at Tracey hadn't exactly been highlights of the meal, but he'd stopped slurring at least. Mark had still pulled her aside at the end of dinner, stopping her before she changed into her newly tailored Mess dress, worn for the first time that night,

"Trace," his face a picture of concern, his every 38 years required to exert the self-control he didn't feel,

"Please let Chris and I take this fool away? I will pay for a room for him myself. Trace…"

He'd taken her by the shoulders as shame stole over her face,

"He's not worth it, don't let him spoil something for which you've worked so hard."

Trace shook her head; regret flooding her even now, a week later.

"I should have listened, I should have let my brothers chuck the tosser in a room and make him sober up, but I just hoped…"

53

She choked, a lump in her throat, the memory raw. Soph reached over, squeezing Tracey's hand, she smiled, taking a breath,

"...So instead I, like an idiot, said no I wanted him there and sure enough, Bill got bladdered."

The fireworks had gone off at midnight and instead of celebrating, euphoric at passing the finishing line and becoming a Commissioned Officer, Trace had wept as her brother Mark peeled off the silk covering over her single pips on her shoulders, she looking round, bleating despairingly for Bill who no-one could find.

"So where the hell was the asshole?"

Tracey shrugged, "God knows, he maintains he 'got lost', frankly it doesn't matter."

"I have to say though,"

Sophie, squeezing Tracey's hand before reaching for her own now lukewarm coffee.

"...I was deeply, deeply impressed by you tearing a strip off him the next morning."

"I think everyone was!"

Percy chuckling, remembering how they'd all listened to the hushed fury of Tracey as she'd explained in intricate detail just how badly Bill had behaved and just how much of a selfish bastard he was. There had actually been some cheers from closed rooms as Bill had tiptoed out in disgrace, eyed dolefully by a disapproving ColourSergeant who had almost wept with laughter as he had listened to Tracey's wrath.

"Yeah well, I'm not quite in the place to find it funny yet..."

Percy paused,

"Not yet hon, but you will."

"I am sorry," Sophie interjected, looking for the waiter, "but he *was* a cock. So how about a toast?"

Three shots of tequila arrived and despite groans, feigned vomitting noises, collectively they threw back the glasses, laughing at shared triumphs.

"To friends!"

10

Belfast, Holywood.

"OH GOD, I think I'm going to be sick."

Her eyes were streaming, chest screaming and all she could think of was putting one leg in front of the other to keep going.

Palace Barracks was a punishing running route, more so for someone who'd spent the last three weeks eating lasagne, lazing in bed and drinking the best part of a bottle of Oyster Bay a night. Complacency Sophie was paying for now as her t-shirt dripped with sweat and she swallowed tears. How was she supposed to have known her Platoon Sergeant would be a running snake? This was trial by fitness; check out the newbie, thrash her into submission.

"Not me."

Through gritted teeth, swallowing back bile, not now.

Admittedly she hadn't known what to expect. Cruising into camp in her Mini convertible, totally impractical when packing for the ferry, squeezing in combat boots, sleeping bag behind seats, wedged anywhere she could find space, the Camp had looked sleepy. This will be a breeze. 6 months here, bit of shopping in Belfast, bit of phys then off to do Special to Arms training. No worries.

She gasped for air like a drowning swimmer, swallowing back vomit now, bile a pleasant memory. You *are* kidding, was that a blister?

How wrong she'd been. The introductions had seemed innocuous, although the CSM with his broad Northern Irish accent, kept giving her an overwhelming urge to parrot phrases like 'I know where you live'. Her platoon Sergeant meanwhile was a force of nature. Frosty at first, he'd offered a hand that engulfed hers, pumping furiously, speaking nineteen to the dozen about platoon training, marching season and what were her plans for Exercises? Sophie's head had spun, any semblance of confidence leaking out of boots. Both men were huge and she was no dwarf. She felt like the new girl at school, intimidated, lost, not even sure where the loo was.

"So Ma'am, how yer finding it?"

Soph looked up blearily at Sergeant Brown, barely breaking a sweat,

"Thought we could do woon mure lap, end then we let the boys cuule down? Or d'yer want ta push uut another cuuple of laaps?"

What the hell was he saying? Something about laughs? Who was laughing? This wasn't funny. What was wrong with this bloke? She'd been saddled with some eejit who was sadistic to boot. Laps? Laps! Right, laps. Despite gasping for oxygen like an emphysemic smoker, Soph nodded,

"Sure," she blurted, "two more laps, lead the way..."

"Yer with me a'course Ma'am, wheeze gotta lead fra'th front."

Oh for God's sake! Please just let me stop here and curl up and die, this is inhumane. Instead Sophie willed her legs on and edged forward with Sergeant Brown. Two more laps? Did she just agree to two more laps? But these laps were epic. How could such a small Camp actually have hills? She jogged beside her Sergeant, his long legs taking one stride for her every two. Behind her was a litany of suffering, coughing, splutters, spitting and curses. At least she wasn't the only one hanging. They turned the first corner,

"So youu's leek running Ma'am? Aiimm quite a farn, go every day, so I's thought you could cum wi'me? We culd talk about training fur tha platoon?"

What? Alarmed Soph pictured hauling herself out of bed at the sparrow's fart of dawn, dragging on Ronhills, scraping back hair into a pony tail. God it would be like Sandhurst. I don't want that she screamed internally, that would be hell!

"Surree."

Why was she rolling her u's like they were r's? Get a grip woman.
"Sure Sergeant Brown,"

Rounding the third corner, thank God,

"That sounds like a plan. S'always good for there to be a united front."

She sounded like something out of the 1950s. Where had that come from? Rounding the fourth corner, Soph took comfort from one more lap, but wait a second? What the hell was he doing? She looked on in horror as Sergeant Brown lengthened his stride increasing the pace dramatically. She could hear collective swearing behind her as they turned to forge up the final hill. Sergeant Brown peeled off leaving Sophie desperately trying to keep up the speed, her legs slowly turning to jelly, lungs bursting.

"C'mon, keep moving, keep up thar, push yuresulves mun, wuurk haard!"

Sophie burst along the road, pushing through the final 100 metres, just staving off collapsing in front of the platoon lines. Bodies piled past her, blokes collapsing on verges, bent double, someone puking into the bushes. Sergeant Brown jogged up next to Sophie, whispering into her ear,

"Gotta be honest Ma'am, thurght yuu'd be encouraging them blokes a bit murre, straight from San'hurst an'all."

Soph mustered a thin smile, feeble thumbs up, then threw up all over his trainers.

11

Aldershot

PERCY PLUCKED RESTLESSLY at her combat jacket, a thin sheen of sweat on her brow, her t-shirt damp. *You'd think by now I'd be used to sweating my arse off.* Instead she shifted in the four tonners front seat, looked around for Corporal Jay, the driver and where the hell was Staff Sergeant Mason?

It was midday. Staff Mason had jumped out for what he called a bit of check navving aka a slash and a fag. Corporal Kay was off calling his girlfriend and as for the rest of the convoy? Percy chewed her lip, as Convoy Commander she didn't feel particularly like she was in command and her convoy appeared MIA. Nibbling on her nail, she flipped open her nyrex, checking the check list. She'd done radio procedure as directed, everyone had acknowledged, she'd hit her RV bang on time. A small drop of sweat trickled down her nose, landing on the waterproof page. The tap at the window startled her, rolling it down Percy peered out,

"Ma'am, they're coming, so you might wanna take errm, a comfort break, we've got a 10 hour stint coming on and you ain't gonna get many chances, know what I mean?"

Percy grinned; Staff Brillo Mason was her, second in command or otherwise known as 2ic and becoming a mentor too. So whilst technically she was in command everyone knew that he was in charge. He was unmissable with his deathly pale skin, hair that resembled a red brillo pad, skin drawn taut over his face, frame wiry from years of hill running and committed smoking. He was smaller than Percy, but what he lacked in height he made up for in attitude. They'd hit it off from the start, a chin up war in the office leveling any doubts he had about her being a Rupert from Sandhurst. He'd been quietly impressed by the blonde, her soft baby blue eyes, quick to smile but sharp as a whippet and fit too, quite the bundle. Question was, could she hold her own in front of the blokes or was she one of those officers who'd shag about or slope shoulders when it all got a li–tt–le bit difficult? So far though she'd not only made the brews, she'd actually written orders, fabloned check-lists and her radio chat was pretty good too. For once, this one pip wonder might know what she was doing...

Corporal Kay swaggered over trying to look tougher than his 19 years, appearing more like a stroppy uniformed teenager,

"Staff 'ow long we got? I got time for a quick fag?"

"Sure, burst into flames, Ma'am?"

Percy jumped out of the cabin, grateful for the breeze, her t-shirt slowly peeling away from her back. Cradling her cigarette she dragged in sharply, hand shading her forehead, peering out to the entourage trucking towards them. It was about 20 minutes late, which meant they would have to make up 30 minutes somewhere, because this lot coming in would need a quick rest before moving on from this RV. How was she going to make up that time?

"No meal breaks, any pit stops get slashed in half and everyone has to radio check in every couple of miles, call it three. How does that sound?"

Percy shook her head wryly,

"Are you psychic?"

Blowing out smoke amused,

"No Ma'am, but I can read your face like a book, and I'll let you into a secret...,"

She leant towards him as he whispered dramatically,

"I've done this before."

Snorting Percy stubbed out her fag, walking over to the first four tonner pulling up behind them.

"You've got 3 minutes to have a pee stop and rehydrate and then we're on the move."

Good girl, thought Staff Mason nodding quietly in approval, flicking his own cigarette into the bush, now to convince the other Seniors to screw the nut and help this little Officer pass her first convoy Command appointment.

12

Southwick Park

TRACEY HUGGED HER coffee mug and sat back. The view was calming, green slopes, manicured lawns, trees thick with blossom. She could just make out some birdsong despite the cleaners singing along to Justin Bieber's latest hit. She took another sip of coffee courtesy of her indulgent Nespresso machine, nestled in the corner of her room. The move in had been easy, everything packed into her clapped out VW van and transferred into this SLAM accommodation. It was the updated single persons living arrangements, with an en suite shower and loo, a designated 'living room' area and a partitioned bedroom. Her kit was stuffed into the sizeable walk in cupboard, the rest stowed away in the storage rooms at the end of the corridor.

The odd familiar face from her intake made things less daunting since she'd completely failed to register that those who'd joined the SPS or ETS would be here doing their Special to Arms training as well. It gave the place a University feel and already a couple of weeks in, there was enough gossip to fill a tabloid, the corridors stinking of booze, illicit fags.

Paperwork. She hadn't reckoned on that; reams of the stuff. Caseloads were her bread and butter. Patrols in Germany would be scarce, she'd be overseeing her Platoon, scoffing now at the word leadership, Trace realized management would be her middle name. She curled a stray hair behind her ear, nibbling her lip gently, green eyes trained on the trees outside. Close Protection,

Special Investigation Branch or General Police Duties. Sighing hard, pushing paperwork to the side, she drained her mug and wondered in which part of the RMP she'd like to specialize. Close Protection or CP was sexy no denying it, evasive driving skills, honed firing drills, they'd all joked about it in syndicates, who'd they'd protect, the blokes acting like Starsky and Hutch. SIB, Special Investigation Branch appealed more: cerebral, more involved. She liked jigsaws and saw detailed investigations as a derivation of the same format, finding the pieces, linking them together, creating coherence out of a chaotic evidence chain. NCIS without the Navy she smiled.

"Hey stranger, you're deep in thought…"

Trace wheeled round to see Dom French leaning against the door. Her heart had sank when he'd pitched up, his friendship with Ben Kitson making Tracey wary. However, slowly Dom had eroded her caution with his forthright openness. His banter was still pretty rubbish, but now that Ben wasn't around he seemed more honest.

"God you finished already?"

"Nooo, just thought I'd come and pester you."

Dom raked a hand through bushy hair, it wasn't quite bouffant, but pretty close. His eyes danced, a piercing blue that matched his current t-shirt of choice, a Super dry favourite he'd worn to death and she hadn't failed to notice clung to his chest ra-ther nicely.

Tracey grinned, even if Dom wasn't her type it was nice to have the attention, after her self-esteem withered away like a neglected vine under Bill's sarcasm and disinterest.

"Have you come begging for another espresso?"

Dom scooted in, flinging himself into the issue 'easy chair', a grey foamed armchair that was ubiquitous throughout the accommodation.

Tracey snapped in another pod to her machine and let the water steam through, Dom flicked through her notes, flagrantly stealing her ideas.

"Struggling are we?"

Eyebrow raised imperiously, snatching back her scribblings.

"No, it's just," Dom flung his head back dramatically,

"...seriously Trace, we're supposed to be the cops y'know? I didn't drag my ass through Sandhurst to become a pen pusher. I wanna be out in Afghan, front and flipping centre, catching bad guys, making sure it's a legal fighting force, efficient killing machine, respecting the military order y'know?"

She smiled, opening her mini fridge, splashing a drop of milk into Dom's coffee, not too much, not too little, habit ingrained by his endless visits.

"Dom bless you," she smiled maternally, "but in the nicest possible way grow up."

He pouted,

"You're acting like we live in some comic, as if the blimin' X-men or Fantastic Four are going to bust through the door and drag you off to kerpow some Taleban ass. All blam blam and blat blat."

She fired off finger guns into the air.

Dom sipped his drink sheepishly,

"Yeah, well it's more interesting than managing case loads, and pushing bureaucratic paper piles. I just didn't think this through I suppose. Once again it's the soldiers who get their hands dirty and we..."

"Oversee." They both intoned, Trace flicking her fingers like speech marks hanging in the air.

"Have you thought about Close Protection?"

"Does Rod hull know Emu? Are you kidding? As soon as we are through this training and I'm in a Unit I'm gonna do my best to get recommended, I tell you."

His eyes shone at the thought, despite the fact that he sat there looking like some washed up surfer dude, all baggie shorts and Cult Clothing.

"Anyways, you were looking pretty pensive earlier? Everything all right? Missing your sheep?"

Trace rolled her eyes, sipped her own tepid coffee dregs.

"I'm fine, actually bit nervous really."

"Why?"

Dom crouched in front of her fridge, peering in at the contents hopefully. Trace reaching over, kicking him with her foot, pulling open a draw and tossing him a tube of hob nobs,

"Don't eat them all."

He tucked in feigning offence, sliding back into the armchair,

"So?"

"Well we've got that exam for SIB selection tomorrow?"

"Now you're being dramatic Trace it's just an aptitude test and a couple of interviews, but yeah I get your 'this means the world to me' gist."

"Well," Trace couldn't help but laugh, "It means the world to me. It really interests me and…"

"Yeah you'd make a fit Tamsin Outhwaite. Not sure you'd look better blonde but I'd do you."

"Thanks for the recommendation."

"You're welcome."

"Never gonna happen Dom my man."

"Can't blame a guy for trying…" He leered grinning, mouth full of chocolate hob nob.

"You're disgusting y'know?"

"Still do you."

13

Aldershot

PERCY SIGHED, BLOWING errant blonde hairs out of her eyes, chewing nails, expertly missing the cam cream smeared on her hands.

"I cannot believe I'm wearing cam cream again. I only commissioned 6 months ago surely there should be some break?"

"Why?" Staff Brillo straight faced,

"So you can pad tactically around a desk? Believe me ma'am..." He mused blowing smoke out of the window, watching the crescent of the moon, thinking of his mrs and her famous banoffie pie,

"...there is plenty of time for barrack action. S'better out here anyway."

He flicked his butt outside, its tip glowing softly in the dark, an orange beacon sputtering into black.

"Train hard fight easy Ma'am, won't be long before we're out in Helmand anyways."

They'd been talking about the rumours flying. Whilst it still depended on which Unit Percy was posted, most Regiments were rotating through Afghanistan at an alarming rate. Logistics first in, last home. It was a brutal tempo of which Staff Brillo was all too aware. Percy meanwhile was itching to get on with the real job, stop the pretend, get amongst it. Brillo appreciated her keenness, but knew it wouldn't take long for the Army to suck her dry, leaving her parched of hope like the rest of them. Drones; too tired to care, too apathetic to leave.

A pair of headlamps flashed dipping and diving in the distance, weaving towards them. Percy flicked a look at her watch; practiced now at time appreciation, fuel consumption, load bearing and its effect on approximating speed. Her navigation had improved as well. Staff Brillo hadn't disguised his astonishment that she could read a map.

"Nothing sexist Ma'am, just normally you Officers are fucking rubbish at navigating. At least you've got the map up the right way."

As was typical he fell into silence, conversation over for another few hours. Percy appreciated his dry wit, insightful quips. He hadn't been a sympathetic tutor, but his attention to detail and industrious nature had proved an effective trainer. Whilst her counterparts had less conscientious SNCOS and it showed. Percy's mentor had meant she was head and shoulders above the rest and whilst theirs couldn't quite be described as a camaraderie, Staff's universal disdain and suspicion of Officers putting pay to that, there was a mutual respect that was enough for Percy.

It was the Final Ex on her course. This, her last Command appointment and it was no easy finish. It had been 3 days straight already and whilst there was no sleeping in shell scrapes, putting up bashers or dodging DS, it was more intense because, if anything, this mattered even more. Percy was acutely aware that the SNCO and JNCO grapevine was faster and more devastating than Facebook. If she failed to perform it would circulate around each of the RLC Units in days, making any new arrival dismal. She had to get this right.

Flicking another look at her watch quietly relieved that things were running to schedule. Turning on the driver's light, she cast another look at the map almost memorized. There were 6 more RVs with at least 2 of those stops being Exercise Patrol bases and one FOB. Rubbing her eyes, palms clean of camouflage she shook herself. It was 50 km to the next RV, at 12Km/h that would be four hours, four hours, her brain was foggy from too little sleep, too much coffee, four hours and 10 minutes constant driving. The drivers had a limit of eight hours a day, they'd already done four...

"Bugger, Staff! Staff,"

"Ma'am I'm right next to you, you don't have to shout."

Brillo frowned, sliding towards Corporal Kay who was dozing in the drivers' seat, the three of them clammed together like peas in a pod.

"Can drivers exceed their hours?"

Her eyes were blazing, maniacally, had she been drinking Brillo wondered? Sure she'd been mainlining coffee, but alcohol? It wouldn't be the first time a Second Lieutenant cracked under pressure. He sighed, he was sure…

"Brillo? Can they exceed their driving hours?"

Brillo's eyes narrowed. Nope not drunk, too coherent,

"Ma'am you know this…why?"

Brillo rolled his eyes, maybe she was pissed, because this was drilled into them via Powerpoint and practised throughout the course. Driving hours were a minefield both in the Army and Civvy street. Contravention could see even the squeakiest Officer hauled up on his arse, so she needed to get this straight. He sighed again, disappointed and about to launch into a lecture, when Percy butted in and reminded Brillo to trust his instinct.

"I know about the 45 minutes mandatory break after 4 and a half hours driving, but my approximations see that these guys will have done 4 hours once they get here and will only need to bang out another 4 hours 10 when they move off! Don't you get it?"

Percy whooped in delight,

"…I'm only gonna bloody get in early. You hear me?"

Her eyes were shining and it was Brillo's turn to feel his brain was mush, though he couldn't help but smile thinly at her hysteria, another Second Lieutenant cracking up, shame it was on his wa….

Wait a second? Brillo pulled out his Iphone and went through the arithmetic. She was bloody right,

"Ma'am…" he looked up, a real grin plastered on his face, "I think you are about to make Final Ex history."

And with raised eyebrows and a little giggle Percy, pushed open the four tonner door to greet the first of the convoy.

The next morning, Brillo was stood around with the other DS comparing notes over egg banjos and coff-tea, the unique Army blend of coffee and tea, a swirling brew, hot and wet delivered in green Norwegians. At 5am no one cared how it tasted as long as it was warm and liquid.

Brillo stood back listening to discussions. Whilst his opinion would likely be sought, he was experienced enough to keep his head down and ears open at the initial deliberations if he cared at all about the young Officer he'd nurtured. He also wasn't naïve, realizing that Percy's performance reflected just as much on him as it would in terms of paving her future posting. He moulded his beret, smoothing it over grade three hair, wiry red curls resolutely bouncey. Agitated, he thrust his thumbs in his webbing belt, paced behind the Officers, ignoring the other Staffies. He sighed, pulled out his B&Hs and flicked his zippo. Snapping it shut, slowly slipped off his beret, folding and unfolding it methodically, until he became conscious his behaviour might be attracting attention, so slid it into his combat jacket pocket, sliding the zip closed thoughtfully. Perching on the edge of the brew table, its rickety legs complaining he watched the conversation. He knew she'd done well. Question was did these Captains?

"Well Willows albeit late was still pretty slick on his drills, got the convoy through the refueling pretty well…"

Willows? Brillo stifled a laugh. Didn't they know Willows was a bluffer? That he leaned on his Staffie like an arthritic old man on a stick. He flicked a look at Staff Butcher, Willow's Staff Sergeant. Butcher was a good bloke, could do with cutting down on the pies, but honest and he thought Willows was feeble, ultimately, worst of all a weak commander. He'd bottled under pressure, turning to Butcher a gibbering wreck begging for advice, his route cards a mass of confusion, his radio procedure shot. It had taken Butchers the best part of 5 minutes just to calm him down. Butcher caught Brillo's look, narrowed his eyes, mouth twitching disapproval.

"Then of course Walters…whilst he was wobbly to start with, he made all PBs within time, course he did cock up the FOB unload…"

Cock up? Brillo stubbed his fag out, reaching for another. Walters was a smug self-righteous arrogant knob. He'd looked down his nose at his Staffie and his soldiers, strutted around like a peacock and blagged a good game. It might have worked for these Captains, but his Staffie fully intended to let Walters' next Unit know about his habit of calling his Senior NCOs 'my man'.

"Then there's Brooks..."

Brillo's ears pricked almost perking his head up like a Meer cat, instead taking quick drags of his cigarette, senses feverish,

The Captain who hadn't spoken so far chipped in. Brillo knew him as Williams, didn't know much about him, apart from his name was Duncan and he had a hell of a reputation; kept his cards close to his chest, but his opinion was highly rated, Brillo noticed the other Captains went quiet.

"She was good, really good. She came in on time, didn't panic under fire, her voice procedure was slick, her routes good. She made all of the RVs, and I mean all of them and she didn't cut any corners. If it were me...,"

He paused, toying with his mug, cheeks wearing a shade of stubble, a reflection of the long days and nights, his eyes an intense oceanic blue, piercing as if penetrating to the heart of any dilemma by his pupils alone.

"...I'd want her on my convoy and frankly I'd take her out with me now."

Brillo could have cheered. Out-fucking-standing. At last, but what? What was this...?

"Yeah, get that Williams and she's fit as well, but Walters has got quite a presence, we're talking about the best second lieuie here."

"Sirs,"

Startled the Officers looked round,

"Hey Brillo, you all right there? Gave us a fright."

"Sorry, look, I don't mean to interfere but about Brooks?"

"Oh yeah, got a bit of a soft spot have we?"

Brillos's glare silenced the innuendos, feet shifting uncomfortably under his gaze.

"I gotta show you something, I think, I think it'll make your decision easier."

Brillo shifted the tea urns and spread out a map.

"See this?"

"Yep, think we all know that Brillo it's the route your Troopie took, in fact they all took because it's the quickest and most direct…"

"Yes, it was, but I don't think you noticed the difference in her route card which allowed her to be a whole 20 minutes quicker than the other wan…junior Officers."

Curious, Williams and the other Captains peered over Brillo's shoulder, scouring the map. Brillo pulled a pen out of his jacket, never using a finger on since it could obscure an entire grid square, he pointed out a vague thread on the route.

"What's…"

"No way."

Williams whistled and stepped back.

"Fair bloody play."

"She found it herself."

Brillo knew eyes were on him, he slowly took his beret out, smoothed it back on, keeping it calm, playing it cool, yet conscious his eyes were blazing with triumph and not a small bit of pride.

"I didn't even know that track was there. She found it, dragged me out to recce it with her at the crack of bloody dawn, it's that, that that gave her the edge, it's that, that that brought her in under time. I just thought…I just thought you ought to know."

"Cheers Brillo," Williams looked at him thoughtfully,

"We'll bear that in mind."

The other Captains nodded, slipping note books in pockets, conversation over.

Brillo nodded his jaw tightening, eyes narrowed saying more than words could ever convey, daring them to go against what he had pointed out, what was so glaringly apparent.

"Right Sirs."

He turned and walked away, because that was all he could do.

Percy flopped on her bed, boots still on, leaving a green imprint of her face on the White Company duvet. Fuck she mouthed into the sheet remembering she hadn't cleaned off her cam cream. Hauling herself off her bed, she stood before her mirror, grabbing a wodge of Wipe-Out, wet wipes smearing green sludge off her cheeks. Her eyes red rimmed, bloodshot, lips cracked from dehydration, eyebrows unruly, in dire need of tweezer attention.

"Well, I think I totally wiped the floor with that Ex."

Walters leaned nonchalantly against her door, hands slung in pockets, eyes haughty and imperious.

Percy turned and scowled. Walters wasn't bad looking in a Mr Darcy sort of way, but there was something about him, the self-righteousness and snobbery that soured any attraction. Whilst he might act like a Cavalry officer, he was in the wrong Corps and she couldn't help but wonder if he was a bluffer.

"That went like a dream..."

Willows drifted into Percy's room. Small, almost puny, his combat jacket seemed to wear him more than he it. He sunk into her grey armchair, picking his nails,

"...no dramas whatever, if that's what it's going to be like in Afghan then it's gonna be a breeze."

Percy's stomach tightened, was she the only one who'd found the Ex challenging? Who'd stayed up long into the night scrutinizing the map, looking for quicker routes, checking her route cards, making sure she'd had alternatives, double checking her checking. Bugger, her spirit sank like a slow puncture, I've obviously really cocked up. She thought shamefully of Brillo, she'd have to apologise for letting him down. Damn, She walked to her mirror, snatching some cotton wool, pulling savagely at her cheeks, dragging the cam cream off in long strokes. I thought I'd done ok.

14

Belfast

THE FOOTLOCKER SHOEBOX sat on his desk. Sophie eyed it, butterflies flapping up a hurricane in her stomach. She sat at the desk trying to ignore the clock. In achingly early, she'd set two alarms to ensure she got in before him he being such a bloody early worm. She inched out a crust of sleep in the corner of her eye, yawned cradling her coffee. God she missed Starbucks. Naafi coffee was disgusting and the Mess wasn't any better. Blimin' Tracey and her Nespresso machine had got her hooked on those espressos, she'd have to log onto eBay later and get one herself.

Sergeant Brown threw open the office door and came to an abrupt halt to find his Platoon Commander sat studiously studying patrol reports. It was 0632 and he had to use every ounce of self-control not to laugh. Hanging his combat jacket behind the door he ignored the trainers.

"Morning tha' Ma'am, ya in errrly."

"Yep Sergeant Brown, y'know, paperwork, like the morning, quiet, can crack on and not be interrupted."

"Raaally?"

He suppressed the urge to continue, like it so much that I've never seen you in before 0830? He sat down at his computer, ignoring the shoebox.

Sophie winced, bastard, he was going to really drag this out.

"Errm, about the run, I, well I've been meaning…"

72

"Don't chuu thank any muure about ut ma'am, yooose impressed tha booze, giving it cha all."

He'd since heard from the Sergeants' Mess that apparently his Second Lieuie had been on the pop the night before the vomiting incident. He'd swallowed a grin at how she must have suffered pushing out those final two laps. Still fair play to her, she probably came damn near close to giving herself heat exhaustion.

"So about your trainers, I was in Belfast over the weekend and…"

"Oh yas? My wife, she luuuves it tha, so she does, bores me rugud all them there shops, but still, think it's a female thang."

"Oh for God's sake Sergeant Brown, will you open the damn box."

Sergeant Brown cracked a grin and pulled it towards him,

"Ma'am, yoose shuuldn't hav', I've pot thum in the washing muuchine, and thaa'll be fine."

Mind you, he thought, pulling out the snappy Nike numbers, these are quite nice and save me a bob or two. This Officer didn't have the usual deep pockets.

"So yooouse recovered ha'ye?"

It had taken Soph the best part of three days to rehydrate and recover from that PT session. Her nose crinkled at the memory, it was, however, entirely her fault she'd struggled so badly. The night before in the Mess she'd gone to the bar for the first time. Normally quick to dive into the formal dinner, nod to the others at the table, wolf down her meal and dash back to her room to catch up on unpacking, setting up Skype and filling in arrival paperwork. That night she'd fancied a wind down, and ambled into have a quiet drink. Three hours later she was racing shots with some Fusilier Captain called Andy, being cheered on by the Camp's Adjutant a guy she could only recall as 'the Rosster' as well as Andy's Company 2iC, a Will Carling lookalike oddly called Will. She cringed remembering the conversation turning cruder and cruder, with gossip about other Mess members and corridor creeping that had had her eyes wide as saucers. The next morning, gulping orange juice like she'd just walked out of the desert, she'd tried to slip out of breakfast unobserved only to walk squarely into 'the Rosster'. Managing a weak smile, he'd sneered at her unkindly, making marked quips about Officerly conduct, leaving Soph open mouthed on the Mess front steps as he took off on his mountain bike.

"Well nice to meet you too."

Gloomy about her hangover, the run hadn't raised her spirits, but at least she'd sweated out the spirits she'd drunk.

"Yeah, am fine now."

"I mus'admit ma'am, Eyes ha' thou you be fitter coming fra'sandhurst an all. If ya'don't mind me saying, yees tried to hide it, bu' I could see yooouse was hanging."

Soph's face reddened, he had a point, but she'd apologized and she had her pride.

"I've bought you some trainers to apologise, I made a mistake getting tanked up. But seriously Sergeant Brown you were out to make a point. Flogging the newbie Second Lieuie around camp like it was a Formula One track? Not exactly subtle or original? So how's about we call it even?"

Sergeant Brown paused grudgingly impressed; he was beginning to like this one.

As the days passed, the unlikely pair began to forge a friendship, largely conducted through a series of daily practical jokes. She'd walk in and find her computer autocorrect changed, with every 'and' adjusted to type 'Sergeant Brown is OC' or if she typed 'the', 'I owe Sergeant Brown a lucozade' would flash up. The initial 5 minutes had been deeply amusing until Soph realized it would take the best part of an hour to undo all the wise cracks Sergeant Brown had so painstakingly inserted. That little joke had upped the ante, so that both of them got up increasingly early to get a head start on the other in the office, be it to re-arrange the other's desk or hide their coffee cup whilst looking on innocently. Then of course there were the runs. Paula Radcliffe would have been subdued at some of the jog outs Sergeant Brown dragged Soph round. Although the pace was steady, with no unexpected lengthening of strides like her first running baptism, the distances were herculean. Who knew that

Belfast had so many hills or that one man could navigate so efficiently to ensure they enjoyed them all?

She lost count of the days she'd be bleary eyed, cheeks puce with effort, quads screaming, looking up only to see Sergeant Brown cresting a hill that may as well have been in another continent. Nonetheless, Soph persisted and although there was little conversation, her insides churning with nervous anticipation before each departure, as the weeks passed she knew her fitness was rocketing. Gradually able to keep up with Sergeant Brown, her breath a little smoother, her pace as fast, her quads less agonized.

The side effects that Soph hadn't noticed were an increase in confidence, composure and a calmer attitude to life on camp. Previously she would have arrived at the office irritated by the misogynistic banter at dinner, aggrieved by the sexist protocol and archaic etiquette that had insisted on livers-in assembling in the bar en masse in suits before moving into the dining room. She would have come incensed at countless roasts where the conversation focused on soldiers who 'would get one' or facile observations on the latest X-box game, or TV celeb's breast implants. Bored to tears one evening, Soph had responded to some inane inaccurate observation about strategic defence and been met with silence; a silence that had lasted the best part of 5 minutes, with only the scraping of cutlery to pierce the quiet. Flush with self-consciousness, she had never been the butt of such outright bullying and rather than be intimidated she did what she had always done, held her head high and met her browbeaters face on that evening,

"So Andy, how were you the morning after those shots? I tell you I was suffering, and I had a PT session from hell to boot."

Soph's heart was racing, hands shaking as she carved pork and crackling, she looked up at Andy, willing her face to remain unmoved, unaffected by the fact he was ignoring her, her question hanging awkwardly. Instead, a greying, lean bloke chipped in, she'd seen him about, knew that he was part of her Unit, the Royal Irish, but hadn't been introduced. She remembered Sergeant Brown warning her a propos of nothing,

"Ba'careful o'tha one, he's a mean piece of work and yoose an easy target."

That evening he looked over at Soph, his eyes narrowing, a thin smile, as he laid his knife and fork down,

"So, does Sandhurst teach you to be sick all over your Senior NCOs trainers these days or did I miss that lecture?"

Soph blushed with embarrassment, meat catching in her throat she reached for her water, hand heavy with indignation,

"Well, it was an introduction neither of us will forget, but Sergeant Brown has really helped with my fitness. He's an absolute running machine."

Her voice was brittle, contrived cheerfulness that sounded hollow, needy. Christ where did this come from? Who was this bloke?

"I felt like rubbish actually Soph, hanging and I'm sure I stank when I went into work the next day. Frankly I'm sure I would have collapsed if I'd been forced to run out that day. I saw you out with your platoon, you at the front, thought it was a good effort myself."

Soph's eyes switched to the speaker who at that moment she could have kissed with relief. It was the Will Carling lookalike, he deliberately focused on his food, not catching anyone's eyes, but for now it was enough to bat off the graying snake, who narrowed his eyes at Will, instead excusing himself from the table but not before throwing Soph a threatening look. Who the hell was that guy?

After dinner, Soph had drifted into the ante room, pouring herself coffee, glad to be away from the boxing ring that had been supper. The Taleban had shown less aggression than was focused on her tonight. Shaking a little from residual nerves, she picked up the Telegraph and slid into the leather sofa nestled in the bay window at the rear of the room. Immersed in stories of Cameron and the NHS, she didn't notice someone place their coffee cup on the table until he started speaking,

"Look, I'm, Will, we met the other night and I just wanted to say sorry about what happened in there."

Instinctively guarded, she narrowed her eyes, defensive, unsure whether he was friend or foe despite his throwing her a line at the meal. His eyes were steady, a rugged face if a little heavy. He was broad with the rugby players' physique that so reminded her of the old English Captain. He looked vaguely familiar, possibly the intake above her at Sandhurst? She sipped her drink and looked at him levelly,

"What was that about? I mean seriously, I've only come to dinner a few times, but if Hitler himself had entered the room he'd have got a warmer reception. And what the hell was with grey haired guy? I've never met him before but he was gunning for me."

Soph felt tears springing to her eyes, quickly glancing down swallowing back the emotion.

"You don't know Grant?"

"No?"

Sophie shook her head, frowning,

"Should I?"

"That's your Adjutant."

Her heart sank.

"Fabulous, so the guy whose responsible for the discipline of young Officers in my Battalion now knows within the first few days of being here I got howlingly drunk and puked over my Sergeant's shoes. Excellent."

Will suppressed a wry grin, then looking more serious,

"I'd be careful with him, he's got an eye for the girls and he can be a vicious fucker."

Will, it transpired, had been in the intake above Soph. The Fusiliers with whom he was a Platoon Commander had been in Palace Barracks for a little over 2 months by the time Soph had arrived. He sat down beside her, thighs squeezed into the brown leather armchair, his suit straining to contain some pretty impressive biceps. Cradling his coffee, he crossed a leg,

"It is bl-oo-dy boring. S'alot of range work, phys and patrols but that's about it. We're pretty much at the back end of Op BANNER, so the interesting stuff is over. Yes we've got the marching season in a couple of weeks, but apart from that we're just marking time until we head off to TELIC or HERRICK. Tricky, because the blokes are getting bored too, so they go into town and get into trouble, which in downtown Belfast, even these days, isn't bright. So what happens? More and more of the town becomes out of bounds until you can only get a bloody drink in MacDonald's."

Sophie nodded thoughtfully, out of bounds, she hadn't even heard about that, and as for the Marching season, the thought of corralling angry hordes was more than enough to focus on, let alone anything more 'interesting'. Yawning she called it a night, wandering upstairs, flicking on her computer, jiggling her mouse, sliding onto her desk chair, slipping off her suit jacket and loosening her shirt. Logging onto eBay she entered a search for coffee machines and assuaged the memories from dinner by deliberating over Gaggia or Delonghi.

15

PULLING ON HER running shorts the next morning, Soph cheated by hopping into her Mini and nipping up the 500 metres to her office. Typically Sergeant Brown was already in, wearing his running kit as if born in it. He handed her a freshly brewed coffee,

"Ooh, muchos grazias Sergeant B."

"Yoouse gonna need the caffeine yoouse addicted to, thought we could go for a slightly longer run today."

"Urgh, God how much longer? Down to blimin Galway and back?"

"Don't yoouse be worrying about tha', jus' yoouse drink yas coffee and we's get going. I've got a message for ya'too. From the Adjutant,"

Soph's hand froze, stomach flipping,

"Oh really? What is it?"

Sergeant Brown looked at her quizzically,

"Why's yer looking all'scared like?"

Gulping coffee, Soph slumped into their illicitly acquired armchair, why were all the issue armchairs grey? So depressing.

"Well, I think I met him last night. Let me rephrase that, I know I met him last night and he was an arsehole."

"Ah, don't let that bother yoouse, he's like tha' with any girl who hasn't fallen for his heavily hidden charms. If yoouse not been flirting with him, he'll be saying ya' a lesbian. So's I wouldn't be paying it any attention."

Sophie mentally flicked over the last few weeks. She hadn't knowingly been ignoring anyone, dashing about in a permanent state of near exhaustion because of these runs with Sergeant....

79

"Oh no…"

She groaned, a foggy memory confirming Sergeant Brown's assessment.

"That night, the one before we went for that first PT run, I think he was in the bar, I think he was being flirty then and I, well I was pretty hammered, I think I may have just blanked him or…"

Sergeant Brown went quiet, his face serious,

"Ma'am, yoourse need to be careful with that one. He's got tha ear o'tha Battalion Commander. He could ma' ya life very difficult."

Soph stared at Sergeant Brown, coffee stewing in her stomach, all humour gone, suddenly feeling very exposed.

"How was I supposed to know?"

She banged down her mug.

"What is it with this place? It's a fucking mine field. Dinner is like some throw back to the 1950s when a woman speaking seems to defy all social etiquette and everyone looks at me like I've got two heads. Now I find out that some bloody Captain who preys on junior Officers and doesn't even introduce himself and is a complete bastard to me in front of everyone could potentially ruin my life. This place is bloody rubbish."

She knew she sounded like a petulant teenager, but there seemed threats from all angles; and politics, of which until now she'd been blithely unaware. Now that bliss was shattered.

"Look, s'no point in worrying yerself and the message woos just ta'say there's a function in the Mess tonight, and yoouse expected to be there to host, no biggie. Now let's eat some pavement."

For once Sophie had been grateful for the distraction. Feet in sync, padding side by side, arms pumping, breath in steady measures, she hung to Sergeant Brown feeling the reassurance of his company. Slowly he began to pull away from her as the miles increased, eating the distance under his long strides. Soph's eyes trained on the back of his heels, up hills, around hedge trimmed fields, around a green, through an underpass, watching his back, following his lead. Her mind empty, attention tunnelled on running, one foot in front of the other, miles and minutes melting away.

It wasn't until she started to feel her mouth slowly dry that she became aware of the distance they'd covered, familiar landmarks had been few and far between for a while now and she began to scour the distance for the comforting sight of barbed wire indicating camp fencing. Her legs were wobbly, her head getting a little woosey. Driving her arms, she laboured up the hill, Sergeant Brown a good six or seven hundred metres ahead, a stick man out of reach, relentless, leading her on and on. Slowly it became a mental battle, Soph wrestling with her inner demons, whining to stop, moaning about a couple of blisters that were nagging her feet soles, whinging about dehydration and an empty stomach reminding her of coffee and a slice of toast for breakfast, hardly enough for a mouse. She pressed on, cresting the hill Sergeant Brown had long since passed, savouring the downhill stride, closing her eyes briefly in the breeze, licking salty dried lips, flexing puffy fingers. Searching the horizon her heart finally soared, there just around the bend at the bottom of the hill she could see the shards of barbed wire. Nearly home.

Panting, legs like jelly, Soph pulled up beside a red faced Sergeant Brown who was running his hand through sweaty hair.

"Tha' was a good one ma'am."

"We…we…"

Struggling to catch her breath, her legs limp and lifeless,

"…must have done bloody miles?"

Sergeant Brown checked his watch both GPS and digital clock,

"Yeah, no'bad, about 12 o' 13 miles tha' one, I'll see yoouse back in the office."

Astounded Soph watched him jog off, looking ridiculously fresh.

God, bloke's a bloody machine, and plodding in through the gate, showing her MoD 90 to the amused guard, she wearily made her way back to the Mess.

Perched behind his desk, as if he'd been engrossed in excel spreadsheets all day, Soph, still red faced, hair still wet from the shower, walked into the office and stared at Sergeant Brown baffled.

"Seriously do you eat? Drink? Are you a machine?"

He looked up briefly, grinning and pointed at a half-eaten granola bar.

"Ah right, yep, just run virtually a half marathon and your tucking into a cereal bar."

She shook her head exhausted, pulling the plastic off a BLT and snapping on her computer.

The afternoon passed, with Soph caught up in reading past annual reports of her soldiers when Sergeant Brown interrupted the companionable silence,

"Errm, Ma'am, I don' wanna be hurrying ya' now, but chew haven't forgotten about chur mess function tonighe ha'ye?"

Soph's face drained and dropping papers she fled the room. Uniform parades and time pressure had taught Soph the art of changing in seconds. Hauling off her uniform as if it had been attached by velcro, she dragged on a pencil skirt, scraped a comb through still damp hair, shook a shirt out of her cupboard, scowling, deliberating over whether it looked ironed, time deciding there was no option and threw it on. Flinging on some heels in need of a polish she ran to her Mini, and sped up the hill, coming to a crashing halt outside her Unit's Mess. Steadying herself, she attempted to walk in looking calm and composed.

The bar was a morass of people, local dignitaries mingled with older Officers who were vaguely familiar. She scanned the room for a friendly face forcing her to close in on the throng, until someone called her name. Looking up smiling, Soph's grin froze,

"Ah Sophie."

It was him. She felt her bowels loosen. Relax she soothed herself, he's hosting local government, he's not interested in you.

"What would you like to drink?"

His fake smile made her feel like a rabbit cornered by a praying mantis, she forced a cheery answer,

"Errm, just an orange juice errm,"

Should she call him Grant? Sir? She took the plunge,

"...Grant."

Grant's smile stiffened,

"You driving Sophie?"

"Errm nooo…?"

She felt a sweat breaking out under her shirt, what was wrong with an orange juice? Was that a trick question? What did driving have to do with anything?

"So what would you like to drink?"

Becoming aware that the general hum of conversation was fading into a lull as interest in their conversation increased, Soph found herself clenching her fists steeling her fading confidence.

"Errm, I'd still like an Orange Juice please Grant."

"Do you not drink Sophie?"

"Yes Grant, you know I do."

Why was he doing this? God had she missed something when out running?

"So what would you like?"

"Grant,"

Soph felt herself flushing with anger, this was ridiculous,

"I don't care how many times you ask me, the answer will still be the same, please can I have an orange juice."

The room was silent and sensing that the audience was beginning to side with Sophie, Grant conceded, but not before he flashed Sophie a look of such pure hatred that she actually stepped back.

"Of course, you must be dehydrated with all your running after Sergeant Brown."

Ignoring the barbed comment and accompanying stilted laughter, Soph reached through the parted crowd and took her glass from Grant, who stared at her, his face cold and chilling. She looked away, backing sharply from the bar, what the hell was that about?

After 5 hours of strained conversation, eating a lifetime's allowance of cocktail sausages and dodging the passes of some septuagenarian local MP, Soph crept out to her car. Flinging herself into the front seat, she sat staring ahead, exhausted. Etiquette had demanded she stay until the CO departed. Watching him expectantly all night, Soph's hope had slumped like the flat beer being served, until drained she'd resigned herself to watching portly Officers getting sloshed whilst trying to elicit more local funding from the Mayor and his minions. Grasping her diet coke like a defensive weapon Soph had tried fruitlessly to scan the room for familiar faces. Until that point she hadn't appreciated there were so few junior Officers in the Battalion, or rather she was the only Subaltern who hadn't managed to swerve this duty. Sighing, she glanced for the 100th time at her watch until salvation passed her on his way home. Watching the CO depart Soph could have danced, and ditching her drink had raced for the car.

Sat absorbing the evening, she started the engine and paused retracing the opening sequence of the night. Sitting back baffled, twiddling with a stray hair.

"What the hell was that about?"

She turned the ignition but not before a wisp of apprehension skittered up her spine.

16

STARTLED SOPH SAT bolt upright. Ringing, she could hear ringing, what the…? It was her mobile, scowling at her watch, just making out it was bloody 0730, she didn't normally get up for half an hour. Padding naked across her room, snapping open her phone,

"Morning?"

"Ma'am, yoouse need to get into work *now*."

Her stomach plummeted,

"Why? What's wrong?"

Poised, frozen to the spot, clutching her hair back from a face etched with anxiety,

"I's dooont know ma'am, but eye've been batting off phone calls frem yer adjutant. He's been calling since 0700 asking where you are."

"0700? No ones ever been in work by 7, but whatever I'll be right up, did he give any idea?" She hopped around the room, pulling on knickers, grabbing a bra,

"Nope, jus'tha he wanted youse in his office at 0800 sharp."

Soph's eyes flicked to her watch, 0738.

"Right, better hurry."

"Bring youse blackthorn as well, I gotta feeling this is gonna be formal."

Soph snapped her phone and eyed the Blackthrorn stick she'd tossed in the corner. It was traditional to carry the wizened black stick around camp. Unwieldy, no one had explained the tradition to justify the practice. Reasons such as 'we always have', 'it's issued', had Soph rolling her eyes. Sergeant Brown's was slightly more adequate,

"I believe ma'am the tradition cuums from the swagger stick, yoouse know? When gentlemen walked with a cane to show their class? It was also useful to bop soldiers on them tha's heads in case they were out of line like. Point is yoouse is my Officer and ya'goona look proper for the platoon, so yourse gonna have to carry it."

He'd ignored Soph's sullks so she had lugged it around, until feigning she'd left it in the car or her room, eventually weaning him off it. Until now.

Sleeking her thick wavey chestnut hair back more scrupulously than normal, she pulled on her combats, and grabbed a brush and polish for her boots at the same time. Hopping around picking socks up off the floor, she kept one eye on the clock. Snatching up her keys and cane she sprinted to her Mini and shot up the hill. 5 minutes to spare she burst into their office, breathless and nervous,

"How do I look?"

Sergeant Brown surveyed his Second Lieuie, hiding his concern; something was seriously awry. The Adjutant was as wily as a fox and just as vicious. He hadn't told Soph about Grant's infamous preference for bagging the new female junior Officer in the mess, seeing it as his Adjutantal duty to break in the newbie. Sergeant Brown had hoped that Soph would have enough sense to avoid his advances, his concerns allayed by his Platoon Commander's no nonsense attitude. She was honest though and that made her vulnerable in the python's pit that was the Officer's Mess. She needed to up her game where politics were concerned.

Pulling her shirt collar down, and straightening her belt, Sergeant Brown cast an approving eye.

"Smart as a carrot. Now yoouse best get over there, and don't forget to salute before youuse go into his office."

Soph nodded, swallowing her nerves. Speed walking over to Battalion HQ, desperate to sprint over, but not wanting to be being picked up for that too, she took a breath and pulled open the Headquarters door. The atmosphere felt prickly, unsure of where to go she peered up and down the corridor finally peeking her head into the post room.

"Errm, sorry to disturb, but can you tell me where the Adjutant's office is?"

"Sure Ma'am,"

A stocky young lad walked over to the bar separating them, pushing aside parcels to lean against it, pointing her in the right direction,

"Up this corridor Ma'am and then take the stairs at the end, and the Adjutant's office is the second on the right, after the admin girls."

Soph smiled nervously, mouth dry, anxiety flooding her limbs as she made it to the next floor. At the top, she came face to face with Grant. Her heart leapt into her mouth, breathlessly stopping mid stride,

"Errm, Sir you wanted to see me?"

Grant's eyes narrowed; nodding curtly he spun round from his conversation with the Admin Corporal and paced back up the corridor. Initially uncertain, Soph paused, then seeing no indication otherwise, trotted after Grant, behind him and into his office whereupon he wheeled round,

"Get the fuck out of my office and do that again."

Frozen, real fear racing through her veins, sick with confusion, she backed out, adjusting her beret, swinging her stick under her left arm then marching in, throwing up a salute after stamping her feet to a halt by his door.

Grant ensconced behind his desk, looked up, pointed to a spot in front of him and continued to scan his computer screen. Feeling formality was safer Soph stuck to the marching and halted again where he'd indicated. Her hands were clammy, mouth dry, staring straight ahead, blood rushing in her ears.

"Sir, you wanted to see me?"

"Yessss."

Grant dragged out the word, leaning back threateningly in his chair,

"Who the fuck do you think you are Second Lieutenant Jefferson?"

Soph's heart thumped so hard she thought it would bolt out of her chest and run screaming out of the room. Her mind careened through possible answers. Silence seemed wisest. She stared ahead, swallowing hard.

"Well?"

The silence hung between them, Soph resolutely staring at a spot just above Grant's head.

"I'll tell you who you are. You are a fucking anti-social little shit. How dare you refuse to socialize like a civilized human being,"

What the...? Soph's face creased bemused, she made to speak then bit her lip. Right, it was going to be like this. Slowly the slivers of fear that had been racing up and down her spine were replaced by a steely resolve. She pressed her lips into a thin line, studiously keeping poker still, refusing to show his remarks registering,

"Who has a drink whilst hosting with the COMMANDING OFFICER..."

Grant's voice rose like a crescendo. Soph thought of Loch Fyne and their Pinot Grigio,

"Who was THOROUGHLY UNIMPRESSED with..."

Percy and Trace, laughing, dipping focaccia into a small dish of olive oil, stirring in the balsamic vinegar,

"...that kind of conduct on a..."

Giggling about future postings, how life would be now they were out of the hard regimented system that was Sandhurst,

"...young officer. YOU WERE A..."

becoming a real Officer. Soph felt tears that she fought back, instead remembering how they'd toasted triumphantly their future, the thrill of walking up the steps. She glanced at Grant, God his face was puce from shouting, flecks of saliva showering his desk. She thought of Sergeant Brown, she thought of home.

"...FUCKING DISGRACE. If you EVER do that again, I will have you CHARGED for insubordination."

Breathless Grant stopped, eyes bloodshot. Stuck up little bitch. The amount of grief he'd got that night about a Second Lieutenant putting the Adjutant in his place, it was humiliating; he could hear the Commanding Officers' voice now,

"I like that one, she's got character and I've seen her out running with her Platoon Sergeant. Excellent example, excellent. She is a credit to her Corps, hardworking and a real team worker. Really Grant you are an arsehole pressing her to drink like that. If she were a little more experienced she would have known she could have your balls for harassment."

He'd paused smacking his lips, cradling his Bushmills, smiling icily,

"Might want to watch that Adjutant."

At that he'd put his drink down and walked out of the Mess, glancing at Sophie as he'd glided by, not immune to the curve of her waist, the fullness of her lips.

Silence hung heavy and Grant stared at Sophie. Bitch seemed utterly unmoved by what he'd said, damn, he'd wanted tears, pathetic sniveling, sobbing and cringing apologies. Instead he was met with her face drawn, back rigid. Fuck.

"You will do Duty Officer every day for the remainder of this month, and,"

Soph's face twitched, 2 weeks of duty for what? She felt the sweet bile of injustice, ground her teeth, face remaining impassive.

"If I so much as hear that you have missed an Armoury check or cocked up an inspection, I will come down so hard on you, you will wish you'd never commissioned. Am. I. Clear?"

Blinking slowly, she turned her gaze, almond brown eyes darkened, narrowed in undisguised hatred, "Yes. Sir. Permission to leave Sir?"

"Yes, get the fuck out."

Turning to his computer as she saluted, her face blank, he surreptitiously watched her swivel round, cane under arm and march out sharply. He followed her bum, swallowing hard.

It felt like she didn't actually breathe until outside the building. Wheeling round to the rear of the HQ, out of sight, slumping against the wall, dropping her stick, sliding down the rough brick, until she sat slumped arms loose on the ground, staring ahead unseeing.

17

Southwick Park

"SIB IS THE domain of the Late Entry Officer, there are few Direct Entry opportunities, although people, as the mighty Dylan said, Times they are a changing."

The syndicate groaned, the ghost of a smile on Tracey's lips, it was a tough crowd for this lecturer. Despite his best efforts there'd been a lot of irritated shuffling. You tell a group of Direct Entry officers from the Academy that, by the way, the best jobs are going to commissioned soldiers from the ranks, well, you're not going to win any laughs. She flipped a look at her watch. This was dragging. She wasn't interested in the attitude of Late Entry Officers versus wet behind the ears Direct Entry Officers straight from Sandhurst. It was patronising and divisive. There was always going to be a grain of truth in it, but her objectivity, untarnished by a 15 odd year long career that may or not have left her jaded, meant that she could bring fresh insight and enthusiasm into the role. Tracey shifted in her seat, flicking a look at the caseload guidance handouts. It was going to be another PowerPoint marathon and her bum already ached from the last 3 hours of lectures. Dark auditorium plus a morning of phys equals damn near impossible to stay awake. Slipping a hand into her pocket she pulled out a tired, raggedy piece of haribo, sucking the bittersweet chew, eyes wandering. There was Bill doing his best impression of a nodding dog, jerking as his dreams took hold, a small spool of saliva slowly etching a path down his chin. Sal Saunders, conscientiously scribbling notes, chewing her biro avidly between jotted pages. Trace baffled at what she was writing in a lecture so far devoid of any substance.

They were days away from finishing the Young Officer course. It would culminate in a Final Ex, a particular case contrived by the fact it would warrant a multidisciplinary approach, but necessary to see if they'd captured the key elements of the course. Rumint had it that they were going to have to run their own investigations from an ops room. Real soldiers, Trace rolled her eyes, would be brought in and Trace and her team, constituting some imaginary SNCOs and Juniors would have to respond to the evidence the DS would provide. Trace was itching to get on with it, to prove she was up to the job.

The SIB attachment they were currently being briefed on was a 3 month stint in a Unit, there would be plenty of time to soak up the reality there, rather than listen to some Warrant officer drone on about life skills and managing your people. Patronising didn't even touch the sides. Her knee was drilling its own beat and she toyed with taking another swig of diet coke, even though she'd downed enough coffee that morning to put Starbucks out of business, another flick at her watch.

"Right that's enough out of me. Your DS have informed me timings have changed. You're all to assemble outside study rooms 1-9 now. So gather your stuff people and make a move. You're in your own time now."

Frowning, what? They'd been told they were going for a beat up run before a Combat Fitness test this afternoon. She caught Dom's eyes, he shrugged, shaking his head. They were all a bit beyond being bemused at timing changes and programmes being turned on their heads. Trace swept up her rucksack, ran a smoothing hand over her scraped back hair, and drifted into line.

Formed up in a gaggle outside the study rooms, gossip was rife.

"I heard that we're getting bollocked for Jackson failing his BFT."

Jackson glowered. Carrying a couple of kilos above his fighting weight, he was invariably glued to the bar, and would be the first to admit that he hadn't even had a gym induction.

"Sprained ankle mate, what can I say?"

Sal chipped in,

"Maybe we're being stood down to prep for the Ex? Stands to reason they give us a bit of study time."

Chorus of jeers. Trace couldn't help but grin at such a hopelessly optimistic idea.

WO1 Stead steamed in and rolled over any morale. His creased face could easily house pencils in the lines, flabby lips, piggy eyes in layers of flesh. His baldhead seemed to be permanently laced in a light sheen of sweat. 5'9" at full height rather than stooped by a weight of woes no one understood but him, he was universally liked and respected. He played fair, took no flack and was a font of information. Everyone recognized him for the masterful mentor he was, but he wasn't around very often and his presence commanded immediate attention. If Stead was here, it was serious.

"Ladies and Gents, this is the start of your Final Ex,"

Exclamations of disbelief, Trace's eyes widened in shock, but they had a few more days?

"Settle down. As you'll find with your Units, investigations rarely happen when it's convenient and hardly, if ever, stick to a neat plan. Each of you will be buddied up. Those pairs will be allocated a room. For the first 3 days of the Ex one of you will be the Officer in Charge with the other their acting 2iC, at the half way point you will swap roles with the 2iC becoming the OiC. Roger so far?"

Nodding in unison.

"You will find your rooms equipped sufficiently to run this investigation to conclusion. You will be fed serials, and pax will come and go requiring interviewing or otherwise as you deem fit. You will notice in those rooms that there are CCTV cameras. These are to record your actions. Gents and Ladies, this is a 24 hour Ex. It will be for you to manage your resources, your time and employ whatever techniques you have been taught that you feel will lead you to an accurate and satisfactory conclusion. Clear?"

More nods.

"Right, will the following go to room 1..."

Names were called as pairs filed off, some happy with their partner, others wearing expressions of naked despair.

"Bonner…"

Trace's heart raced, who?

"French."

Dom grinned at Trace and despite her reservations, she smiled back, could be worse, could be a lot worse.

Their study room was laid out sparsely. A large fold away table straddled the centre. A white board with pens hung on the wall opposite the door, with a flip chart cradled on a stand in the right hand corner. There were no windows and the CCTV camera fitted into the top left of the ceiling made a whirring noise as big brother homed in on them and their reactions. There were a couple of plastic chairs that promised discomfort. All in all functional was generous and the prospect of being stuck in this room for the best part of a week was depressing.

Trace wandered over to the table, Dom letting the door slam shut, making Trace jump and tut at Dom who shrugged sniggering. He flung his bag on one of the grey plastic chairs and sighed staring up at the camera.

"Mooooorning!" Waving theatrically. The camera seemed unamused.

Trace leafed through the array of paperwork spread over their bird table. Maps, profiles of people, interview sheets, proformas for interviews, blank paper, some biros and a small recording device. There was guidance on legal policy and a number of other piles of paper that demanded some judicious reading. Before Trace could raise the issue of organizing the running of the room, a tannoy blared along the outside corridor,

"The following pax will assume the role of OiC for the next 2 and a half days. Saunders, Jackson, Bonner…."

As soon as Tracey's name had been called Dom and she locked eyes.

"The Ex will commence in exactly 30 minutes. If you have additional kit you would like to retrieve, now is the time. Note however that no written notes from lectures or assisting documentation other than that with which you have been provided is permitted. You are allowed issued aide memoires."

Trace nodded at Dom and raced back to her room. Scanning her desk, she grabbed her carefully fabloned aide memoires, then paused and grinning pulled down a cardboard box and started to fill it with her essentials.

A few hours later Tracey was staring at the white board, cradling a Nespresso considering her options. Dom had been bowled over by the coffee maker. He producing essentials like hobnobs and laptops. Trace was mildly surprised at at Dom's amenability. He'd assumed the role of 2iC without question, assisting nimbly in blue-tacking pictures to the white board, making helpful but not interfering suggestions about the room layout, acquiescing to whatever Trace preferred.

The room was now more ordered. The left handside had been made into an interviewing area, the plastic chairs group around a small coffee table with recording device and paper to hand. The bird table remained central, but they'd both purloined issue grey armchairs for the downtime area in the right hand side of the room, where the prized coffee machine sat, with mugs and Dom's biscuits. The whiteboard opposite the door would be the Ops board, cataloguing their progress, suspects, key intelligence and future leads. The bird table had maps laid out, key locations marked with red labels. The flip chart was open, the first page showing a basic link analysis which, whilst at this point read a lot of FNU SNU (First Name Unknown Second Name Unknown) showed they'd incorporated the key named pax. Trace felt a flush of satisfaction, she felt organized. Sticking a thumb under her combat belt, sipped her brew and absorbed the scenario that she and Dom had read repeatedly over the last few hours.

It was a rape. A female Private, named as Private Smith, had leveled the allegation. Private Smith however was no angel; she had a record of drinking, verbal abuse, assault and an attitude that would make a New York gangsta blush. The accused was a Corporal, namely her Phase 2 training Corporal Clark. As expected he was denying all charges and, Corporal Clark, to complicate matters, was an exemplary Junior Non Commissioned Officer, did everything by the book, had outperformed his peers on his JNCO cadre, was a hard worker, punctilious and had a girlfriend. The investigation was based in Germany, Sennelager, a large garrison town that didn't embrace the RMP and wasn't overly keen in assisting their enquiries. Both soldiers were part of 102 Logistic Brigade and were supposed to be concentrating on pre-deployment prep for their imminent HERRICK Tour. Both were due to deploy in five weeks and there was talk that Corporal Clark might deploy sooner owing to a shortage of manpower on the ground in Theatre. That meant Tracey's investigation was under pressure to get a result and get it fast, as soon as Corporal Clark was out of area the whole case would have to be put on hold, and whilst Trace had the right to delay Corporal Clark's Tour date, her reasoning had to be air tight.

Five weeks, therefore meaning each Exercise day represented a week. She already had the interviews of both key individuals. It was the character witnesses and other players that she needed to focus on. Trace chewed her lip; green feline eyes narrowed scanning the white board, looking at the four other faces that stared back at her.

Private Samantha Price, best friend of the victim. Equally as belligerent publicly, but when on her own was more pliable. She was struggling as a soldier and had been taken under Private Smith's wing. There were rumours of lesbianism.

Corporal Walker was Corporal Clark's best mate and had been with him in the night in question, in fact they'd been celebrating Corporal Walker getting his second stripe. Beers had been coming thick and fast at the popular dingy nightclub in garrison called Go Gos. Corporal Walker wasn't quite as squeaky clean as Corporal Clark. Good looking and one for the ladies, he was happy to pay for sex as well as sleep with his own girlfriend when she visited from the UK. He was a regular at The Strausse, a known brothel. His recollection of the evening was hazy owing to the consumption of his bodyweight in tequila. He swears, however, that Corporal Clark had gone home, alone, when Corporal Walker had suggested a bit of whoring to polish off the evening.

Sergeant Metherall. Tall, imposing he ran a tight ship and was allegedly appalled that his Juniors had brought shame on his troop. A disciplinarian, he had a fearsome temper, was known to sneer at the female contingent and encouraged boozy nights out to cultivate 'Esprit de Corps'. He had been in Go Gos on the night in question.

"Her Majesty's finest eh?"

Dom leaned on Trace's shoulder, his face amused, scrutinizing the various snapshots.

"Hmm, we've got both Corporals Clark, Walker and Private Smith's interview transcripts, which means we've still to interview Sergeant Metherall and Private Price. Given Sergeant Metherall's form, you might get more out of him than me and I can be the good female, sympathetic cop with Private Price. Sound fair?"

"Nice one guv."

Slumping in grey chairs they batted lines of questioning back and forth, areas to focus on and key parts of the evening.

Trace snapped her black moleskin notebook shut, pulling her knees to her chest frowning.

"What's your gut instinct?"

Leaning back, still nursing what had to be a cold coffee, distractedly, he reached for a hob nob munching, a fine spray of biscuit crumbs escaping his mouth.

"Personally? I reckon Corporal Clark has got form, that's of course if we're gonna run with this being a kosher accusation. There is the very real possibility that little miss nasty didn't get the nasty."

Trace snorted glancing at the CCTV camera, feeling it zoom in on their discussions,

"Hmm, fair one. I think we need to finish the interviews and then re-interview Private Smith, get a feel for the authenticity of her story, y'know the form, repeating the same points, keeping eye contact...?"

"Open body language, guilt remorse, I geddit Trace, I was in those lectures too. What about you though Boss? Who's the bad guy or maybe girl?"

Trace had her thoughts, but she wasn't going to share her cards entirely. This was an Exercise after all and whilst Dom was playing fair so far as 2iC, it was all about passing, and passing well. Guts and glory she thought guts and glory.

"Let's get on with it."

Picking up their internal phone, she called the Exercise 102 Logistic Brigade HQ and requested the presence of Sergeant Metherall and Private Price.

18

AN HOUR LATER there was a knock at the door. Trace had been thumbing her way through hours of interview reports, digesting notes and link analysis that introduced yet more people into this increasingly complicated scenario. Scribbling notes, mainlining coffee, she was chewing the end of her pencil like an incensed gerbil. The knock made her jump.

"Right if it's Metherall you lead, if it's Price I'm on, ok?"

Dom nodded.

"Come in."

WO1 Stead strode in and Trace's shoulders sank. His face was blank, inscrutable apart from chewing something that made his fat lips gently smack a rhythm.

"You wanted to see me Ma'am, Sir?"

Dom strode forward, suddenly in command.

"Yes Sergeant Metherall, please take a seat."

He ushered WO1 Stead to the plastic chairs, eliciting an unscripted scowl all too familiar with the school chairs.

Dom slid opposite him. Trace perched on the bird table.

"I'm Lieutenant French, this is Lieutenant Bonner. We're investigating the alleged rape of Private Smith,"

WO1 Stead snorted.

Trace flushed, was he snorting at Dom's preamble? Or was he in character? It was hard to tell the difference. Pulse racing, she focused on calming, remain detached, she sensed this was going to be a provocative encounter. Silently she repeated a mantra, don't rise to his bait, don't rise to his bait...

"As the SNCO of the Troop we'd like to ask you a few questions. This interview is being recorded are you aware of your rights?"

A desultory nod from WO1 Stead.

"Where were you on the night of July 13th?"

"Why? Do you think I screwed that little gobshite?"

Trace flinched; Dom blanched but continued not missing a beat.

"Please mind your language Sergeant Metherall and answer the question."

"Been here, told your colleagues this, why you wasting my time? I've got a CO's inspection, so if we can move this along?"

"I'll be the judge of timings Sergeant Metherall and we are aware of what you have revealed thus far. So again. Answer. The. Question."

There was a pause as Sergeant Metherall/WO1 Stead sized Dom up as if deciding whether or not to ramp this up or do what the one pip wonder wanted, despite his eyes still narrowed he smacked his chewing gum and answered,

"On the alleged night in question,"

Drawing out the word alleged, making his point,

"I was in Go Gos drinking Peroni with Sergeant Crossley from 12 Squadron. We'd just had an ECI and got the green light, so we're were having a bit of a celebration,"

An Equipment Care Inspection brought chills to most Commanding Officers. The ad hoc check was key to the fighting power of a Unit and involved the closest scrutiny of the upkeep, records and daily maintenance practices of any given Unit. It was as thorough as CSI analyzing a crime scene. Each vehicle was spot-checked, each record forensically examined, every wheel, brake and engine eyed for shortcuts and substandard performance. Careers were made and broken on ECIs, it didn't matter if you had a wall of Military Crosses, if your Equipment Care was not up to scratch, your posting to the depths of Falklands was as good as signed. Celebrating after a successful ECI was an outstanding alibi, easy to verify and entirely justified. Trace winced.

"So I was there after knocking back some pops in the Mess from about nineteen hundred. I think we exited the building,"

Voice dripping with sarcasm,

"About zero two hundred, but I'm not 100% on that, you can ask Crossley."

"We will."

WO1 Stead shifted in his chair, raising his eyebrows at Dom's tone.

"You mentioned in previous notes you'd seen Smith and Clark talking?"

Folding his arms, WO1 Stead nodded,

Dom remained impassive almost but not quite hiding his irritation.

"And? The content of their conversation? Their interaction? How did it appear to you throughout your time in Go Gos?"

"Well, *Sir*,"

His attitude getting under Dom's skin shifting in his chair, face reddening,

"It looked to me like Pricey liked a bit of Clark action and old Miss Smith wasn't happy about that, being a dyke and all."

"Sergeant Metherall, I'm not going to remind you again."

"Sorry Sir, lesbian. Clark also looked quite up for some Pricey nookie which I think was pissing his mate off mister Walker, who frankly prefers to pay for beaver, thinks whoring gets him a better class of pussy. Me? I think if you can get it for free why the fuck would you part with hard earned cash?"

Trace bit the inside of her cheek. There was no point getting precious about the language. This was how it would be, basic, scatological, nauseating. She might not like it, she might object to it, but getting squeamish was not going to solve a case and if she had a weak stomach at this stage, she may as well pack her bags and go and join VSO.

She sat taller, keeping her face blank, meeting squarely the gaze of WO1 Stead as he turned, his eyes lazy, insinuating. He licked his lips, then slowly turned his gaze back to Dom, looking at his watch insolently. Dom's tone was getting tighter, shorter. Hold it together Dom hold it; don't let him wind you up.

"Did you go to the Strausse?"

"Sir, I was wasted. There was no way I was going to get myself back to the Mess and to the Strausse in one night. So no, I didn't go looking for some action."

He looked at Trace as he said action, borderline leering. She narrowed her eyes.

"Did you see any of your Squadron leave Go Gos?"

"Well…I saw Miss Price, she was stumbling about a bit, leaning on Mister Clark who in my drunken opinion looked like he was quite enjoying her stumbling. Miss Smith meanwhile was being her usual gobby little self, mouthing off some obscenities like the little princess she is,"

Trace couldn't help but allow the hint of a smile at WO1 Stead's adopted double standards. Damn he was playing this part well.

"…mister Walker meanwhile looked like he was going to thump her. At that point I thought it best I retire and allow the children to play unwatched. What I don't know doesn't need AGAI-ing."

Army General and Administrative Instructions, the bane of any SNCO or Officers' life. Don't see, don't tell, was an unwritten rule and often why seniors and Officers didn't go out drinking together, neatly avoiding chest prodding a few Carlings down the road.

"What was the state of your Squadron on parade the following morning?"

WO1 Stead sighed, feigning (or perhaps not thought Trace) boredom,

"They looked shabby, and to be honest I felt shabby too, so I wasn't about to start rattling cages. They were, however, all on parade which I think is what you're asking about?"

Dom nodded. Trace began to get the sense he was losing his way, momentum dying and WO1 Stead was making the most of it, adopting a distracted uninvolved attitude.

Dom hesitated, flicking through notes, swallowing. Shit, he hadn't expected this, hadn't, bugger.

"Sergeant Metherall,"

Trace waded in, Dom looked up his face flushed, embarrassed,

"Your Juniors reflect on you, so you'd just let this happen, whilst you're at the same club? You admit," Trace listed points from her notes,

"You saw the pax in question, you could see that tempers were getting short, that all parties were clearly intoxicated and as you left you admit you witnessed an altercation. So at no point during that, did you think, I'm a Senior NCO, these are my soldiers, perhaps I ought to be gripping this, before 'the children' get out of hand?"

WO1 Stead eyes widened, he sat up, glaring at Trace,

"Or Sergeant Metherall were you, that night, one of the children? Not the grown up you are trained to be in Her Majesty's Forces?"

"I thought they'd figure it out themselves, it looked like a squabble,"

"A squabble?"

Trace pushed harder,

"A squabble? With Private Smith a known troublemaker? A potential lesbian couple being infringed upon by Corporal Clark, with his best mate on hand, unimpressed, and ready to steer his mate to trouble at the Strausse?"

"What are you asking Ma'am?"

WO1 Stead eyeballed Trace, bolt upright now, the atmosphere tense.

"What I'm asking is what did you do? Because the belligerent Sergeant we've seen here today wouldn't just walk away from a scene where I believe you could throw your weight around."

WO1 Stead caught off guard at Trace's insight, almost smiled, then slipped back into character, pausing. Crossing one chubby leg over the other, barely keeping it propped on a knee, he crossed his arms responding,

"I did have a word now you mention it. Yes... I remember now,"

Dom rolled his eyes. Trace didn't move,

"Yes, Crossley and I walked over, pulled little Miss gobshite off Corporal Walker, propped Miss Price up against a wall that she promptly slid down and told them to get a fucking grip, sober up and stop making a bloody scene or the German police would go medieval on them."

"And how did that go down?"

"Like the proverbial bag of sick. Walker got all pushy on me and Crossley and Corporal Clark looked like he wanted to run. I don't recall Miss Smith shutting up at any point during proceedings. Yes I remember her rambling pretty vividly."

"And what were those rambles?"

For the first time WO1 Stead/Sergeant Metherall started looking shifty, eyeing the recorder, unfolding one leg, only to cross the other over again. It wouldn't take an expert to read his body language. The silence dragged, but if Dom just left it, just a few more minutes maybe, just maybe...

"Sergeant Metherall the rambles what was she saying?"

And with that the shutters came down.

"Ooo you know what Sir?"

Metherall suddenly looking like the cat who'd got a vat of double cream and some single to boot.

"I just shouldn't drink so much should I? I think I've got drinkers amnesia. Now are we done here?"

The interview was brought to a close and WO1 Stead sneered at them, before waddling out. Dom couldn't meet her eye, mindlessly shuffling papers on the bird table,

"Well, I thought that,"

"You fucking idiot."

"What the...?"

"You totally cocked that up. You let him get to you,"

"Oh give me a break Trace, he was riding me."

"Of course he was! He wasn't meant to make this easy, but you were supposed to let it wash over you. He was deliberately,"

"What? Being a cock? Offensive? Insubordinate? Honestly Trace? Really? I thought he was totally pushing it beyond the realms of believability, we're Officers."

Trace was sure she could see the CCTV camera zooming in, relishing the row like some scene out of a reality TV show.

"Are you kidding me? We're Lieutenants. How often have we been told that we basically have no credibility AT. ALL?"

"Yeah, but,"

"No yeah buts, you just cocked up a key interview because you were getting pissy at a pretend Sergeant deliberately delaying the questioning. If you'd given him some space WO1 Stead would have dished, because if it had been a real interview, the interviewee, AS WE HAVE BEEN BRIEFED, does not like silence and will inevitably FILL THE GAP."

Trace flung her notebook on the table, groaning through gritted teeth slumped in the grey armchair, snapping on the Nespresso maker. Looking up at the camera she nearly screamed.

19

THEY SAT IN silence for a few hours. Dom doing his best impression of conscientiousness, pointedly writing up notes from the interview, replaying the tape, the squealing of rewind and fast forward making Trace seeth. She sat and mused, thought over what had been discussed, rubbing her temples chewing haribo. She stretched her legs, thought longingly of going for a run, striding out, sprinting off the frustration, allowing fresh air to replace the staid coffee atmosphere, clearing her mind, giving her space to think, because there was something not right about what they'd been fed by WO1 Stead, not right at all.

"Look, I was thinking, we need to get on with interviewing..."

"Shut up!"

Trace bolted out of her chair, two strides in front of the whiteboard,

"Sergeant Crossley, why hasn't he been interviewed?"

Dom hands in pockets, the hint of a shadow darkening his jaw, shrugged raking his hair,

"Dunno, s'good point actually."

"We need him in next, we need him in now."

Trace was suddenly working on all cylinders; time to drive this investigation forward.

It was close to ten o'clock when Sergeant Crossley turned up, another instructor from the course. Although a familiar face there were no pleasantries on this occasion. Red haired and built like a rugby player he loomed into the room and demanded attention. Where WO1 Stead had played the laid back cocky Sergeant, the Staffie who was playing Sergeant Crossley had decided that injecting a bit of ADHD into proceedings would be a nice test for these two Subalterns.

He took a seat, knees jigging, chewing nails, eyes narrowed, darting around the room, until resting on the whiteboard.

"What's this got to do with me?" Hint of a Mancunian drawl.

After Dom's flop, Trace was taking the lead. She got straight to the point, recognizing speed was of the essence; moving fast would force a mistake.

"Go Gos, afterwards, about 2am. You and Sergeant Metherall were leaving,"

"So?"

"So you saw some Juniors from his Squadron?"

"So?"

"So what did you do?"

Knees still drilling a beat, Crossley shifted in his seat, threw Dom a cursory glance, then went back to pulling the best part of his thumbnail off.

"We went over, calmed them down. They were getting a bit excited like and we didn't want any German police raining on our parade after we'd had such a good ECI."

Finally corroboration, Trace pushed on,

"What was said?"

"Y'know, usual, keep it down, go home, sober up, you need to be on parade tomorrow, y'know the kind of thing. Well,"

He paused, sizing Trace up, flicking a look at her rank side,

"Maybes you don't."

Tracey blinked.

"That it?"

"Yeah…we went home then."

"Sure about that? How did you get back?"

"Taxi."

"How much?"

"30 euros"

"The 5 miles from Go Gos to camp cost you 30 euros?"

"Rip off merchants those taxi drivers."

"What time was that?"

"About 2 am…"

He paused, finding his index finger incredibly interesting.

"2am? So it took you zero time to move locations? Sound a bit odd Lieutenant French?"

"Very odd Lieutenant Bonner."

"So do you want to rethink that Dr Who transfer at warp speed?"

"I was drunk! What can I say, I don't memorise my timings at stupid o'clock in the morning."

Crossley's belligerence wasn't quite enough to mask a hesitation. Trace smelt blood, went for it.

"You didn't speak to them did you?"

"Wha…?"

"You followed them didn't you? More interested in how it was going to turn out, not in being SNCOs."

"Now wait a min…"

"You followed them and you saw didn't you? What really happened?"

Dom was transfixed, he hadn't seen any of this coming. Crossley's reaction was showing that this line of questioning was bang on. How did she know?

Crossley ran a hand over his cheek, rubbing his chin, chewing his lip, virtually chewing anything that came near his mouth.

"Look do I need a legal rep or lawyer or something…?"

"I don't know, do you?"

Crossley's head sank between his knees, cupping his forehead he spoke to the floor, where his hopes had sunk.

"It was Metherall's idea. He didn't want to go back to camp and he flipping hated that Private Smith. She was always giving him slack for being sexist or homophobic. He was itching to teach her a lesson but knew that if he laid a finger, well he'd lose his stripes over it. He also knew that Walker hated her…so we followed and…and I bottled it. Look I've just picked up, I didn't want anything to screw up, it just seemed dodgy, and after being treated like a God over the ECI I wasn't about to get busted over some slag. So I left him to it. Shit bust."

He looked up imploring.

The recording tape snapped off. Dom walked Sergeant Crossley out. Closing the door, looking at his watch.

"Mate its 1am."

"Yeah, I know,"

She was pouring over her notes, tiredness tugging the edges of her eyes, slowing her thinking, wading through treacle.

"Trace…?"

"No, seriously Dom, I'm right behind you, you go. I'll see you back here after breakfast yeah? Early."

Dom nodded, raking his hair again, feeling agitated, he glanced up at the camera, had the urge to flick it two fingers. Instead, shaking his head went as if to say something, then closed the door behind him.

20

WO1 STEAD TOOK a long slurp from his mug, painfully sweet instant coffee with just a suggestion of milk. Reaching for another chocolate digestive, he leant back in his chair and nodded to himself. All the DS for the Final Ex had laid bets on who'd perform. Saunders had been surprisingly near the top in his opinion, although he did have to bow to the girl's attention to detail. He'd known that she'd fall over in the interview, and as sure as mice like cheese, she'd crumbled tearful and offended when 'Sergeant Crossley' had got a bit choice with his powers of description.

Jackson had been another one mentioned, but again Stead had kept quiet. Lazy as a young Officer where phys was concerned meant he was likely to be lazy on the more unsexy paper pushing side of the job and sure enough, he'd stumbled red faced down rabbit hole after rabbit hole through lack of proper preparation for his interviews. No, his money had always been on one person and one person only, and right now as he stared at Tracey stretching and yawning loudly, re-reading a report he knew she'd read three times already, he was pretty convinced that come the end of this Ex he'd be £100 up.

"That's my girl." Eating the digestive whole.

21

"No, you have got to be kidding me."

Trace slurred awake, groaned as pain sliced through her neck. Rubbing her shoulders, she slid upwards, got her bearings.

"Seriously mate?"

Dom sat perched opposite her, clean-shaven, fresh faced and smelling vaguely of Persil. Trace cringed hating to think how she smelt.

"...Have you actually left this room?"

His tone implied concern, but Dom was irritated and marginally alarmed, his eyes flicked to the CCTV camera and then to the bird table, whiteboard and Trace herself. There were scribbled notes and link analysis proliferating every spare inch of space, work generated by Trace in his absence which aka made him look like a slacker and his absence would have been recorded to boot. Bugger, little miss conscientious here had just raised the bar. He needed to claw back some credibility before he took over the reins.

"Right how's about you slip off and do some personal admin, means I can catch up with your lines of investigation and then we're on the same page to take it all forward. Sound like a plan?"

His smile was steady, professional; he didn't want anyone in the observation booth to think the 2iC was doing anything other than offer support.

Trace rubbed her eyes, stretching, and glanced at her watch,

"Jesus Dom its 0900, how bloody long does it take you to have breakfast?"

Her eyes narrowed, guard up, smelling his bluff, so convincing yet so self-serving.

"Y'know what? I'm ok."

Dom ground his teeth.

"I'll just knock some coffee back and slip out for a freshen up later. I hadn't appreciated it was so late. Just as well I've given us a head start eh?"

WO1 Stead and 'Sergeant Crossley' otherwise known as Staff Benlow both laughed, warm brews steaming by the monitors, they'd turned up the volume in their booth, munching on egg banjos supplied by Stead.

"Cheeky bastard eh? Less than 24 hours in and he's already showing his true colours."

Stead shook his head, wiping some yolk from his chin,

"Devious bugger. Blatantly realizes he's stymied himself by slouching off early. Lazy git too, rocking up at 9 O'clock."

He took a slurp of coffee, so sweet it would make a diabetic shudder.

"So how are they doing Stead?" Benlow between mouthfuls.

Popping the last of the sandwich in his mouth, Stead delicately licked his fingers, taking a look at the overhead clock.

"Well by all accounts they, or should I say Lieutenant Bonner are streets ahead. The way she's going they could have this wrapped up by tomorrow lunch. But therein lies the killer, that's when slacker here,"

He tapped the screen gently with a pudgy finger as a small Dom walked across to the Nespresso machine wearing a scowl not out of place on a two year old,

"Takes over and I'm willing to wager a small bet that things could take a stunning turn for the shit. Up for a small bet mucker?"

Staff Benlow shook his head grinning,

"What? And get fleeced like I did last Ex? I will never know how you foresaw that girl was gonna have a complete nervous breakdown and cock up, she looked fine to me, right up to the final brief."

"Argh Watson, it's all in the voice, and her's, my little amateur friend, was shaking like the proverbial leaf. Anyway's best get on with the next line of interviewing, they said who they want to see next?"

Benlow looked at his notes,

"They've asked to reinterview Smith."

"Best get Lindsey lined up then."

Sinking back in his seat, Stead studied the screen, watching the dynamics between Dom and Trace steadily deteriorate.

22

By lunch the atmosphere was downright chilly, any colder and there was risk of frostbite. Dom sullen and irritable, feigning offence at being excluded from Trace's analysis, was more afraid he couldn't keep up with her train of thought with a growing sense of dread that in the next 24 hours the investigation would be his. His to lead, to tie up and to deliver the conclusions and right now he hadn't got a clue.

Trace meanwhile was immersed in transcripts. She knew time was running out, had a pretty good idea of what had happened but didn't want to preempt her findings. A knock at the door interrupted them and in walked Private Smith as played by Warrant Officer Class 2 Sally Rosebloom. Whilst her name might have cultivated pictures of a kind, willowy type, WO2 Rosebloom was cut from the same cloth as WO1 Stead. In fact, there was a running joke amongst the DS that in a previous life they might have been brother and sister, with Sally Rosebloom being the brother. Appearances could be deceptive and although, as she walked through the door Sally Rosebloom had the expression of a truculent teenager who'd just been told they were grounded with no allowance for a month, in reality she was a jovial, considerate and calming DS. Nonetheless, she quite enjoyed tapping into a darker streak and wasn't holding back for Dom and Trace.

Trace was leading the interview and beginning to struggle. Her head was fuggy, mouth dry, the beginnings of a headache needling her right temple. Dom was perched on the bird table, one eyebrow arched in a sardonic frown, his pencil poised, as much support as a soggy biscuit.

Mentally shaking herself, Trace drove the interview forward until they got to the point all named personnel left Go Gos,

"Did you see Sergeant Metherall?"

Sally's eyes widened, her alter ego of Private Smith was scared, whilst Dom frowned confused. Trace sat back relaxed.

"Errmm, no why?"

"You seem awfully nervous about that."

"No, I just don't recall seeing him there."

Private Smith began to fidget, chewing nails.

"Private Smith can you tell us what happened that night?"

Like a rabbit caught between headlights Private Smith froze then shut down completely.

"Y'know, I think I'd like to retract my statement. I'd like to just take it back and go back to work. I was pissed and errm, I think I got muddled."

She made to leave.

"Sit down Private Smith. You, by retracting your statement, could be charged with making false allegations, you know that?"

Private Smith nodded, deflated.

"I don't want to do this anymore."

All her attitude, ranting and fighting spirit seemed to have dissipated like a flaccid balloon. Trace tried to shroud her own panic,

"What I suggest is you go home, think about this and we can discuss this again tomorrow?"

Nodding, Dom and Trace watched her and their case disappear through the door.

23

IT WAS WEDNESDAY lunch time, time for Dom to assume the lead and as far as Trace could see, systematically dismantle everything that had been achieved to date.

They sat grim faced matching the grey arm chairs, Tracey's hair in need of a wash, her face pale, bags under her eyes big enough to carry a Tesco shop.

"Dom, seriously, competition aside, I think you are making a big mistake. This is not about me trying to 'win' the Ex, this is about us coming out with a credible final brief on Friday. What you're suggesting is,"

She shook her head in bewilderment, struggling with disbelief,

"It's just bloody stupid."

Dom was wiping off half the whiteboard; earlier findings he believed were now obsolete. Fresher, shaven and fragrant, to the uninformed it might have looked like Dom and Trace were on different Exercises.

"I'm OiC Trace. I know what I'm doing. I suggest you go and shower, get some sleep and then you can join me for the shift tonight."

Trace peered up at him, baffled, a small spot reddening on her cheek, her lips cracked. Shaking her head,

"Whatever. It's your lead now."

Sucking her cheeks, Trace left the room.

When Trace returned early evening, she walked into a dark room. Backing out thinking she must have made a mistake, she checked the door number and realizing there was no error, reached in and flicked on the light.

"What the…?"

No Dom, no notes, no progress. She looked back out in the corridor as if Dom would magically materialize and then closed the door behind her. At that point she registered the post it on the white board,

Couldn't think clearly, so off to do some phys. Reckon we should just both start fresh tomorrow morning.

Trace sat on the grey armchair, utterly astonished. This was complete kami-karzi, what the hell was he playing at? The gentle whirring of the CCTV camera reminded her she was not alone in watching Dom drag their investigation down in flames.

"Well fuck that."

Pulling out a note pad from the mass of papers, she walked over to the interview area, flicked on the recording device and listened to Private Smith and Sergeant Metherall again.

24

THE ENTIRE NEXT day had passed with Dom popping in and out like he was a Dr on rounds taking a desultory interest and then disappearing again under the auspices of phys or clearing his head or getting some shut eye. Trace had been round eyed with wonder. This could not be happening and on Thursday night she'd ignored Dom's yawns and talk of an early supper by blocking the door.

"Sit the fuck down."

Dom's face flushed, he made to protest but changed his mind seeing Tracey's eyes.

"Seriously, what the hell are you doing? It's like you're flushing your career down the loo. This is the Final Ex, if you don't pass, its reshow. Y'know? As in backterm, repeat, do again geddit?"

Dom crossed his arms, face impatient, fingers tapping a beat on his arm.

"You finished?"

"No, but I'd like to hear you explain."

"I've just got this sussed mate."

Waving his hands expansively round the room.

"Look, they've given us a whole raft of notes, leads whatever and y'know what? I think the whole thing is a red herring. It's testing our ability to spot time wasters, to recognize false allegations and to check that we have got the moral courage and strength of character to say a rape did not happen. It's got to be about the hottest potato of them all rape, and crying wolf, well everyone tip toes about it and investigates it to death even if we know in our heart of hearts that the piece of work throwing allegations around is doing just that, making allegations."

Trace's eyes widened, convinced her blood was slowing in her veins,

"Jesus Dom, seriously, you have got this *so* wrong."

"Have I? Really? 2 Senior NCOs witness an altercation and freely admit they interceded, watched and left with nothing having occurred. They've got far more to lose by lying than a bunch of pissed up juniors. As for that Private, she just got stroppy because her lessie lover took a bit of a shine to the cock."

Trace winced, flicking a look at the CCTV camera.

"So she makes some trumped up charges to scare her little girlie and remind her who's boss. Simple. Then when Smith gets called on it, she realizes that she has bitten off way more aggro than she can chew, and lets it drop. There my friend is where it ends. You are simply looking for complications and conspiracies where there are none. Trace, simple truth is human behaviour is sometimes just simply crap, but simple is the operative word. This isn't a movie."

Trace sighed, her head feeling heavy. She could not believe that Dom had gone so way off the mark.

"Dom listen to yourself. If that is the case, why would they split the Ex command appointments? *If* what you are saying *is* true, the last 2 days or so would just be a waste of time, as you've so effortlessly shown. How is that a test?"

She shook her head,

"Look, I've been doing some more thinking and gone over the transcripts, and I think I know what really…"

"Drop it Trace, I'm giving our conclusions tomorrow morning and I'm not deviating and,"

His face darkened, eyes narrowed,

"If you try and out manoeurvre me I'll accuse you of insubordination."

WO1 Stead and Sally Rosebloom sat in silence, watching the Mexican standoff in study room 1. Both initially bemused, confused and then infuriated at Dom's cavalier action. There was little if any logic in his approach and his slap dash attitude was anathema to the methodical and thorough techniques that had been drilled into the subalterns.

Stead noticed his hand was vice-like around his mug. Sally looked at him thoughtfully,

"He's writing his own sentence Bob, we've all seen it before, nothing new here."

"Yeah, I know," Stead gruffly, surprised at his own strong reaction.

"I just, it's just fucking selfish. They're a team, his findings, his actions will reflect on her."

He jabbed a chubby thumb at the screen.

Sally sat back reflecting on Tracey's predicament. Young Officer, wanting to make an impression at the end of her training, she was entirely aware that the Army was a small organization and any Unit would be given the heads up as to how she'd performed. Right now her introductory meeting with the Commanding Officer might be sans coffee, not a great start.

They both stared at the screen gloomily.

Trace sat stiffly, staring at Dom.

"So that's it, you're going to just kick all this into touch and fuck over my career?"

Dom winced, he hadn't thought this might affect Trace, he hadn't thought at all about the ramifications if his theory was wrong, because, well, it wasn't.

"S'ok mate, seriously, I'm doing you a favour. I've steered you away from making a monumental mistake. Seriously,"

He sniffed loudly, standing and stretching without so much as a glance at the CCTV,

"We're going to rock. Now I'm going to get an early night, I suggest you do too."

And with that Dom left, Trace feeling her career skulk after him.

She sat there for hours staring into space. She'd pretty much got the case nailed, a slick link analysis chart and report capturing her thoughts. It was neatly compiled on her laptop, along with a PowerPoint presentation conveying the key points and areas that she'd follow up if she'd had more time.

Chewing her nail she flicked a look at her watch 0400. In about 5 hours Dom may grace her with his presence, they'd sit, twiddle their thumbs, then at about 1000 they'd be warned off they were to deliver their findings. Trace raked a hand through knotty auburn hair, chewing her nails again. Her foot tapped the air. Suddenly it froze, hand slowly slipping to her side. It was a huge risk, big, but it might just work. She flew out of the chair and the room, leaving both Stead and Rosebloom baffled.

25

AT 0900 DOM sat opposite Trace. Freshly pressed uniform, clean shaven, smug. Trace was calm. Whilst her cheeks had hollowed from a diet of coffee and biscuits for the best part of 4 days, her eyes sparkled and there was the faintest whisper of a smile. She passed Dom a Nespresso coffee, piping hot, just a hint of milk all hostilities from yesterday gone.

"Ah cheers mate."

He sat in the issue grey armchair, confident in his course of action, every inch the victor. Trace blowing on her coffee, her face bland,

"So you seem happier Tracey, less frantic, come round to my wisdom?"

He took a large slurp.

"See? Told you it made sense. Just had to get you out of that rabbit warren."

Trace offered him a flapjack,

"Oh don't mind if I do, you're being very hospitable this morning."

"Well want to make sure my boss has the energy to deliver his killer speech."

Dom snorted, draining more coffee, taking a bite of sugary oats.

"Yeah, no dramas, be fine."

He paced over to the whiteboard, noticing a different link chart.

"What's this?" Pointing his flapjack at the chart.

"Oh just some doodles from last night. You know me, can't let it go."

Dom shrugged, drinking more coffee, pacing the room. Licking his fingers he swallowed the oat bar, draining the rest of his coffee. Smacking his lips he plonked the mug down and stretched like a contented cat.

"I tell you what, I am so looking forward to a few beers this weekend, going to get le-ath-ered, utterly smashed and that's just for starters. Then I reckon I'll get some of the boys together to hit Infernos, y'know? Over in Clapham? If you can't pull in there you aint' never gonna pull. Yep, get the shags in, watch a bit of footie. Class…"

His face froze.

"Everything alright?" Trace eyes vague, glassy,

"No."

Dom took a short breath,

"Just felt bit weird there."

He put a hand on his stomach,

"Nothing to worry about."

His tone less confident he walked back to the easy chairs, a thin sheen of sweat on his forehead. He paused midstride grunting, this time holding his stomach,

"What the fu…?"

Trace cocked her head at him, "You all right?" Voice devoid of concern.

Dom was bent double, hand clutching the back of a chair, groaning, he stared up at her, face green, eyes bloodshot,

"What the hell have you done?"

"Done? Nothing Dom, I had a cup of coffee just like you, and there's my flapjack, big bite out of it, so no idea what you're talking about. Maybe you should have a lie down?"

Her smile. Comforting as a snake.

Dom squatted groaning loudly, then blood drained from his face, he sprang to his feet and sprinted out of the room.

Picking up his mug, shaking her head in confusion for the benefit of the CCTV camera, Trace proceeded to set up her laptop, and order her notes, it was show time.

"...And your OiC is happy for you to brief?"

"Well yes Mr Stead, he, he sort of rushed out about 10 minutes ago and as 2iC I thought it only right I take over."

Stead studied her face. He had a rough idea of what she'd done and was having a hard time swallowing his laughter. This one was better than he'd given her credit, a lot better.

"Well Ok Miss Bonner," exchanging looks with Sally Rosebloom,

"Commence, you have 10 minutes to deliver your findings."

"Bottom line up front there was a rape. But it wasn't Corporal Clark or Walker or Sergeant Crossley. It was Metherall. He did follow them. Crossley was with him. They were drunk and they did break up the fight. All parties involved testify to that. Clark and Walker if you look at the transcripts, both admit to going home after things were broken up, the guard room can verify this. Sergeant Crossley and Metherall I believe, offered to take the girls home, but rather than accept this invite I suspect that Private Smith made a scene and possibly assaulted Sergeant Metherall. Sergeant Metherall being three sheets to the wind and already having admitted that he wanted to treat, I quote, the 'gobshite' a lesson, raped Private Smith. I believe, he created a circle of complicity by threatening Private Price because she witnessed it and also that he would probably threaten to rape her too if she said anything. He prevented Sergeant Crossley from speaking, because he was newly promoted and was an accessory to the fact. The latter I gleaned by Sergeant Crossley's reluctance to discuss events after the breaking up of the initial altercation and I suspect on further cross examination both Price and Crossley will corroborate."

Stead and Rosebloom sat quietly, Sally scribbling notes. They looked over Tracey's report, asked a few questions about secondary interviews, nothing too probing and then offering back her handouts, got up,

"All right Miss Bonner, we're now going to listen to the other findings. At 1200 you need to be assembled in the main classroom and I suggest you find Mister French."

And with that they were gone, leaving Trace exhausted in her chair.

26

SHE FOLDED CLOSED the cardboard box, stereofoam keeping the Nespresso maker snug. Her room now bare apart from the odd piece of stubborn blue tack. Outside her car resembled a stuffed Christmas stocking, kit packed to the hilt. Sellotaping the box lid she stood up, holding it in her lap, perching on the desk. There was one last thing to collect and it stared back at her, silver, glinting, the figure of a red cap Officer on one knee holding a rifle, aiming at an unseen enemy. Very apt Tracey had thought. The plaque under the soldier was engraved, Second Lieutenant Tracey Bonner Best Red Cap, Young Officer Course Nov 2010. She grinned picking it up, then, lifting the coffee maker made her way to her car. Imperceptibly she slowed her step, passing Dom's room. Untouched, fully furnished, Dom head in hands at his desk. He looked up, their eyes locked, then Trace was gone, out and off to her first posting as a Royal Military Police Officer.

27

PERCY PULLED AT her collar nervously staring at herself in the mirror, reflection almost unrecognisable. A long black dress that skimmed the floor, blonde hair swept up into an elegant chignon, she hugged to her the tailored black embroidered jacket, the colour of her Corps. There was one pip lovingly sown onto each shoulder and the golden brocade glinted in the overhead glare. Officers' Mess dress, a thing of tradition, a thing of pride and an outfit that Percy hadn't donned since pissed at the Commissioning Ball. However, even then, the barely concealed looks of admiration and respect were evident amongst her civilian friends. As she stood twirling in her room, she could hardly suppress a smile at how far she'd come, and this was just the start.

"The beginning of the end of my training."

Taking a stand in front of her bathroom mirror, kohl pencil in hand, mouth in an 'oh' shape, carefully drawing liner round her impossibly blue eyes. It was the final night of her training and the dinner this evening would herald the announcement of their future postings. Apprehension and excitement permeated the air, nervous banter carried along the corridor.

She flicked a look around her room, bereft, boxes were scattered about resembling a shabby storeroom more than the home it had been for the best part of six months. For a moment her spirits sank, sinking onto the end of her bed wistfully, she thought back to the Exercise results, Brillo's gruff words of consolation, her own confusion over his disappointment, coming second out of a cohort of thirty was no disgrace and even if Walters was patronizing and dismissive of his soldiers, he wasn't given the top Subaltern plaque for no reason. Brillo however hadn't seen it like that, muttering about Officers and their favourites and injustice before he'd given her a stiff handshake and a large box.

Percy smiled as she looked at her desk. It wasn't packed away, such a generous and carefully thought out gift. Light refracted through the crystal tumblers, the decanter heavy and opulent, the centre piece carefully presented on a beautiful piece of oak, engraved with the words,

Second Lieutenant Brooks, The Best Second Lieutenant on Course 051. SSergeant Brillo.

Percy had been speechless, standing before Brillo only the day before, the gift open in his office, biting back tears, Brillo shifting papers, looking studiously disinterested.

"I just hope, well that I did you proud. Thank you so much Brillo, I really learnt a lot."

"Well's you's best make sure you remember it, don't want my name to be associated with a one pip wonder wally."

He glanced at her briefly, gruffness gone for a second, replaced by the shadow of a smile and eyes that shone with pride. Then back to his abrupt self, shoeing her out of his office muttering that Senior NCOs ran the Army and didn't she realize that yet?

Percy pulled on her heels, smoothed her jacket one more time and made her way to the bar.

"Gin or tonic, Pimms or white wine Ma'am?"

Smiling gratefully at the waitress, she stood by the door to the Mess. Clutching her drink, she took a breath and plunged into the maelstrom. The foyer was a mass of black tailored jackets. The blokes stood around awkwardly, surreptitiously pulling at collars that choked and cummerbunds that squeezed like corsets. All the trousers were painfully tight, forcing Walters to walk around as if he were on stilts, Percy suppressed a smile and wandered in. Guests were not just Junior Officers, as was tradition, all Directing Staff were there, stern faces that for so long had judged, berated and directed were now softer, smiling with even a hint of solidarity. Conversations were mixed, some forced career laughs at Senior Officers' clumsey jokes, others where Captains stood in groups having serious discussions on Helmand, rumours of which Unit was deploying next and news from the ground. Colonels and the Brigadier formed a predictable gaggle, the Colonels fawning over the Brigadier, the Brig's face already flushed from wine, preening like a peacock; his length of time in rank diminishing his recollection that his subordinates were a captive audience, not because he was interesting but because he wrote their annual reports.

Percy kept to the edges, perching gently on a ledge, flicking a look at her watch, sipping nervously, noticing her glass was virtually empty, smiling self-consciously at the waiter as he paused to give her another, the bitter sweet of the juniper and tonic easing the knots in her stomach.

"I always think this bit goes on a bit too long y'know? Far too much career chat and frankly I'm hungry."

Percy blushed, Captain Duncan Williams. She'd seen him on Exercises, even exchanged pleasantries on occasions, but he'd always appeared so distant, aloof. She wondered for a moment if she'd become like that when she was a Captain? Seemed such a lofty rank compared to her Second Lieutenant.

She swirled ice cubes in her glass,

"Oh I don't know I'm sort of grateful for the delay, pretty nervous about the posting announcement."

There was a sudden guffaw in the corner of the foyer, Percy and Duncan's heads jerked up, Percy more to see who else was with Walters, recognizing his laugh immediately, subjected to it for months. Duncan's eyes narrowed muttering something under his breath, unaware that Percy had noticed, interest piqued.

"Thought he was your golden boy?"

His lips thinned, taking a large gulp of gin,

"Not mine. No. Certainly not mine. Anyway," slurping more drink,

"How about you? Nervous about postings? Don't be. Your first one will be what it'll be, no point worrying. Is there anywhere you'd like to go?"

"Well,"

Percy mentally listed all the possibilities, deleting those that didn't appeal or downright horrified her, highlighting the places that sounded interesting,

"Germany would be somewhere I'd quite like. I know that we're all moving back from there, so I guess I'd like to get the German experience whilst I still can. Plus, I think those Units are more likely to deploy."

She blushed, embarrassed at sounding cocksure in front of someone she admired,

"Well, errm, that's what I think is the case."

Duncan flicked a look at his glass, oddly touched at this Second Lieutenant's self-deprecation. He wasn't used to it and was pretty sure he hadn't been so humble when he was her rank. In fact he admitted humility probably hadn't featured in his vocabulary.

A long bugle call silenced the collected hub announcing dinner, and with the Brigadier leading the way, everyone filed into supper, Percy secretly hoping the table plan had her sitting near Duncan.

"You having some port?"

Percy's bladder was bursting. Finally at the end of the meal, she was woozy from too much red and white wine. Swallowing uneasily she narrowed her eyes in a bid to see one not two tables of people,

"Ooh no you don't! Come on Simon, women don't touch the port remember, you pour it for them and then they pass it on."

Foggy Percy struggled to keep track of who was saying what. She needed the loo and felt bloated from a heavy roast lukewarm by the time it got to her plate, potatoes dauphinoise thick with cheese, French beans laden with salt. She scanned the table for water, fumbling to slide on the port.

"You heard about Spearhead?"

Duncan tore his eyes away from Percy. On the table opposite her, he'd watched her all evening as she'd tried to chew politely and talk, listen to conversation he knew would have been agonisingly banal, the Captains either side of her pouring it on thick as Directing Staff. He could tell she was drunk, struggling to remain focused and the way she kept shifting in her chair he guessed she probably needed a comfort break. His heart softened.

"Spearhead? No what about it?"

Duncan moved out of the way of the waiting staff as they cleared the table for the loyal toasts, pouring himself a large port, turned to face Paul. Out of shape, sweating in his Mess dress, with too high an opinion of himself, Paul was not Duncan's kind of bloke. He talked too much, dodged taskings and gossiped like an old woman. Duncan wondered why he hadn't joined the INT CORPS.

"Well I've heard on the QC,"

Paul tapped his blackhead peppered nose conspiratorially,

"That they're deploying to Bosnia."

Duncan shook his head groaning,

"Not the bloody Elections again?"

Disappointed that his tip top secret news was no surprise, Paul continued pompously in his element,

"Well," lowering his voice unnecessarily,

"It's a key mission that the UN clearly sees we are adept at executing. Whoever goes to..." He floundered for the location of the Unit undermining his sanctimonious soliloquy.

Duncan flicked a look at Percy who was sheepishly glancing around in the hope no one had noticed she'd spilt some port. Dabbing at it discreetly he felt a smile involuntarily take hold, his face creasing with affection, irritated he turned to Paul,

"The mission is one that is rotated through all nations. We've done it before, and we're adept, as you so condescendingly say, because Spearhead train for it, hard. As for the Unit, I think Abingdon was the Camp you were groping for, is a shit hole, the accommodation is condemned, that includes the Mess, the showers rarely deliver the delights of hot water and the only place that serves anything that is sanitary is the bar."

The gavel hammering on wood brought Duncan's diatribe to a close.

The President of the Mess Committee, Lieutenant Colonel Heavenly, a name he firmly contradicted, stood heavily, Mess trousers bulging,

"Mr Vice, the Queen."

Mr Vice was Second Lieutenant Walters. Whilst he wasn't the youngest Second Lieutenant, on this occasion he'd been appointed in recognition of his achievement. However, Walters had clearly forgotten amidst the flowing alcohol and self congratulatory chat that he was due to make the Loyal Toast; a toast that warranted both solemnity and more fundamentally, sobriety. Staggering to his feet, his eyes watery, swaying gently, Walters nearly knocked over his glass, eliciting a small gasp of horror from his table, before he caught it with a grin sloshing it jerkily upwards, slurring,

"Chiirrs, Laaaychies and Chentlemen, peas be upsshhtanding for her Maychessty the Queen."

Chairs scraped back, transfixed the room rose, attention riveted on the Second Lieutenant who seemed to be defying gravity, leaning back precariously. There was a pause, as Walters lazily looked round the room, oblivious to the next line in his role, he grunted at an elbow in the ribs,

"Ooh, shhorry, The Queen."

Everyone lifted their glasses and returned,

"The Queen."

Sipping from their glasses, Walters drained his, slumping unceremoniously back into his chair. The show wasn't over yet. Percy watched in morbid captivation. Walters was reaching for more port, clattering the decanter on the table as he poured Tawney both into his glass, on the table and his trousers.

Another hammer of the gavel. The room was torn this time from looking at the PMC or watching Walters dabbing uselessly at the pool of Port now soaking through his trousers.

"Mr Vice,"

Colonel Heavenly's expression intimated hellish consequences for Second Lieutenant Walters,

"Our Colonel in Chief,"

Walters face drained. Colonel in Chief? Who the hell was the Corps' Colonel in Chief? Someone had told him before the dinner, he'd repeated it to himself mantra-like and now it had fled into the recesses of his Port soaked mind. It was HRH something?

Unsteadily he rose from his seat, what to do? He held his glass swaying and then from nowhere, felt a rising tide of hysteria. His eyes widened in horror realizing he had absolutely no control over what was happening to him, desperately trying to swallow back giggles bubbling at the back of his throat. His hand shook, his face flushing with the effort, the room unearthly quiet,

"Laaaychies an chen, Sirs an Cheeentlmen, HRH our Colonel in Chief!"

And with a flourish he triumphantly held his glass in the air accompanied by a giggled hiccough. The room paused, everyone frozen, until one male officer rose in response,

"HRH the Princess Royal." Tipping his glass.

Heads swiveled as if watching a Wimbledon match, tearing away from Walters grinning inanely, to the Officer who'd saved him, Williams, who stood there composed, as if this were the most normal state of affairs in the world. Everyone stood following Duncan raising their glasses in salute and waiting for the National Anthem.

Bedlam was the best description for the conversation that broke out afterwards. A five minutes comfort break had been announced and whilst many fled to the loo, those who stayed tucking into the cheese and biscuits, gabbled about Walters' performance that would undoubtedly go down in history as the most stunning career torpedoing that had ever been so spectacularly witnessed. Percy sat stunned, whilst busting for a pee she was equally appalled at Walters' kamikaze conduct. Feeling as if she'd been sluiced with cold water, she levelly regarded the top table, eyeing the huddle of Senior Officers and mused over just how diabolical the consequences would be for Walters. Rising she took herself off to the loo, softly shaking her head.

Everyone re-assembled; the Brigadier began his address,

"Ladies and Gentlemen, we are gathered here tonight in recognition of the not inconsequential achievements of our Junior Officers. After completing Sandhurst they, as you are all aware, are put through their rigorous paces in order to meet the exacting standards that Combat Operations demand today. We are under pressure from all quarters and there is no space in this man's Army for a free loader.

Each and every Officer right from the outset will be expected to execute his responsibilities to the very best of his abilities; responsibilities that are as wide ranging as assisting the construction and teardown of Patrol bases in Sangin to commanding Combat Logistic Patrols as they traverse through some of the most hostile terrain in the world. We, in this room, are under no illusions. Much is expected of our newest Subalterns today.

It is with that in mind that my Chief of Staff and the Headquarters at Directorate Royal Logistic Corps, think very carefully about where we should appoint our newest members. The first posting is pivotal in sculpting the Junior Officer. It will be where he or she makes both their best and worst decisions, where they will come face to face with their troop and all the expectations that come with leading 30 Loggie Soldiers.

The Op tempo is unrelenting at the moment and shows little sign of letting up. Whilst for some the departure from Helmand is a slowing in Operations, for us it will be our most trying hour as we try and retrieve the best part of a decade's worth of kit in a window of only a handful of years. Yet it is not just Afghanistan that demands our support. Bosnia and its volatile elections are still a UN priority and one of our most esteemed RLC Units is currently training with Spearhead to be in a position to deploy. Working at the height of readiness with such a prestigious Unit, that demands the very best from all, especially its Troopies. There are of course our Units in Germany, gearing up for their own HERRICK deployments, pre-deployment training exacting a grueling training programme for those manoeuvring to deploy.

That brief snapshot shows the breadth of requirements and the need to ensure we place the right Junior Officer in the right position to ensure that both Subaltern and Unit get the best results.

It is with that in mind that here tonight, at the eleventh hour, my HQ and I have made some changes to our choices."

Murmuring rippled across the room, more than a few looks flashed at Walters guzzling port and chomping on cheese, oblivious to the impact of the Brigadier's words.

"Maturity, presentation and the very highest of standards are required at all times in this Corps. Know your audience...I therefore have decided that the following Young Officers will go to the following appointments,"

Percy's heart was in her throat, she cradled her coffee to her chest, unaware Duncan's eyes were on her.

"Second Lieutenant Willows 245 Squadron Gutesloh..."

Percy scanned the room for Willows, sunk in his seat, his face ashen. She pinched her lips, remembering their conversation the night before. Willows munching on a bag of hula hoops, trying to hide his apprehension, the mask slipping for a moment,

"I just don't want to go to Germany Perce, flipping *do* not. I've just scraped together a deposit for a house and my girlfriend, well she's said if I don't start seeing her..."

He'd clammed up, shoveling crisps into his mouth.

Percy saw his eyes drop to the floor, as if somewhere done there hope lay.

"Second Lieutenant Banker – 23 Squadron South Cerney."

Percy didn't know Banker very well, but judging by his grin, this was not bad news. The names continued. Each time Percy's heart would fly into her throat thinking her posting next. Each time Germany was announced a sliver of disappointment glancing through her when her name didn't follow.

"Second Lieutenant Walters,"

Walters' head jerked up, wobbling on his shoulders like a puppet on a string. He'd obviously get Spearhead, he'd come top, the Brigadier had just been eulogizing about the criticality of that Unit in its mission to Bosnia. Perce shivered thinking of the freezing conditions out there, the need to kick your Troop into shape, the multifaceted nature of the role. Daunting? It was downright terrifying.

"24 Squadron Deepcut, Postal and Courier Troop."

Walters' jaw dropped. Percy's eyes like saucers. She didn't know what else to do but stare at her lap. Postal Troop? Deepcut? Not even an Operational one? Christ that was a penal posting. She shook her head; he'd only got pissed for God's sake.

"Second Lieutenant Brooks,"

Percy's head shot up, blood racing, Duncan fixed to his seat, oblivious to his knuckles whitening as they clenched in his lap.

"26 Squadron Abingdon,"

Percy gasped, but that was,

"Spearhead."

Duncan let out a breath. He was thrilled for her, but he couldn't ignore, slowly relaxing his hands the anxiety in his stomach. Bosnian Elections had Spearhead supporting them for a reason and it wasn't to help people form orderly queues. He nodded up at the waiter as he poured more coffee, eyes still centred on Percy.

"And that is the lot. Good luck to you all and if you have any queries please direct them to your Directing Staff. Your Admin Instructions will be in your pigeonholes tomorrow morning. Enjoy the rest of your evening."

As the Brigadier bumped back into his chair, the room broke out into a cacophony of noise, reactions torn. Percy aware all sorts of comments flying at her,

"Wow, Percy good on you mate, hell of a first posting."

"Your urban patrolling skills up to scratch Percy? They want to be!"

"You like the cold Percy? Bloody freezing out there!"

Smiling, nodding distractedly at the advice and observations, Percy was a maelstrom of emotions. Disappointment at missing out on Germany, pride at being appointed to a demanding post that was traditionally for the best Junior Officer and a creeping sense of awkwardness that Walters' fall from grace served as her trajectory to triumph. She looked up startled by Captain William's piercing look. Their eyes locked, he slowly winked and gave her a smile that melted her concerns and for a beautiful moment, she felt remarkable.

28

SOPHIE STARED AT her Body armour, her combat jacket hanging neatly off the back of her chair, rifle sling wound tightly into a wad as per training. Weapon cleaning kit beside her black issue notebook, boots polished ready by her Combat 95 uniform. Her stomach was a churning mass of nerves; outside she could hear the revving engines of Saxons and Snatch Landrovers. It was 0500. It was Marching season.

Walking up to the Platoon lines carrying her rifle collected from the Armoury, Sophie slid the sling through the eyelets and went through again in her mind's eye the drills for providing support to the Police Service of Northern Ireland (PSNI) during the next week. Largely they'd be on standby as part of the process of reducing the UK Army footprint on the streets. Op BANNER was drawing down, looking to close entirely within the next 18 months, so heavy handedness at this stage would be frowned upon. The first thing she had to do was issue orders, scrambling around in her pocket, rifle hanging from her shoulder, she read through her notes, Enemy Situation, Friendly Forces, Scheme of Manoeuvre. She knew it was formal, probably a little over the top, but she'd been too embarrassed to ask Sergeant Brown what he thought. After all wasn't she supposed to be the Platoon Commander?

Breezing into the office, a practiced look of nonchalance, Soph grew anxious at the unexpected quiet. Where was everyone? Noticing a post it on her desk she ripped it off,

Knew you'd forget, we're in your Mess grabbing some scoff. Sgt B.

Oh fuck.

Pushing open the Mess Scruffs bar, Soph feigned a professional yet disinterested look as if she delivered orders for potential riots every day, another day in the office and all that. Sergeant Brown looked up, fork piled with eggs and beans half way to his mouth, nodding at her, shovelling it in. The Company Commander was there, Major Leonard, to Sophie simply Sir. As a Second Lieutenant she found the rank of Major intimidating, which was ridiculous because Major Leonard wasn't that much older than Soph, but at this point she was so nervous that a sheep in uniform would have had her quivering with respect.

"Right, see you out there, Soph you happy with your Platoon's mission? Any questions?"

Soph blushed. Questions? Should she have? It took every ounce of self-restraint to resist looking at Sergeant Brown in panic. Instead, she thrust her hands deep in her combat jacket pockets and adopted a studious, been here done that expression. Sergeant Brown swallowed back a laugh.

"Errm, er-uh, nope, everything seems just dandy."

Dandy? Did she just say dandy? God kill me now.

Major Leonard nodded, distracted and strode out of the room. Soph slipped some bread in the toaster, not even sure she was hungry. Coffee sloshed into a cup handed to her by Sergeant Brown, who was gulping hot sweet tea.

"The boooyss aress all ready. They's in the lannies waiting for youse orders. Shall I say 5 minutes?"

Soph blinked. Their dynamics seemed to have subtley changed tonight. She was in charge. He was stepping back.

Soph gripped her coffee, nodded,

"Yep, 5 mins is fine. Just have a quick piece of toast."

She watched the door rock to and fro, alone in the room and for the 100th time told herself she'd been trained for this.

29

"RIGHT LISTEN UP,"

Landrovers were in semi-circle, headlights illuminating the area like floodlights. The soldiers were assembled in a huddle in front of Soph, Sergeant Brown off to the side. She'd never felt so exposed.

A sketch map of the area they'd be patrolling lay before them. Pointing at the street with a stick, Soph forced her voice to keep steady,

"We've been tasked with Ben Gaully Street. So we're going to break down into our three sections. 1 Section, you'll be point, sweeping behind the sniffer dogs, I will be with you. 2 Section you will follow 1 Section in 2 lannies, 3 Section you'll position yourself here,"

She pointed to the end of the street,

"Ready to pick everyone up or be called in as a Reserve in case anything kicks off. H Hr is 0900 for this task to be complete no later than 1130."

Soph was sweating, thighs screaming from crouching, hands red raw, cold in the chill of the morning. She looked up at the faces of the Section Commanders, the three Corporals at least a foot taller than her, more than a handful of years older too. But they were playing the game, taking her seriously as she was treating this seriously. For that, she was grateful.

"Yep Ma'am, got it."

"Sergeant Brown, any points?"

Soph got up, looked over at him, hoping she'd made a good impression, got it right.

"Nope Ma'am, that was bang on the money for me. All right booys youuuse heard the Boss, let's get on with it."

Sat next to Sergeant Brown, they waited in the Landrover for the other Platoons to move out. Soph finally relaxed, wound down a window and had a cigarette; Sergeant Brown frowned at her,

"Those'll kill ya ma'am."

"I know, I know," She waved the smoke outwards, "but this morning, well..."

She blushed not sure if she should be admitting how staggeringly nervous she'd been.

Sergeant Brown played with the gear stick, pushing up his sun visor, adjusting his beret then turning to her,

"Well, you's did fine to me Ma'am."

Soph blushed, turning to hide her grinning out of the window, brown eyes glinting with delight.

Sergeant Brown brought the Landrover to a stop. They jumped out, scooped up their weapons, adjusting straps, putting on personal radios, checking channels. Soph tightened her belt. Scanning her notes she did a voice check with Sergeant Brown,

"Echo this is Charlie One, Radio check over?"

"Charlie One this is Echo One, Roger Out."

He grinned, in his element. The other Landrovers, pulled up behind them, the layby suddenly a hive of activity. Corporals dishing out directions to their Section, Sergeant Brown distributing radios, checking kit, chivvying the guys along. Soph loitered by the Landrover, wanting another cigarette, flicking a look at her watch. 0830. Her radio crackled,

"Charlie One this is Sunshine are you in position over?"

Sergeant Brown looked over at Soph, she nodded,

Answering Major Leonard crisp and clearly,

"Sunshine this is Charlie One, Roger that, we are in position and ready to move, over?"

"Wait out."

Soph paced up and down, chewing her nails looking at the sky, the clouds brooding but no rain. Jogging over, Sergeant Brown gave the thumbs up,

"Ready to move Boss, hurry up and wait I guess?"

"Yup."

Leaning against the Landrover door, she rested an elbow on her weapon. Now wait for her Platoon to be called forward.

They were in the midst of discussing the merits of Cheryl Cole's singing performance versus that of her role in Girls Aloud when the call came through,

"Charlie One this is Sunshine over?"

"Sunshine this is Charlie one, Roger over?"

"This is Sunshine, move to your position and conduct sweep now over?"

"This is Charlie One, Roger out."

Sergeant Brown had started the engine before Soph had finished. Bowling along the streets she soaked in the scene. The roads were awash with people, music blaring from houses, banners draped from balconies championing religious groups. She felt a creeping sense of anxiety, not helped by a tension in the air. Sitting up straighter, fiddling with her jacket zip, the weight of the task ahead heavy, the risk all too apparent.

Drawing up at the end of the Ben Gaully street, Soph pulled out her rifle, yanked her jacket and hoped she didn't look too much like Private Benjamin. Sergeant Brown stood beside her.

"We're behind time by 30 minutes, so we need to make this slick. I'll move up the road with the reserve. If you need me just radio."

He tapped his PRR smiling.

1 Section assembled around Soph. She let the Section Commander take the reins, eyed the sniffer dogs thoughtfully as they leapt out of the white Dog Unit van. This was real now. There really could be IEDs out there. When the Corporal had finished his brief he flicked her a look,

"One more thing, keep your 5 and 20 metre checks tight. I know you've done this before, but we're running behind time and we need to keep this slick."

Grim faces nodded back, crossing the road with half the unit, Soph and the Section adopted a staggered formation slowly walking up the street.

Every sense tingled, she felt like her eyes were on stalks, legs wading thorough treacle. Turning to look behind her she walked backwards a few strides and then circled round to face front, repeating this motion, feeling like she was back on Exercise, half expecting Tracey or Percy to make some witty quip on the radios. She kept her rifle snug, looked warily at the undergrowth by the side of the road, cheeks flushed from concentration.

1 Section's Corporal walked up beside her,

"Why don't we go in and ask them to turn down that music? It must drive everyone mad?"

The Corporal smiled at her, white blonde, in his mid-thirties, stocky to boot, with eyes that spoke of years of experience, he drawled with a thick accent,

"Because Ma'am we arrr not the PSNI, the Police have jurisdiction harr, we'd be just causing truuuble. Ploos, if we asked tham to do'tha, the moment we walked ou'that building theys only turn it roight back up."

Soph rolled her eyes,

"But that's so childish not to mention provocative?"

"S'kinda tha point Ma'am."

They walked on in silence, both of them watching the dogs as they furrowed their muzzles into every nook and cranny. Soph scanned her immediate area looking for both the abnormal and the absence of the normal. Anything that looked out of place, disturbed gully grates, rubbish bins with full plastic bags, all of those were perfect hidey-holes. She was sweating despite the chill in the air.

Glancing to the other side of the street, feeling proud at the diligence of her soldiers, impressed by their uniforms, their drills, the air of professionalism they exuded. Suddenly one of the dog team shouted and Sophie's heart nearly shot out of her chest. She put a fist in the air and everyone froze, taking one knee, crouching to see what the dogs had discovered.

Blood raced in ears, she felt sick, struggling to control her breathing. Glancing over at the Section Commander she noticed how composed he was, chewing gum, inspecting his nails.

The dog handlers gave their canines a long lead as they whined, tails wagging, enjoying their work, oblivious to the implications of their actions. Soph steadied herself. Think of home, think of Trace and Percy and Loch Fyne, think of a nice cold Pinot Grigio, moisture condensed on the glass, chilled to perfection, a nice warm pasta dish, fresh and tempting.

"All clear."

Blinking Soph came back to reality, wincing getting up, she waved forward as they moved off, convinced she could hear a sigh of relief from behind her.

"Charlie One this is Echo one over?"

Recognising Sergeant Brown's voice, Soph pressed her pressel,

"This is Charlie One over?"

"This is Echo One Charlie One, Reserve is in place, there seems to be a delay. All ok over?"

"This is Charlie One Echo One, dog's false start, all clear, moving off now over?"

"Roger, out."

Sergeant Brown shifted uneasily in his seat, frustrated at not being in the thick of it, anxious for his Platoon Commander. He chewed his nail, pulling the ragged skin from the cuticles, eyes flicking to the rear view mirror, checking the other Landrover was parked up, ready to move; his blokes aware and prepared. Things could turn sour any minute. He'd done this long enough to know that you could be waiting for hours, and just when you got complacent, yawned, relaxed, all hell would break loose. So he was wired, every nerve on tingling. Trouble was, he was like this most of the time, found it hard to be any other way.

His thoughts drifted, remembering when he'd been called forward leading the clearance part of a patrol. He swallowed hard torn between the now and the past, grounding himself by checking his PRR, pushing the pressel, hearing the click in his earphone, the crackle of readiness.

It had been a standard patrol, seven years before, Marching season again. Sent out, a Corporal to lead the Dog Unit, his Section, his guys, he'd been full of himself, blinded to the risk, blasé about the drills. Until the dog whined, wheeling round, seeing dog and handler crouched low, the spaniel poised, leg pointing, handler's face ashen, shaking his head, waving them back. Sergeant Brown hadn't registered, focused, he wasn't concentrating, his head foggy from the beers the night before jogging over, one of his Lance Jacks joshing to beat him to it, Jimmy Mcshea all of 22 years racing ahead only to be blown to bits. Sergeant Brown blown on his back, his coccyx smashed, not stopping him from leaping up, racing to Jimmy whose torso in its mangled twisted mess had made his stomach spasm. Jimmy whose face was frozen in shock, his eyes staring, his leg hanging from a tree, left arm blown to the other side of the road, the sound of the guys in the Section shouting, someone vomiting, the smell of cordite, smoke and piss. The whine of the dog howling, the Handler sprinting over to Brown checking he was ok, his own face black, bloodied.

Sergeant Brown had cradled Jimmy in his lap, training kicking in, propelling him to tie a tourniquet around the stump of his leg, the remains of his left shoulder joint, knowing it was pointless, that most of Jimmy's blood was on the road and the ambulance wouldn't get here in time because of the Marching blockades. Jimmy had looked at Sergeant Brown, eyes wide with fear then just glazed over, emptied and he was gone, all that was left a lifeless corpse, mangled and misshapen; all in the space of a few minutes.

Shaking away the ghosts, Sergeant Brown looked ahead relieved to see Sophie in the distance. He'd recognize her gait anywhere, feigning confidence, she was a plucky Commander and he liked her for it. Admired how she faced her fears face on, respected him, looking to him for advice and standing up to those in charge including that cock of an Adjutant. Sergeant Brown had heard through the NCO grape vine what had happened and still contorted in fury at the abuse of power, the sheer injustice. Soph had never mentioned a thing. Just come back to the office white faced and pushed on through the day minus her usual banter and giggles. He could have punched Grant. How was that supposed to teach or achieve anything except infuse a sense of bewilderment in a Young Officer learning the ropes? Officers, he shook his head baffled, he just didn't understand them at all.

Sophie's figure was growing larger, rest of the Section emerging along the road. The false alert had had Sergeant Brown almost chewing the wheel off with apprehension, but thankfully the Operation looked like it was going to be uneventful. In days of old Sergeant Brown would have been disappointed, itching for excitement, a fight with the crowds, chance to get out the riot shields, wield the batons, put training into action. Dodge petrol bombs, a junkie in the face of the violence, thriving on the adrenaline, pumped, lined up in the row, holding the line like some extra from Gladiator as they would have stormed down the road, steaming through anything that stood in their way. Jimmy blown to bits put pay to the appeal of that. These days Sergeant Brown was quite happy getting his thrills from beating a particularly long and steep hill, thrashing the blokes on a decent run, smashing out some burpees then cracking on with another few miles. No, the thrill of the smash and grab a protestor had grown old, as had he.

Soph's face was beaming, Sergeant Brown's heart swelling gently with paternal pride. Realizing she might have looked a little like a child after an Easter hunt, he tried not to chuckle at her composing her features into an expression of earnest professionalism.

"Well, that's complete. Dog had us there for a minute, but thankfully it was just a nice distracting pile of discarded KFC rotting chicken, can't blame the poor pup! So any news from the other units?"

Soph pulled open the Landrover door and jumped in, Sergeant Brown noticing the sweet smell of sweat, recognising the patrol had taken its toll.

"Nope, their all still out there. I thinks one of the streets haas got a bit hairy, thank the Fusiliers maay ha'their hands full. Mind yooouse, they'd rather chew tha'hands off than call in for support fra'tha Royal Oirish."

Soph smiled, feeling suddenly exhausted, not wanting Sergeant Brown to see. God hope I don't smell.

"So errm..."

Fiddling with her combat jacket reaching for her cigarettes then stopping seeing Sergeant Brown's frown. Sinking into her seat blushing,

"What happens now?"

"Now we wait."

The Landrover warmed with the rising sun. Radio traffic punctuating the silence, providing updates of activity in other parts of the city; Platoons calling in their positions, confirming the completion of tasks, Major Leonard coordinating movements. Soph watched distractedly as swathes of people lurched past clutching cans of beer, throwing the odd bottle, throwing up fingers crudely, so much so she started to count the number of times. She checked her watch, it was about 2pm, itching for a bath, tired and irritable, she chuntered to herself about having a measly breakfast, hammering herself for forgetting the basic lesson of training, you never know when your next meal is, so eat up. She sneaked a look at Sergeant Brown. He never seemed to eat, just shifting gently in his seat, as if he couldn't get comfortable.

"I know!"

Sergeant Brown leapt out of the driving seat and strode over to the troops. Cigarette butts littered the area, travel mugs clutched with empty thermoses. Sergeant Brown talked animatedly, pointing around the now empty street. Vehicles were moved, Sections repositioned, Soph looked on bemused, too tired to do more than watch.

"Come on Ma'am!"

She looked up, sighing, grabbing her weapon and jumping out of the cab. 100 metres away in an abandoned car park, her Platoon was stood in a triangle. The vehicles, with their gunners aiming GPMGs out of the roofs, providing top cover, were assembled in front of a wall painted with an IRA Mural. In front stood 2 Section, standing firm, weapons slung, Sergeant Brown beckoning her to the front. Suddenly feeling sheepish, Soph hesitated,

"Come on Boss! This'll be a great photo for yer!"

Self-conscious Soph jogged over, touched at Sergeant Brown's idea, amused at her posing soldiers. Stood at the front, gesturing for some to move in, checking his camera sat astride a couple of ammo boxes. Sergeant Brown pressed the flash button and dashed over, edging in besides Soph,

"Three, two, one."

30

BERGEN IN THE middle, black battered roller bag by its side, body armour flung on top. Soph stared at her room. Three pyrex boxes neatly stacked to the side of the door, full of notes and paperwork. She perched on her desk. Bed stripped, duvet stuffed in the back of her Mini, pillows thrust between seats, uniform poking out of gaps, the car bursting at its seams and she still had to find room for this lot. She picked up the photo beside her, wiping the glass of dust that wasn't there. It still brought a lump to her throat. The frame contained a Royal Irish Second Lieutenant rank slide mounted underneath the photo taken all those weeks before during the Marches. She grinning like a Cheshire cat, surrounded by her Platoon all serious and war-ry. Sergeant Brown chin up, chest puffed out, proud of his men, the vehicles and weapons making the scene impressive, captured perfectly; quite a memory.

Clearing her office, Sergeant Brown had been more agitated than normal, moving papers about, up and down, he was like a small child after too much birthday cake and lemonade.

Pressing note pads and mugs into a battered cardboard box, Soph had paused, resting on her possessions,

"What is going on with you? You're like a toddler with a sugar rush!"

Sergeant Brown feigned offence.

"All very well for you swanning off, but some of us have to keep this Platoon ship shape, boss or no boss. Now are you going to inspect the guys? I's told you they's were needing an inspection, their uniform is in a shite state."

Soph had rolled her eyes, irritated that Sergeant Brown had insisted she wear Service Dress on her last day; starchy, scratchy beige shirt, tights and the brown skirt. Brown, brown, brown, sooo grim.

Pulling her hair tight, buttoning up her Service Dress jacket she had to admit she looked smart; a Sam Brown belt, burnished and bronze, its leather spanning from her right shoulder to her left hip, tradition borne of General Sam Brown who'd lost his arm in battle and had no way to carry his sword, so the Sam brown had been devised, a means by which a weapon could be carried without needing to be held. Nowadays the Sam Brown was worn on its own, snug around the waist, the leather a smart contrast to the dark khaki of the jacket and skirt. She stepped into her heeled court shoes, grateful at least not to be clumping around in combat boots.

Now here in the office, on her last day, she felt over dressed, a track suit more appropriate for the humping and dumping. It was the only time she'd have preferred the green pyjamas of Combat 95.

"Ma'am, c'mon,"

Sergeant Brown popped his head round the door. Slinging on her jacket, she adjusted her beret and pulled the knot of her tie tight. Frowning she followed Sergeant Brown.

"Platoon, Platoon Shun!"

The Platoon stomped to attention, and Soph strode out, feeling a bit contrived, inspecting her troops.

"Ma'am, we've assembled today, not for you to inspect, but to say goodbye."

She froze, stunned.

"As a way of saying thank you to our Boss, whose run us ragged around the Camp,"

A few nods and ayes in agreement. The Platoon Commander's fitness now undeniably equal to Sergeant Brown's, making PT sessions a thing of dread.

"But shown us proud in front of the other Platoons of the Battalion and the Fusiliers. So,"

Sergeant Brown glared at one of the Section Commanders, who stared back,

"Oh! Sorry!"

Peeling out of the body of men, he retrieved a brown package behind the tree to the rear of the Platoon, handing it to Sergeant Brown apologetically, who rolled his eyes in despair.

"Here's a little something to remember us by."

Soph stepped forward, immediately saluted by Sergeant Brown who thrust the parcel forward. Soph almost forgot to salute back, overwhelmed by the occasion. Throwing up a response she took the present.

"Can I open it now?"

The Platoon looked at Sergeant Brown who studiously unmoved, nodded.

She ripped off the carefully wrapped brown paper and gasped at the portrait, blown up from weeks before, all of them posed in front of the vehicles. Held in front of her, eyes wide, watering slightly, cheeks flushed,

"I,"

She lowered the frame, looking at her guys.

"First of all please relax."

"Platoon stand at ease!"

Arms crossed behind backs legs set apart, the Platoon eyed Soph cordially,

"It has been a pleasure working with you all. I've learnt so much and I've been so impressed with your commitment and dedication. You have shown me how to be a real professional, and Sergeant Brown has dragged me to a new level of fitness I'm not sure I wanted."

Jeers and laughter.

"But I'm certainly grateful for now. I wish you all the very best and I cannot thank you enough for such a wonderfully thoughtful present. Thank you."

She turned to Sergeant Brown,

"Thank you Sergeant Brown, I know this would have been your work. You have been a remarkable teacher and...well,"

Her voice cracked,

"I just, thank you."

She saluted and nodding again to the Platoon walked away; 31 pairs of eyes following her go, not wanting her to leave.

Slamming the boot of her Mini, Soph placed her treasured picture on the passenger seat, wrapped in her dressing gown, snug between handbag and kettle. She looked at the Mess, the place where she'd grabbed orange juices after epic runs, the accommodation where she'd had too many beers in the bar and weaved back to her room. The place where she'd prepared for Exercises, dreaded facing training and retreated after the day the Adjutant had bawled her out. This hadn't been a home, but it had sometimes been a haven and most of all, it had been a place of learning. She would miss Sergeant Brown and his practical jokes, his advice, solid unwavering support and obsession with running. Actually no, she wouldn't miss the running smiling. It was time to move on, to go home and start her Special to Arms training. She wondered what that would entail, learning the ins and outs of being an INT CORPS Officer and after that? Her first job as a qualified Intelligence Lieutenant. Slamming the door, she reversed out of her spot and drove up the hill, glancing at her old office, then as she approached the gates slowed, raising two fingers at the Adjutant's office, before speeding out of the barracks.

31

"MATE, SERIOUSLY PROBABLY shouldn't be talking as I'm on the Autobahn and fuck me people drive fast, my combie van is rattling along at 60 miles per hour, no idea what that is in kilmometres over here. Saunders is behind me in her car, since she refused to share this van, says it stinks of dogs, bitch."

Tracey grinned down the phone, scowling with the smallest hint of envy as a Mercedes flew past the best part of 100 miles per hour. She was looking forward to doing the defensive driving course over here. Apparently in Germany you could really floor the pedal, and still have some to spare. Flicking a look at her rear view she saw Saunders puttering along in her blue VW Polo. Everything neatly stacked, the car a mobile testimony to an organized mind, or anality as Tracey liked to tease. Trace and Sal had grown close during training, with Sal sitting open mouthed in horror as Trace had recounted the events of the Final Ex and Dom's refusal to play the game. In between huge mouthfuls of pasta at Strada in Covent Garden, she shook her head,

"I don't understand, you basically offer him an easy cruise through the Final Ex and he decides to go Banzai. I mean seriously? What the hell was the bloke thinking?"

She threw her curly red hair back, oblivious to the glances from waiters, her grey eyes firmly trained on Tracey, posture taut, that of a trained dancer, a secret she'd only shared with Trace.

"So you spoken to Soph or Percy?"

"Yep, Percy is on her way to Abingdon and I think Soph starts her Special to Arms training with the INT CORPS next week after a bit of leave."

Sal's face looked bemused, taking a sip of coke, resolutely a non-drinker, Trace had ignored her pinched lips and ordered a G&T,

"It's because the INT Corps only work at Brigade level, junior Officers don't really operate within a Battalion per se, they work at a more strategic level."

"So?"

Sal still looked confused,

"Well Soph has just done an Infantry attachment, I think it was the Royal Irish in Belfast, it means she actually got to put into action all the Platoon Commanding we got trained on at Sandhurst. Otherwise she goes straight into either singleton posts or bang into a Brigade and doesn't get the chance to make mistakes at the billy basic level, well, like we're about to!"

Sal laughed, ignoring the gentle bubbling in her stomach, the fear of living abroad, living in a virtually all male Mess, but that was all good right? A challenge? She couldn't quite shake her misgivings.

"So how are you?"

Trace floored the pedal, signs to Antwerp sailing by, even at the best part of a kilometre in front of Sal, she could feel her disapproval burrowing into her back. She loved the girl, but was pleased Sal was off to Gutesloh, further North, whilst Trace would be based in the Garrison town of Sennelager, or Sunny-lager as it was nicknamed. German summers and German beers, a winning combination, but one that Trace was well aware would also spell more work for her as RMP.

Soph grinned, spread out on her issue bed, well ensconced in the Young Officer or YO basic training. Fast and furious, the pace had seen them off to a sprint start.

"Ah you know, the accommodation is shit, box room, with a bathroom that is riddled with mould. Get this,"

She sat back leaning against her pillow, pulling her duvet around her, painted toenails peeping out, thick chestnut hair spread out around her, eyes sparkling, mouth dancing with laughter, looking every inch a young woman that no one would believe was military,

"I moved in and wanted a quick hair wash before the first day. I couldn't work out why there were two pint glasses in the bath. Odd. So I turn the shower on and literally a dribble tried to escape the shower head. So I turned on the taps in the sink that gushed out, and then realized why there were glasses in the bathroom. Un-bloody-believable!"

Trace cackled down the phone, eyes peeled for cameras and lurking Belgian police. God this country just went on and on and yet there wasn't anything here apart from very clean empty Services serving chips and mayo. She flicked a look in her rearview mirror, Sal bobbing about in her seat, likely singing to her latest obsession, Enrique Iglesias.

"So how long is the course?"

"Six months. The other people seem pretty sound, course Percy is still in this country, so I'm going to hook up with her once she's found her feet at Abingdon. Have you heard anything?"

Trace carefully changed hands, lodging the phone between her left ear and shoulder, stretching out her shoulders, swearing she would buy a hands free, hair getting tangled in the handset,

"Wait a second,"

She plonked the phone in her lap, peeled off the ever present elastic band from her wrist, twisted her hair back into a bun, brown and golden strands framing her face in long waves,

Picking up the phone, she continued,

"Yep, it aint good. If you think your accommodation is bad, you have to speak to Perce. She's being her usual upbeat self, but Christ, she said something along the lines of condemned Mess, no hot water, can you believe that? No hot water and apparently the Quarter Master was overheard saying in the bar after a few Carlings that, "Why should he give a toss if there wasn't any hot water because he lived in the married quarters where there was plenty thanks very much, and, if those in the Mess didn't like it, they should get married like the rest of us and move onto the patch!" Can you believe the fucker?!"

"Nooo!"

Soph's eyes widened,

"That is flipping outrageous!"

Trace nodded emphatically, almost dropping her phone, swerving into the nearside lane to rebalance herself, scaring a French couple who were cruising close beside her in their newly purchased Peugeot. Trace waving apologetically trying not to laugh at the mass of Gaelic hand gestures.

"What's worse is, apparently there is some poor pregnant Captain in the Mess whose husband is deployed and she's there unaccompanied, having to huddle up in her room as she gets bigger and bigger, dodging the dead flies floating in the sinks. Grim."

Soph shook her head, clutching her duvet, casting a look around her room, acknowledging whilst minimalist, it was at least warm and without a pile of insect corpses.

"So how did the Final Ex go? Rumour has it you stormed it?"

Trace flushed with bemused delight, green eyes gleaming, unsurprised at the speed of the army net. She filled Soph in, Dom's kamikaze attitude, the consequent awarding of best red cap.

"So I got Sennelager, the cream of the German postings. I'm pretty chuffed, although I'm nervous as hell. It's supposed to be mega busy, and squaddies in Germany don't half drink a lot, there's a reason it's called a German stone."

Soph scoffed,

"There is no way you'd put on that much weight even if you were boozing loads, you're a phys monster and you know it. Plus it gives me lots of excuses to come out and see you at the weekend. Helps me get an idea of whether I want to put down Germany as a first posting too. So you heard about Percy?"

"No?"

Trace indicating to overtake the Mini Clubman that insisted on keeping a snail's pace in front of her, despite the fact it had the acceleration to leave her munching dust. Powering past she peered down at the driver and admitted, as she clocked the 80 plus year old driver, that perhaps she wouldn't be burning rubber at that age too. Great taste in cars though.

"I'm convinced there's some bloke in the picture. She was telling me this hysterical story about some Junior Officer getting utterly mullered at their final dinner, so much so his posting actually got changed as a consequence,"

"No way?"

"Way. Anyway, there's definitely someone, because, well you know Percy, she just went all quiet and wouldn't say. He's definitely senior to her too."

"Oooo, well we're going to have to do a bit of dig about that with the perce-meister. Look, it's great to talk, but I really should probably concentrate on driving."

Trace accelerated hard and then pulled over to the left to allow an angry BMW driver speed on.

"Let's definitely catch up soon and good luck with your course honey."

"And you, let me know how Sennelager is, I'm so flying over when you're settled in Orrificer!"

Laughing Trace flung the phone onto the passenger seat, whilst Soph picked up the pile of papers next to her and, duvet firmly wrapped around her to keep out the creeping chill, began memorising the distinguishing features of an Infantry Armoured vehicle, sighing heavily and wondering if a cigarette would be a bad idea.

32

PERCY SAT WITH a Marlboro light wedged between her lips, blue eyes narrowed, trying to read a map by red flashlight, tactical but a nightmare on ordnance survey maps since it distorted the colours. Blood shot eyes from the effort, hair slicked back partly through the grip of her clips, partly through grease accumulated from 4 days of no washing. She was conscious her usual Issey Miyake odour was fading, replaced by a fug of coffee, stale cigarettes and undeniable BO. Right now however, as Convoy Commander, she was more focussed on her convoy than perfume and for the hundredth time wishing Staff Brillo was here.

"Staff Mackey, seriously, I'm pretty sure we should have turned right back there."

Staff Sergeant Mackey sighed, his barrel like chest rising and falling in exhausted dismay. Salt and pepper hair, a chiseled jawline and eyes that were both piercing and attractive, he could have almost passed for a military George Clooney if not for the extra stone or two he was carrying. Crisps, he just couldn't resist them. Right now however, he was resisting the urge to raise his voice at this particular Officer, who he hoped could read a map.

"Ma'am, do you have any idea where we are going? It's just I know we're on Salisbury plain and not causing a traffic jam, but you've stopped a convoy of 20 four tonners, not exactly tactical and suffice to say I'm not convinced the dwellers of down town Bosnia are going to love this kind of major interruption to their nightcaps."

Percy rolled her eyes, looked up, then back at the map,

"This is Delta One Zero, Contact wait out."

Percy froze, Delta One Zero was one of the trucks about half a kilometre down the convoy. A Contact meant either an ambush or an IED strike, either way the whole convoy would have to go static and Percy would have to lead a way out.

She and Staff Mackey sat in breathless silence, waiting for an update, their actions directed by the Sitrep fed in by Delta One Zero.

"Delta this is Delta One Zero Sitrep. Situation: we have hit an IED and are currently taking incoming fire. We are returning suppressing fire. We have one casualty requiring immediate casevac possibly Cat 2,"

Percy groaned,

"MERT requested and fire support needed over?"

Percy frowned, she wished Staff Brillo were here, she wouldn't be afraid to look to him to advice, but she'd heard he was in Afghanistan now and all she had was Staff Mackay who was clearly looking to her for direction and not entirely sympathetically.

"Delta One Zero this is Delta, roger that, wait out."

"Charlie this is Delta over?"

"Delta this is Charlie send over."

"Delta requesting immediate medevac in our position. Grid figures…"

She waved to Staff Mackey for the map, grabbing the sheet and turning down the folds to see the grid lines more clearly. Noting her position she calculated that Delta One would be about a kilometre away, possibly more, but she couldn't risk the MERT going in too short. Accuracy was as key or she'd risk the MERT being exposed whilst it found the correct location or the casualty potentially being life-threateningly delayed.

"…83469765, I say again, figures 83469765, Currently one pax requiring immediate evac, Delta One will be providing suppressing fire, over?"

"Roger that Delta, MERT eta figures 4 over?"

"Roger that Charlie, out."

Breathless, she couldn't help notice a look of surprise on Staff Mackey's face,

"Not just a junior no hoper after all?"

Grinning, feeling a flush of satisfaction, she snatched up the radio, relaying all the details to Delta One and calling for all other call signs to confirm their status. No other element was experiencing difficulties, which was good, meaning the Contact was contained and like a quarantined contagion, unlikely to spread. At this point, having relayed to HQ aka call sign Charlie all call signs within her convoy were safe, all Percy could do now was wait.

They sat there at the mercy of the radio, both chain smoking, the cabin prickling with tension and stale smoke. Finally, Delta One radioed in the successful casualty extraction,

"....CAT 2 now downgraded to CAT 3. MERT extracted, contact ended at 1453, ammo replen ongoing over?"

"Roger that Delta One, good news, prepare to move in figures 10 over?"

"Roger that Delta out."

Percy sighed with relief. Ok it was an Exercise but downgraded casualties were always a feel good, and right now she could do with feeling good.

As they rolled into the Exercise Forward Operating Base or FOB, Percy's stomach groaned at the sweet aroma of baked beans. She couldn't remember the last time she'd eaten. Whilst it was her poor admin adrenaline had curbed any hunger pains and now her stomach reminded her that *that* was a state of affairs not to be repeated. Exhausted, she jumped from the driver's cabin trotting to the FOB gates counting in her vehicles, oblivious to the approving glance from the Company Sergeant Major impressed by her diligence, but would rather chew his arm off than tell her.

Kit dumped, hair looser and coffee in hand, Percy looked at the queue of soldiers waiting patiently for their cooked breakfast. Each looking ragged and tired, yet bursts of laughter and the chat that drifted over, reassuring that whilst this Exercise had been intense, morale was high. She lit a cigarette, savouring the nicotine hit glancing around for any other Company Officers. This had been quite an isolating experience in terms of command. Used to the camaraderie of her fellow Junior Officers, it had been hard to adjust to standing alone literally and metaphorically. Right now if she made the mistake of drifting over to groups of soldiers, conversation would die, their backs stiffen and the stifling blanket of formality would descend, rendering any small talk hopelessly contrived with the subtext of piss off. Percy took another hit of Marlboro lights and realized that, although surrounded by so many people, she felt lonely.

Someone parted from the gaggle of queuing soldiers and marched towards her, his walk giving him away immediately. Percy braced up.

"Morning Sir."

"Morning Percy, well done, that convoy was pretty tricky but you were right on the mark. How did your guys do?"

Blushing at the unexpected praise she scanned mentally back over the week's Ex. There was the Corporal who'd left his rifle at one of the RVs when he'd jumped from his vehicle's cabin for a quick piss, causing the entire convoy to halt whilst he retrieved his SA 80. There was the Private who'd been caught giving a Lance Jack a blowjob in the back of their four tonner. Something which had staggered Percy, given they hadn't showered for three days. Then there was Staff Mackey's constant sarccy comments, generally apathetic demeanour and uninspiring conduct as a senior soldier or SNCO.

"By and large Sir, I think they pulled together really well."

The Company Commander narrowed his eyes, knowing full well Percy's troop was full of colourful characters. He reached for his own cigarettes, pulling off his beret, shoving it in his combat jacket. Hands cupping the flame as it licked his cigarette,

"So I hear you were a bit of a hero on your YOs course?"

Percy stubbed out her fag thrusting her hands in her pockets, looking longingly at the breakfast, conscious her Commander wanted to talk. She glanced at his smock, flashes peppering his sleeve, each badge a testimony to completed Infantry courses; the All Arms Commando, P-Company. Those slides were earned from blood, sweat and tears. Percy folded her loose hair behind her ear, mindful of her single pip and inexperience. She wondered if having another smoke would make her a chain smoker, fishing them out of her pocket she realized that that debate had been decided long ago.

"Well Sir," Percy kicked a stone with her boots. They needed a polish.

"I think I was more a benefiter of circumstance if that makes sense?"

Major Buchan's eyes narrowed, curious,

"Well the star of the course got leathered at the final dinner, and DRLC was there who, ahem, wasn't very impressed. So I think there was a bit of musical chairs on the night because well,"

Percy coughed embarrassed and feeling for Walters. Rumour had it he'd hit the booze hard at Deepcut, depressed at being Officer in Charge of post. She didn't blame him. Percy caught a whiff of sausage and her stomach cramped.

"He got posted to Deepcut as OiC of Courier and Postal services and I, well, I came here."

Major Buchan barked a laugh, grinding his cigarette into the ground, stooping to pick it up, entirely aware that whilst his Company were studiously avoiding his gaze they were scrutinizing his every move.

"And? Must have been a bit of a surprise for you...? Pleased?"

Percy hesitated. Pleased would not be how she'd describe the current relentless training tempo. Nights out of bed were meant to be minimal during a Unit's time in Barracks. For Percy it felt like it was the other way round. She couldn't remember the last time she'd had a night on a mattress. Camp cot or vehicle cab yes, duvet and mattress, not so much.

"Absolutely, Sir. There's no denying the tempo is pretty fierce, but Spearhead is an exciting place to be. Do you think we'll be called forward?"

Percy's OC looked over at bodies strewn round the base. Most were smoking or chatting, long since having scarfed their brunch. He knew the high readiness took a toll on all of them, that the training was savage, but it needed to be. For all of their sake he hoped they would be deployed to give all of this rhyme and reason, or his wife, for one, would be nagging him for months about the pointlessness of it all.

"I hope so Percy, I hope so. Now go and get yourself some scoff, oh and have you heard?"

His tone dropped, Percy's skin immediately prickling,

"No Sir?"

"We lost one in Afghan, a SNCO, I don't know him personally, but I heard he was a good bloke. Staff Sergeant Mason I think, anyway bloody travesty as ever."

He walked away, Percy staring after him, the smell of bacon drifting over as she held her breath.

33

TRACEY COULD NOT believe the paperwork. In post for 4 months, she had just about mastered her Platoon's work allocation and the matrices on the system, endless excel spreadsheets that needed updating. But the caseload, it was enormous. Drink driving, verbal and physical assaults, theft, rape, alot of rapes and accusations of rape. It was a veritable litany of the worst of humanity. She drained her fifth coffee of the morning and taking her ISAF mug to the percolator poured another.

Up since 0600, a squad steady state run, followed by the morning update or Prayers as it was known, appraising her of the progress on her team's investigations. She was a desk jockey and she knew it; juggling reports, updating her OC who seemed to prefer the gym, running, or basically being out of the office to any real involvement, leaving her to manage the oversight and approval of following up leads. It was a far cry from tabbing around Salisbury Plain at Sandhurst and she felt a stab of nostalgia for being out on the Area, bitching with her old Platoon mates about carrying the radio and the latest patrol orders.

It had become pretty apparent on arrival that as OiC she didn't get out on the ground much. Her's was a managerial role and one her Sergeant Major was heartily grateful to hand over. Her post had been gapped for the best part of 6 months, meaning he'd been the paper monkey. Now he was out shadowing the guys and happier for it. Tracey meanwhile drank her body weight in coffee and looked longingly out of the window. Highlights were interviews and she

162

did her best to sit in on those under the auspices of 'ensuring best practice', meaning she was away from her desk, and better, her phone.

Padding back to her seat her phone rang, suppressing a sigh,

"Lieutenant Bonner, OiC 12 Platoon speaking."

"Morning OiC! How the devil?? They keeping you busy? I'm chained to my desk! How much bloody paperwork?"

Tracey grinned, sinking into her chair,

"Hey Sal, how are you? God mate its crap!"

"I know, cannot believe I dragged my ass through the lakes, literally, at Sandhurst to be sifting paper. Anyways, down to the more urgent business of social life. In a couple of weeks there's a big Mess do here, think it's in aid of the Octoberfest, not sure, either way it would be cool if you could make it?"

Tracey tugged over her diary and flicked through the pages, each looking bleakly blank.

"Welll, I'm a bit booked up…"

"You are such a liar Miss Bonner! Get yourself up here and see what Gutesloh has to offer! Honestly the town is actually quite pretty, even found a fairly decent coffee shop that I just may frequent a little too often. Oh go on? Say you will? There aren't many females here and the blokes are gagging for it!"

"Well… when you put it like that, how's a girl to resist?"

"Great, you're in! I'll let you know the details by email; in fact I'll drop you one now to put in your calendar so you've got no excuse. Look after yourself."

Tracy slipped the phone back, her email immediately pinging,

Insert into diary now-drinking session and general debauchery in October, date to be confirmed with Sal. I shall not let her down.xx

Trace shook her head, and copied the email into her personal calendar. She thought about Soph and wondered how much time she still had to push out on her YOs course. If her timings were right, she'd be about 8 weeks away from ENDEX. Everything would be getting pretty serious as they started the slow sprint to the finish.

God, that seemed a lifetime away, although the last four months hadn't been all work. Her arms, a dusky brown from sunbathing out the back of her flat, legs toned from long runs. Her face honey brown from nights spent giggling and sipping Steins of beer in the Officer's bar, or popping round to each other's flats, beer in hand from the Naafi, sharing stories of exhaustion and deprivation from Sandhurst; trips to Dusseldorf, Amsterdam and Berlin over the weekends that had left her giddy from sightseeing and the sweet taste of freedom. It was exhilarating, and whilst the current monotony of work was a grind, the promise of further adventures with the other Subalterns of her Battalion was a panacea that was hard to beat.

"Ma'am?"

"Yep?" Startled, Corporal Dancer looked at her amused,

"The interview is about to start, you said you wanted to sit in?"

Trace's mask descended, stomach flipped. Damn, she'd forgotten. Her mouth dry, she sipped some coffee, cradling the tepid drink following Corporal Dancer into one of the interview rooms.

Bare except for a wooden table and 4 basic chairs not made for comfort, Trace dragged hers into a corner, Corporal Dancer assuming the chair opposite the accused, a table dividing them. Trace's Senior NCO was seated beside Corporal Dancer, letting her take the lead. She was good and this was her chance to really spread her wings on an investigation, even if it was a particularly unsavoury one.

Trace placed her mug on the floor. Nodded at Sergeant Baker. 6'1" he didn't need to do much to exude a presence; hair cut a fierce grade one and biceps that looked like they could bend steel rods for fun, he was an imposing figure. Although Trace knew that in reality he was a complete softie, who drank herbal teas and owned a cat called Charlie. Right now however, the accused, a Corporal Jon Dowley didn't know that. Right now Sergeant Baker just looked scary.

Corporal Dancer however wasn't daunting, in fact quite the opposite. Delicate features and a slight frame, she looked like she over did the phys and ate too little. Her face drawn, cheeks too hollow to be attractive, borderline emaciated. Her dark brown hair was taut in a fierce bun, the Essex facelift. Trace knew again, looks could be deceptive. Corporal Dancer did not have the nickname 'Rottie' for no reason.

"Commencing interview with Corporal Jon Dowley, 2 Battalion the Fusiliers. Corporal Dowley stands accused of sodomising a female within the same Battalion. Corporal Dowley is also accused of theft, namely the stealing of said female's wallet containing 200 euros and various cash cards as well as her military ID. Corporal Dowley is aware of his rights."

Trace winced. When this case had first come in, her eyes had widened in disbelief, the taste of bile clipping her throat. She hadn't been sure if the lack of response from her soldiers both Junior and Senior NCOs alike wasn't more concerning.

"Corporal Dowley, would you care to reiterate your whereabouts on the night in question?"

"Well,"

Corporal Dowley had a strong scouser drawl, a face pocked from acne, red from rubbing, eyes slitty from too much smoking, lips thin and dry. He sat back in his seat, all skinny and attitude. He'd been known as scroat rather than the accused throughout the case, it seemed more appropriate. Trace tried not to think of the photos of the victim, tried not to remember her tearful statement, the split lip, the fact she hadn't been able to sit still, that sitting at all had initially been a cause for embarrassment and then distress. That interview had been a baptism of fire.

"You'd 'ave to tells me which night that was, being not guilty of anything yoouse have said, I wouldn't knows what youuse talking about."

Sergeant Baker shifted in his chair, Trace could almost feel his self-restraint.

"That would be the night of the 18th of August, a Saturday, Corporal Dowley. And you know how we know you were there? We recovered the wallet from your room, as presented to us by your roommate,"

"Yeah wells he's a fooking grass, youuse should be looking to him fur this."

"And do you know how we knew it was the victim's wallet? I'll tell you Corporal Dowley, it contained her MOD 90, the ID she had left in there."

"Like I said, my room mate is a dodgey foooker, 'e stole it."

"Well you see,"

Corporal Dancer lent back in her chair, unphased, crossing her arms, icy,

"I have a problem with you accusing your roommate."

"Whys?"

"Well because he was back in the UK for a long weekend with his girlfriend, who has in turn testified to his whereabouts."

"Well of course she would, she's a lying scroat too."

Corporal Dowley's eyes flitted nervously to Sergeant Baker who shifted ominously in his chair, metal legs screeching on the floor, voicing the same disbelief Corporal Dancer was containing. Trace reached for her coffee, Corporal Dancer took a sip of water,

"Well oddly, catching him on CCTV camera at Dover was sufficient collaboration for us. Cameras don't lie Corporal Dowley, although I'm beginning to suspect you do."

Dowley swallowed, eyes more slitty, arms wrapped tight around himself, he resembled Smeigel off Lord of the Rings, all limbs and wiry, slippery with deceit. 'Rottie' waited, space in an interview, guilt in the gaps. The air thick with tension, no one moved. Dowley shifted, uncomfortable, eyes darting around the room, cornered like the rat he was.

"Look, she was fooking asking for it. I just wanted a snog, but she made such a fooking song and dance about it. Look can't we come to a deal or something? You know? Like they do off the Bill? Honestly I was off my head I'd drunk that much beer. Doesn't that count for something? Anyway, I paid for her kebab, so she owed me money! That's why I took her wallet y'know?"

Trace picked up her coffee, the cup cold, her hands clammy. Dowley's whining continued as she walked out, letting Dancer and Baker wrap it up. They'd all talked about this final interview. Dowley had been a bit tougher to break than expected, but Dancer had wanted one more crack at the whip. She was convinced he'd squeal like the underhand thieving rapist he was. Trace had struggled being in the same room.

Back at her desk, grateful for the distance, she drank in the quiet, staring at her screen, then grabbing her combat jacket and beret marched for the door. Fresh air, she needed fresh air, her lungs were screaming from sharing the same room with the dregs of humanity.

Marching across the camp, she returned salutes and ignored stares from soldiers as they eyeballed her warily. A red cap was rarely welcome and she'd come to adopt a defensive stoop. She hoped it portrayed a sense of grim focus and determination, to some she just looked intimidating. Pulling off her beret, she took a deep breath of freshly baked pastries that perfumed the Naafi. The local shop come coffee bar, it was the haunt of choice and there was a lot of banter over the sheer quantity of coffee Tracey consumed. Making a beeline for the queue, dropping her guard to take in the scene. Soldiers' families peppered the seating area, screaming children, toddlers staggering around, falling under tables, Squaddies grinning sheepishly at chubby wives. Tattoos were ubiquitous as were black leggings and scraped back greasy hair, gold earrings dangled, whilst fizzy Tango was slurped. 'Fuck' was every second word and the set volume for conversation was loud. Trace grimaced, concentrating on whether she'd go for an extra shot in her latte. She patted her bun, smoothed her jacket, wondered if it was too early for a pastry.

"Do you think it's too early for a pastry?"

Lips twitching in amusement she turned to face the stranger who'd read her mind. He was Army, moulded beret to perfection meant he had to be some kind of Infanteer or judging by his height possibly a Guards' Officer. She clocked his rank slide, a Captain. His eyes danced, as he watched her size him up. Pulling off his beret, revealing a full crop of brown hair he raked awkwardly, he put out a hand,

"Hi I'm Dan, just posted in, I'm one of the Adjutants here, or about to be; mid handover, had to duck out to get a coffee, there's only so much send you can take, y'know?"

Tracey smiled. She knew exactly what he meant, handovers could be tortuous; either too quick as the current incumbent raced for the door, sketching over the barest minimum, or the obsessive who wouldn't let go and wanted to make every element clear so you realized *just how important* the job was to the future of the Army. Turned out Dan was a Gunner, Artillery, hence the confidence and public school boy haircut. Trace vaguely remembered a discussion in the bar that one of the Adjutants was moving on or being deployed. There'd been loose chat about the replacement; fresh blood in a tired camp always kindled curiosity.

"Tracey, I'm the OiC of the RMP Det here. Welcome to Sennelager. You done a German tour before?"

Dan nodded,

"Yep, when I was a subbie, s'good isn't it? Though I don't intend to drink quite so much beer this time."

He patted his stomach,

"This took quite some effort to reduce to hilly rather than mountainous, I'd like to keep it that way."

Tracey snorted, turning to scan the drink list.

The cashier inspected them with a bored expression, chewing her nail, thinking of the 5 hours yet to go and whether her boyfriend had scored some weed.

"Can I have a Latte with an extra shot?"

Tracey raised an eyebrow expectantly,

"Coffee, sorry, Americano, with space for milk please,"

"And,"

Trace paused,

"A cinnamon swirl."

She grinned,

"Now you're gonna have to help me eat that."

"You're on."

Seated at a formica table, stirring their drinks, the eating area had cleared, the din of sugar high kids diminished, allowing Trace and Dan the opportunity to talk rather than shout. A slightly awkward silence descended as they cradled their drinks. Dan shifting in his chair, Trace sipping self-consciously,

"So… you've been to Germany before? Where?"

"Ah Gutesloh, bit further up, not quite so easy to get back to the UK, but the Mess life was better. Mind you it was a damn sight more sociable than Hohne, God! Those guys, felt sorry for them. Most of them went blimin' feral stuck out there in the sticks. Any efforts to get back to the UK involved such an epic car journey just to get to an airport that it was hardly worth it for a weekend. Unlike here of course, Paderborn just down the road, best of both worlds isn't it?"

He pulled a chunk off the pastry and munched.

"How about you? First posting?"

"Hmmm."

Trace nodded, sipping more drink, flicking her eyes to the clock above the main door, aware of how long the interview would have taken to wrap up. Realising she shouldn't be absent for too long, enjoying how nice it was to talk to a bloke about postings and not their criminal history.

"S'good, been really good. Living arrangements are all right too. I thought we'd all be piled into a Mess, not have our own little flat on a patch because the Mess is full. It's nice, more personal space than I thought, very civilized!"

"Yep, s'what I thought too. Stuck in Battalion back home meant the same small places, spaces and faces, and whilst we've all moved here en masse, it's given a bit of time out, well before the next deployment at least. You been warned off?"

Trace's stomach squeezed, she tugged a bit of sweet bread and chewed slowly,

"Not yet, but there are whispers about, the next few months. What are we now September? So the next rotation is due out in…?"

"April." Dan finished "and we're on it and there's rumours of Tours being extended from 6 to 9 months as well."

Dan shook his head. He'd managed the last 6 month tour, but at a cost. He pulled another section of cinnamon swirl remembering his ex-girlfriend moving out, the accusations, acrimony, the consolatory beers in the Mess, solving nothing, just numbing the fall out. He shook away the ghosts. At least this Tour he wouldn't have to worry about leaving someone behind, 9 months would exact a terrible toll on any loved one doing the waiting back home.

"Wow."

Trace took another mouthful of coffee, aware Dan had gone noticeably quiet, preoccupied.

"Anyway, Mess dos here are quite a laugh, probably see you there?"

Dan brightened.

"Yeah, sure, look thanks for the coffee."

They scraped back chairs, Trace folding invisible hairs behind her ears, eyes, on the floor, Dan moulding his beret, stretching the moment.

"Well errm, thanks, I owe you a coffee and something unbearably sweet to eat."

Trace blushed,

"So we'll have to make sure we do this again?"

"Sure."

Sweeping on her own beret now at the door, they smiled sheepishly at each other, walking away, wondering if the other was looking back, not wanting to look in case they were caught. Yet Trace grinned because she could feel his eyes on her back, she walking a little straighter, a little happier.

34

THE GERMAN SUMMER, hot and dusty, flying beetles and cool beers slowly passed into a distant memory. Soon replaced by protracted rain, gloomy clouds and chilling winds that urged even the most dedicated to stay in bed and press the snooze dial just once more.

Tracey's alarm went off for the third time. She slapped it back, groaning, snuggling up to the warm body comatose next to her. She was pushing it, the last month had seen her have more than her fair share of late starts and she was beginning to take the piss. But right now, this moment, was a little slice of heaven. Breathing in Dan's inimitable smell she smiled to herself, grimacing only when the buzz of her iPhone interrupted their sleeping bliss for the fourth time. She couldn't ignore this and nor could Dan. Throwing back the covers she ignored his pawing her bum, pulling at her skimpy t-shirt,

"Babe, seriously already pretty close to the wire, you've got to get up too. Haven't you got some brief with your CO this morning?"

"Oh shit!"

Dan dived out of bed, hauling on his combats, shaving beside her in the tiny bathroom, still finding time to grab her bum and nestle her ear.

"You seeing that mate of yours tonight? The one just posted to Rheindahlen, HQ ARRC?"

Tracey mouth full of toothpaste shook her head, and spitting white paste, leered at Dan,

"No, the one up in Gutesloh. Gotta let Soph find her feet. Think this is an early Oktoberfest or something"

"Ok," Dan kissed her on her cheek, "look so attractive with toothpaste smeared over your face my RMP fox. I'll see you tomorrow, enjoy the girly drinks."

Then he was gone, the door slamming behind on their domestic bliss.

35

SOPHIE EYED HER room. Average? Generous. She dumped her box on the bed. Freshly highlighted chestnut hair desperately trying to burst out of its elastic bands, Superdry grey sweats and hoodie making her look younger, vulnerable.

The Mess had been huge, long corridors devoid of people, giving it the feel of an abandoned hotel. She had shivered thinking of The Shining, hearing 'red rum red rum' echoing down the corridors. As a Junior Officer her accommodation was unlikely to be palatial. Sticking her head out of a still empty corridor, she padded out in search of a loo, shower and anything vaguely ablution. Sure enough there was a single toilet at the end of the building, opposite a laundry room that smelled of Persil and clean sheets. She stumbled into a drying room and then opened a door into a chaotic scene that must have been the stores. Finally she peeked into the showers and was relieved to see they weren't unisex. You never knew in Germany.

Trotting back to her new home, she picked up her duvet cover, plugged in her iPod and rolling up her sleeves, began to make her room cozy, with West life pouring out their hearts loudly promising that tonight they were gonna make love to her. If only.

A few hours later, in front of the full length mirror Sophie straightened her shirt. Ironed badly, she tugged at the tramlines sighing and ignored her butterflies. She'd heard movement in the corridor earlier, banter and whoops of laughter that at least confirmed others of a similar age. She looked at her watch, 1905, one minute later than when she'd last looked. Rummaging around in the pile of shoes hurled into her cupboard, she pulled out some black leather pumps. Smart, without trying too hard, adhering to the irritating Mess rules about dress at dinner. At least with a suit you couldn't go wrong. After all who the hell knew what ladies equivalent to a lounge suit was? In fact for that matter, what *was* a lounge suit?

Roast lamb wafted down the corridor and Sophie's stomach reminded her with a huge leap that food hadn't starred highly in movements over the last 8 hours. Licking her lips, patting her hair and throwing her shoulders back she walked into the dining room. A hot plate blasted heat to her right, to her left was an immaculately laid wooden table, including flickering candles, populated by a handful of people. Starters appeared to be laid out and judging by the heavenly smells, the main was roast, roast and more roast. Even in another country the Military menu remained the same. Sophie suppressed a smile, and eyed up the table. Walking over to a seat opposite a few young blokes, she beamed widely,

"Hi I'm Soph, just arrived today."

"Hi,"

Dark slightly ruffled hair, gleaming white teeth and eyes that danced with amusement,

"I'm Joe." He stood up offering his hand.

Grateful Soph shook it hoping hers wasn't too clammy. She looked to the other two. Red haired, with a roundish face that suggested a heavy drinker, he had a warm grin,

"Hey I'm Jeremy, you can call me Jerry."

He smiled up at her, as Soph pulled out her chair.

Her face flushed with relief at how welcoming the blokes had been, she realized the third one had just glanced up and did he grunt? Then carrying on, shaking his head, muttering something like NIG. What the...? Soph's face dropped, she trained her eyes on the smoked salmon neatly rolled into an appetising ensemble before her. What a knob.

Jerry noticed her blushing,

"Ah, don't mind Tom, he's an antisocial git and doesn't talk to subbies."

"Oh."

Soph nodded, feigning indifference, whilst her stomach rollercoastered with hurt and even more annoyance that it had been Tom, with his grade 1 hair, rugby build and eyes that seemed to stare right through her, whom she'd most wanted to say hello. Wanker, who needed him and what was a NIG anyway?

"So?"

She said brightly, ignoring the shaking of her hands, disguising how flustered Tom's easy dismissal had left her,

"What's this Mess like then?"

Standard practice was to finish supper in the bar, so over wine and pints Soph was regaled with Mess exploits. Propped up against the bar she grinned as Joe in the Engineers and Jerry, a Loggie tried to outdo each other with drunken tales of debauchery. She did her best to ignore the brooding body that was Tom; the feeling appeared mutual.

"How's about you then Soph?"

Joe grinned easily, interested,

"Well straight off the YO's course, join my Section tomorrow. Quite lucky, because a few of my intake from Sandhurst are here as well, Sennelager and Gutesloh. Anyway, guys thanks for being so friendly,"

Soph flicked a baleful look at Tom, who resolutely ignored her,

"But I'm pretty knackered so going to call it a night, good to meet you."

"Night mate."

As Soph walked down the corridors she heard snorts of laughter and hated the fact that she wondered if it was Tom who'd been interested in anything she'd said.

The next morning, tightening her belt, peeling yet another stray hair behind her ear, beginning to wonder if any of her hair was actually held in her bun, she grabbed her wallet and shoving it in her combat jacket, slipped out the back door of her corridor. Despite a steady drizzle the main thoroughfare was teeming. Cars rolled up the road, bikes raced by, plenty of uniforms walking into work as well. Soph was in the 'Big House', the main red brick building found at the top of the camp near the main gate. Her pulse racing, adjusting her beret one last time, she pulled open the security gate and wheeled out her bike. A black mountain beast, she was secretly quite proud of it. Slinging her leg over, she flicked her eyes to check the path was clear,

"Seriously?! Look where you're going!"

Soph hauled her bike backwards, narrowly avoiding what seemed a streak of silver, all screaming rubber and swearing. The rider, who'd just avoided smashing into Sophie came to a juddering halt and turned glaring,

"Oh, it's you."

Cheeks burning, her stomach flip flopped like a fish out of water.

"God I am so sorry, I swear I thought…"

Tom glowered, eyes sizing up this subbie. She was more than pretty. He'd hardly been able to keep his eyes off her last night, and what she'd talked about? It was disarming. He hadn't encountered someone for a long time who seemed, well, so genuine, nothing to prove and not a hint of arrogance. She was staring at him now, her gold flecked brown eyes filling, lips shaking, chin wobbling just a fraction though determinedly hiding it.

"Errm, look like I said, I really am sorry, I'm a bit nervous, it's my first day,"

Why couldn't he say something bloody arsehole just standing there, straddling his bike all sexy and glaring at her?

"Ok, so well, errm,"

She pulled her jacket closer, straightening her beret,

"So, yep, sorry about…"

"If you stopped blathering for just a second you can buy me a coffee later. I'm sure you'll get shown where it is in the Big House. Don't worry I'll come find you. Latte be fine"

Eyes full of mischief and the ghost of a smile, he smoothed his beret and was gone, leaving Sophie doing her best goldfish impression, watching him speed off.

Today was handover, as would be most of the week. She'd already spoken on the phone to the girl who was currently in post. Bubbly, friendly and not a little relieved at Soph's arrival, she'd promised an easy introduction with plenty of coffee and down time for Soph to find her feet.

"Seriously, the job is fine. The OC is a bit of a character, but he likes females and as long as you make sure there is a steady supply of biscuits and smile at his jokes he'll be eating out of your hand. I'll see you at about 0900."

Locking her bike into the shelter, and a quick check round for senior Officers Soph bolted for the main door and began the bureaucracy of building passes and security interrogations.

"Hey, welcome to the Big house!"

A petite blonde beamed at Soph as she peered round an office door. Resisting the instinct to throw up a salute, Soph grinned hesitantly,

"Sam?"

"Yeah, come in come in. I bet you were even thinking about saluting?"

Blushing, Soph avoided answering instead installing herself into the grey easy chair in the corner. Swiveling on her leather seat Sam smiled,

"So how was the Mess?"

"Cool, friendly, big."

"Yeah it is isn't it? Look, I'll just give you the quick intros and then let's get a proper coffee over in the Naafi. I can show you admin stuff like the Bank and Post Office as well."

The classified working areas were windowless, computers lining one side of a room, a handful of soldiers and a Sergeant Major seated at the desk nearest the door, opposite Soph's soon to be office. Overjoyed to see she was going to actually have some private space and equally pleased to shake the hand of her future Warrant Officer Soph stepped forward smiling. The response was less enthusiastic. Athletic, her face lined, eyes tired and cynical, she regarded Soph luke warmly.

"Ma'am, welcome to the Section."

The handshake limp.

Soph's smile faded, she turned her attention to Sam's introduction of her soldiers hopeful of a more welcoming attitude,

"We've got Lance Corporal Green,"

"Ma'am."

Ruddy faced, cheeky Corporal Green was a bit of a looker. Thick dark hair, cheekbones and a face that would fit in a boy band, he knew it and flashed Soph a flirty smile.

Soph remained impassive; distance at this stage was probably not a bad idea.

"Lance Corporal Sedley,"

"Ma'am."

Tall lanky, with wire rimmed glasses he fitted the stereotype most people probably had of an INT CORPS soldier, he also looked older than both of the other soldiers, and not a great smiler either. Soph liked him immediately.

"And Lance Corporal Fulston."

"Ma'am."

Mousey hair with a nervous disposition, Corporal Fulston looked like she was on the brink of bolting from the room. G1 thought Soph grimacing, welfare case in the making.

"Where's Sergeant Leg Sergeant Major?"

WO2 Ryan shrugged,

"I think he's on his way in, probably been checking the Lannies down at the bays."

She stared balefully at Soph, an attitude that whilst Soph understood, oddly irritated. Didn't she realize that her new Boss was stood right in front of her? Shouldn't she at least try to be a bit deferential rather than so unashamedly unimpressed?

Sam meanwhile was oblivious to Soph's righteous indignation and grinning at her Section, filed out to the Naafi. Grabbing her beret, Soph traipsed after, disappointed at an underwhelming number of introductions.

Minutes later, clasping mugs of steaming fresh coffee, Soph blew gently on her steaming drink and rephrased her question,

"I guess what I'm trying to say, is, well, errm…WO2 Ryan, she's a bit…?"

"Cynical? Jaded? Couldn't really give a toss about the new Boss? More interested in playing sport?"

Soph bit her lip, nodding,

"Am I way off the mark here?"

Sam snorted, slurping merrily,

"Look I won't lie. You are effectively a one pip wonder, no let me rephrase, you ARE a one pip wonder until you promote to Lieuie in a few months' time. She looks at you and just sees someone who hasn't got a clue."

Soph sputtered indignantly,

"And before you go on about Sandhurst and how hard the Final Ex was not to mention the YOs course, that's not what I mean. Look,"

Sam sat back, sipping thoughtfully, Soph trying not to let her eyes flick to the Captain's rank slide; those 2 extra pips seeming to move her into an almost other universe of seniority.

"We don't know what we don't know when we leave Sandhurst. The Young Officer's course whatever the cap badge tries to minimize the damage, but the same is true of any business you go into, at the start, no matter what training you've had, unless its learnt and proven on the job its worth diddly squat in real terms. WO2 Ryan has been in the best part of 20 years. She's seen people like you and me come and go two a penny. It makes no difference to her, well no..."

Sam smiled, gulping more hot brew and waving at someone before turning back to Soph,

"Sorry, what was I saying? Oh yes, we do make a difference, we make her job harder, because she is supposed to show us what to do, and, well, WO2 Ryan couldn't give a toss. She's not a great teacher, she's not interested in making you look good so,"

Soph felt her heart slide towards the floor like jelly down a toddler's bib, this was turning out to be the posting from hell. She sipped her coffee gloomily,

"Look I'm sorry, I'm making this sound like you've got some kind of herculean task ahead of you. You don't think that everyone, and I mean everyone, be they juniors, seniors or even the Company Commander don't know that Sergeant Major Ryan is a slacker? What they are more interested in is what you are going to do about it. So the fact that you've already clocked she is a waste of space, means that you're not going to waste any time looking to her for guidance. You'll go straight to the source, namely Sergeant Leg and the Juniors and you know what? They'll respect you more for it. So finish that and let's go and get your bank account opened. Pay is morale remember!"

There was no natural light in the office, no window to open, just four walls and a fluorescent strip that Soph was sure gave the room a slightly greenish tinge. Sam had gone to the gym, leaving Soph time to have a bit of a rummage around her new working space. Banter drifted across the corridor, jokes and laughter that made her feel left out. The loneliness of leadership right? She rolled her eyes at her pompousness. Yawning, she stretched, leaning back in her chair wondering what the hell she should be doing.

"Ma'am?"

Soph's chair slammed to the floor.

"Yes?" Composing her features into a suitably 'Boss-like' expression.

"It's Wednesday, so the lads and I, we're gonna go off and do some phys unless?"

WO2 Ryan let the question hang in the air, a token effort at formality. Childishly, Soph paused, looking deliberately quizzical as if racking her mind for some urgent task the Section should be intent on completing. It lasted five seconds, until she dissolved into a 'please like me smile' and hating herself for being so pathetic, nodded and within what felt like seconds the office was silent. Eyes flicking to her watch, looking around the office, she pushed some paper about and then gave up and went hunting for a kettle and a cup of tea. Locating both a kettle and a cup, Soph discovered that there was no milk and no tea bags. Tutting, she grabbed her wallet and headed back down to the Naafi to grab a quick coffee and then get back to her desk. She wasn't quite sure where to start, but reading through the handover notes Sam had compiled was probably a good idea.

"So, you gonna get me that latte?"

Soph pulled up in the corridor with a start,

"Jesus how do you do that? You following me?"

Tom swallowed a grin, he wasn't about to admit that he'd been loitering for the last hour outside her office waiting for her to emerge. Or that he'd stopped Sam to check that Soph at least knew where the Naafi was, much to Sam's amusement,

"Ooo, bit of a fan of our new subbie are we Tom?"

"Oh sod off Sam, just asking."

She'd walked off sniggering, a wolf whistle echoing down the corridor.

Soph for the second time that day felt her cheeks crimson, she composed herself, come on get a grip, he's just a rude Captain. Nothing special and you nearly knocked him off his bike, so least you can do.

"Sure, course, least I can do…glad that you're deigning to speak to us subbies."

Finally Tom met Soph with a smile, so gorgeous and easy it made her pulse race,

"Well, charity starts at home…"

Despite herself, Sophie creased with laughter.

36

PERCY SHIFTED IN her seat. There was little relief a small shuffle could provide for a bum numb after over 8 hours of sitting. Spearhead had been called. 24 hours of checking that she'd packed everything then unpacking to check again, before going through the MCCP or Movement Control Check Point that really equalled Clerks messing around with medical documents and dog tags, then shuttling them to Brize and onwards to Bosnia.

Elections, who'd have thought they could be a source of so much potential violence that UN intervention was required? Percy mused over the question whilst pulling out her cigarettes. Norgie poloneck, thermal vest and elegant thermal underwear, coupled with a buffalo jacket all squashed under her combat jacket, she now resembled something like the Michelin man's wife. She was still cold.

Staff Mackey was silent next to her, equally unimpressed by the temperature, but knew better than to moan, made you colder somehow. He flicked a look at the dashboard clock rolling his eyes.

"Fuck me! We've been sat here 8 and a half hours! I mean who the fuck is going to kick off at 3 in the bloody morning?"

Cupping her lighter Percy suppressed a snicker, savouring the smoke which provided some semblance of warmth and woke her up. A bit.

"Some local Mafioso, pissed up on wodka."

Amused at her own mob accent. Staff Mackey, or Mackey as he'd now let her call him had grudgingly acknowledged that as Bosses went, Percy was all right. Comfortable banter and mutual back watching replaced burgeoning hostilities from the last Exercise. Percy appreciated the shift in dynamics and was secretly pleased she'd won the, albeit reluctant respect of a Senior NCO. She must be improving.

"The last I heard from the OC was a holding of positions until,"

She pulled back her padded sleeve and pinched the side of her watch. The display glowed green, 0303,

"Until about 0500. Then it's all back to HQ for tea and medals."

Mackey snorted.

"More like chips and tea, ooh actually bloody love that, chip butty and a warm cup of NATO tea."

Percy rolled down her window, cold air bursting in through the crack, the fug of smoke in the cabin demanding an exit.

"NATO? What's with that, tea NATO? I've never got that."

Mackey looked incredulous,

"You serious Ma'am? God you really are a newbie. Milk and two sugars Ma'am, milk and two sugars. It's from the 1950s Ma'am, when the military was taking the piss out of NATO wanting to standardize anything. Don't you subbies know your history?"

He shook his head, appalled at Percy's ignorance. She grinned and turned to stare out of the window, frost had made the windows opaque, barely discerning the barren landscape beyond. There wasn't much to uplift a tired, sleep deprived soul anyway. Snow covered spindly wood line, with slushy piles of dirty snow by the road. The odd burnt out car broke up the monotony, but other than that, being held on the limits of the town wasn't really a place to keep the mind active. Percy flicked a look at her watch, 0333. She groaned. Time was crawling and she was knackered. They'd been out here a few weeks now and whilst a tentative timeline of 3 months had been levied, only a fool would hold their breath. Percy had deliberately avoided making Christmas plans, but judging by the plunge in morale when they got mobilized, a lot of families hadn't been so cynical. She rubbed her palm against the icy window and stared out into the evening. Too early for the crack of dawn, no birds would be singing yet and she wondered if the locals as they slept even appreciated or for that matter registered their presence. Did it make a difference? Right now any sensible Election rioter would be tucked up in bed, dreaming warm fantasies of violence and electoral disarray, not outside in this freezing night actually wreaking havoc. Sighing she resisted the urge to look at her watch again. Glancing at Mackey who was doing nodding dog impressions, she pushed her radio pressel,

"Charlie 49 this is Delta 5 Zero, radio check over?"

Mackey looked over at her wearily, yawning loudly, rubbing his newly stubbly chin,

"Delta 5 Zero this is Charlie 49 Ok over?"

"Charlie 49 this is Delta 5 Zero out."

"Enjoy that did we?"

"Oh fuck off Mackey, it's called being professional, rather than sitting there farting and snoring and bitching about being bored."

Mackey's jaw stiffened. Pulling out his thermos, he unscrewed the metal lid, letting the warm aroma of coffee flood the cabin.

"Bit harsh Ma'am. Coffee?"

Refusing to feel guilty, Percy relented not one to drag out a point.

"Sure, love one."

"Then you can make your bloody own."

They both laughed as Mackey poured the hot liquid into tin mugs.

"So your missus all right about you being out here?"

Mackey slurped noisily peering ahead, sniffing,

"I wouldn't really say she was all right about it, but it was hardly a surprise. It's just a bugger that we've been deployed at this time of year. I was sort of hoping we'd make it past Christmas, even nudge past the New Year, but y'know…"

He drifted off, looking out the window.

Percy chewed the side of her cuticle, kicking herself for raising the subject. As Mackey spoke it had rushed back to her his wife's pregnancy, his feigned indifference, which ridiculed by his friends in the Sergeant's Mess, who happily relayed back to Percy that her Senior NCO had gone soft on her.

"Sorry Mackey, that was thoughtless."

"Nah Ma'am, don't worry about it, anyways you must have some Rupert tucked away, missing your fine self? Playing scrabble?"

This time it was Percy's turn to blush. Duncan had been a surprise and even now she felt a naughty tinge at going out with a bloke who had been her Directing Staff. It felt illicit, which was ridiculous given the fact that she was now a Lieutenant, a measly one pip away from Duncan's three pips. Although he would tease her as she pulled on his combat shirt in the Mess.

"You should really be sitting to attention there in bed Lieutenant; there is a Senior Officer in the room."

Percy had laughed unable to resist,

"Think you'll find it was you who was stood to attention a few minutes ago."

Duncan groaned, nuzzling her,

"Ah my crude little subbie, such a cliché."

They'd giggled, drinking coffee in bed together, before Duncan had made his way back to Deepcut to DS another YOs cadre, something that made Percy's heart tighten. Stupid really, but that had been where they met, oddly though it had been Duncan who had reacted badly when she'd been warned off about Bosnia.

"Oh for fucks sake!"

He'd stomped around the Bank Hotel room in Oxford booked as a romantic getaway, made all the more poignant by the imminent Tour. All muted beiges and brown throws, understated chic that did nothing to distract Duncan from his mood of petulant rebellion. He flicked on the kettle, pulled out the cafetiere looking at Percy with an eyebrow raised,

"Yeah, please. Don't Duncan. We both knew this was coming and well, the OC reckons it'll only be for a few months. So it's not like we're talking 6 months here."

Duncan spooned heaped piles of coffee granules into the cafetiere, steaming water releasing the delicious smell of freshly ground beans. He pulled open the mini fridge and reached for the milk, standing, wearing only his Bank Dressing gown and nothing else, Percy couldn't help but grin.

"Hot water and nudity, taking a bit of a risk there aren't we Sir?"

As ever, Percy with her gentle jokes, nudging him out of his bad moods, he knew he was being pathetic, God he was the more senior here. It's just he knew what it was like on Tour. No, let's be honest, he knew what blokes were like on Tour and Percy, God Percy was so damned nice. Honest, open, vulnerable, eyes that you just made you want to dive in. Yes she played the game, and was getting better at holding her own, but underneath that professional veneer, she was the cute girl, who'd spilt port on her Mess dress at her dining in and hoped no one saw. God if any bloke even looked at her. He gripped the cafetiere tighter.

None of this was lost on Percy and whilst Duncan had banged around making a ham fisted effort at coffee, which was really an attempt to distract himself from his own anxiety about her first tour, Percy had mentally chosen the words, considering how to calm them both.

In bed carefully cradling a mug, he handed her her latte, nicely milky, just how she liked it. She was touched how it had only really been a handful of weeks and already they knew each other's little foibles. That was the Military, no time to waste. Courting was fast and furious, because you never knew when you'd be leaving.

"Look Duncan, oh for God's sake will you take off that bloody bathrobe, I can't take you seriously."

Duncan laughed, and finally with Percy tucked next to him he stopped her soliloquy.

Swallowing his pride, taking a slug of brew,

"Look Percy, you don't need to soothe my ego, or come out with some platitude about how it's going to be ok and it's not long. Blah bloody blah. I like you and well, I know what blokes are like. They're bloody dogs. Loggie soldiers are disgusting. They'll be running a book on you from the moment you board the C17. Bosnia, Elections, it's a load of bollocks and for the most part you'll be sat in some bloody freezing vehicle, on standby for fucking ages, just in case some fat Eastern European decides he wants to kick off, which of course he won't because any self-respecting mobster knows better than to make a move when the British Army is there and most importantly when it's so cold outside that your knob can drop off just from taking a piss.

"I don't have a knob."

"Oh shut up!"

He hit her with a pillow.

When the pummeling with pillows had subsided, they lay looking at each other, Duncan pushing away golden strands from Percy's face, she silently adoring.

"Duncan, I know I haven't done this before, but I'm not an idiot, I'm not naïve..."

"I beg to differ."

"Y'know what I mean. I'm not going to be some bloody conquest."

Her tone changed, more serious,

"Please, you know me better than that?"

Percy stared out of her window, the small section she'd wiped now covered with frosted condensation, smiling wryly, remembering Duncan's words about sitting in freezing vehicles; if he only he could see her now. God she missed that shower in the hotel, and after, her cheeks reddened. Suddenly the radio crackled.

"Delta 50 this is Charlie 49 over?"

Mackey and Percy bolted upright, exchanging bemused expressions, thinking the same, only hours to push, come on, not now. It had been stupidly quiet, and here they were within a few hours of cots and sleep.

"Charlie 49 this is Delta 50 send over?"

"Delta 50, Sunray ordering all call signs back in, I say again, all call signs to return to Sunray now, over?"

"Charlie 49 Roger that, out."

"Wahoo!"

Percy had barely released the pressel before she whooped with delight,

"Get that engine on and let's get the fuck out of here!"

Mackey didn't need to hear it twice. Revving the engine he got them moving yet at the same time feeling an unease he wouldn't voice, not wanting to spoil the Boss' mood. Question was why was the OC calling them back in?

37

Tracey gripped her drink. The drive down here hadn't been as bad as she expected. Her Combie bumbled along at a fair old whack and the autobahn was surprisingly clear, given that she'd poorly timed her departure to coincide with German rush hour. Gutesloh was an attractive camp as camps go, woody, with wide roads. She'd swept up to the Mess and leapt out, abandoning her van and hunting down Sal's room, expecting a euphoric reception. She hadn't expected Sal to be drunk. At 6pm.

"Mate!"

She woozed at Trace, bleary eyed, grinning,

"Come in, come in. Sshhoo glad you could make it."

Breathing fumes all over her she thrust a glass into Trace's hand and swung back to face a precariously balanced mirror on some issue chest of drawers. Trace took a breath,

"Hey, I know it's a big night and all, but don't you want to pace yourself? I mean it's,"

Sal's face soured,

"Hey! Don't come down here and lecture me!"

Stumbling back to pour more wine, she nearly deposited half of it on the floor. Squinting at the mirror, she dabbed kohl pencil at already heavily made eyes.

Trace shifted awkwardly. Putting down her glass, peeling off her jacket glanced around the room. It had the feel of someone who'd started with the best intentions and then either got distracted or given up. Clothes lay everywhere. The sofa whilst scattered with cushions had a fair helping of girly detritus from magazines and empty chocolate wrappers, to a rolled up combat jacket and some dessie socks. Trace took her glass and sipped the wine, wincing at the sweet Riesling. Since when had Sal been into such sweet wine? For that matter when had Sal turned into a domestic slut and lush to boot? Something felt wrong.

"So errm, I parked my van out back hope that's ok?"

Sal hardly seemed to hear, which would normally have irritated Trace. After all she'd driven a far distance and hadn't seen Sal for a while, but there was something, what was it?

Sal seemed to either admit defeat to the eye liner or was content with the blackening. She turned grinning at Trace,

"Sooo, how are you? How's it down there?"

Swaying gently, barely focusing on Trace, who slapped her glass down exasperated.

"What the fuck Sal? I mean seriously? You are leathered and you're not speaking to some tee-total puritan. You're not going to last ten minutes at this do, not to mention you look a bloody car crash. What the hell is going on?"

Sal's face blanched and despite the makeup she suddenly looked young and vulnerable. Slumping into the easy chair, she cradled her glass carefully.

"I..."

She bit her lip, tucking her feet underneath her, sipping more wine,

"I'm not sure I know what you mean. Yesshh I've had a glass or two."

She wiped back a stray hair, smudging blusher, making her botched make up seem more clown like. Tracey had seen this before and her heart sank.

"Oh God Sal, what's happened?"

Sal's eyes brimmed,

"Nothing Trace, ssshtop trying to figure me out. So I'm pished? Well it's the bloody Oktoberfesh."

She blushed at her slurring. Trace leaned forward, concerned, her tone softening, feeling sadly like she was back at work. Come on, not here, not to her friend?

"Tell me what happened."

Sal seemed to waver, as if deliberating whether to continue the charade, then her demons caved in and she surrendered. She curled her knees up to her chest, pyjama bottoms baggy, striking contrast to the strappy top. A half-finished ensemble that just emphasized Sal's chaotic state.

"Oh hell Trace, I…I don't know what to do…"

She seemed to sober up as she began to talk, as if resigned to telling her friend the sorry truth.

"There was a dinner, about a month ago…"

Trace nodded,

"It was one of the first Mess do's I've been to here and I was a bit nervous, so I probably drank a bit too much. But I wasn't hammered you know? I was talking to loads of people, most of whom I was meeting for the first time, and well, pretty much everyone was more senior than me. But, well, they were all so nice y'know?"

Trace felt herself stiffen, how many times had she heard this?

"Well I was talking to this Major, I, he, well we were flirting, and I was sort of flattered, he was a Major and here was me a one pip wonder and well, I guess, I sort of enjoyed the attention."

She paused, reaching for a glass that Trace wanted to rip out of her hand, but not wanting to interrupt the flow. Sensing Tracey's disapproval Sal only took a small sip,

"So I realized I was drunk and when we finished the dinner I gave the bar a miss and weaved back here. Everything gets a bit blurry then but,"

She paused, Trace waited,

"And well, I woke up and he was on top of me…ah God inside me. I was so drunk, I could barely push him off and so he finished and then pulled himself off me and did up his trousers and left. I couldn't believe it, I thought I'd fucking imagined it. But I lay there and well, I crawled to the door and locked it, sobbing."

Sal paused shaking her head, looking at the floor, oblivious to how she was chewing a nail that was already down to the quick. Trace winced, waited for Sal to continue.

"Well after that I just went into my shell, but him. He…he came back to my room the following night, knocked on my door, and when I opened it, well I slammed it in his face. He was drunk and he tried to get in. I locked it, but he wouldn't leave, hammering, demanding to come in, acting as if I was the one being unreasonable. I stayed there all night, leaning against the door, barricading it, terrified he'd get in."

"Jesus Sal, why didn't you tell me?"

"So what? You know how this goes? It's our job for God's sake. New subbie arrives, flirts with every bloody Officer going, seen doing it at a dinner and then what? Accuses one of the most well regarded Majors in the Mess of rape? I'd be laughed out of the building and the Camp for that matter."

"Not necessarily?"

Trace felt frantic for Sal, raging at the injustice, helpless in the face of her very real and tragically pragmatic evaluation of the situation.

"So, how have you left it?"

"Left what? I took the morning after pill and I've booked some leave. I'll be damned if that fucker knows I went to an STD clinic on Camp because of him. No thanks. I'll do that back home with the NHS. Anonymous."

Sal looked at Trace her face a picture of despair and Trace knew then that Sal had never wanted to go to the Oktoberfest. She'd wanted her friend and so with Sal curled up beside her, she rocked her friend to sleep as she wept bitter tears of hurt and disillusionment.

38

15 KG IS not much to carry really. It's heavy but manageable. However, over 8 miles that 15 kg can feel more like 25 kg and if it isn't packed right, so it rests evenly on your back, it can feel more like 10 men sliding around having a piggy back. Soph moved from one foot to the other. She knew she was fit; she'd even started trotting around Camp on runs to explore. But there was something about forced physical training, PT, which made her stomach turn in knots and give her the urge to have a nervous pee; an urge she was currently ignoring.

She looked around for a friendly face. Sam had been a bit evasive about whether she'd come, maintaining that since she was now moving into the Battalion HQ, strictly speaking Soph's job was double tapped and really Company PT wasn't her bag anymore. Chewing her nail, Soph pulled at her t-shirt. Tucked into combat trousers, with the usual boots, it wasn't the obvious gym kit. But loaded marches were by and large steady state, they weren't meant to be a race, so wearing boots wasn't overly onerous. She spotted WO2 Ryan, hesitating about wandering over. The Sergeant Major had seen her new OC and whilst she had at least nodded in her direction, her preference to keep her distance was clear as she turned to continue her conversation with the Company Sergeant Major. Soph sighed and tried to ignore her bladder.

"Morning Ma'am, don't think we've met, I'm Sergeant Leg."

Blonde, Cheerful and a good 6ft plus, Sergeant Leg was a welcome relief from the ambivalent reception Soph had so far had from her Section. Grinning she put her hand out,

"Lieutenant Jefferson."

Firm handshake, smiling,

"Honestly Ma'am, I'm not a real fan of loaded marches. Well I am at the end. Especially hitting the bar afterwards, earning a decent pint."

"Hitting the bar?"

"Don't y'know Ma'am? This is OC's PT, and since it's a Friday and this is going to take about 2 hours, if the PTIs get it right, we'll be done by lunch. So we all slope off with the OC and Company HQ and the rest of the Company to the Dutch Bar. They serve a cracking pint, and the chips and mayonnaise are a weird combo but awesome."

Soph hid her surprise. She knew that Germany was quite boozey but beers after PT? Well it suited her, though she felt a twinge of uncertainty about hitting the drink with her soldiers. She vaguely remembered some brief at Sandhurst about maintaining professional boundaries. Or was this bonding? She pulled her rucksack up her shoulders,

"So where were you before here?"

Distracting herself from the mild back ache already starting,

"JARIC, up near Lincoln Ma'am. God I tell you,"

He ran a hand through his hair,

"If anythings gonna drive you to the bar, living up there will. Odd bunch of people, there are no windows in any of the offices,"

"Not that different from here then?"

"No, but you've got things to do here. Lincoln is dead. Its miles away from anything and the locals, well reckon 11 toes is pretty normal."

Soph snorted, "Hey looks like we're being briefed."

Gathering around the Physical Training Instructor, Soph couldn't help but think of Trace and Percy. This reminded her of the laughs they'd had, jostling and mucking about before phys at RMAS.

"Sirs, Ma'ams, Ladies and Gents. Please keep the squad tight, if you spread out it means those at the back have to run further and longer and that's not the point of this exercise. It's steady state march, 8 miles in 1 hour and 50 minutes. Myself and Staff Hattersley here,"

"Awight Roy!" shouts from the Company causing much laughter, Staff Hattersely rolled his eyes,

"Intend to keep it within a few minutes of that time, so there should be no need for long bursts of running to make the time. Right are there any injuries?"

"Does a broken heart count?"

More laughter and then it was time to form up. Soph knew from experience that being at the back was, despite the PTIs assurances, invariably harder work. People would start to string out, and the lagging would necessitate jogging. For the odd mile that wasn't a problem, over 8 it became painful. Just as she was about to sidle into the middle of the squad she heard someone barking her name,

"Lieutenant Jefferson, over here."

Darting round she spotted the OC, firmly stood at the back. Oh. Soph swallowed, I missed that, Officers at the back. Taking a breath, she pushed back her shoulders and jogged smiling, despite the jabs of her rucksack, to join the OC at the rear. This was going to be hard work.

The OC was round. There was no other way to describe Major Campbell. Fat would potentially be another and likely more accurate, but it didn't do justice to his uncanny resemblance to the Fat Controller in Thomas The Tank Engine, and the Fat Controller was just a round Lego figure. So fatty Campbell's nickname, unbeknownst to him was Controller Campbell. When Major Campbell had overheard his nickname in the Naafi, he'd smiled wryly, thinking of his tight command style. The truth was far more entertaining. The good news was Controller Campbell lived up to the fatty cliché; good-natured and liked a joke. Whilst he barely drew breath in between sentences, he was a likeable Company Commander, with most under him quietly despairing at his example, but still working hard for him simply because they liked him. It was enough to keep the Company in a good state from what Soph had heard.

"So how are you settling in?"

"Good Sir, Sam is making it very easy and the Section have been very welcoming."

Soph's eyes flicked to WO2 Ryan at the front, arguably the easiest place. She pinched her lips, a pattern emerging.

"Excellent, glad to hear it. There is something we need to discuss as well. I thought I could have your introduction interview after this? Let the rest of the Company have a quiet drink, we can join them later, go over a few things."

Her stomach flipped, the natural pessimist in her expecting something wrong, RMAS teaching her to prepare for the bollocking.

"So how was your YOs?"

Walking now, moving up the road, heading for the forest; PTIs set a brisk pace, arms pumping, nervous chatter rippling through the ranks.

"It was good Sir, long,"

The course had dragged, 6 months being way too long.

"But I'm glad I'm here now."

Major Campbell barked a laugh,

"Bloody vehicle recognition, loved it but there's no denying it's a bit dry. Helped I'm a bit of a spotter!"

They turned into the woods, the shade providing a chill; Soph's cheeks beginning to redden.

"Have you met the CSM yet?"

"No Sir, jus' been focusing on my guys so far."

"He's a good bloke, tight rein with the troops, but makes my life easier. Sergeant Major Haver is reliable and experienced, good head on his shoulders. If you need some advice, he's your man. Your WO2 however…"

Soph turned, surprised, but Major Campbell thought better of it,

"We'll talk about it later. I'm sure you've already formed your own opinion. Anyway, what do you make of Germany so far?"

Soph grinned, lengthening her stride; conscious the squad was already beginning to spread out.

"Well the Mess seems pretty friendly,"

"Yes it's a young Mess, fun."

"Absolutely, and the accommodation seems fine."

"Better than some Messes."

"Food is fine."

"That matters!"

"The camp from what I've seen over the last few days is very pretty, green, leafy."

"Have you got out yet? Been to Dusseldorf? Lots of things for singlies to do here, in the thick of Europe, Amsterdam down the road, France a few hours' drive, it's all for the taking."

Soph nodded, she'd been focused on finding her bearings, getting into work, she hadn't thought about traveling around. Her spirits lifted thinking of the exploring ahead.

The conversation came to a close, largely as a result of Major Campbell's laboured breathing. Soph noticed the CSM was jogging up and down the squad urging people on. The cynic in her wondered if it was for appearances.

It was already the back end of October, and despite the unseasonable warm weather, November was closing in. She'd already thought about Christmas, whether she'd go home. She mused over catching up with Trace and Percy. How were they? Be nice to have a bit of a reunion, swap stories. She'd heard that Percy was in Bosnia as part of the Spearhead. Wincing, the thought of deploying daunted her. She knew it was futile to avoid, going on Tour was de rigeur for those serving now. The days were long gone when you could lounge in the bar, and spend long weekends waiting for the Russians to come over the border. Afghanistan demanded a punishing rotation and Soph knew her turn was just around the corner. She focused on breathing, feeling a thin sheen of sweat on her back. Still she'd only just arrived, she wouldn't deploy this soon.

39

PERCY JUMPED OUT of the 4 tonner looking around for the CSM who jogged over. His face wasn't reassuring, his words less so.

"Ma'am, orders in 5 minutes."

She turned to Mackey who didn't even let her speak,

"Ma'am, you concentrate on what you need to do. I'll get the boys sorted."

Managing a half smile she made her way to the Ops room, anxiety plucking at her stomach.

The warmth was welcoming although the pinched faces of concern didn't match the temperature. A palpable sense of urgency, Percy could see Troop Commanders gathering around the bird table. Her stomach flipped, what was going on?

She went over to one of the Troop Commanders, guy called Sam, thickset with a serious face he turned nodding a hello,

"What's going on?"

"Int suggests there's gonna be some kind of bombing, not sure what, but obviously intended to throw a spanner into the Elections. The OC is putting together orders to interdict."

Percy's stomach dropped. Bombing?

The Ops' room buzz quietened as the OC entered, he strode over to the bird table. Everyone braced.

"Relax relax."

He looked exhausted, a far cry from how he'd been on Exercise all those months before. His face drawn, shadows under blood shot yet piercing eyes. Percy wished she'd grabbed a coffee, she could have done with the caffeine.

"Gentlemen and lady," managing a half smile at Percy,

"I'm sure you've all heard that Intelligence has indicated an imminent threat."

A ripple of acknowledgment.

"Well, these are my orders, pin your ears back, it's going to be a long night."

Pulling out her notebook, she was fishing in her pocket for a pen when a steaming cup of coffee appeared on the table before her. Whipping round to Mackey, eyes locked, she smiling gratefully.

The orders were long and comprehensive. Timings were tight. The plan was to create a ring of steel around the Town Hall, Election central. Nothing and no one would get through unless they'd been searched so thoroughly they may as well have stripped. Each Troop was assigned a task. Percy's was to manage the entry point, arguably the most dangerous and essential. No pressure then.

Wearily she focused on grid references, scanning the map laid out on the table, mentally assigning her guys to roles, thinking of how she could best manage the containment of a large area with not enough blokes.

"The threat is real people, but this is what we trained for. Good luck."

The gathering broke up and Percy stood a moment longer, gaze trained on her area of operations. Sergeant Mackey appeared at her shoulder,

"I didn't get all of that, but it sounds heavy, what's the plan Boss?"

Pausing,

"I'm still figuring that out. Look thanks for the brew, could you possibly get me another, sorry, I wouldn't ask if time weren't so tight, but I'm hanging."

"Hey Boss, no worries, I'll get the boys stood by ready to take your orders."

"Thanks, should only be about 15 minutes."

Percy pulled up a stool scrutinizing the map. Mentally drawing rings around the central point of her designated area she worked out ratios and points of risk. It was going to be tight, but a way of containing the scene began to emerge, one that would allow people through without it being overly porous. She rubbed her eyes, thinking longingly of her sleeping bag. Sleep out of the question. Major Buchan had stated that the first rotation, which she would lead, would last about 8 hours. It would be a long time for all of them.

Half an hour later, sat in front of a white board scribbling schemes of manoeuvre, allocating sections to areas, defining timelines and protocol, Percy shared her plan.

"Is everyone clear on the SOPs?"

All of the Corporals, the Section Commanders, nodded.

"Right, form up in vehicles outside, 15 minutes. Make sure everyone has eaten and had a hot brew, over to you Sergeant Mackey."

Leaving the room she headed back to her own pit. Sinking into her sleeping bag, she allowed exhaustion to engulf her. So tired she could sleep on the spot. Then Duncan slipped into her mind and for a few precious moments she let her mind dwell. How he smiled, the banter they had, how for a while things had been peaceful together, that the time had been fun.

"It will again." She muttered.

"Sorry Ma'am, you talking to yourself?"

Sergeant Mackey leaned against the door,

Percy blushed, "Only person who listens to me."

Sergeant Mackey snorted,

"They were good orders. Here, I filled your thermos."

Percy was touched and pushed it into her Bergen, no time to drink now.

"What do you think?"

"About what?"

"The threat, everything...?"

He rubbed his stubble, a heavy shadow spreading around his jaw, eyes hollow and teeth stained from too much tea and smoking. Pulling his softie jacket around him, he blew into his hands,

"I think we're in for a long night."

Exhaust fumes filled the air. Percy was bundled in her softie, combat smock and helmet. No more training, no more Exercises, this was real, and she stared ahead hoping her orders were enough. The four tonner moved with a judder, fumes freezing in the chill of the morning. Slowly the convoy edged out of the HQ and made its way the 8 miles to the town centre. Percy scanned empty streets, the odd drunk tottering about clutching a brown paper bag, others less discreet, waving bottles of vodka, some thrown at them. Too exhausted to feel threatened, Percy watched disengaged, gazing over the general bleakness of the surroundings, wondering why they were here and if their help really made a difference? Chewing a nail, she swallowed her nerves. The bombing that Intelligence had disclosed could be in any guise, a car, IED, even a suicide bomber, though that was deemed unlikely. There had been some derisory rolling of eyes at the vagaries surrounding 'The Threat', the J2 bod blushing as some of the Troop commanders waved hands over the map after the OC had gone, saying loudly,

"There is a threat, somewhere in this vicinity. Yeah Cheers."

Percy had stood back, feeling sympathy for both, but marginally more for her fellow Loggies who were going to have to hit the streets whilst the green slime Intelligence Officer sat in her comfy seat. It made Percy think of Soph, was she subjected to this? Suppressing a smile knowing that Soph was more than capable of holding her own.

The four tonner slowed to a halt, reaching for her radio she carried out checks whilst slipping the sling on her rifle, and checking her chest rig. Sergeant Mackey slid out of the cabin, throwing on his webbing, sloping his rifle round his front, pushing in his PRR earpiece whilst waving in the other four tonners. The convoy was staggered, each lorry leaving equivalent space between them. A soldier was to be stationed in each gap, rotated with his or her buddy. The other would watch in the cab, eyes on both sides whilst also allowing for a break from the cold. Sergeant Mackey and Percy would patrol up and down ensuring the electorate, as they approached, was searched before proceeding through the gaps in the lorries. A basic sieve, but given her scant resources, it was the best Percy could do.

She pushed open the door and caught a glimpse of herself in the window. Startled she paused transfixed by the hollowed cheeked reflection. There was a furrow on her brow that was new, her eyes seemed a darker blue, more serious, shadows under her eyes stark, as if smeared make up from a night out, skin pale with the beginnings of a spot on her chin. She looked run down. Right now aside from wolfing down a chocolate bar and draining the thermos dregs she'd have to do. After all it wasn't like she was heading down the runway, no just your average life threatening Bosnian high street. Tame by comparison. She'd watched America's Top Model.

40

BLOWING IN HIS hands, pacing down the file of lorries, Sergeant Mackey listened to the chatter on the PRR. Laddish banter that kept people awake was no bad thing; distracting chat was a different story. It was a delicate balance. He nodded as he passed each pair. Pale faces atop thick padded uniforms, tired eyes peering out of cabins.

"Awight Sergeant Mackey."

Corporal Cox was a jock who reminded people on a daily basis of the supremacy of Scotland. If he could have his way his face would be painted permanently blue and the uniform would allow kilts instead of troosers, as he called them. He was a hard worker, all bald headed attitude and piercing eyes giving him an intimidating command presence that he used to good effect in his Section. Right now he was grinning, pulling hard on a Marlborough red.

"Fookin freezing enough for yer Sergeant Mackey?"

Mackey nodded, pulling out his own cigarettes, eyes panning the streets, doing his 5 and 20 metre checks. He flicked a look up at the driver cabin and saw Lance Corporal Ham lent against the window, or should that have been more licking the window? Raising an eyebrow at Cox who spun round appalled, smacking the door, making Ham jump so much he banged his head,

"Serves you right you fookin lazy wanker!"

They both turned and eyed the street. Elections started at 0700 sharp, obscenely early for even the most civic minded. The intention was to capture people on their way to work, ensuring a high as turn out as possible. Mackey wasn't sure he'd bother given the weather.

"What's the score then Sir? D'yer think it'll be on our watch someone will make a move? I fookin hope so! Don't want Bravo troop getting all the glory."

Mackey snorted quietly pleased at Cox's enthusiasm. As soon as a soldier went quiet, be it no shinnfing or banter, then he knew morale had gone through the floor. Cox's chat showed that, whilst tired, he was still on the job. Mackey wouldn't expect anything less, but he was paid the pop stars' wages to keep an eye on those indicators.

Finishing their cigarettes Mackey nodded at Cox and continued his checks. A bit of banter with each soldier, seeing that they'd had hot brews, their weapons were ready, they were in warm kit without over doing it. It never ceased to amaze him that soldiers could still give themselves heat injuries in subzero temperatures by wildly over-layering. He was the sort who preferred to be a little bit cool rather than padded up, otherwise he'd start sweating like a pedophile in a playground. He grinned to himself walking slowly back to his own four tonner. Time was passing, and slowly he could see that the great unwashed were finally in drips and drabs coming through their barricade to vote.

"Everyone all right?"

Percy looked so small swaddled in softie, jacket, cheeks glowing in the chilled wind. Sergeant Mackey nodded. He pulled open the truck door and grabbed his thermos, Percy jumping out to join him. Stood in silence they watched locals drifting up the line. So far there had been little chatter on the radio which was good. Percy cradled her hands, blowing warm air, trying to heat her icicle fingertips, her nose gently throbbing, toe tips long since lost their sensation, she quietened her mind, centering herself, learning to distract from the very real discomfort. Stamping her feet, purgatory was not hers alone. There would be others feeling this more, focusing on the cold, the icy breeze sending spasms of shivers through you; the thought of having to endure this for another bone crushingly boring and freezing 6 hours morale sapping.

Minutes crept by, turning into hours. Percy ensconced in the four tonner cabin.

"Err Charlie zero this is Charlie three over?"

Bolt upright, her eyes flicked to Sergeant Mackey, as she pushed her pressel,

"Charlie three this is Charlie Zero send over?"

Charlie Three was Corporal Cox and right now he didn't sound his usual brash self, right now he sounded unsure and that wasn't Cox at all.

"Charlie Zero, this is Charlie three we have a male civilian who is refusing to be searched. He is also showing signs of acute anxiety and there appears to be...wait out."

Percy, nerves jangling, jumped out of the cabin.

"I'm going down, stay here."

Sergeant Mackey went to protest but thought better of it, watching Percy jog off, apprehension etched on his face.

Pressing her beret tight against her scalp, pulse racing. Focus. Focus. They had only an hour to push, an hour. For fuck's sake. She saw Corporal Cox and his buddy partner, Lance Corporal Ham. They were stood talking to what looked like a fat little person, crazy white hair, animated. She could hear voices from here and wasn't impressed by the crowd forming.

"Charlie Zero Bravo this is Charlie Zero Alpha over?"

"This is Charlie Zero Bravo, send over."

"Charlie Zero Bravo we're going to need a cordon here, approximately 8 pax required, over?"

"Roger that out."

Percy tried to control her breathing, slowing to a walk, face bland, impassive.

"Everything all right?"

Corporal Cox looked up, eyes wide with adrenalin,

"Ma'am, he, he just won't show any ID, or back off and he's got something under his coat, but he won't show it."

Lance Corporal Ham was trying to engage the man, calming him to defuse the situation. Language was clearly a barrier and judging from the white haired man's face, Lance Corporal Ham may as well have been speaking Klingon.

Percy stepped forward, the man's eyes locked on her with a flash of unadulterated hatred that made her almost step back. This was not good.

"Sir, please, you need to show ID? ID?"

He shook his head vehemently, gesticulating wildly, gabbling something incomprehensible, stepping forward,

"Whoa whoa whoa. Step back!"

Both juniors made ready, the cocking of rifles stopping him in his tracks. He froze then slowly brought his hand up beneath his coat. Percy's eyes widened,

"STOP!"

Cocking her own weapon, she felt a rush of fear, everything slowed.

The man froze, hand in coat, eyes trained on Percy, Mexican stand off.

"Mackey we need an interpreter down here. Now!"

Percy sacked off the radio voice procedure, clarity was key, as was carefully measured behavior; her rifle now at her shoulder, iron sight on the man, cross hairs targeting his head, centred between his eyebrows.

"Interpreter on way, eta 2 minutes."

They stood there, juniors' weapons targeted at the man's head, Percy leaning forward into the weight of her SA 80, finger resting on the safety catch.

This could not be happening.

"Take your hand out of your coat...slowly."

Uncertain Percy was sure she saw a glint of comprehension. He stared challenging her, daring her. Percy flicked the safety catch off; the gesture unmissable. He blinked. Slowly pulling out his hand, grasping the unmistakable form of a grenade.

No one breathed. Percy felt the surge of adrenaline, her hands shaking, cheeks blazing, biceps screaming holding her rifle level. She stared at the man, seeing red thread lines in the whites of his eyes, hardly daring to move her gaze,

"Corporal Cox, pin? Is the pin still in?"

Silence, Percy swallowing, she couldn't feel her feet. A bead of sweat slowly dribbling down the side of her cheek,

"Captain Brooks, sitrep over?"

Ah Jesus, she thought, that was the last thing she needed, the OC. Sergeant Mackey must have let HQ know there was a situation.

"Corporal Cox, wake the fuck up and tell me, is the pin still in the grenade?"

"Soo...sorry Ma'am..."

She heard his sigh of relief,

"Yes Ma'am, pin intact, still in grenade."

Her heart seemed to relax its thundering. Thank God.

"Lower your arm and put the grenade on the ground. Ground. Grenade. Now!"

Thinking about it for a second, the man slowly bent to his knees and rolled the grenade onto the ground. Corporal Cox leapt forward checking it was safe.

Lowering her rifle, arms screaming from lactic acid build up, she looked at him, his face pale, lips purple, equally exhausted by the encounter.

"Corporal Cox, get the RMP to detain this man, have him removed and then get yourself a hot brew."

Turning away she left the Juniors to wrap up, concentrating on taking one step after the next back to her four tonner; waves of relief and exhaustion flooding through her.

41

TRACEY DUMPED HER kit in her room, ripped off her trackie bums and ran for the shower. If quick she'd be able to wash her hair as well. The drive back from Sal's had been time to reflect. Hardly a relaxing weekend, but Sal had had some catharsis. They'd wandered into town the next morning, Tracey pleasantly surprised by down town Gutesloh, the hustle and bustle, pleased to find a decent bakery serving real coffee and warm croissant. Conversation had been slow. Sal knew what Tracey was going to say.

"Trace,"

She wavered, her face red and puffy from floods of tears and beers the night before.

"I know what you're going to say,"

She put her hand up to stop her,

"I'm not going to do it. I know we're both RMP, for fuck's sake, I know. But being here,"

Her hands shook, spilling coffee into her lap, a sight so pitiful Tracey wanted to hit the table in frustration.

"But being here…the other side, where the,"

She paused searching for the word. Tracey knew victim was all wrong, but defendant suggested a prosecution…

"Look, I just, I'm not going to do it. In fact I know what I'm going to do."

Tracey froze, mouth half full of warm pastry, hands clasped round her coffee for warmth. Then it dawned on her, groaning she shook her head,

"You're going to sign off aren't you?"

"The Army's just not for me."

"Bullshit Sal! This bloke is not the Army! He's a fucking scroat who raped you. End of. It's not the Army, it's not the RMP, it's nothing other than a crime that could have happened anywhere. Don't jack in your career because one twat took advantage when you were pissed. Seriously Sal, this could have happened on Civvy Street, in an office. Don't throw out the baby with the bathwater."

She slammed her mug down,

"If you throw in your towel mate, he's won. Checkmate, flipping carte blanche."

Sal stared hard at Tracey, her friend so sure opposite her, sat in unviolated shoes, a little too sanctimonious for Sal right now, but even where she was she could see it was well intended. Sighing, she looked around her, a garrison town in a foreign country. Only a few weeks ago she'd walked around this precinct intoxicated by the newness of it all, excited by the language, the foreign shops. It had all felt like such an adventure. Now? Now it just felt overwhelming, alien and unwelcoming. She wanted to go home. She wanted out of her uniform and preferably never to see Combat 95 ever again.

Slipping 20 euros onto the table, she slid her bag over her shoulder, smiling weakly.

"I'm sorry Trace, my mind is made up. Let's walk back."

Trace had grimaced in frustration when home in the shower, hot water sluicing over her but doing nothing to assuage her own bubbling poker red rage. She'd begged, cajoled, and almost threatened Sal until they'd got back to her camper van. But Sal had remained impressively resolute waving Trace off, who'd in turn watched her in her rearview mirror turn, shoulders slumped to walk the path back to her room, and draft her letter of resignation no doubt.

"Bloody wanker!"

"But I haven't seen you, how can I have pissed you off already?"

Nearly jumping out of her skin, she squealed in delight as Dan jumped in.

In bed hazey with contentment, she cradled against his chest. "Wow."

He lay there, arm flung under his pillow, head resting on it.

"I don't know what to say babe, hell of a weekend. Would have thought you definitely need a drink now!"

"You and me both, kipping on Sal's sofa was not what I had in mind. What do you think? I mean c'mon you see my point, she's got an obli..."

Dan turned sharply pulling Tracey's head up, cupping her chin,

"Tracey my darling, I think you are delicious, but no, she is not obliged to do anything and it is not your place to force her either. It sounds like she's been through fucking hell, and whilst I'd gladly like to wring the neck of the fucker who did this, if Sal just wants to bury it, and that helps her, then fair play. Two words. Leave. It. Now enough of the pouting and suck my willy."

42

THE TEA WAS disgusting. So strong a spoon could have stood upright, but at that moment, Soph was grateful for the tannin and sweetness. She flicked a look round the room; the OC was leading prayers, CSM Haver to his right. The two other Section Commanders were also there. Al Green, a Late Entry Officer who'd been on leave, hence why they'd not met. A ready smile and easy humour he was a welcome relief with it apparent that what he lacked in height he made up for in experience. Giles Bannister meanwhile, tall lanky and RAF was the other Section lead who took himself way too seriously, and was imperious in his attitude towards Soph, deeming her beneath him not only in rank but in capability. They hadn't hit it off. Finally there was the 2iC, keen, energetic, rarely sitting still; he'd been out of office focusing on his first love, the maintenance of kit and vehicles or G4. Although INT CORPS, he was really a grease monkey and silently rued the day he'd passed up on a commission in the REME. He listened to Major Campbell, his foot tapping a beat in the air, nervous energy crackling.

"Right I'll get down to business; first of all, for those of you who haven't met our new OiC NIC, please may I introduce Lieutenant Jefferson, Sophie."

Soph smiled, a grin returned by all apart from Giles, who rolled his eyes.

"Ok, I think most of you are aware," he nodded at Sophie,

"Apart from yourself Soph, that we've been warned off for deployment; dates to be confirmed but likely April, possibly March next year, so not long folks, just over 5 months. We've got plenty to do and here is how I'd like us to do it...."

Although Soph heard the OC continue, for her it was largely white noise. Deployment? She was going on Tour? But she'd only just got here! Wasn't she supposed to have some boozy first year? Get to know the ropes? Make stupid Junior Officer mistakes? Where was the FORM cycle everyone spoke about? Force Readiness Mechanism that did what it said on the tin, got the Forces ready?

"...lion's share of the Company will deploy as the Operational support Team in Lash Gahkar. The other elements will be in either Kabul providing support to the Majority of the ARRC or in Kandahar..."

Lash Gahkar? Sophie hoped her rush of fear went unnoticed. She knew this day would come, but not immediately and felt embarrassed at her intimidation.

"...training forecasts as soon as possible. Is that clear?"

Soph's head jerked up, realizing she'd largely missed all of the OC's direction, equally aware her WO2 had dished out some tenuous excuse to avoid these forums; an absence that just amplified Soph's isolation. Her panic hadn't missed Al, who gently steered her out of the office.

"You need a coffee."

Two steaming lattes, and the smell of bacon permeating the air, Sophie finally came down from a thousand feet.

"I'm just,"

"Nervous." Al answered.

"Relax, its normal. You're just out of training."

Soph balked at the 'you're still in nappies' suggestion, even if true.

Chuckling Al continued,

"Y'know you are going to have to try harder not to let everything show on your face like some news flash. Poker face? More like preview face."

Soph blushed, "Sorry."

Al softened, "Hey relax, look I know it's a quick flash to bang, but you're not stupid from what I can tell..."

Soph raised an eyebrow, Al laughed unphased,

"You've just got to get organized and look to your Warrant Officer to…"

"But that's just the problem Al! I don't want to make excuses it's just…well have you met WO2 Ryan? I don't,"

Stirring his coffee, Al sucked his teeth.

"Oh. Right. Hmmm. I didn't know she was still in, or I thought she was in Brawdy. Right, you do have a bit of a problem. Whose your Staffie?"

"I, I don't have one, though I've got Sergeant Leg?"

"Oh Jesus,"

Al slapped his forehead,

"Look this is going to be a pretty steep learning curve. I suggest you do this…"

The suggestions went on for 2 lattes and another round of toast. Bloated from bread and wired from caffeine, Soph buzzed gently. Grateful but slightly overwhelmed by all his guidance, the amount of work needed seemed nigh on impossible.

"Hey, it's not impossible; you're just going to have to step up."

He paused, as if hesitating but continued.

"Afghan isn't easy Soph. I'm not going to lie to you, for a first tour, you're going to have a bloody steep learning curve, more like a cliff and you've been royally screwed with WO2 Ryan being on your team. Your OC knows this and," more pauses,

"Well there has been talk of replacing her for a while, but when you're that senior, the case for effectively sacking someone has to be air tight, and the audit trail, it's, it's just not strong enough. Everyone's been brushing this one under the carpet and you love, well you've been shafted with the spring clean. What you do have are some outstanding soldiers, they're cracking. So just get your head sorted and it means you can hit the ground running when you get out there, which frankly is all we can all hope to do."

"Right, gotta go, been blathering far too long! S'good to have you on board."

Ruffling her hair, Al bounded off whistling, leaving Soph staring ahead shell-shocked.

"You look like you don't need another coffee?"

Looking up with a start she blushed then groaned inwardly. The last thing she needed was some arrogant Logistics Captain patronizing her.

"Hey, Tom… look nice to see you but, I'm, well, I'm not really up to being given a hard time at the moment."

Oh bloody hell were her eyes welling up? Too much caffeine had to be. She looked away embarrassed.

Tom pulled up a chair, face concerned, something not lost on Soph who was oddly pleased.

"Hey, what's the matter?"

"I…I…"

Unaccustomed to his gentle tone, she burst into tears, leaving Tom bewildered. Sitting patiently, he waited as she dabbed her face with a bit of scrunched up loo paper. Taking a deep breath more than a bit embarrassed, she grinned at Tom sheepishly,

"Sooo errrm, feel a bit silly…"

Tom shook his head, his heart squeezing at her coyness. He gripped the side of the table to stop himself from leaping out of his seat to give her a hug. Get a grip man.

"Hey, s'not a problem. What's up?"

Soph slowly relaxed in the face of his kindness, nibbling a nail, quietly thrilled.

"Well, it's like this…"

They spoke for over an hour; mostly Soph unloading her until now, silently held fears and apprehension. Tom sat nodding, listening attentively or so it seemed, when in fact Soph's words just washed over him, his eyes instead trained on her lips, tracing the contours, then moving up to her eyes, the most blissfully brown and golden flecked irises he'd ever seen that sparkled as she spoke. Oh no he thought, oh no, I'm lost and he smiled weakly wanting to tweak her button nose and tell her she was amazing.

"So I'm being pathetic right?"

Tom nodded in agreement and then saw Soph's face darken in disappointment and kicked himself out of his reverie.

"No of course not."

He gazed at her a fraction too long in the silence, Soph blushing, eyes lowered, stomach a storm of butterflies, a smile dancing on her lips.

"I don't know that much about Int Soph, but you seem like you have your head screwed on and Al is a good bloke, sure he'll have your back."

Soph was ridiculously pleased at the comment and tried to tone down her beaming smile, failing miserably, making Tom almost laugh.

Soph chewed her lip, squirming for a moment as if undecided then blurted out,

"What about you? Aren't you warned off? You not coming? I…"

She cast around for words that would moderate the obviousness of her question, lace them with a veneer of professional courtesy,

"It's just I thought most of the HQ was coming?"

Tom's heart soared at her question, he drained the dregs of a cold latte to hide his delight and flicked a look at his watch; a gesture that unintentionally deflated Soph.

"Sorry, we've been talking for ages, do you have to go?"

She felt stung. Tom mortified instinctively reaching across the table, ignoring the sly glances from other Officers mindlessly gawping in curiousity at this attractive couple so engrossed in each other for the last few hours.

"Nowhere I'd rather be."

43

PERCY STARED OUT of the coach windows, torrential rain relentless, coursing down the motorway. She felt numb, conscious that it should be a relief to be home, equally aware that being home wasn't registering, a ghost of a memory from training whispering that this wasn't normal, wasn't right. Street lamps flashed past, cars speeding, occupants irritated by the slow coach, oblivious to the exhausted uniformed passengers. An hour and they'd be back in barracks; she leaned back, vaguely aware that as each car had overtaken she'd scanned the people, held her breath. How long was that going to last?

She wondered about Duncan, when they'd get to see each other? She'd dashed out a quick email before they'd got bundled on the transport. Her mind whirring, eyes focussed back on the streetlamps, looking for threats. He'd been on some kind of ceremonial duty, mostly in barracks or out boozing. Boozing? Percy licked her lips at the thought of a drink; would that stop her mind racing? Stop seeing the white haired man? The grenade? She blinked, focus, look at the streetlamps. You're home now, relax and she held her breath watching another car.

44

"TRACE CAN I see you when you've got a minute?"

Scowling, she jerked her head up. There was a mountain of paperwork to do, she was hoping to nip out for a decent coffee and she'd been holding a pee for the last hour. Now was not a good time.

"Sure Boss."

Ignoring her bulging bladder, she waited for the news that she'd been pinged with Duty officer again. God I hope it's not bloody Garrison officer, Dan and I were hoping to get away for the weekend.

"Trace you've been trawled."

Her stomach fell through the floor. The office clock ticked seconds past, the rev of traffic on the garrison road outside drifting into the office.

"Look, everyone here has been deployed within the last 9 months and well, I know you are just out of Sandhurst, so I thought you'd be keen, and frankly I have no reason not to release you."

"When...Sir?"

"In about four months' time. I know, I know, it's pretty quick flash to bang, but often it's the best way, less time to dwell. I've got the paperwork, including your Pre-Deployment Training itinerary."

He slid across an ominously thick manila folder,

"I suggest you take a look over it, then wrap up your own work, you'll need to do a hand over and get yourself on PDT from the start of next week. Any questions?"

Shaking her head numbly, she walked out of the room clutching a file that felt too heavy to accomplish in 4 months. Thumping it down, she flopped onto her chair ignoring her screaming bladder. Instead reaching for the phone, dialing the number now engrained.

"Adjutant."

"Babe it's me."

Trace felt tears welling, instantly Dan's voice softened,

"Hey what's up?"

"I've been trawled."

"Oh fuck, how long?"

"4 months."

Sitting back in his office chair, the cushioned backing squeaking, running a hand through his hair, he shook his head. Why be surprised? This was going to happen at some point, just…he should have known better than to get his hopes up.

"Hey look, it was going to happen,"

Leaning forward, head resting in his hand, phone clutched to his ear,

"We just make the most of the next few months."

Tracey nodded, his support making her feel both upset and reassured.

"Babe where do I start? I've got so much to do for PDT and I've been told to just crack on and do it myself?"

She looked up, grateful for the quiet office, her moment of vulnerability private.

Dan frowned at the knock on his door, waving away the Chief Clerk who stomped off cursing Officers and Adjutants in general. Who the hell did they think they were? The Commanding Officer?

"I think the best thing you can crack first is OPTAG. Get on a course and get it done, you'll have to do a Weapon Handling Test before, but I bet your SA80 drills are a damn sight better than mine."

Tracey doodled mindlessly, range targets and figures of eight. Her shoulders sagged, she flicked a look at the clock,

"Look do you reckon you could slip out and meet at the Naafi?"

Dan frowned,

"Hey I know you're busy," anticipating his excuse, "it's just right now, I need to see you and you're buying."

"Ok see you there in ten and *you're* buying, including a bacon buttie."

Twenty minutes later, bacon rind on a plate in front of him, licking lips, Dan smiled softly at his red-eyed girlfriend,

"Hey c'mon it's not that bad, you're surprising me how you're falling apart here."

She gripped her latte, stung.

"It's just, things are really good right now, between you and me, the job is going well and I've only been here what feels a few months. So give me a break. I'm not falling apart, I'm, well, a bit stunned and be fair…"

She took a gulp of her second coffee, caffeine jolting through her system, pride kicking in, clawing back from whining,

"4 months flash to bang for my first tour and as an augmentee, it's pretty full on."

Dan had to agree, being an augmentee was tough for anyone. He sat back, trying to look positive and failing; flying out as a newbie into a formed Unit who'd deployed as a oner was never easy, not for a Captain and certainly not for a NIG straight out of the factory. No, he'd been harsh, wind your neck in Dan he thought, she's a corker, cut her some slack.

"Look I'm sorry, you're right, it's a shitter, but we'll be fine, it's not like I'm going anywhere."

Despite the tooing and froing of soldiers and other ranks, he reached out and held her hand.

"Now get your ass booked on OPTAG and book some leave off too, we're gonna have to get some serious loving in before you go."

For a moment they relaxed and laughed like a couple at ease with the world, sharing a coffee in a military café.

45

A WEEK IN Camp. In uniform. Percy paced around like a caged animal. She knew this was protocol, a way of ensuring gradual acclimation before people were released to their own devices. Decompression had been borrowed from the Yanks when it was realized after a number of fatal domestic shootings that letting a soldier march home with no break, no breather, no chance to adjust was as bad as giving him a grenade with the pin pulled and pushing him in the direction of his nearest and dearest. Still Percy chewed on the end of her biro; it didn't make it any more bearable. She wanted out, she wanted home. Sergeant Mackey rubbed his chin, staring wearily at an empty cup of tea and trying to ignore Percy's restlessness.

Padding over to the kettle that nestled in the corner of their pitiful excuse for an office, he yawned,

"Ma'am, just let it go, don't fight the white. You've gotta do your time here like everyone else."

He snapped on the kettle, pulling open the little fridge bought for £40 from Tescoes, affording the luxury of cold milk and the odd beer stashed for after hours.

"Now do you want a brew?"

Percy tutted nodding,

"I wouldn't mind if we had something to do, but we've cleaned and accounted for kit, debriefed, done some phys, I mean how much running round a camp can anyone do Mackey? C'mon you've got to admit it's annoying?"

Pouring boiling water into two stained mugs, splashing some milk in to both and spooning enough sugar to make a diabetic comatose, he handed Percy a stained mug.

"The way I see it is, well, it was a tough time Ma'am. Not long, but,"

He eyeballed her knowingly,

"*We* had a surprisingly tough time of it. We didn't lose anyone, but we, and I mean we, had some fairly hairy moments."

Percy sipped thoughtfully, ignoring her butterflies, the now too familiar clammy feel that had sprung to her hands, that couldn't be blamed on a mug that almost scalded. She was ok wasn't she? Everyone felt like this didn't they? But then she hadn't asked and no one had asked her either, so she'd let it lie, pushed it down, ignored it, better that way wasn't it? The butterflies thought otherwise, sputtering around in her stomach, preventing her from eating much and right now she could really do with putting pounds on, not losing any more.

Mackey slurped his tea loudly leaning back in his chair,

"Y'seen the OC?"

Shaking her head,

"No why?"

Sucking in his cheeks, taking another slurp,

"Rumour mill."

Her heart sank, anxiety exhausting her as it screamed around her system, making her want to sprint to anywhere but here. The silence hung in the room, not wanting to push, to hear the answer to a question she didn't want to ask. Mackey sat staring at his desk, eyeing a coffee ring as if it had all the answers to their problems.

The OC knocking at their door made them both jolt.

"Sorry to interrupt folks; need you in my office in ten. CSM is rounding up the Company."

Major Buchan paused for a moment to check both Sergeant Mackey and Percy had registered, then nodded and strode off.

Percy and Mackey's eyes locked.

Major Buchan marched purposefully back to his office. Stride firm, his every muscle screaming don't bother me, his face inscrutable.

Fastidious about professionalism, he walked into his office after nodding at the recently returned CSM, who nodded in return. So, everyone was on their way. Ensconced in a chair 'procured' by the Company's Quartermaster, Major Buchan made the most of the few minutes to focus. The leather soft beneath him, he swiveled the chair to stare outside. A stony grey sky, bleak, balding grass, and cars spattered with a light drizzle hardly inspired. He could have done with some morale, something to bolster the spirits. Instead he looked back at the flickering screen re-reading the email from the Commanding Officer of the Battalion. He knew the words verbatim, since he'd spent all morning arguing about them with the CO, whom he'd thought of as one of the good guys, not quite a friend, but damn near close. Their conversation however had been nowhere near amiable; in the end it had been one way.

"Major Buchan, and it is *Major* Buchan still isn't it? Not suddenly wearing a pip above that crown?"

Startled into silence, Ben Buchan bit his tongue,

"Ben, just listen to me because I'm not going over this again. This is a direct order, I'm not happy about it either, but I've told you what I know from PJHQ and there is no avoiding it. So just get on with it because the last time I checked, I was the fucking Colonel around here."

The line went silent; Ben had replaced the receiver and stared out of the window, knowing his CSM had heard everything, knowing that every minute counted.

Bracing himself, he looked towards the door as his recently returned Staff filed in. All tired, drawn, expecting the worst, because since when did the OC call in all his staff two days into decompression to tell them a joke?

Ben swallowed hard, flexing his toes in his boots, his feet damp from sweat, throat irritatingly dry. Pushing a biro to one side, he sat up looking at his team, his boys and girls, damn near dead on their feet, who deserved more than he was about to tell them.

"We've been warned off folks. Deploying to HERRICK, four months time."

46

SERGEANT LEG SAT enthused before Sophie. WO2 Ryan meanwhile looking as interested as if Cebeebies was playing a rerun. Sophie resisted the urge to ask if they were keeping her from something more engaging, like skiving for example?

"So what I'm saying is we need to put a training matrix together, or rather," hastily correcting herself,

"*I* will put together the training matrix, but well, I'd like your input."

More like I need your help. Casting her mind back to Sandhurst, it had all been about making it through Exercises, learning academic theories of war, but actually training your Section? Preparing your platoon for a deployment? Nope, she must have missed that lesson, EVERY DAY FOR A YEAR.

WO2 Ryan looked at her watch, four months?

"Right well we best get ourselves booked on OPTAG. When you planning to tell the boys and girls,"

She paused deliberately, "Ma'am?"

WO2 Ryan's barely concealed sarcasm was as antagonistic to Sophie as a stick to a camel. Struggling to calmly return her baleful gaze,

"Grateful if you could actually action that WO2 Ryan, y'know rather than just talk about it?"

Stunned at Sophie's directness in front of Sergeant Leg, WO2 Ryan's face froze, eyes blazing, she shifted in her seat, swallowing back a bitter response. Fucking Junior Officer, what the hell did she know anyway? She'd been out of Sandhurst for what? Five minutes? Did she know what it was like on Tour? Christ, WO2 Sheila Ryan bit the inside of her cheek, already raw from gnawing. She was only three years away from retiring. Three lousy years from a pension that would see her brown, fit and happy in Greece. The last thing she needed was a tour to HERRICK. She'd managed to avoid it the last few rotations, so she knew it was going to bite her eventually but still...she shifted in her seat, ignoring her own anxiety, her own, call a spade a spade, fear. Glancing at her watch she blocked out the conversation around her. This was not happening. Four months? Four lousy months to prep for a six month thrashing in Helmand? Bile raised in her throat. God. She was terrified.

Sergeant Leg scribbled notes furiously. He couldn't believe his luck. He'd done TELIC, bit of Bosnia and he'd been trying to get on a HERRICK tour for flipping ages and boom! Straight in his lap, first posting to Germany. Awesome! He listened to his young OC. She was pretty fit, tall, serious eyes, clever. Definitely do her given the chance. Yep, she'd get one. Shame they were deploying in some ways though, Germany was a bit of a gift. He'd heard the whores were out-fucking-standing in Dus, and he was like what? Few hours drive from Amsterdam. He wanted some of that. Oh well, he wiped his forehead, smooth gleam of sweat, glanced up at Sophie, listening, still thinking that hey at least Amsterdam wasn't going anywhere, he could hit the whores when he got back, and he'd have more money too. Grinning he leaned forward, yep, deployment win-win.

"So I think that covers it. WO2 Ryan, sort OPTAG, I'll tell the Section this afternoon and I'd like dates by then please. Sergeant Leg, like you to start thinking about who should be allocated to what area of interest, you know their strengths. Basically who do you think should be a subject matter expert on what? Just roughly at this stage and then I'll draft up a layout and an intelligence overview. Ok? All clear? Right I'll talk to everyone after lunch? Say 1330."

WO2 Ryan and Sergeant Leg exited, Sophie turning to her screen, jostling the mouse, looking purposeful, the door closing behind them, leaving her silent, alone, overwhelmed. She reached for the phone, dialed a number that had become nicely familiar,

"Hey," she smiled hearing his chocolatey voice, all professional answering from his Battalion HQ,

"You free?" The question a formality, the answer assured.

"For you? Always. See you in five."

Snatching up her beret, not bothering suppressing the smile that always played across her face just hearing his voice, she marched out of the office, for the time being deployment was shelved.

47

Operational Training Advisory Group, aka OPTAG provided a week's package that covered key elements of entry into any given military Theatre. There was some range work, basic drills and skills, a lot of briefs and a little cultural immersion. It was also delivered at the grimmest location in the UK, Shorecliffe, lending the whole proceedings a distinctly depressing tone from the outset. Not that anyone turned up to OPTAG with a spring in their step. No, they were there to jump through a hoop, another mandatory tick in the box that ensured yes, they knew they were going to a dangerous place and no, the locals weren't friendly.

Sophie dumped her Bergen on the transit bunk that would be her bed for the week. Squeaky plastic covered mattress, single bed in a dormitory for thirty, the Hilton it was not. Pulling out her gortex and gloves, she slung her day sack over her shoulder, grateful at least that her rifle was stowed in the Camp's Armoury and rumour had it wouldn't be needed for a few days. Barely looking up when the door was flung open, she burrowed in her Bergen for a Twix stashed for much needed morale.

The stomp of boots, a blast of cold wet air, another Bergen being slung on a mattress near Sophie, finally catching her attention she looked up.

"No way?"

Percy and Sophie laughed and lunged into a hug.

"How the hell are you? What are you doing here? You deploying?"

Questions spilled from them both, when the door was pulled open again and a tall welsh voice was heard muttering complaints,

"Bloody dump, what a... no way??!"

When all the hysteria and garbled questions had settled, the three girls sat in a circle, perched on the edges of beds. Tracey had shared the content of her thermos, Percy dishing out chocolate digestives, but despite the food, the conversation had become sombre.

"I'm just knackered y'know? I've not seen Duncan for what? A month?"

"Oh?"

Tracey smiled, munching, always an ear for the gossip,

"You two an item still?"

Percy blushed, "Sorry, yeah, not one to y'know..."

"No I know you Cotswold girlies, keep it between you and the horses."

The giggles were welcome, the laughter healthy.

"What about you Soph?"

Soph slid back on her bed, boots hanging heavy, coffee in her right hand, left propping her up, tendrils of hair framing her face, softening the harshness of the obligatory bun.

"I just feel so...so under prepared. I mean 4 months guys, it's crazy and I don't know about you, but did I miss the lessons at Sandhurst that actually taught you how to train your section? Y'know put together a training matrix, all that jazz? Don't know about you but my YO's course, didn't really cover it either."

Rueful they sat in silence, the smell of coffee making the dank dormitory almost homely.

"Bloke wise though? Gotta be some fitties in Germany?"

Tracey's eyes sparkled making Sophie squirm, smiling,

"Well..."

She couldn't help the reddening of her face, Percy and Tracey jeered at her in unison,

"Ok, Ok, there's this Loggie Captain, he's, he's..."

"What?!"

"He's nice, he's been nice, I, I dunno...maybe..."

Dodging further interrogation unprepared to discuss something even she hadn't labelled she turned the question to Tracey,

"So how about you? Going strong with you and your Adj?"

Tracey visibly turned to mush,

"Oh guys, he's just so…"

"Arrrgh stop!"

Percy and Sophie bundled their loved up friend. When the play fighting stopped, the conversation turned serious again, Sophie asking,

"You guys know where you are going? Bastion? Lash Gahkar? Kandahar?"

Tracey nodded,

"Based out of Bastion, probably fly in and out of locations."

"I'll be bringing you guys blankets and bullets, be out of Lash Gahkar, but mostly CLPs."

Percy's smile faded, something not lost on Sophie who held back from probing further.

"As for me?" Soph looked pensive,

"Not sure, but think Lash as well."

"Well guys, that is pretty cool y'know? Means we at least get to see each other? Maybe?"

Tracey's tone didn't match the optimism of her words. Although all were touched by the prospect of knowing they would be close, anxiety at the unknown and the threat of a warzone where there was no front line, with an Operational tempo that demanded close to twenty hour days left them quiet. It was what Sandhurst and the last few years had prepared them for, yet felt woefully inadequate when faced with the reality of Afghanistan.

48

WHAT SEEMED LIKE only a heartbeat later Sophie was staring at the threadbare floor of Brize Norton. Cheap faded black carpet, her boots worn and creased, a contrast to the newness of her sandy coloured desert combats. She leaned forward, elbows planted on knees, concentrating on a ragged nail, zoning out the nervous chat around her. She hated this Military airport. It reminded her of waiting around to fly to Cyprus for the final Exercise. They'd been there an hour, likely be waiting a few more. The check in margin before a military flight was ludicrously long and made a mockery by the RAF who would invariably turn around and tell you the Herc had gone U/S or some other woefully inadequate explanation as to why they wouldn't be flying. U/S, unserviceable or useless slackers as most thought of the RAF movers, always the harbingers of bad news and delivered with a cocky attitude that had seen more than one filled in by a tired Para.

She glanced up, looking for those in her Section flying out with her. Corporal Green had already found a target for his charms, flirting outrageously with some Logistics Private who was blushing and squirming in front of her peers, joshing her for being embarrassed.

Lance Corporal Sedley was rather predictably reading a book, looking as if he was about to board a flight to some corporate meeting in the States rather than a warzone. Soph sighed, envying her soldiers blasé attitude. Glancing at the ancient coffee vending machine, she pushed herself out of her chair, foraging for some coins wandering over to have her third brew of the morning.

Major Campbell eyed his young Officer thoughtfully. He knew she was good, better than that in fact, but he still felt nervous for her, felt nervous for them all. This was going to be a steep ask. Expectations were high and the intelligence picture in theatre made for ugly reading. They were taking too many casualties and the overall strategy seemed to lurch around like some drunken sailor, with no clear end in mind. He chewed a nail pensively, slid his eyes over to WO2 Ryan who was flicking through some trashy woman's magazine, taking no interest in her soldiers or young OC. She was a problem and Major Campbell felt guilty for not making more stringent efforts to sack her. Sinking further into his seat he knew that regret was futile. The fact was, WO2 Ryan was bullet proof and she knew it. Three years to pension point with nothing to lose, she ensured she did just enough, just in time, a career style that had defined her journey through the ranks. It meant that Major Campbell had not been able to gather sufficient evidence to prove her ineffectiveness and people like Sophie had to carry this baggage of a Sergeant Major. It wasn't fair, but it was the system.

Scanning the room he saw Sergeant Leg walking back in from probably his tenth cigarette of the morning. Lolloping to where Corporal Green was showing off, Major Campbell realized he also wasn't a great asset to Sophie's section, not as bad as WO2 Ryan, but hardly razor sharp. No. It would be down to Sophie to steer her team. He just hoped she had good instincts and didn't drown in caffeine before they flew.

WO2 Ryan scowled. Bloody RAF, bloody tour, bloody Army. She flicked another page of Woman's Own and thought about her husband. He'd laughed when she'd told him about her Tour, pushing sausage and mash about on his plate, slurping from a mug of luke warm tea, his eyes dancing, teasing,

"Ah come on love, its six months. I'll send you some parcels if you're good…"

She rolled her eyes,

"…and then when you get back it's not even eighteen months and you're out, home free, me too and we can move to Greece. So c'mon, why are you so worried?"

WO2 Ryan had put her knife and fork down, cradling her own cup of tea and been surprised by the tears that sprang up,

"Because I'm nervous Bob, seriously, in fact, I'm not nervous, I'm terrified. I've not been on Tour since Bosnia and we both know that was a piece of piss by the time I was out there. Afghan is a different show entirely and the Int piece is really bloody important. We're working eighteen hour days out there as a norm, people are dropping like flies from the stress and that's not even including the mortaring and rocketing that's regular as clock work."

Bob stopped grinning and reached for his wife's hand,

"Love I'm sorry, I didn't realize you were that nervous. Look it'll be ok, you've got a good team and…"

"Bob," shaking her head irritated, "you know what it's like, as the Warrant Officer I'm supposed to run the show…"

"So?" Bob looked confused,

"So,"

Blushing WO2 Ryan looked down at her plate,

"So I haven't, I've not had my eye on the ball. I never thought for a second we'd deploy and now…now I just don't know the intelligence picture, I've got a new young Officer who can sense it and I…"

Focusing on the magazine in front of her, WO2 Ryan pinched her lips. It was six months, she could do this, six months, get a grip and focus on Greece. Yes, think of Greece and then all this would be over. Feeling a little more relaxed she started to read about Tiffany and Bill who were actually father and daughter but were in love and having a baby.

49

DUNCAN SMILED, FOLDING a stray hair behind her ear,

"We'll go somewhere nice, somewhere quiet, just chill eh? The two of us."

Percy reached out to him but he seemed to move away, reaching further her arm stretching like elastic man off the Fantastic Four and yet Duncan got further and fur…

"Ma'am? Ma'am?"

Jolted awake, a small stain of dribble on her cheek, eyes gritty, she stared at Mackey blankly,

"You were moaning, sorry."

He turned back to the horizon, endless desert, PRR gently crackling static in his ear, eyes red from lack of sleep. He glanced at Percy,

"Bad dream?"

She pushed herself up, bumping around her seat as the Mastiff rode over boulders and God knows what else that was better not to think about. She tried to shake off the grogginess,

"Thanks, I'm ok."

Unscrewing her black water canteen she peered through the dust. They'd been driving thirteen hours straight. For once she wasn't the Convoy Commander, she was doing one of the other Subbies a favour. One of his guys had gone down with D&V, so they were one person short for this CLP. It was a relatively quick run, one FOB to the next and back, just resupping food and water. Critical, but not a long haul. Percy hadn't thought twice when Paul had asked, instead simply asking,

"I'm there, what time do you leave?"

Mackey had been horrified. They'd just got in. Finally getting some desperately needed down time. What was his OC thinking volunteering for another trip even if it was a sprint? Hadn't he taught her anything?

"Er Ma'am, remember that whole volunteering thing?"

They'd drifted to the vehicles to check the Section were doing routine maintenance as SOP between runs.

Percy smiled thinly, eyes almost piercingly blue with her now light tan,

"I know, but I hate sitting around. I'm not asking you to come, I'll be back in a few days, you guys can get some shut eye without me pestering you."

Stubbing out his cigarette, Mackey stopped Percy in her stride.

"Ma'am, You go, I go."

He turned to the troop,

"Corporal Brown, you're stepping up as acting Sergeant for the next three days, the boss and I have got a quick errand to do, don't fuck it up."

So there they were, 45 miles out in the desert, thirsty, tired and Mackey knew there was nowhere else he'd rather be. His wife hadn't occurred to him for the entire three weeks they'd been out here. The only person he'd become focused on was his Boss. Just being professional right? He shifted uneasily in his seat, not ready or willing to explore these new emotions. This was work right? Who are you kidding Mackey?

The explosion stunned them both. Mackey slammed the brakes,

"Contact! Wait out."

"Fuck!"

They both sat there waiting for QBOs, knowing any movement had to be coordinated centrally, sitting tight the only excruciating option.

"This is Zulu 3 Zulu, Zulu 4 Zulu has struck an IED, all call signs go into all round defence. Wait out."

Mackey snapped round to Percy,

"Did you hear that?"

Percy who'd snatched up her PRR as soon as the blast hit, nodded, pulling on helmets and grabbing rifles, they both threw open doors, pausing, adrenalin screaming, looking left and right, hurling themselves out of the cabin. Down the line pax were propelling themselves out of vehicles, hearts racing, heads down, soldiers leopard crawling out a few feet, eyes trained on sights, scrupulously checking the ground for anything that might resemble moved earth or telltale signs of an IED. Percy's breath was coming in gasps, her mouth dry, eyes squinting out into the glare of the sandy landscape. The radio was silent, but she knew there would be a hive of activity in the lead vehicle. Shit, shit, shit, was anyone hurt? Had it just blown an axle? She hated this bit, the no news, the not knowing, it was worse than being in the thick of it.

"C'mon Paul, c'mon, what the hell is going on?"

Mackey tried to calm his breathing, pulse racing, he squinted through his sight, moving slowly left and right checking arcs. The Taleban were cowards by and large, hit and run or shoot and scoot, knowing full well that Allied numbers were higher in ratio. Still, static like this made them vulnerable, irresistible as a quick win. It scared the crap out of Mackey. He'd been talking to the guys in the canteen the night before, Three Para who had just come into Bastion from one of the Patrol Bases for logistical meetings. They'd grabbed a cup of average tea and smoked fags outside the front of the DFAC.

"Fucking Wasps."

Sculley, a wiry racing snake tom, odd nose and sunken eyes that made him look like an alien caricature.

"They're like fucking wasps. One minute nothing, the next a swarm and the thing is,"

He sucked hard on a Marlboro light, blowing out a thin stream of smoke, staring into the distance,

"The thing is, they don't give a fuck."

"It's like,"

Tomo continued, short squat broad as a rugby player with a baby face that had grown serious in only a few months,

"It's like they don't have any tactics y'know, I mean," he sucked on his Marlboro stamping it out and pulling out another,

"I mean they just don't give a toss about hitting one of their own, running about in full view. Basic self-preservation doesn't seem to occur to them, it's fucking mad."

Sculley had nodded grimly and Mackey had felt his stomach clench with fear. He didn't have to go out on patrol like these fellas, but as he watched them both fall silent and stare out into the distance, eyes scanning for an unseen enemy, he saw the toll only a few weeks under had taken on his mates. Gone were the easy jokes, replaced by chain smoking, eyes darting, all business.

Mackey licked his lips, shifted his feet; one of his legs had already gone to sleep. He wondered if Percy was all right, he seemed to wonder that a lot these days.

Percy's PRR crackled alive,

"All call signs stand fast."

She heard the call sign for the MERT and groaned. Bollocks. That meant injuries or worse.

"Bastards."

A shiver of fear piercing the intense heat. I hate this fucking country, shifting her elbow from a stone, shaking her head, eyes trained on the horizon. They could be like this for a while.

50

"WE ARE NOW beginning our descent into Kandahar. All personnel ensure they are wearing their combat body Armour and helmets."

The lights flickered; Tracey snapped the chinstrap of her helmet.

Bit of a far cry from BA she thought as the lights went out for the tactical night landing. She stared out of the window, gripping her seat. The Tristar lurched downwards, a heavy plane overused and out of date, juddering from the strain of a steep approach. The lights of Kandahar flecked the landscape below, few and far between, light discipline tight since KAF got rocketed and mortared far more than Bastion, which, as a more isolated camp, was harder to target.

Butterflies flapped up a hurricane in Tracey's stomach. I can't believe this is happening, that I'm landing in Afghanistan, six month tour. No more Dan except through email and general welfare comms, which apparently were up and down like a yo-yo. She'd heard on the grapevine that morale was pretty low in theatre. Focus on extraction but no clear date, a feeling of leaving a job undone and more casualties caused by Taleban in Afghan police uniforms. The latter meant serious internal investigations for RMP, Trace knew she'd be busy; it was just a tragedy it was usually as a consequence of lost lives.

Swallowing hard she flicked her eyes to the left. Some loggie SNCO who'd farted most of the way if he wasn't troffing, sat snoring, mouth wide open. Trace had envied his lack of nerves. He was coming back off R'n'R, he knew what he was going into, Trace didn't have that luxury. Ignorance was bollocks.

Tyres hit tarmac and with a sigh of relief, she undid her helmet. Everyone remained seated, stock-still, no conversation, here to do a job. This wasn't RyanAir.

As the flight came to a halt there was a jostle for kit bags and queues slowly filtered into the aisles. Exhaustion suddenly hit. Trace read her watch, 2100. Was that local? She couldn't remember if she'd changed it. Either way she wasn't getting her head down anytime soon.

Boots slapped against metal stairs as various ranks walked down onto the air pan, rucksacks flung over shoulders, helmets hanging loosely or slung under arm. Chat was at a minimum, the air palpably tense, the warmth of the evening making most feel a thin sheen of sweat underneath their combat shirt. The fetid smell of excrement drifted over to those waiting for their bags by the hull. The sewage lake across camp, gave Kandahar airfield's infamous unique aroma, a stench no one got used to nor could ignore.

Trace wrinkled her nose, peering across the tarmac, scouring for a familiar face emerging out of the dark. The red nightlights cast an ineffective glow making most people look the same.

Frowning, Tracey found her Bergen; differentiated from a 100 other identical bags by her little green ribbon bow, and marching towards the gate joined a gaggle who seemed to be making their way to the transport. As an augmentee you had to fend for yourself. The daunted anxiety of a new place was not mitigated by having your muckers about as was usually the case for most formed Units. As an individual, it was all down to setting the conditions before you arrived and hoping your oppo turned up when promised, timings dictated by Operational tempo rather than Trace's desperate need for both the loo and sleep.

Hopping gently from one foot to the other she stood by the coach that would take most people to the transit accommodation. Any new arrival was given the tour of Camp, a familiarization that confused rather than clarified. Then newbies were unceremoniously dumped at the transit accommodation, a warren of self-contained air-conditioned drash canvassed tubes; a free for all to find a cot that wasn't littered with proprietorial kit or a sleeping body. An additional concern when navigating this labyrinth were the chorus of tutts and swearing, making it crystal clear that night noise wasn't welcomed by those getting precious kip in between shifts.

Tracey jumped on the coach, guessed it was best just to get some sleep, she'd find the RMP cell in the morning. Sunk in her seat she secretly hoped the journey would go on forever. This was all too real and intimidating not to mention huge, how did anyone find their way around here?

51

LASH VEGAS WAS everything Soph had hoped it wouldn't be. Iso containers galore, dust peppering everything and heat that made her eyes crinkle. She was virtually asleep on her feet, but the OC had insisted on a brief before everyone thinned out for scoff and sleep. She tried to listen to his well-intended attempt at rousing words, but like most felt they were a hurdle to getting some shut eye.

"So early start tomorrow please, I want everyone in for a central brief at 0800. We've got a lot to organize, not to mention the basics of just assembling tables and laptops. Until then, CSM carry on."

CSM Haver barked orders, Soph looked around for her seniors and spotted Al looking relaxed and unphased. How was that possible?

"Hey,"

Al grinned at her,

"It'll feel better after some sleep. Tomorrow will be easy drills anyway, s'just about getting the whole layout plugged in properly. How you feeling?"

"Nervous."

Soph rubbed her eyes, stifling a yawn.

"Bound to, be weird if you weren't, but hey,"

He nudged her with his shoulder,

"We're all in this together."

They walked back to the accommodation village, corrimecs piled on top of each other, a maze of rooms and ablutions. Soph knew she was lucky; she was sharing a corrimec with a Major from another

Unit. She'd yet to meet her, which boded well for personal space, something at a premium on a small Camp.

"See you at brekkie." Al disappeared off into the fading light.

Lying on her bed, head on folded hands, too exhausted to get changed, Soph thought about what lay ahead. The advance party had erected most of the infrastructure and there were already a host of corrimecs wired up and used by her fellow Intelligencers. It was just slotting her team in, keeping them focused and setting a battle rhythm. She swallowed hard at the prospect of the threatened eighteen hour days. She hated the whole sleep deprivation thing. Sighing she heaved off her boots, pulled up her duvet and passed out, but not before she pulled out a well-thumbed note scribbled on the back of a bar chit from the mess.

Hey NIG, you keep safe out there, be thinking of you. I'll buy you a coffee on RnR. Tom x

She'd found it tucked into the top of a jetpack on the side of her Bergen. Singularly the most romantic thing she'd ever had, she kept it in her pocket wherever she went. Smoothing it closed, she slipped it on the cabinet by her bunk and slid gratefully into a deep sleep, the ghost of a smile glancing over her lips.

52

"TAKE COVER! TAKE COVER!"

The tannoy boomed jolting Soph awake. Eyes bleary, mouth dry she threw off her duvet and yanked on boots,

"TAKE COVER! TAKE COVER!"

Masking her concern as the siren wailed, Soph followed the other females down to the lower level, where most slumped onto the corridor floor and promptly fell asleep. Piled on top of each other, the corrimec had corridors between each room with fridges containing water and the odd cooling towel. Sinking to the floor Soph wished she'd grabbed a fleece. Boiling during the day the temperature plummeted at night and coupled with a handful of hours sleep meant she was already shivering.

"Here."

WO2 Ryan handed her a softie jacket. Soph's mouth dropped,

"Err thanks."

"Could be here a while."

The smallest hint of a cessation of hostilities, but as they sat there ignoring the alarm, neither made small talk. Instead, they each slipped hungrily back into fitful sleep, Soph grateful for the softie, replaced by a need for unconsciousness.

An hour later, WO2 Ryan shook Soph,

"S'over."

Pushing herself up, she walked back down the corridor to her corrimec. Soph baffled, wondered why she'd come out and then remembered her borrowed softie,

Well I never…

The 0600 alarm felt cruel and premature. Clawing the air to slam it off, Soph rubbed her eyes and flopped back on her pillow. The siren from the middle of the night felt like a bad dream, although the whisper of a smile drifted across her face as she saw the softie hanging from her locker door.

Pulling on trackie bums and a loose t-shirt, she slipped her feet into flip flops, and shuffled outside into the glaring sun, joining the other stragglers on the morning ablution run. The shade in the shower block was a relief. Plonking her wet bag on the sliver of a shelf, Soph brushed her teeth, staring blearily ahead. The other females in various washing states were equally quiet, the odd greeting pierced the relative silence, but by and large consensus was that 0600 was no time for talking. Teeth brushed, Soph waited patiently in line for the shower, when everything stopped.

"Oh shit! NOoo!"

A chorus of howls went up in the shower cubicles. Practiced sighs from those on Camp for a while indicated this was nothing new. Most shook their heads sagely and made to leave,

"What's going on?"

Soph asked a stern faced brunette, hair scraped back, eyes sunken with exhaustion,

"It'll be the engineers, they've either hit a pipe or more likely the contractors have after failing to ask the engineers for a layout plan. Likely be no water for the rest of the day."

She tutted, shaking her head resigned to the drought.

Soph appalled quietly said a prayer of thanks that she wasn't the young Corporal in the shower currently using a bottle of water to rinse the shampoo out of her soapy hair. Note to self, store some water bottles in the room for emergencies. She headed back to her room, grateful for her clean teeth.

53

THE COOKHOUSE WAS buzzing; scrambled eggs, toast and porridge creating a potent morale raising mix. Self-conscious Soph reached for a tray and browsed the hot plates, hyper sensitive to the shameless staring that met her arrival. Newbies always attracted attention, especially women. Soph had been warned, but hadn't expected a wall of scrutiny. Chewing her lip she reached for the porridge and scanned around for coffee. Scouring the canteen for a familiar and ideally friendly face and failing, she threw her shoulders back and spotted a seat at the end of a bench. Tucking into her oatmeal, Al slapped his laden tray down in front of her.

"Fucking engineers is all I can say."

Soph grinned,

"Managed to brush my teeth at least."

"Fuckers, desperate for a shower and not a dribble. I heard on the grapevine it was some afghan contractors playing hari kari with a new drill. How's you?"

Soph shrugged,

"Y'know, bit tired, could have done without the mortar alarm."

"Still day two week one, time is passing."

Soph snorted. The ubiquitous chuff chart characterized most conversations and laptops in theatre. The count down was both motivating and depressing depending on how far you were into your tour. Right now Soph thought it was best to avoid. She cradled her coffee, grateful for the caffeine and warmth,

"So, what do you think the OC will have in store for us?"

Al chewed on bacon and sausage, throwing down some coffee in between bites,

"I heard he was up till about three planning and liaising with the other local J2, so probably quite a lot."

Nodding, she stared down at her plate, nerves forming a knot in her stomach.

"Anyway, either way, Op MAXIMISE starts today."

Soph cocked her head.

"Ah c'mon, y'not that green Soph? Everyone does it, six months in the desert, sod all to do, everyone gets into their phys. I'll be smashing out the miles and weights in Camp to get back to my fighting weight."

He smacked his belly,

"You'll be letching after me in no time. Talking of letching, you were getting a fair bit of attention as you were checking out the hot plates."

Al's eyes twinkled mischievously, Soph blushed.

"Oh you saw? Hmmm, well I'm new, new face and all that, sure the novelty will pass…"

"Don't you believe it."

Al forked in the last of his egg and bacon and pushed his tray away. Slurping he looked at her levelly, tone serious,

"You be careful, you're not exactly the back end of a bus and after a few months, those around here, who haven't seen a female for flipping ages, well you'll be like a bloody super model. Dogs on heat Soph…"

Uncomfortable at the attention Soph flicked a look at her watch, thoughts of Tom crept into her mind, wishing he was here, missing their lattes, the reassurance of his voice, comfort of his hand. She wondered what he was doing, whether she had crossed his mind.

"We better get moving."

Major Campbell rubbed his eyes. The J2 architecture out here made a mockery of the word. It was more like a shantytown, erected and torn down depending on the whims of the latest Brigade

Commander and his Priority Intelligence Requirements or PIRS. It was no great secret that a lot of the 1 Stars saw their tour in Helmand as a career defining moment. Glory rather than continuity was top of the agenda.

Simon rubbed his eyes again, holding gold wire rimmed glasses he looked more like an Academic than a Company Commander. He'd been up all night talking to the other SO2s, Majors from different cap badges getting the lay of the land. Gossip, truth, vagaries, the overall feeling was anxiety and uncertainty. What constituted over watch? What was the latest mission from Whitehall? When were the Yanks going to pull out because everyone knew their timelines defined NATO's. It was a dance with little direction and sporadic movement, and on this occasion his partner was the CSM, his confidante and a capable Warrant Officer, but no innovator of ideas. That was Campbell's job. He stretched, arms thrown up, yawning loudly. He'd got an idea of how things were going to work, it was a new concept, strategic intelligence at the tactical level, but he knew it could add real value, and he had confidence in his team. They needed to link in with the J2 that was already here, prove their metal. Synergy was the buzzword, finding the nexus another. Draining his now cold coffee, the sound of boots and chat, he replaced his glasses.

Soph filed in with everyone else. The set up basic, a huge dome like air-conditioned tent would house the section, she'd be at one end, overlooking the process. The OC was in a separate corrimec, the CSM seated at a desk outside like some henchman. Desks and laptops lined the centre of the room, white boards and chairs in assorted areas. There was a smoking area outside the tent and a kitchen corrimec to the right of the OC's office. The area in front of both corrimecs was also covered and provided a central pitch for the CSM and Warrant Officers to meet and chat from the other Sections. Al's Section were in a similar set up but with the operational intelligence section on the other side of the OC's office. Their classification was lower, so technically no need for them to be quite so cordoned off. The wire was both a source of amusement and irritation to those not in J2. It indicated the sensitivity of the information being analysed but equally seemed an obstacle to accessing it. Although the tangible fencing was no prevention to the electronic dispersal of intelligence, the perception remained that intelligence was hoarded and not cascaded down to those who in need. Major Campbell's mission was to ensure that that myth was shattered and that all intelligence, no matter the classification, was somehow fused into the overall picture and disseminated to a level where it was required. After all what was the point of having lifesaving information if it didn't save lives?

Perched on her desk cradling another coffee, Sophie watched her Section sprawled before her, chatting excitedly, enjoying the lack of responsibility. The CSM looked on, arms crossed over his barrel chest, bearlike at the back, WO2 Ryan sat looking bored. The 2IC was acting as rear party back in Germany, which was a shame, because Soph would rather have had him than Giles who was smoking, head darting in and out at the back of the tent.

"Sit up!"

Soph straightened as the OC walked in,

"Relax, relax."

He looked tired and it was only day one. She sipped more coffee.

"Ladies and Gents, We've been given a heavy responsibility,"

Soph flicked a look at Al who winked. She squashed a smile,

"Fusing strategic intelligence with operational is no mean feat in terms of classification and adding value rather than complication,"

Giles stubbed out his fag stepping into the tent, the CSM scowled,

"I've spoken to all of the J2 elements here and as I thought, they welcome our contribution. I'm going to brief your OC's now. In the interim the CSM is going to guide you on setting up, formatting and organising this room for work as well as liaising with your Warrant Officers about stagging on rotas and PT. We will all do PT together as a formed Unit. It's important we remain fit and vigilant no matter the tempo. I want you to look out for each other. Make sure you get enough sleep and exercise, it's a way of getting out of the office and managing stress, it's non-negotiable. I wish everyone the best of luck and I know this Company is going to set a high bar for the future practice of fused intelligence here in Lash. Any questions?"

Silence was quickly filled by the CSM as he barked orders, leaving Giles, Soph and Al to file behind the OC into his corrimec. Metal chairs with khaki canvasbacks squeezed together like throw backs from some film scene from Casablanca, they sat notebooks ready. Major Campbell rubbing his balding head, opening a bottle of water,

"I'm not going to lie folks, we've got a fucking hard job ahead, but this is what I want us to do which is essentially an extension of what we roughly agreed in Germany. So for once planning early has not meant planning twice. Soph…"

Three hours later, they emerged.

"Jesus I need a fag."

Giles marched off to the smoking area, head bowed leaving Al and Soph sombre,

"S'pretty clear at a least? You ok?"

Al looked concerned,

"Seems like a lot got laid on your plate in there."

The same had occurred to Soph as task after task was levied in her direction. Notebook heavy, she was hanging for a coffee, she glanced around for Sergeant Leg or WO2 Ryan.

"Hey,"

Al put his hand on Soph's shoulder,

"You can do this and if you need any advice just let me know, after all I'm just outside the wire."

They both laughed. Al wandered off, letting himself through the gate and out into the adjoining tent where his section waited, greeted immediately by his Warrant Officer eager for information, itching to support. Soph looked on, envy slicing through her; she couldn't even see her Warrant Officer.

54

SHOVING KIT INTO her Bergen, brown dessie t-shirt sticking to her gently sweating back, Trace scraped back her hair into a bun and scanned the tent. Row upon row of cots. Leaving her Bergen packed and enviably organized, Trace picked up her beret and followed the crowd hoping they were making their way to breakfast. The blast of heat from outside stopped her in her tracks. Unrelenting, like a wall of fire, tinged with the smell of excrement,

"Jesus."

Smoothing her beret and collecting herself, she squinted into the light, and made her way to the cookhouse. Jackals and Humvees piled past, Americans openly leering from trucks, weapons hanging loosely by their sides. Clenching her teeth, Trace stared ahead ignoring the catcalls, focused on getting coffee and some shade and finding out where the RMP SO3 was who had been supposed to meet her. It seemed to have all gone to pot and she had only a vague idea of where in Kandahar she was based. The smell of bacon and eggs guided her into the cool of the cookhouse, heads bowed, chowing down porridge and crispy toast. Trace scanned the tables looking for a familiar face. Finding none, she homed in on the coffee and was pleasantly surprised to see a real espresso machine with quite a queue of people. At least she'd get a decent caffeine hit.

"Tracey? Tracey Tracey?"

Wheeling round Trace camp face to face with Dom French.

"No way!"

Relief flooding through her,

"I cannot tell you how pleased I am to see you!"

Quickly ensconced with coffee and toast, Tracey munched contentedly whilst Dom filled her in.

"Look I'm so sorry that we didn't get to meet your flight. It's just been manic and,"

Dom looked around shifting in his chair,

"We've got that many investigations going on at the moment ranging from sexual harassment, rape and NDs that there's not enough hours in the day. I cannot tell you how grateful we are that we've got you. I thought you'd probably be able to get yourself a cot and some scoff this morning, so we weren't that worried."

Trace smiled thinly, irritated at his assumption. Not liaising was not ok, a hint of paranoia wondering if this was YO course payback; a question for another time.

"I told the crew that if I caught up with you in breakfast I'd be back a bit later, use the canteen as a space to induct you if that's ok?"

Sipping on a rich coffee blend, eyes occasionally drifting to the sea of faces behind Dom, she nodded, still adjusting to the noise and heat.

Dom outlined the Reception, Orientation and Induction everyone received upon arrival at Kandahar. It was standard stuff, zeroing rifles in case the sights had been knocked in transit; shooting in a straight line was pretty crucial in contacts.

Next there were the IED drills, mortar attack drills in camp, first aid reminders and health and hygiene sanity checks. D&V could send a whole unit U/S, spreading like wildfire if there wasn't stringent attention to basic hygiene at ablutions and toilets. There would also be endless power point presentations about NATO rules of engagement and Camp regulations. Movements in and out of Theatre were also back briefed, after all, end of tour dates and rest and recuperation were front and centre of most people's minds from the moment they arrived.

"...the job is intense Trace I'm not going to lie,"

She studied his face. Dom had lost a lot of weight since the RMP course. Borderline gaunt, his eyes were sunken and didn't sparkle how she remembered. There was a sober tone to his voice that was new. Overall Dom had aged since being out here, his boyish banter gone and it didn't altogether suit him, instead seeming oddly premature.

"We're not exactly seen as friendly forces and to be honest I sometimes question whose side we're on."

His voice tailed off, eyes drifting bleakly down to his cold coffee. He flicked a look at his watch and sighed, raking a hand through thick hair now flecked with the odd grey hair that Trace registered was most definitely new.

"We can probably blag one more coffee and then we'd best get back."

Fresh cups, they moved outside. There were a few benches with picnic like tables, a touch of home amongst the inhospitable.

Stirring two sachets of sugar into his double espresso, Dom yawned and nodded at someone. It was a bit early for idle conversation.

"Essentially Trace we investigate any time there is anything involving casualties on both sides, Afghans and us, we of course being brothers in arms."

His voice dripped sarcasm.

"There is also the small issue of kit going missing, be it being flogged, lost,"

Miming apostrophes with his fingers in the air,

"Or just plain nicked. You can imagine that doesn't go down well. When your mucker has just lost his legs, most of the Toms don't appreciate us nosing about asking about a few stray rounds and some rations. You get the point."

She swallowed uneasily. Trace had always reconciled the internal friction between Forces and the RMP as a necessary evil. She saw her role as guaranteeing cohesion of a fighting force, letting everyone else get on with their job without recrimination. From what Dom was saying she was moving into murky waters.

Dom came to a close. Shoulders slumped, she was struck simply by how exhausted he looked,

"Dom how long have you been out here?"

"4 Months and 27 days. R'n'R due in about 4 days, I'm shattered. But I wanted to push it out y'know? Less to do when I get back, but the OC…"

Trace frowned,

"OC what Dom?"

He sipped some more coffee, pulling out cigarettes,

Tracey raised an eyebrow.

"Yeah I know, but when you're working the hours we've been working, you use anything you can get your hands on just to stay awake. Nicotine does that."

He cupped the flickering lighter, inhaling sharply,

"I'll be honest Trace, it looks like we're all going to get extended."

Her face paled.

"I know this is not exactly what you want to hear when you've just arrived, but there's no point dodging it. Fact is we're all likely to get pushed out by another month,"

Dom paused, dragging in the hit of Marlborough light,

"Could be more."

"More?" Trace sputtered.

"But I thought it was Major and above who were doing the nine monthers?" She knew she wasn't going to get much sympathy, but the best part of a year in this hellhole? The smell of crap drifted across their table as if emphasizing the point.

"Oh Christ."

Dom laughed at Trace burying her nose in her sleeve,

"You better get used to that, cause that ain't gonna get any better."

"Look the good thing is,"

He stubbed out his cigarette looking around for his beret, sculpting it onto his head, darkly amused at Trace's stricken expression.

"The good thing is, you do get to go out of the wire a lot, and I mean a lot. You'll probably go out to the FOBs at least once, if not twice a week and likely stay there for a few weeks. Then you might also have to duck into any of the PBs if shit kicks off there. Put it this way your heli embark and disembarkation drills will get pretty slick.

S'a lot better than some folk who get serious cabin fever out here because they can't justify getting outside the wire. It's fair enough, be a bit of a shocker to get hit by an IED when you're doing some military tourism, to be honest that is some of the things we have to jump on. You're gonna get to see plenty of this beau-ti-ful country."

"C'mon grab your beret, it's time you met the OC and the rest of the crew."

55

THE SOUND OF rotor wings jerked Percy awake. She'd drifted off in the sun, the boredom of watching arcs that were just empty horizon too much. A huge grin slowly spread across her wind-chapped face.

Thank fuck.

Apaches were called wasps by the Taleban, they were the ultimate top cover and Percy could feel the palpable sense of relief drift down the convoy. While they had those big birds in the sky everyone could relax. A bit. It wasn't just Apache, the MERT flew in fast, so quick was its descent that Percy barely had time to turn her face from the tornado of dust. She heard voices shouting, the Whop Whop Whop of wings and the surge in the engine as it took off and tore through the sky back to the cutting edge medical facilities at Bastion. Percy made the sign of the cross. As the dust settled a voice crackled through her PRR.

"All call signs this is Zulu 3 Zulu, all call signs are to re-embark vehicles. Departure time figures 5 minutes. Wait out."

Percy sighed. Her muscles ached from lying prone and her back screamed at the prospect of getting up. Laying her rifle down, using her elbows to push herself up, she winced. Her face was sunburnt, mouth dry as sandpaper. Pulling up her SA80 and ignoring cramp in her calf, she hobbled back to the cabin at the same time Mackey yanked open his door.

"All right Ma'am? Don't know about you but I'm fucked."

Slumped in seats for a few minutes, both slurping from warm water canteens, they sat staring ahead like zombies.

"Think that's my sunbathing done for the Tour."

Percy slowly turned to face Mackey, unblinking they looked at each other and slowly began to laugh, belly aching, gasping for breath, eyes squeezed shut, no dignity gulps of laughter and damn did it feel good.

56

"Ma'am? Ma'am?"

Soph put her hand up, Just one more second…then,

"What?"

She looked up, eyes screaming this better be worth it, lips a thin line of irritation.

Sergeant Leg barely registered.

"Ma'am, General Freeman is here."

"Now? He's early."

"Yeah, well, Generals sort of do their own thing, but if you want I can go and tell him that he's early and he can wait?"

Her face froze then cracked into a smile.

"No, fair one, sorry, bit stressed. Is he in the conference room?"

Sergeant Leg nodded, his face a picture of exhaustion.

"Hey when was the last time you got your head down?"

Skeptical, blood shot eyes searching for the trick question he answered hesitantly,

"I'm not sure, yesterday at some point, might have been during the day. Why?"

He groaned inwardly, just because she could seem to manage on sod all sleep didn't mean he could, and if he was about to get another bollocking…

"Because you look awful. Go to bed for God's sake. I need you."

He looked at his OC who'd matured in the last few weeks beyond anyone's recognition. He felt a small lump in his throat.

Hastily he braced himself, get a grip man, but as he turned to grab his corrimec room key he couldn't quite wipe the smile off his face.

General Freeman, robust, took no prisoners and insisted he be briefed by Sophie. He sat stiffly in the conference room, air-conditioned, real coffee, for most it was luxurious, for a 3 star it was standard, even in Afghanistan he expected no less. He looked at his watch and felt a wave of anxiety. Things were not going well, no matter what kind of positive spin PJHQ wanted to paint. The fact was, progress was infinitesimal. Admittedly this had been a good week for casualties, only heat stroke and an ND that narrowly missed someone's carotid artery. However, the temperature was rising which meant the ferocity of the fighting would too. He shifted in his chair, looked at his watch.

"Afternoon Sir."

Soph breezed in all business and perfume.

For a moment General Freeman's face softened. He liked this Captain, she was no nonsense, young and intelligent and he wasn't going to lie, nice to look at too. A General had to have some perks.

"Have you been given coffee Sir?"

"Yes, thank you Sophie, how are we?"

"I'm good Sir."

She placed his reading file down, appraising him of the headlines. It was a bit of a game, he knew the intelligence picture as well as she did. Before he saw Sophie, General Freeman received a briefing from her US counterparts, whose intelligence reach was considerably more comprehensive. Soph's job was to give the UK perspective and frustratingly it was never pretty.

"Have you been out on the ground Sophie?"

Sinking slowly into her chair, curling a hair behind her ear feeling oddly self-conscious, the General's question felt more like an accusation than a query.

"Well,"

She coughed,

"No Sir, I can't in all good conscience find justification to go outside the wire, especially with the threat state being what it is, it, well it's not really essential Sir."

She shuffled her papers wishing they could return to business.

"Don't you think perhaps you ought to get a foot on the ground to appreciate more fully the PBs and locations you're briefing on?"

He pushed his chair back, knowing full well he was making her embarrassed. She was right, if there was no valid reason to leave Camp then it was irresponsible, but part of him wanted to know if she was curious or maybe if she had the backbone to face the enemy she so knowledgably briefed about.

Furious at what felt like implicit criticism, she stiffened. How dare this bloody General make out she was hiding behind her desk. Didn't he realize she was crawling up the sides of her corrimec from cabin fever? Didn't he appreciate in his bloody ivory tower that being cooped up was just as stressful as cutting about all over the hinterland? She had a job to do and that job was Camp bound. It was bad enough having to pacify her frustrated Corporals that the closest they were going to get to the enemy was emailing a Patrol Base, without having to justify herself to some pompous 3 Star.

"With respect Sir,"

Disrespect hanging in the air,

"I think it would be grossly irresponsible, borderline military tourism to leave Lash without having good reason. Not to mention that the guys and girls in the FOBs and PBs have enough on their hands without some Intelligence Officer adding to their ration roll."

She snapped her mouth.

General Freeman sat forward, allowing the silence to last just too long. A small bead of sweat slid down her spine.

"Your point is valid. I, however, think for situational awareness you should get yourself on the ground. So tell your OC that for my next briefing I'd like an update on PB Sanghole and FOB Pearson, derived from your eyes on the ground. Clear?"

"Crystal Sir. Can I guide you to page one?"

57

STIRRING HIS COFFEE, putting in more sugar than was strictly wise or necessary, Major Campbell pinched the bridge of his nose, concentrating on what Soph was saying, whilst willing the emergent migraine squeezing his sinuses to go away.

"So," pushing his glasses back up his nose,

"He's basically told you to go to FOB Pearson and PB Sanghole? Excellent."

He rolled his eyes, scowling,

"Any idea regarding the sudden personal interest in your movements?"

Resting her elbows on her thighs, she hung her head down at the floor, exhaustion washing over her. Racking her mind she replayed the conversations she'd had with General Freeman. He came weekly, sometimes for hours at a time. They often talked nothing but shop but sometimes...

"Oh...I might have said something last week."

He raised an eyebrow.

"Please, do go on."

Soph rubbed the back of her neck leaning backwards, grateful for the quiet of the room, the space, escaping the glare of her computer screen, relentless pinging of emails.

"I might have said...that I was feeling a little removed from the battle, ermm..."

She dodged her OC's eyes,

"And that really I ought to have eyes on a location that I was briefing on."

"Oh bloody hell Sophie!"

"Oh come on Sir! I thought we were just passing the time, I didn't think he was really listening! Plus I'd just banged out an eighteen hour stint, I was feeling a…"

"Bit sorry for yourself? So you thought you'd have a whinge to a 3 Star?"

Major Campbell shook his head, irritated by her naivety.

"Sophie it's bad enough having to keep the guys motivated without you whining to a General."

"Ah c'mon, I never imagined for a moment that he would pay attention to the rambling of a Captain?"

"No, no c'mon."

His tone turned frosty.

"We've got a situation, effectively a direct order I cannot ignore. When is he next due for a briefing?"

Her heart racing, she was stung by her OC's disappointment. She'd worked her arse off the last month getting everything organized, motivating, guiding, setting an example. She was hanging and it was only a month in. How was it her fault that some sex starved General liked to perv on her whilst she briefed the Intelligence update?

"Not for another fortnight Sir, I think he might be going back to the UK for some talks at Main Building, so it could be three weeks."

"Ok well let's try and get some clarity on this, two or three weeks, I want a concrete answer and then the next thing you need to do is identify who is going with you. I want Sergeant Leg to be one and then choose one of the Juniors, no more, no less. I don't want it to be seen as some kind of jolly you've scored that they can't benefit from. Then liaise with PB Sanghole and FOB Pearson, you're mates with that Captain in the Ops room, so I'm sure he can help."

Sophie blushed embarrassed, she'd met the Infantry Captain in the canteen, Sam, said she had nice eyes. God, what a mess.

"And one last thing. No more talking out of turn. Focus on the task in hand."

Smarting Soph returned to her desk. It was long past dinner and she'd lost her appetite anyway. The tent was quiet, with only one junior at his desk. WO2 Ryan was, as ever, making herself scarce and Sergeant Leg was taking Soph at her word and hadn't been seen for hours. She wandered out into the smoking area and stared up at the stars, then turning, she snatched her beret from her keyboard and dived out of the gate.

58

SAM WALTON WAS smoking his third cigarette in an hour. Running a hand through dry, dust encrusted black hair, he flicked a look at his watch and wondered if he could squeeze in one more fag before going back inside. Three months and five days, he was weeks from R'n'R and wasn't sure if he'd make it. Blue eyes scanning the horizon, always watching the gate, patrols returning and departing, he was like a caged animal, wired for action, eyes constantly darting about. He needed to calm down, this was not going to help him get through the next couple of weeks. Still he couldn't shake the feeling that something big was brewing. It had been quiet over the last day or so and whilst no casualties was a God send, it made him nervous.

"Hey."

He spun round, his face immediately softening, stomach suddenly plagued by butterflies, he ground his cigarette into the dust.

"How's you?"

Casualties, Op reports and stag rosters all suddenly paled into insignificance, he just wanted to know how she was, if they could perhaps go for a coffee, maybe get the hell out of dodge?

Soph rubbed her temple and his heart squeezed. His eyes quickly flicked about doing a five and twenty metre check. Someone was always watching day or night, for a second he couldn't care less.

"I was hoping you could help?"

He tried to look nonchalant, secretly delighted.

"Sure."

He motioned to a makeshift bench outside the Ops room. It was hardly private, but offered some respite from the burning sun during the day. It was such a clear night that the moon cast enough light to walk confidently, the stars a nice sideshow.

She flopped down next to him, rubbing her nose, trying to ignore the lure of cigarettes. Over a month, she hadn't succumbed, but damn she was beginning to enjoy the smell.

"It's General Freeman."

Sam tutted,

"Him again?"

His knee jogged a beat in the air. Neither of them noticed.

"He's pretty much ordered me to go and visit PB Sanghole and FOB P…"

Sam exploded.

"What the fuck?"

He jumped up, agitated, angry,

"He can't do that!? Jesus we are CONSTANTLY pulling people up for trying to wangle military tourism jaunts and he's fucking ordering you to take one? Are you kidding me?!"

Soph blushed, "Ok ok, calm down…"

"Calm down? Do you know how many bloody IEDs are out there? Do you….?"

Soph looked at him eyebrow cocked,

"You do know."

"Yep and I'm not happy about this either, nor is my OC. Bloody brilliant, he thinks I've been moaning to this 3 star to wangle a way out of Camp, s'rubbish."

Sam slumped back onto the bench, realizing there were few options available.

"When do you need to go?"

His stomach churned, a whole range of graphically unpleasant scenarios racing through his mind. Fumbling at his packet of Marlboroughs. Oh for God's sake why Soph? She'd just bloody got here. He had always been secretly so relieved that she never had any need to leave the wire, that she was as safe as you could be in this unforgiving hellhole and now, now this. He kicked a stone away in the dust, twisting away from her as he lit his cigarette. Stupid. He wanted to protect her and this fucking 3 Star was screwing it up.

Soph chewed a nail and scowled at a mouthful of grit. She looked up at Sam noticing the anxiety painted on his face. She blushed with embarrassment, feeling awkward but needing his support.

"I'm sorry Sam, you've been a real rock in such a short time. I, well, I'm sorry to upset you. If the truth be told,"

She glanced about self-consciously,

"I'm a bit scared, silly eh?"

Sam's heart damn near exploded.

"No," he whispered, "not silly at all."

59

TOM WOKE GASPING for air, thrashing with his duvet, sweat pattering his forehead. Bolt upright, awareness slowly returning, he slid back onto his pillow, anxiety still wrapped tightly around him. It had been a nightmare, indiscernible figures but an overwhelmingly palpable sense of fear, of something being wrong.

He turned to check his watch glowing in the darkness on the little wooden table beside his bed. Its neon face read 0100, about 0430 in Afghanistan. He wiped his brow, kicked off the duvet, cooling his legs, taking the heat from his emotion but leaving untouched his apprehension.

He knew what it was about. There was nothing he could do. He'd never been in this position before, it had always been him leaving, him deploying, leaving others behind not the one being left behind. He loathed the impotence. She was ok, she would be ok and what could he do right now anyway?

Sighing, rolling onto his side, he thought over the last few weeks since she'd gone. He winced, castigating himself as was now his habit. Why hadn't he done more, been more open? Damn it. He'd marveled at her, quietly adored and cherished their coffees, how they'd become close. He knew deep down that her small gestures, the blushes, suppressed smiles and eyes shining that it was mutual, yet somehow both of them had just shied of voicing it?

Shaking his head he cast back, thinking how he'd mooched around the office, his CSM looking at him quizzically, making cracks about him behaving like some lovesick teenager, Tom refusing to

263

register the possibility. Each time the phone had rung he'd snatched it up, gabbling hello, face falling, spirit crushed when a normal tasking was relayed, when it wasn't her.

He smiled, what did he expect? Did he secretly hope that she'd find his number, ask about, figure it out, then be near some welfare comms and feel compelled to phone him at the exact same time he was in the office? The planets and stars being in perfect alignment? He may as well howl at the moon and yet that was what he hoped and he felt a fool for it but still hope nagged at him and the embers of the dream stayed alive.

Clutching his duvet to him, he closed his eyes, willing sleep. Hoping that just for one day he'd awaken without that knot of dread in his chest, buzzing like some wasp hammering against his solar plexus, beating out an anxious rhythm, is she ok? Is she safe?

"Please keep safe, please…"

Finally the bliss of unconsciousness crept over him, stealing him away to a land where faceless figures loomed large and threats seemed real and her face was just out of reach.

60

"Ah Dom, nice of you to join us."

Dom's face flushed.

"Trace,"

He held back the tent flap as Trace walked into the air-conditioned drash tentage,

"This is Major Laurent Corneille or Roger, whichever you prefer."

"Roger?"

Trace looked confused and then shaking the OC's hand clicked.

"Apparently I…"

"Look like Roger Federer." She finished. He did and if anything marginally better which was not ideal. Distractions from good-looking Majors on Tour when she was trying to make an impression were not ideal. Roger however was not interested in pleasantries and dodged introductions, carrying straight on briefing the small team gathered around a central table.

"So in short we need someone out at FOB P within the next week and the week after PB Sanghole is due an inspection. There have been reports of some pretty dodgey ammo handling and storage of Milans or accounting of them at least. Plus it's always good to remind those guys that they're not the last outpost of the Alamo."

Grunts of laughter,

"Any questions? Right crack on. I want those reports on the PBs and FOBs recently visited on my desk soonest please. HQ at Bastion is keen to get an update."

On that Laurent turned and squared up to Trace, standing his full 6'3", something Tracey hadn't registered when he was bent over the map in the centre of the tent.

"So you're our new recruit? I hope you are well rested because you are going to get thrashed. Dom filled you in?"

Snickers of laughter behind Laurent. Trace ignored the innuendo, acutely aware her every reaction was being scrutinized to judge the kind of female she was. Are you going to be trouble? Unjust and unfounded didn't make the prejudice any less prevalent. Women were a distraction to a lot of Infanteers and RMP alike, clearly Major Corneille was one of the old guard who preferred women in the Nurses Corps. Well he better suck it up she thought, I'm not going anywhere.

"Dom has given me an excellent brief thank you Sir, and I am pleased to be able to help in any way I can."

"Ok get the brews on, mine is white, one."

Laurent wheeled back into the far end of the tent, a sectioned off area, lifting the flap and disappearing without a backwards glance. Trace's eyes narrowed to slits.

"Easy tiger, you know what things are like."

Dom eased Tracey's shoulder,

"He's just trying to provoke you, test the ground, C'mon you know the drill."

"Doesn't make it any less bullshit. Now where are the fucking cups?"

It was dark by the time she came up for air. Reading through old reports, familiarizing herself with the layout of troops on the ground and learning call signs her head was spinning and she was gasping for a brew. She looked about and noticed that most people had sloped off for food. Flicking a look at her watch it was gone 8pm, and Dom had already thinned out for food, asking her to join him she'd waved him off absorbed in casualty reports and investigation summaries.

"You're going to have to manage your admin better Lieutenant Bonner if you're going to last the distance."

Snapping her head up she was about to sneer some terse come back when she saw Roger Federer staring back at her. Cool brown eyes, raised eyebrow, was he laughing at her?

"C'mon, I realize I haven't really given you an intro chat, we can do it over some scoff. I think its surf and turf tonight."

"Surf and Turf?"

30 minutes later she was staring at the OCs plate laden with steak and lobster. Question answered.

"First tour then?"

Pushing around pasta, scanning the canteen for Dom, feeling anxious at the amount of reading she had yet to do, a filing system she needed to memorise, and she wasn't even sure where her bed was tonight, having just dumped her kit in the tent, she nodded.

Laurent pushed back his plate and took a breath. He eyed Trace thoughtfully, her anxiety tangible. She was right to be nervous and Laurent was not about to assuage those concerns.

"Look,"

He took another bite of steak, piling some chips onto his fork, time was ticking and he was briefing the Logistics Colonel from Bastion in about 20 minutes.

"This is not going to be an easy first Tour for you."

Trace pushed her plate away. She wished people would stop saying that.

"I'm not going to mince my words. We need you out on the ground and we need that to happen quickly. You are not going to get a warm reception everywhere you go and what you see and hear ain't going to be too pretty either. I don't know what work you've done back home, but this is going to need you to raise the bar to a whole new level. I'm not going to lie, the fact you are a female is not going to help."

Anger rising, she could really do without this perverse pep talk. Did he think this was helping?

"S'no point getting all self-righteous and indignant about it, I'm just telling you how it is. This is not the most democratic of countries no matter our best efforts. This is a patriarchy. Fact. Most women are beaten with a stick first and no questions asked later. It will work against you. Fact. I am behind you 100%, so is the team. You know that, but we can't be with you every waking moment, so I would make sure that that,"

He nodded at her 9 mil holstered on her thigh,

"Is not just there for show but you are pretty damn slick with your short arm drills. Capice?"

She felt sick and irritated, this wasn't the Godfather and she was no little Bo Peep. She sat a little straighter, her jaw tense, green eyes flashing,

"Right,"

Laurent scraped the last morsels of fish and meat onto his fork whilst pushing back his chair.

"We best get going, grab us a coffee on the way out, we've got an evening brief to get to."

We?

Colonel Jones was red faced, piggy eyed with wild grey hair bristling out from underneath his beret. A loggie who'd been through the ranks and was now a Colonel, he was happy to remind anyone, that he'd been soldier first, Officer second and he'd seen it all. Unpopular with his peers, universally loathed by his soldiers, the Colonel was everything the modern Army was trying hard to shed in terms of image. Anachronistic, misogynistic, he was a belligerent senior who was happy to shout first and think later, if he thought at all. Sheer determination and aggression had propelled him through the ranks, frequently promoted to just move him out of locations, Colonel Jones was not a force to be reckoned with but rather one to be avoided. Sadly for Trace that was not an option.

"Good evening Sir."

"Where's Laurent? Who the hell are you? Why am I getting fobbed off with some wet behind the ears Lieutenant?"

Trace blushed as Laurent bustled in saving her from having to reply.

"Evening Colonel, Tracey here is just getting your coffee, black please Trace, you know mine."

The Colonel softened. He threw his beret on the table and shook his head, nasal hair peeping out of his nostrils, adding an additional repugnant element to his features.

"S'pretty quiet out there Laurent, hope your reports haven't dug up any more dirt about my boys? They're doing a bloody hard job under some shit conditions; can do without you guys going around and turning over stones that are best left well alone."

"Sir, we can't ignore weapons and ammo disappearing, but yes you are right. Conditions are tough and I'm pleased to report that currently things are reasonably quiet. Here are the results of the last visit to the PB line. In fact we're planning to send Tracey out there in about 10 days, get a feel for the situation on the ground."

Colonel Jones' eyes narrowed,

"Think that wise? Putting a filly like that in the field? No time for carrying baggage out there y'know?"

Laurent sighed, bored of the Colonel's inappropriate remarks that in any other field of work would at best see him fired, at worst facing a sexual harassment and bullying tribunal. In his opinion he should be facing that anyway.

"I think Tracey is more than capable of handling herself. How are things over at Bastion?"

"Oh busy, bloody Tristars are giving everyone a headache, keep bloody going U/S and causing an almighty queue for R'n'R. if the papers get hold of how long these blimin' lads are now being held on the pan before they even board their flight…"

Trace placed coffees in front of the Colonel and Laurent and slid into a seat at the rear of the conference room.

"Well I'll get down to business…."

Laurent began a list of findings from recent PB and FOB visits. Allegations of child pornography amongst Afghan troops mentored at PB Freeland barely raised an eyebrow, as did the talk of animal abuse and bestiality amongst Afghan police in FOB Allegray. Trace tried not to show the colour draining from her face. She'd heard rumours before she'd come to Theatre, but still...

Laurent pushed back the papers and sat up, he looked tense and Colonel Jones' eyes narrowed.

"What aren't you saying Laurent?"

"By and large things are genuinely quiet for this time of the year. We both know that. Traditionally we'd be experiencing a pretty unpleasant time with fighting season and well,"

Laurent rubbed his face, draining a near full cup of coffee, raking a hand through his hair, he caught Tracey's eye for a refill, she paused gripped by what he was about to say,

"The problem is we've received some Intelligence to suggest that there maybe something big planned."

Colonel Jones didn't move,

"A couple of pairs of Afghan Army and Afghan police uniforms have been stolen."

Tracey exhaled, appalled, Colonel Jones' eyes widened.

"When?"

"About a week ago."

"A week ago?"

The Colonel's spittle settled on the table between them.

"Why the hell wasn't I told?"

"Because, Sir, the Intelligence wasn't confirmed. These Afghans do their doby all over the place and some of them just loose it. J2 just wasn't sure until today, when, well it was too glaringly obvious to deny."

"Has this been cascaded down the chain?"

"As we speak."

Colonel Jones closed his eyes, breathing deeply.

"Bollocks. We can really do without this. Any more for me? I need to go and tell the Commander, think there is a heli leaving shortly. Want to tell him myself. Shit Laurent. This is not good."

Laurent pulled his briefing papers together, shoulders heavy.

"No Sir, it isn't."

61

IT FELT SO good to be back at the FOB; Percy visibly relaxed in her seat as they drove through the gate. Even Mackey's jaw seemed to relax.

"Do you think they put the kettle on?"

Smirking, Mackey jumped down from the cabin, she stretched and scanned the compound. It felt like they'd been away for weeks not days and dehydration had left her eyes feeling like little pieces of gravel. Mackey peeled round from his side, watching the remainder of the convoy pour into the Camp. Sandwiched between 2 Mastiffs was a badly mangled Jackal. 2 wheels missing and a hole the size of a small car in the middle, Percy winced, Mackey whistled.

"Shiiiit."

The Camp seemed to go quiet as those who hadn't been part of the convoy registered the vehicles. Bodies jogged over, offering help, soldiers stepping up, unloading vehicles, handing bottles of water to their peers, quiet exchanges, nods, sharing of Marlboroughs.

Walking over to Paul who was heavily caught up in a conversation with the FOB Sergeant Major, his face serious, he nodded at Percy as she approached.

"MERT has them both, not sure, think it was Nobby who was worse, both CAT B, bloody hope it stays that way, though it didn't look…"

Implication hung heavy in the air. The Sergeant Major, a huge truck of a man nodded at Percy, his arms thick as tyres, tattoos wrapped his biceps, face bronzed from hours in the sun,

"Ma'am…"

The Sergeant Major nodded, flipping his small notebook shut,

"Right Sir, I'll sort the casrep. You squared?"

He stared at Paul, concern masked in one word.

"Yep, squared."

He watched the Warrant Officer march away, heavy with purpose.

"Hey look,"

Paul pulled off his PRR, rubbing his yes, hair knotted with sweat and dust,

"I wanted to say thank you. That…that was not good and well, you didn't need to come…so…"

"Hey,"

Percy stopped him, cupping his elbow,

"You ok? Got pretty noisy out there."

Paul shook his head.

"S'a mess, bloody mess, good blokes Percy."

His voice caught, looking down at the ground, kicking the dirt.

"Is there anything I can do?"

It was all Percy had.

"No, s'ok the Sergeant Major is all over it. I just need to get some water and get the vehicles squared. Thing is we've all got some good news, gotta go back to Bastion for resups, can chill there for a bit too, bloody need it."

Relief washed over Percy and for a moment she felt her knees tremble with fatigue and emotion. Bastion. They had canteens there with fresh food. Cots too. She watched Paul pace over to the Ops room, pause and then almost imperceptibly brace himself before going in. Turning herself, she wandered across the compound.

"Hey."

Mackey looked up, sat on a wooden bench he was draining the contents of a chilled litre of water, handing Percy one.

"Thanks."

In silence, gulping cold water, Percy came up for air first, wiping her mouth, clearing a whiter patch of skin on her face, something

Mackey caught, made him smile, liking the fact she didn't care, wasn't feeling the need to fill the silence.

They stared at the mangled Jackal that had been hauled to the side of camp, no one wanting to turn the tragedy into some sort of spectacle; business as usual.

"You heard the news?"

Mackey leaned forward on his knees, hands hanging loosely, one wrapped round the near empty bottle of Evian.

"Bout Bastion?"

"Uh huh,"

She drank some more water, wiped her face again, more white skin.

"Hear they have fresh fruit in Bastion."

He nodded smiling, squashing the now empty bottle,

"Heard that too."

62

"Need you out there Trace."

Tracey nodded unsure whether excited or terrified, bit of both.

"Need better understanding of how this happened. The uniforms are from troops who are mentored, they've got an OMLT with them. So question is how did this happen?"

More nodding.

"Few more days bedding in, you zeroed?"

"Yep."

"Good. Make sure you get some extra ammo. Don't take much, just a gonk bag, day sack, whatever you think for a few days. Don't want to be dragging your Bergen off the heli especially if you have a heavy landing or you get a welcoming committee. You need to grab your stuff, weapon cocked, then sprint onto the back of those quad bikes, which will speed you into the PB. Taleban are usually too far out of range to actually cause any damage, still, you can hear those rounds zipping past you and I can tell you, at that point you're not thinking about weapon ranges."

Tracey's eyes widened, clenching her jaw refusing to let him scare her.

Laurent emptied his third coffee of the morning, he seemed to mainline the stuff and show no visible effects. Rumour had it he didn't sleep much. Not surprised Tracey had thought, tricky when your blood is 90% caffeine. He picked up his mug, dark eyes troubled, tall frame seeming shorter, less daunting more of an equal to Trace. Suddenly she felt awkward, blushed.

"Morning Sir."

Dom pulled back the flap, pausing, face questioning at seeing Trace and Laurent stood together, in silence. Odd.

Trace turned embarrassed,

"Erm, just gonna grab a coffee from the Boardwalk, want one?"

"Yep thanks."

Laurent butted in before Dom could answer, both watching Trace dart out of the tent.

Timmy Hortons was always busy, but the boardwalk was light relief from the intensity of the tent. Different nationalities mingled, queuing for fat Subway sandwiches, coffee or pizza, weapons slung, sunglasses adding a relaxed edge to the scene. A few females on a corner table eyeing up the talent, being eyed right back.

Waiting impatiently for the lattes, she glanced around her for a familiar face, not really seeing any, preoccupied with absorbing the OCs direction. Patrol Base. Few days. She scooped up the drinks, paced back,

TAKE COVER! TAKE COVER!

Bollocks, breaking into a run Tracey made it back into the tent, thrusting coffees at Dom and Laurent, scanning the room for her CBA and helmet, poised to move, then noticing the attitude around her was entirely unmoved,

"Where are you going? We're just going to get into the conference room Trace, closest hard cover, your CBA is over there with your helmet."

Dom nodded to Tracey's right,

"C'mon."

Sat in the conference room, sipping on lattes, the siren wailed outside followed by, THUMP! THUMP THUMP THUMP!

Eyes wide, Trace looked round at Dom,

"Mortar attack."

She nodded, mouth in an O shape, clasping her CBA a little tighter, coffee tasting bitter. She glanced at Laurent oblivious, leaning against the wall, sipping his latte, eyes gazing into the distance.

TAKE COVER! TAKE COVER!

"Bit late."

Trace muttered, Dom sniggered,

"So I hear you two have a bit of history?"

Laurent eyes danced as he sipped his coffee.

Stunned Dom and Trace blushed, Trace more amused, Dom clearly awkward.

"Think it's fair to say that was a while ago and ahem, I may have learned a lesson or three…"

Dom suddenly became engrossed in the top of the conference table, Laurent seemed tempted to continue, traces of humour gone Dom looked up at Trace,

"You've been loaded onto the next heli to PB Sanghole, you'll likely get bumped off the first slot, so I reckon you'll be on your way by the end of the week. Don't take much,"

Tracey put her hand up,

"Yeah, got it, need to be able to sprint to the Quad bikes. Thanks."

Dom raised an eyebrow.

"The girl is learning."

"Yeah, lessons I can do without."

She drained her coffee listening to the faint thud of mortars hitting the ground.

63

SAM LOOKED THROUGH the Ops log and barked a few questions at the watch keeper.

"Looks like the best option is PB Sanghole. It's been pretty quiet over there recently, a heli is due out of there in a few days. Get in, get out, can't really have you taking up too much living space."

"Can I take my Sergeant and Corporal?"

"Soph this is not some school trip."

"OC's orders."

"Yeah, well bugger that, tell your OC that if he wants you to have a foot on the ground before General Freeman comes back, this is the best bet over the next fortnight. Anything after that, well,"

He looked down at the log,

"Soph its resups, rounds and food, all are more important than you."

"Thanks for that."

"Sorry, one more tea before you go?"

She softened, "Sure."

Back on the bench, Soph cradled her cup, enjoying this brief respite, kicking a stone as she swung her feet she found herself thinking of Tom, wondering how he was, feeling strangely guilty sat her with another bloke. She took a sip of coffee and thought of all the coffees they had shared. Not for the first time she slipped a hand into her pocket and thumbed the well-worn note he'd written. Was he thinking of her?

Sam blew another smoke ring, paused as if thinking twice,

"So you gotta bloke back home?"

She paused, unsure if she was ready to share Tom with anyone else. He was her private pleasure, there was so little here that was private, so little personal space. She wanted to keep him close.

"Ermm, well…" She drained the last of her coffee, allowing the question to hang in the warm air. Was it anything? Her heart squeezed. The Mess back in Germany seemed another world.

Sam stubbed out his fag and looked straight at her.

"He's a lucky man, I hope he realizes that."

Then he got up and walked away.

64

THE HUB OF Bastion was overwhelming for Percy, she looked around blearily, clutching her rifle, bag slung over a shoulder, unused to the heavy flow of traffic, the noise. Struggling with an unfamiliar rising panic, she looked around for Mackey, as ever by her side, rubbing his stubble,

"Pretty full?"

"Hmmm, shall we see if we can get a coffee? Blokes sorted?"

"Yeah they're squared, most have peeled off to the accommodation or welfare comms. Coffee sounds good, scoff wouldn't go amiss either, fucking starving."

Percy smiled, a dull ache reminding her she hadn't called Duncan in a while, more than a while? She shook her head not wanting to analyse right now. Spotting a stream of Brits walking towards the canteen she nodded in their direction.

Plates piled with pasta, salad, vegetable and all things fresh, Mackey spooned in food like he hadn't eaten for a week. Percy paused, pleased with her own bowl of fruit salad, glistening and fresh. She sipped her tea,

"So week here right?"

Mackey nodded, scooping more food, barely pausing for breath.

Scanning the canteen, always scoping for a familiar face, Percy wondered if she'd bump into Trace, what was Soph was doing? Where were they?

Spooning in apple and banana, a sense of calm descended. When every slice had been eaten, every piece chewed and deliciously swallowed she put down her spoon and sat back contented.

"I'm going to make a call. I'll see you back at the TransCoy HQ? Think the QM may have a few cheeky things we could 'borrow'."

Mackey picked his teeth grinning,

"Sounds like a plan."

He watched her go feeling a pang of jealousy, searching for another bowl of fruit salad to distract from the confusion buzzing in his head.

"Hey, can you hear me?"

"Hey! Percy!"

The line crackled, echoing.

"Hey Duncan, I've just got into Camp, how are you?"

Long Pause.

"I'm fine! Missing you!"

Percy hung her head, tears rising, his voice made her feel vulnerable, brought up what she had tried to keep buried so she didn't have to feel like, well, this. She couldn't do this; she couldn't focus here and back home.

"Look I'm sorry, but I've just been called, I've got to go, I wanted…"

She could hear his silence, almost touch his hurt. He knew, how could he not?

"Percy, you're going to be ok, I'm here, you're going to be ok. Don't cut me out baby, I can help."

Tears rolling,

"I miss you Duncan, it's hard out here,"

"You can do it Percy, it's not forever,"

"I'm…I'm…"

She hung her head,

"I'm so tired Dunc, so tired…"

The silence hung between them, words inadequate, the distance almost unbridgeable.

She gripped the edge of the phone, coiling the lead around her fingers, as if reaching down the line, touching him,

"I thought you had to go?"

His voice soft, tender,

"I'm sorry, I just found it overwhelming hearing your voice, being here, you there, I've still got months Dunc before R'n'R, I, I feel a bit lost,"

"Percy listen to me, you're stronger than this. It's the heat, the hours, you aren't lost, you're tired and you have got to look after yourself. I'm not there to kick your arse and make you."

A weak smile.

"How long you in Camp?"

"Few days I think,"

"Well phone me again, touch base, reach out, it'll make you feel more grounded. I promise you."

Percy stood straighter, feeling a little stronger, she was glad she called, glad she made the effort. He did understand.

"Hey," Tone softer still,

"I don't know what it's like for you Perce, but it is tough for everyone the first time. It's still early days, you've only been out there just under two months. You're getting through it. Will you get some sleep for me? God I miss you, do anything to touch you right now."

She nodded, silent, same she thought, same, just want to go home.

The pips went

"What? Oh bollocks! I think Op MINIMISE is about to go on."

Casualties meant immediate cut comms ensuring no one leaked details before the families knew.

"Damn it, Duncan I really do have to go, I, I…"

"I know, me too."

And then he was gone, the phone dead between them.

65

MACKEY'S FACE WAS thunder, glaring at the Transport Company Senior NCO who shook his head almost taking a step backwards.

"Have you got any fucking idea when we last slept? You actually step out from behind that comfortable desk of yours?"

Percy caught the Sergeant's face harden, caught Mackey's shoulder before he was punched.

"Hey what's going on?"

"*Sergeant,*"

Mackey emphasized the rank,

"Worsley here has just kindly passed on that we have to do one more run before we can actually get some shut eye."

"What?"

Percy used every ounce of self-restraint to stop hysteria surfacing. Duncan was right, she needed to sleep, badly and not for one night, she needed a few nights in a row in a cot, preferably in something air conditioned.

She stared incredulous at the Sergeant, who shuffled uncomfortably, his pudgy stomach straining at his belt, unlikely to have been outside the wire, or indeed inside a gym during his tour.

"Sorry Ma'am, PB Sanghole, they need a resup, heli couldn't, called away so didn't drop in their ration crate. S'not that far…"

His voice trailed off, realizing platitudes were only going to make his position worse.

Percy closed her eyes, breathing deeply, letting the news wash over her.

"When do we have to go?"

"S'about a day's journey, so day after tomorrow."

Broken, she nodded,

"Right. Ok"

Turning she walked out, head down until she found her cot. Collapsing into it, curling into a fetal position, too exhausted to think or cry.

66

"Only me Sir."

Major Campbell rubbed the bridge of his nose, sinuses throbbing, eyes red,

"Only you?"

"Yes Sir."

"Why?"

"Rations and rounds priority."

"Yes thanks for that, but this is a 3 Star's direction, so I'm going to ask again, why not?"

Soph stood taller, irritated at her OC giving her a hard time for something beyond her control,

"Because Sir,"

Anger rising,

"That is the only space I could get within the next fortnight."

Major Campbell slid on his glasses, wire frames gently bent out of shape, delicate on his round face.

"Right."

He seemed to weigh up the situation, duty of care, Soph going alone. He could sense her discomfort; he wasn't having a great time with this himself.

"Ok, so day after tomorrow?"

"Yes."

"Well you better get ready then."

He looked back at his screen. Conversation over.

67

SOPH KNELT BY her bedspace, stuffing her rucksack. Sergeant Leg hovering unhelpfully,

"Ma'am, seriously no way I can come with you?"

Sleeping bag, basher, ammo, what else?

"No, just me, can you see my spare pistol holster?"

He crouched down, pulled it out from under a pair of combat boots. Slid over her morphine, thin tubes stabbed into the wounded. Sophie looked up at him significance of morphine not lost on her in that moment, pushing them into her webbing, combat jacket bulging with kit.

"You got enough ammo?"

"As if I am taking on the Taleban myself."

He nodded, shifting one foot to the other,

"First field dressing?"

"Sergeant Leg, you're not helping."

She knew he was anxious, just trying to help. Equally she was having a hard time holding it together whilst he was there, not wanting him to see her apprehension. She was meant to be the Boss.

Crestfallen, he chewed his lip, desperate to help, painfully jealous he wasn't going too.

"Look,"

She stood up,

"The best thing you can do for me is keep an eye on the guys, make sure the Intsum goes out and I'll be back in a day or two. I'm not staying out there any longer than necessary."

He nodded, envy rising,

"Ok ma'am, well y'know…"

He wandered out, shaking his head, mixed emotions, concerned for his OC.

Soph sat on the edge of her cot, checking her 9mm magazine, all rounds snug, aligned. She stroked them thoughtfully, live rounds, this was real, no more ranges. She took a breath, loaded the weapon and shoved it back in the holster.

68

IT WAS DARK, exhaust fumes poured into the cool of the morning, stars peppering the sky, creating a peaceful panoply at odds with the soldiers and Officers loading weapons, bombing up magazines, checking night vision goggles, deciding who would be on top cover.

Mackey and Percy sat, words painfully inadequate. Red eyed, muscles aching, nostrils already blackened from the dust, this was a punishing ground hog day and PB Sanghole wasn't a place to recharge batteries either. They were getting air cover for the last part of the journey. Enough said.

Mackey revved the engine, flinging his rucksack behind him, the back of the wagon full of rations, water and ammo. He flicked a glance at Percy who was staring out of her window, clutching a flask of coffee nabbed from the canteen. He squinted through the screen, gauging distances, timings, checking his dashboard that the vehicle had been admined, which of course it had, plenty of fuel, grease monkeys had been all over it. Still he liked to be thorough. He felt a nudge,

"Hey, s'only coffee, already drank buckets in the canteen."

"You'll be bursting for a pee before we've even left Camp."

Percy grinned,

"Caffeine addict, can't help it."

Grateful he sipped the coffee, hot, milky, bitter kick flooding his veins, jolting him awake, he gulped some more, savouring feeling human if only for a moment. Engines revved and started forward. He handed the mug back, wiped his forehead, pressed the accelerator.

"Here we go."

69

"Hey! Can you hear me? Dan?"

"Hey! Thought you'd bloody dumped me!"

Laughter.

Trace smiled cringing, she'd been so focused on getting her feet under the table that she'd put all thoughts of Dan out of her mind. Felt weird talking to him now. She kicked the dust on the ground, self-conscious, not wanting to feel like this.

"What?"

She put a finger in her other ear, straining to hear him over the noise of passing Humvees.

"I said how is it going?"

What could she say? Oh just brilliantly? Time of my life? Miss you dear, be home soon. She hadn't expected this and resented him for asking a stupid question. He should know what it's like.

"Well you know…"

"Oh."

Wounded. Damn this was not how she wanted the conversation to go. For God's sake Dan, make me feel better, I'm scared. Instead, she muttered a half arsed apology.

"Hey look,"

Voice clipped, withdrawing. She shook her head, silently asking him not to do that, don't pull back, I'm no good at this, this distance thing, this thing where I'm the girl and I'm the one in the war zone. I don't know how to deal with it this way.

"You sound busy, shall I leave you to it? Maybe email be better, 'spect you've got a lot on."

Heavy with accusation.

"Dan, I'm just, y'know, it's a lot to take in..."

"I know I know, culture shock, at least you can find your feet a bit before you go out on the ground."

She bit her lip, wanting to tell him the situation had changed, knowing she couldn't, couldn't say anything on welfare comms except the mundane, the useless. OpSec ensured nothing was shared that would actually give those at home an idea of what you were doing, where you were, which made divides feel bigger, further away.

She looked at her watch, swore,

"Look Dan I'm going to have to go, but I'll..."

It hung in the air, I'll what?

"I, I..."

She blinked, emotion rising,

"I really miss you."

Pause, had he heard?

Sigh.

"I miss you too Trace, I don't know how to deal with this either y'know? Used to it being me out there, and now, well it's you and I, I...well its hard, hard for us both, but let's not take it out on each other eh? You stay safe, time is passing, you'll be back before you know it."

She blinked back tears,

"Thanks Dan..." pips,

"...bollocks the Pips are going, You stay..."

Gone, she stared at the phone and swore.

70

WOCA WOCA WOCA WOCA,

Soph's head bent low, dust billowing upwards as if the ground itself was a sheet shaken in the down draft.

WOCA WOCA WOCA

The Chinook landed, its rear rotors reaching down almost caressing the ground, the front nose arching upwards. Aircrew stood goggled, beckoning those on one knee, shielding heads from the dust, to run up. In file they jogged on, rotors still moving, filing up the centre of the heli, hearts pounding, dust obliterating everything.

Shunted shoulder to shoulder, shuffling along the Chinook's deck, slung rifles facing downward in case of a negligent discharge, ensuring the rotor wouldn't get hit even if somebody's foot did. Soph itched her chin, the sweat in her chinstrap already making it prickle, eyes slitty from avoiding dust. Her stomach was a bundle of fear and excitement. There was no denying it, Chinooks were bloody cool, she surpressed a smile.

Air crew gave a thumbs up, then the Chinook was rising, swirling dust behind it, steep ascent, climbing into the sky, noise of the engine deafening, blades WOP WOP WOP, steady rhythm as the big bird carried them upwards. Eyes were drawn to the gaping hole beyond the ramp, seeing the barren landscape sweep out behind them. It all looked so harmless up here, disarmingly peaceful, eerily beautiful. She scanned the terrain, dusky yellows, beiges, flashes of green, the odd blue glinting in the sun, tin shanty roofs smattering the ground. Sticking her lip out as if pouting, Soph shifted the chinstrap in vain to ease the pinch of the coarse material. Glancing around she saw heads bowed, eyes closed, some staring back, faces taught, thin mouths. She tried twisting a little in her spot, her rucksack digging into her back, pulling on her shoulders, mouth dry remembering longingly that glass of water Sam had offered before she'd dipped out of the Ops room.

"How long you going for?"

She'd squirmed, feeling awkward by his interest, yet grateful for the concern in a place that had left her achingly lonely.

"3 days I think, but you know that, you've booked the transport."

He'd turned, half smiling, pinching cigarette between his lips, blowing a smoke ring. Grinding the fag into the dirt, he'd stepped forward, gently touching her arm, rubbing it softly,

"Be fucking careful out there. You know the threat better than I do. All I can really go on is my guts and well,"

He squeezed her arm, Soph taken by the affection, finding it exquisitely painful as she looked into a face etched with concern, wishing it was someone else's, that the intimacy was shared with someone a thousand miles away.

"I don't want to scare you, but…it's been pretty quiet and I've just got this nagging feeling. I can't explain it Soph, I'm probably talking shit, but be extra vigilant eh?"

She'd nodded, tendrils of fear slowly caressing her heart, clasping it gently, bringing fear to where previously had been excitement. She'd blinked, a flash of annoyance,

"Thanks Sam, I could have done without that."

He blushed, embarrassed. Damn he didn't normally do that, it's just…

"I'm sorry, yeah, look,"

His hand dropped, stepping back,

"Sure it'll be fine."

Soph pulled the strap of her rucksack up higher, sliding her helmet over her bun, tabs hanging loose.

"See you soon Sam."

"See you Soph."

Putting aside Sam's unnerving warning, Soph pushed against the bloke next to her as she jammed a hand into her pocket. Righting herself, smiling apologetically at her neighbor, she carefully unfolded the dog-eared scrap of paper. Smoothing it onto her leg, achingly careful so it wasn't whisked away by the downdraft. She read the words again and felt a flood of comfort, a deep yearning,

Hey NIG, you keep safe out there, be thinking of you. I'll buy you a coffee on RnR. Tom x

You thinking of me Tom? I'm thinking of you. She ran a finger tenderly across the paper, carefully folding it, slipping it back in her pocket, her neighbor rolling his eyes as this girl kept jabbing him in the ribs.

WOP WOP WOP, Soph's stomach yawned uncomfortably as the Chinook swerved in the sky, a rollercoaster feeling, suddenly nose down, it descended rapidly. Movement amongst those on board, first stop, PB RYAN. Soph looked around, expressions pale. A cloud of dust, the aircrew waving people off, soldiers sprinting down the ramp, carrying bergens as if they were full of duvets, adrenaline powering quads, glutes screaming as they flung themselves up and out.

Ping, ping, zip.

What the hell was that? The Chinook rose up and Soph's blood ran cold. The sound of incoming Taleban rounds. Live rounds. She closed her eyes, swallowing vomit.

71

THE TERRAIN WAS awful, pot holes the size of a cow's head made slow moving, visibility low, Mackey craning to see only a 100 yards ahead, Percy irritated by the agonisingly poor speed.

"You got anything to eat?"

His voice ever hopeful. Rifling in her rucksack, she pulled out a packet of biscuit brown,

"Seriously? Biscuit bloody brown? My shits are fine thanks, I don't need that kind of internal binding. Anything normal?"

Percy shook her head, feigning disapproval, smirking at Mackey's derision, instead reaching into her rucksack and pulling out a rather sorry looking banana,

"Fresh fruit?! Give that bad boy to me!"

Despite, large patches of blackness, Mackey snatched the bruised fruit, within seconds having ripped off the skin and scoffed it down.

"Anything else I can help you with there?"

Wiping his mouth grinning,

"Yep bit of that coffee you snaffled from the canteen be nice."

Sipping from a mug, Mackey looked at the convoy ahead, heartened by the steady increase in pace,

"You spoken to your bloke...Ma'am?"

The Ma'am surprised Percy, she raised an eyebrow,

"Hmmmm."

Trying not to remember the awkwardness, the distance, how far away he was.

"How about you?"

Percy looked at Mackey over the brim of her own mug, curious about her Staffies' personal life suddenly. Well he'd started it…

"Looks like I'm getting divorced,"

She gripped her mug. Mackey glanced over snorting,

"Yeah you and me both, but there you go. She doesn't want this amazing life any more."

He waved a hand out in front of him. Percy shook her head,

"I, I'm sorry…errm, when?"

"Yesterday, when we had all that precious down time, thought I'd give her a call, check in, usual stuff and well turns out she'd been doing some thinking. Never a good sign and well, she's been busy it would appear, been to lawyers already. Not sure where I'm going to live when I get back, she doesn't want me in the house…"

Mackey fell silent, grimacing, feeling the same flood of shock when she'd announced it on the phone, not surprised, but never believing she would actually do it.

"Mackey, I'm so sorry. What about your son?"

Mackey paused, grinding his teeth, not wanting to think of his little toddler, how excited he'd been, how thrilled at their little child and now it was all being taken away and there was sod all, sod all at this moment he could do about it.

"Yeah well, these things happen."

Percy felt a flash of anger, this bloody wife who had no idea what he, what they, were going through. Couldn't she at least wait until he got home? Talk it through face to face? Over the phone was so? Callous. So bloody callous.

Percy stared ahead grimly. Bloody country, people trying to kill you out here and now people abandoning you back home. What a life. She sipped coffee as they sat in silence together.

72

"WHERE THE HELL have you been?"

Trace looked up surprised lifting the flap of the tent. Dom's face flushed with alarm,

"You haven't been bumped off the heli at all. I'm sorry I thought you would be. You packed? You are leaving in 30 minutes, need to get you down to the pan, people are ready to go and they're gonna give your spot away if you don't get there now."

Trace turned, sprinting back to her accommodation, snatching her packed rucksack. Racing back to the tent, grabbing her helmet and rifle with Dom dashing her down to the heli pad. Pulling on her helmet and thrusting arms through body armour, she spotted a line of UK soldiers on one knee in herringbone, heads down, the gentle thud thud thud sound of a heli approaching.

"Shit, run, go for it, I'll sort your admin."

She raced to the line, head bowed, assuming the position. Clutching her rifle, shielding eyes from the storm of dust. Adrenaline raced through her, she clocked her watch, what day was it? Pulling on her rucksack, she watched as the Chinook's tail bumped down, rotor wings whopping against the sky. Damn it was cool.

The bloke at the front looked up, crewman beckoning; he lurched forward with each figure peeling in behind, thundering up the ramp avoiding taking in gulps of dirt. Trace, gripped her rifle and with hamstrings squealing legged it up to the heli, pushing up the ramp and squeezing down next to the last guy. The Aircrew counted heads then shouting down to the pilot the engine surged and the heli lifted up off the ground, one crewman grinning at Trace, nonchalantly gripping a leather sling hanging precariously from the ceiling. Casual in his green jumpsuit and helmet, knowing he looked cool against the backdrop of the swirling ground disappearing beneath them.

Trace rolled her eyes watching Kandahar shrink as they rose into the afghan sky.

73

THE BLAST CATAPULTED the chassis six feet into the air. Percy was flung forward like a crash dummy, seat belt burning a line across her chest, eyes finding Mackey as he was forced into the steering wheel, his neck flicking backwards, floppy like a puppet. Smashing down heavily onto the ground, they sat there in shock, the smell of burning rubber, exhaust, cordite filling the cabin. A hissing in the background, Percy trying to get her breath, wheezing her lungs paralysed in the grip of shock.

"Zulu 1 this is Zulu 3 sitrep over?"

"Zulu 1 this is Zulu 3 sitrep over?"

Percy winded gasped a huge burst of air and pushed her pressel, anxiously staring at Mackey through eyes brimming with shock, reaching over to shake him, he lay draped over the wheel,

"Zulu 3 this is Zulu 1, possible IED, wait out."

Percy released her seat belt, ignoring the stench of burnt clutch, ripped metal and dust.

"Mackey?"

She clasped his biceps, squeezing, shaking gently, conscious undue motion could exacerbate any injuries. Gasping, winded, still sucking for air as if caught in a plastic bag.

Mackey moaned and Percy felt relief flood through her, thank fuck.

"You ok Mackey? Can you raise your head? You injured? Where does it hurt?"

Mackey slowly shook his head,

"Motherfucker...."

Percy grinned, he was ok, she sat back her chest finally easing, breathe in, breathe out, God it felt good.

"Zulu 1 Zulu 3, ok this end, vehicle damage may mean we are U/S, checking now, over."

"Zulu 3 this is Zulu 1, convoy halted, we're calling in for support, all round defence, stay where you are, over."

"Roger that, out."

Percy rubbed her neck and for the first time surveyed the vehicle. Bloody hell. The whole rear of the truck had a huge bulge where the explosion had catapulted the suspension upwards. Rations and boxes were a jumble of food sachets and scattered tins. Percy thanked God they hadn't been carrying any ammo, would have been a bloody disaster.

Mackey groaned flipping off his seat belt. He rubbed his forehead, shaking himself, wiping eyes,

"Urgh, my head."

Massaging the back of his neck he peered at his boss,

"You ok Percy?"

Smiling weakly, the first strain of shock passing, emotion flooded her system. He called her Percy for the first time.

"Yeah, I'm ok, bit winded, you?"

"Bloody head hurts, gonna have a wicked bruise from the seat belt, but hey rather that…"

He let the question hang. He turned around surveying the wreckage.

"Blimin' heck, that's mad! Thought the thing would be totalled, sure we must have jumped 6 feet! Looks pretty ok back there, well…"

Percy raised an eyebrow,

"Well apart from the obvious."

He turned back to the wheel, and wiped the instrument panel.

"Y'know we're looking ok."

He was relieved there wasn't a panel of emergency lights flashing. Looking hopefully at Percy he turned the key, the engine burst into life and they both laughed.

"No fucking way!"

"Hey wait a minute," Mackey warned, "not sure if we can actually move though. Wheels could be fucked."

He put the truck into gear and edged forward, stunned they felt the tonner balk then sloppily, lurch forward, but undoubtedly moving.

"Well, fair play, these new vehicles ain't bad!"

Slapping the dash with delight Percy called in the good news to the Convoy Commander. An hour after hitting an IED, Percy and Mackey drove away in a vehicle that had weathered the entire blast. Perhaps there had been investment in kit after all.

74

SOPH PEERED OUT, light beginning to fade. There was one more stop and then PB Sanghole. She felt drained, tipping up and down, watching other pax sprint off the craft. Oddly wishing the flight could go on forever, that others would get off and she'd just remain, safe, enjoying the anticipation without facing the consequences. The idea of hauling her rucksack up and careening down the ramp filled her with fear. Her legs were heavy, back ached, arms tense from clutching her rifle.

Her lips were now cracked from dust sucked in by propellers and inhaled by those sat cramply on the deck. She felt like she hadn't had a clear gasp of air for hours, virtually smoking earth instead. Shaking her head, eyes red, she wandered for the 100th time what the hell she'd been thinking. All gung-ho, jumping on a heli, geed up by the adrenaline of Afghanistan, wanting to prove herself. This wasn't a game, who was she fooling? She was no Infanteer, this was life and death and now she was in the thick of it. Swallowing hard her eyes raked across the other cargo; eye whites peering out into fading light, the sun slinking away over the horizon, taking the last dregs of Soph's courage with it. Hurry up Sanghole, I'm losing my nerve.

Then she was sprinting down the ramp, rounds flying, swallowing screams as she leapt onto the back of the waiting quad bike, a burly looking 18 year old soldier, telling her to get her head the fuck down as he hit the pedal and they screeched into Sanghole. Welcome to hell.

The patrol base gates slammed behind them, Soph lurched forward hard into the back of the Private who'd driven her so skillfully under fire. Both sat panting, he peered over his shoulder, mischievous grin, eyebrow raised,

"You comfy back there?"

Soph blushed, pulling herself back,

"Sorry."

She slid off, almost toppling under the weight of her Bergen, swaying uneasily holding out a hand,

"I'm Captain,"

"We don't bother with rank around here, let's just say the Taleban don't care if you're an Officer or not, they'll still kill you. I'm Turk."

Then he was gone, bike wheeled beside him as if a pushbike from Halfords.

Uneasy and not quite sure what to do next, she stood for a moment taking in her surroundings. The patrol base was tiny, a piece meal wall cobbling chalky stone; wood and brick forming the only barrier and not a confidence inspiring one at that. The Camp was based around a gutted building, few rubbly walls marked out what could have been rooms, creating natural sleeping quarters. She pulled her Bergen up a little higher and walked towards one of the walled areas, hoping to lay claim to what little remained of sleeping space, ideally with some kind of top cover. Although she wasn't sure what was more dangerous, a derelict roof or stray Taleban rounds? As she crossed the base she spotted an ISO container with antennae peppering the roof. Ops room and made her way over.

Craning round the door, she saw a young Lieutenant, a Captain, Warrant Officer and Major gathered round a weathered map spread across a fold away table.

"So they'll be coming from here,"

The Major pointed at some feature on the map.

"Apparently the IED strike was here and they're planning to bring in the damaged vehicle here so Turk can take a look at it and hopefully work his grease monkey magic."

Gravelly voiced, tanned to a near leathery hide, the Major exuded a swarthy calmness learned from weathering too many high stress situations. The Warrant Officer glanced up, piercing blue eyes, cheeks hollowed, furrowed brow, his expression searing. He raised an eyebrow,

"Errm, hi, ahem, I'm Sophie...I mean Captain Jefferson, the Int Officer, here to talk about the situation within this AO?"

All four wheeled around, a near visceral response to hearing a female voice.

The Captain smiled amused, hair a sandy blonde, spikey and not seen a wash in some time. Broad, he looked like a young Robert Redford. Soph swallowed and thought of Tom, stroking his note unconsciously in her pocket. The young Lieutenant seemed the least confident, eyes darting around, anxious to follow the lead of the others, visibly mimicking self-assurance, failing to make it real.

The Major nodded, raking a hand through thinning black hair, his eyes dark brown, serious.

"Welcome Sophie, I'm Major Pat Pearson, this is Captain Ed Chacksfield,"

Ed nodded, eyes dancing, irritating a self-conscious Sophie.

"Lieutenant Adam Clarke,"

Adam smiled nervously,

"And WO1 Jack Cranham."

Jack nodded,

"Ma'am." Drawled without sincerity.

"Think best bet is go and find a gonk space Sophie, grab yourself a brew, then come back and join us. I'm just briefing a convoy we're expecting in, well part of one. There's been an IED strike, one of the vehicles is limping here. Turk, one of our JNCOs is a pretty nifty mechanic and the good news for us is they've got a lorry load of rations and we are running seriously low, so good bit of morale. In fact, didn't you say,"

Pat looked at the Robert Redford lookalike,

"That we're expecting another female?"

Ed laughed,

"Drought to flood eh Pat?"

They all chuckled, Soph blushing again, sweating softly in the heat.

"Yeah, I think some RMP Captain, something to do with some investigation needing ground truth. Know her?"

Ed looked quizzically for a moment, as if chasing a thought,

"What's her name? Something like Lacey, nooo…"

"Tracey?" Sophie almost yelped the name.

"You mean Tracey Bonner?" Her face broke into an enormous grin,

"I know her really well, welsh lass, great laugh, she'll be good for morale too."

"Good, we could all do with more of that. Adam why don't you show Sophie where the bed spaces are? If you can use the word bed around here."

Pat turned back to the table and the three men continued as Adam walked Soph over to one of the walled off areas.

The heat was intense, shimmering above the dusty sand; Soph's shoulder ached from the Bergen, tiredness suddenly engulfing her.

"How long have you been here?"

Adam led her towards a corner of a wall that extended out from the main perimeter. It ended only a few metres from the entrance, anyone could see why it wasn't a popular spot, you were only marginally protected from the entrance gate, noisey, but beggars couldn't be choosers.

As if reading her mind,

"I know it's not ideal, but there's about 25 of us squeezed into this space, personal space is at a premium. You need a wall to give you some cover, but I appreciate your pretty much face onto the entrance. To be fair there isn't much traffic, most patrols go out in the morning and you'll be up by then anyway."

"When are you expecting the convoy in?"

Soph dropped her Bergen, groaning with relief,

"Any minute, same with your mate, think she's supposed to be on the next Chinook from KAF. Anyway, look I need to get back; you ok getting yourself a brew? The cookhouse, is just over there in the corner, if you're lucky there maybe some leftovers from lunch."

Peering over to where Adam pointed, a cam net lay draped over some wall, creating a small alcove, she could smell tea, coffee and cigarette smoke.

Stretched, easing off her shoulders, glad to be up right, feeling more relaxed now she'd met the key people, she pulled out her roll mat and looked out towards the main gate, all of ten metres away she tried to gauge the best position, suddenly a roar of wheels.

"Incoming!"

The gate was pulled open and in raced Turk, billowing dust on his quad. Soph shaded her eyes, tyres screeching to a halt. Then a voice that made her heart soar,

"Fuck me! That was awesome! Thanks mate, what a rush, thought those Taleban bastards had us, you drove like a legend."

Turk already besotted, grinned up at Tracey as she slid off the seat throwing her Bergen on her back. She looked around the base, jaw dropping as she locked eyes on Soph.

"No way!"

More shouting from the sentries was accompanied by the thunder of engines as two 4 tonners gunned in. Rolling into the base, the two lorries barely fit into the small encampment, the gate only just closing behind the second vehicle. Soph covered her ears at the revs and exhaust. Eventually the engines fell silent. The cabin door opened, an exhausted driver dropping out, another slighter figure jumping out the other side, standing, stretching, rubbing her eyes. Tracey wandered around the front of the lorry,

"No way!"

Percy's face strained with exhaustion transformed into joy as she saw her old friend. Clapping arms around each other they laughed with delight as Soph started walking towards them. Suddenly pulling up short, what the hell...? Who was he? Someone shouting sprinting up behind Sophie. Percy and Tracey turning around.

"What the hell?"

Tracey's voice baffled, walking towards the small boy, whose expression was too dark and angry for anyone that young. Then Percy's shouting,

"No! Tracey! Don't!"

The sound of rifle fire then everything went black.

75

SHE COULD TASTE blood, the smell of cordite, urine. Why could she smell piss? Everything seemed to be in slow motion, groans, air acrid from explosive, voices, what the hell had happened? For a moment she lay there, dazed, piecing together the previous minutes. What? A child? A child had wandered in behind the lorry, sliding in between the gates, the sentries on Sangars distracted by all the focus on two women. Sophie had called out to Tracey and Percy, both had wheeled round, exclamations of delight. Tracey then turning back towards the child who had seemed odd, fearless, angry, until Sophie had slowly clocked he was a young teenager, head shaved short, sweating, bulky frame. Why was he so bulky? Then,

"Oh God oh God, get the fuck down!"

Turk who'd brought Tracy in sprinting from behind his bike, ironsight pinned to his eye, rifle trained on the child. Tracey had looked appalled, instinctively protective. Percy had spun round to Sophie, face draining, eyes wide, realisation dawning,

"No! Tracey! Don't!"

She'd sprinted forward to grab Tracey, Sophie had sprinted hadn't she? Wanted to help, help her friend? Felt oddly light on her feet, cooler. Why did that matter? Why was she light on her feet?

"Suicide bomber get down! Get down!"

Percy had wheeled round, Sophie watching as if in slow motion, her own legs suddenly like jelly. This cannot be happening? You read about this in Int reps, this could not be happening. Small boy, so young, so young. How had he got in? Who could do this? What was strapped to his chest?

"Get the fuck down!"

Turk's voice.

Percy grabbing Tracy, pushing her to the ground, the boy's ashen face obliterated in the explosion.

Sophie tasted blood, tried to push herself up, arms weak. Her legs, they weren't responding, she felt tired, woozy. Where were Tracey and Percy? She could hear voices panicked, fear, shouting,

"Casualties!! Medevac!! Call in the MERT, fucking get on with it! Ma'am, breathe breathe!"

"Percy listen to me, hold my hand, come on Ma'am, don't you give out on me now."

Damn it, Sophie couldn't see, couldn't push herself up, too tired…

Turk suddenly beside her,

"Ma'am, look at me…look at me…"

Why was he saying the same thing to her as Percy? What was going on? She looked up, Turk's heart almost breaking as he saw this young Officer's eyes fill with tears, fear.

What's going on? What was that God-awful gurgle? Why couldn't he understand her?

"Ma'am, shushssh, just hold my hand, concentrate on breathing, the MERT is nearly here…"

She coughed, twisted, spitting, red raining down on the ground, terrified she looked up at Turk. Unphased he held her gaze,

"Ma'am you are gonna be ok…"

"Percy! Don't you fucking dare! Get the bloody medic!! Medic!!"

Turk looked up torn then his face awash with relief as Warrant officer Jack Cranham sprinted over,

"I've done as much as I can, it's, there's, just hold the pressure here,"

Where thought Sophie in a daze, hearing a far off voice,

"You've done what you can, go, go!"

Turk sprinted away, leaving Sophie staring into the eyes of Jack,

"All right Ma'am, need you to stay awake now, gotta few minutes to wait here, place is a bit of a mess, we've all been caught out here but you are gonna be just fine, just fine…"

He looked down at this young pretty Officer, her golden brown eyes misty with shock. He couldn't see if she was in pain, Turk had been quick with the morphine, not too much. God what a mess. He almost gagged on his own bile.

"Percy! Look at me! Look at me! It's Mackey and I am NOT driving all that way back on my own, you hear me?!"

Mackey's voice shrill across the compound, emotion straining, Sophie could hear a female sobbing,

Whop! Whop! Whop!

The MERT blowing sand across the debris now littered across the compound. More voices, suddenly a flurry of activity around Sophie, shouting orders, coordination, was that Lieutenant Clarke? He sounded scared Sophie thought dimly…so tired…just a small nap…

"Ma'am! Fucking stay awake! You bloody Officers! I've been in the army 22 years and I tell you where is your fucking backbone? I told you to stay awake, so bloody stay awake!"

Sophie's eyes widened in horror, embarrassed, then angry, how dare…?

"Jack you ready? We're gonna have to make this tight."

Pat Pearson, clear, calm.

"Got it here Sir, on your count."

Sophie looked up, people around here, lifting her now and oh my God who was screaming like that? It was shattering the…then the icy realization it was her, white agony raking through her body like a chainsaw, slicing huge swathes of pain. How? How was this…. what had happened?

She was being jogged, shrill screams with every jolt. Where was Percy? She could hear someone crying, blearily she caught the back of Tracey's head.

"Percy pleeeeasee…."

A senior NCO jogging alongside Percy, his face white, peppered with red spots.

Sophie turned, wanting Jack, wanting the security.

"…Help me."

Jack there, holding her hand as they ran her up the ramp, surrounded by medics, mask on her face, turning her head to the side seeing Percy next to her, unconscious, limp like a puppet, her face almost angelic, the ragged stump where her left arm used to be, blood soaking the blanket, her leg a ragged angle.

Sophie groaned,

"Oh Jesus, oh Jesus."

What was wrong with her? She wanted to move her hand, her legs weren't moving. Why weren't they moving? She coughed spattering the mask with blood, pulled off her face, replaced with a fresh one.

"Pleassshhh…" She hissed to Jack.

He knelt beside her as the Chinook lifted, the ping of Taleban rounds as they gain height, the big bird taking them higher.

Jack looked at her, his face etched with pain, exhausted, he couldn't disguise his own fear, this was as bad as it got.

"Pleasshhh…"

Then she remembered. The boy detonating, Turk trying to shoot him before the suicide vest could explode. The chilling rage on the teenager's face, horror on Percy's as she saw Sophie's alarm, understood her warning and then was toppling Tracey, the blast catching her side and tossing Percy high into the air like a rag doll, just as Sophie, Sophie who'd been rolling out her roll mat, Sophie who'd been prepping her sleep area, Sophie who'd dumped her combat body armour thinking she'd be safe, thinking she could just rest for a minute. Sophie who'd run to help, so deliciously light on her feet, wearing no body armour. Sophie who had caught the full brunt of the blast and been blown backwards like a newspaper in the wind, her stomach ripped out and hips shattered so badly they barely held together, her legs limp. Sophie who'd saved her friends and was now looking at Jack remembering the sequence of events before she slid gratefully into the blessed oblivion of darkness, clutching a small thumbed crumpled note, until grip loosened, it slipped from her bloodied hand, flitting across the floor of the heli and blown out into the sky.

76

THE MED TEAM were grim faced. Hands scrubbed, red raw...two females coming in, life-changing injuries. There was nothing to talk about. They knew the drill; every second counted. Cutting edge technology helped, the extreme injuries that they faced on a regular basis meant that trauma care in Bastion was the best in the world. Here lessons yielded experience that got results, that got equipment. The two young Lieutenant Colonel surgeons stood side by side, they'd talked about who would focus on whom, where their skills best suited the injuries described. Information was patchy. One female had lost an arm, possibly spinal injury and her leg was hanging by ligaments. The other female had lost almost all of her intestines; stomach punched through to her spine, spleen obliterated, hips still in place, just...

Whop! Whop! Whop!

The tremor of adrenaline through the group was like a shot of caffeine. Eyes widened, irises focused, feet twitchy.

Once the Chinook landed, both casualties would be transferred into the ambulances on standby. Any second there'd be the scream of sirens, dust signaling their arrival.

Wheels squealed to a halt.

"Female...Cat A, one arm severed, no sign of limb, spinal movement nil..."

The surgeons nodded, one jogging beside each patient, taking in every detail, blood group, pulse, vital signs, responsiveness, both unconscious. Damn. That wasn't good.

Boom! They burst through the swing doors, swabs holding wounds, falling to the floor red rags marking a path, packets of fresh blood hanging ready, transfusions almost immediate, blood loss lethal.

"Surgery, stat!"

The surgeon held out his arms, a nurse pulling on gloves, helping him with his mask, glancing at the girl, so young, prone on the gurney, her body a mangled mess.

The other surgeon leaning over his blonde patient, inspecting the arm stub, looking at the side of her body, her hipbone jutting out, buttock blown off, femur exposed. He winced: this was going to be a long night.

"Let's get on with it."

77

THE DOOR WAS thrown open, bubbly blonde grinning at him,

"Can I help?"

Dan swallowed,

"My name is Captain Dan Grey, I was hoping to speak to Mr and Mrs Jefferson and Mr and Mrs Brooks?"

"Jesus! How the...how did you know they were here? Oh my god it's Sophie!

What? *And* Percy? Mum...!"

Her voice shrill, terrified, made Dan wish he was anywhere but there.

Thundering footsteps then a sea of anxious faces on the doorstep, staring at Dan. People who only moments before were enjoying a glass of Chablis, sharing pride over the achievements of their daughters, delighted to have made such good friends during their daughter's careers.

"I,"

Dan swallowed,

"I need you both to come with me. Now. Your daughters they are both in SellyOaks, both have been injured. Seriously. I'll drive you, but if you would like more of you to come please follow. I need to speak to Mr and Mrs Brooks and Mr and Mrs Jefferson separately."

Mr Jefferson, tall, aquine nose, intelligent brown eyes ushered Dan in, calming the storm of questions with a hand.

"Let this young man do his job. Let him speak."

They turned, four parents, hearts pierced with terror, this young Captain holding their future in his hands.

Dan breathed; he'd thought carefully about this on the drive up, how to choreograph this bit, who should take primacy? There was simply no way to gauge. The severity of the injuries was equal.

"There is no fair way to put this, so if I could just default to the alphabet as the best judge of who I brief first? I'm sorry, it's clumsy but the best I can do. I'll keep it short because we need to drive. Soon."

Mr and Mrs Brooks followed Dan into the kitchen led by Mr Jefferson. Mrs Jefferson stayed ashen faced in the front room unable to move, clutching her daughter's hand.

Mr Jefferson nodded, leaving all three alone in the warmth, an Aga throwing out heat in the chill of the evening.

Dan held their gaze, Mrs Brooks, clutching her husband's arm, he, roundfaced, balding: farmers, solid stock, tough and tender people. Why was he having to do this to them?

"Your daughter was involved in a suicide attack at the patrol base she was visiting,"

Gasps. Mrs Brooks' muffled sobs.

"Sustaining life changing injuries. She has lost an arm, her buttock has been hit badly by the blast and damage to her left leg."

The blood literally drained from Mr Brooks's face, he closed his eyes. Mrs Brooks eyes an almost turquoise blue simply stared, as if her very life had been sucked away.

"She is on life support in SellyOaks. I'm so sorry, but I need you to prepare yourself to say good bye."

Dan bit his lip,

"Please, excuse my crassness, but I'll leave you to absorb this whilst I speak to Mr and Mrs Jefferson."

He left them both frozen, almost stumbling out of the kitchen. He could not fucking believe this. CNO was bad enough, but a double whammy? On his own? This bloody sucked. I cannot wait to hand in my papers muttering to himself, filling with dread as he made his way back to the Jeffersons.

They stood huddled in the room, Mr Jefferson stiffly upright, his face fixed, expression inscrutable. Mrs Jefferson sat on the edge of the sofa, springing up at Dan's arrival, her daughter by her side, the silence in the room deafening.

"Mr and Mrs Jefferson,"

He nodded weakly at their daughter embarrassed he didn't know her name,

"Tess, I'm Tess."

"I'm going to keep this brief because we need to move. Your daughter, your sister was caught in the same suicide bomb attack as Mr and Mrs Brooks' daughter. Your daughter has suffered life changing injuries, losing a kidney…"

"Oh God!"

Mr Jefferson caught his wife as she staggered, braced by her husband she looked at Dan as if he were aiming a pistol between her eyes. Dan felt sick,

"Severe intestinal damage, including her colon and spleen, spinal trauma and her hips have been dislocated. She is on life support at SellyOaks. I need you to prepare to say goodbye. I'll wait by the front door. I am so sorry."

Dan turned, closing the door, hearing the sobs and sound of heartbreak in his wake. Dazed he almost didn't hear his phone, moving out of earshot to both parties, he scrambled to answer. Pulling open the door he stood on the doorstep, drizzle dampening his face, nodding at the news. They needed to go. Now.

As he turned, urgency etched on his face all four parents met him.

"Ok, ready?"

"That phone call?"

Mr Brooks, a foot shorter than Mr Jefferson, let the question hang in the air.

"Yes, we need to get a move on. Let's go."

78

Six months later

HEDLEY COURT IS the Army's rehabilitation centre. Located in Surrey, the surroundings are a soothing balm to the personal struggle that epitomizes the lives of many of those in recovery. Humming the latest number one on the charts, Tracey steered her VW van down the drive, grinning as a squirrel scampered across the road. Slowing she pulled into a parking space, sitting for a moment, hearing the engine ticking over as it cooled. She'd lost count of how many times she'd visited. When she was in Germany probably about once a fortnight, now back in the UK working at Northwood made the journey a lot easier, something for which she was grateful, though she would have travelled no matter the distance.

Pulling open the huge wooden door to the front entrance, she smiled at the sound of laughter and healthy banter, the screech of trainers on wooden floors. Her regular visits made her impervious to the bleached corridors, the smell of trainers, the stench of sweat. The front door opened to a carpeted reception area, which led up to the rehab suites on either side. The largest room by far was the gym, decked out with cutting edge equipment pumping loud music punctuated by bursts of laughter.

Tracey paused at the door watching her friend throwing a med ball to Mackey. Mackey who was always here. Unlike some. Trace's mood darkened for a moment.

"Call that a throw yer big Jessie? Pah can tell yer just looking for sympathy…"

Her face glowing, Percy laughed. Blonde hair scraped back, she caught Mackey's toss easily, her left prosthetic comfortable, near natural. It was state of the art, bionic arm with a fully articulated hand that was wired into Percy's nervous system by a subtle web of optics hidden under her jumper. Her tracksuit bottoms were still skewed where half her backside had been blown off, but plastic surgery was going to take care of that in the next month. Apparently the desire for J-Lo bums had made buttock cosmetic surgery quite in demand. Who knew?

Tracey was in awe, every time she visited. Her friend's grit and determination through pain that was hard to imagine had been humbling.

Glancing over, Percy's eyes sparkled with delight,

"Hey! Tracey catch!"

She flung the med ball with enough thrust to make Tracy grunt.

"How goes it you two?"

Mackey blushed. His devotion to Percy was undying, the bond between them profound. Tracey didn't know if it had grown into anything else, but the love that shone in Mackey's eyes was hard to miss.

"Yeah really good,"

Percy ambled over,

"We ready to go?"

"Yeah, ready when you are?"

"You ok Mackey? You gonna hang around for a while? We're going up North? But I'll be back tonight?"

Tracey's heart squeezed as the question hung in the air. Would Mackey leave? Seriously? Was the Pope catholic?

Mackey tried abysmally to disguise his puppy like adoration,

"Well pretty busy y'know, but…"

He coughed, trying not to grin,

"But guess I may be here when you get back."

Percy squealed trotting over to him, unashamedly throwing her arm and prosthetic around him firmly. He pushed her off half-heartedly,

"Get away with yer…"

As the two girls walked outside, Tracey resisted the urge to help her friend with her coat. The prosthetic was still new, Percy feeling her way, but her pride not welcoming any help, as Tracey had discovered, wincing at the memories.

"So?"

Percy clambered into Tracey's van, a flash of pain skittering across her face, forgetting for an instant the lack of cushioning on her butt. Tracey grimaced; bit her lip, turning the key, keeping silent. They'd been here before, words of sympathy didn't go down well.

"S'all good."

The pain easing, Percy speaking more for Tracey's benefit than her own.

The journey was familiar, only a couple of hours. Sometimes peppered with chat, other times easy silence. Today wasn't. Today was tense.

"Have you heard anything?"

"No, I've not had a chance to speak to anyone. I've…I've been warned off again."

"Oh shit mate, seriously?"

Tracey nodded,

"Yep, few months then back to Helmand."

Percy stared out of the window, demons whispering around the edges of her mind.

"Your Counsellor ok with that?"

Tracey's jaw clenched.

"I'm ok with that and that's what counts."

It had been a sore point for a long time; Tracey surviving, unscathed, yet battered by waves of dark and tortuous dreams, causing pain more enduring than a lost limb. Survivor's guilt; pernicious in its grip.

The miles fell away, Percy flicking radio channels, Trace lost in thoughts about PDT. She indicated to overtake a VW Golf that may as well have been going backwards.

"So, any…?"

The question hung unfinished. Percy blinked, looking away. She barely recalled much of the casevac from PB Sanghole. How she'd woken up in SellyOaks surrounded by family, searching the sea of anxious faces, stunned at the absence of the one person she'd thought would have been unwavering. Rehabilitation had been excruciating. Harrowing times, pierced with thoughts of a more permanent escape, languishing in too many a dark nights of the soul.

It had shaken her that someone who had been so central, so intimate to her existence, just excused himself from her life. Exit stage left, no reason, no answer, not there. Biting her lip she had her theories, her suspicions, but they made for such disappointing conclusions, that she'd shelved them in a distant part of her mind, visited infrequently, adverse to the predictable sting of betrayal.

Then Mackey. She smiled, Mackey who'd been there from the start, unobtrusive, calm, dependable. Mackey who'd kept his distance in the early days as her parents flapped. Mackey who'd stepped forward more as their visits lessened as her health improved. Mackey who'd realized that although the healing on the outside was progressing, the demons on the inside had nearly destroyed her. Mackey who hadn't let her down.

"Hey, can we leave it?"

The thing was Tracey hadn't left it. Tenacity that served well in her role as RMP was hard to just put to one side. Instead she'd done some digging, phoned some friends, the Army was a small place.

Dan had whistled slow and long when Tracey had outlined her findings. Dan who'd been there for her every step of the way, committed, focused, a total rock, even when her demons had challenged them both.

"He's in the Falklands,"

Dan raised an eyebrow, prompting her to go on,

"Apparently when he heard the news, the full news..."

The scale of Percy's injuries were immense and testimony to her personal grit and courage. The implications however to others less brave would have been daunting and tragically repellent. Just because those serving faced extremities of danger on the battlefield, didn't mean that that same bravery extended to their home life. Cowardice is a trait of all humanity.

"He went straight into his OC, looked him in the eye and asked to be deployed. Duncan knew there had been some trawls so he volunteered himself. He was on a flight within a week. I just…how do I tell Percy?"

Dan's eyes hardened and his tone became uncharacteristically stern. He held Trace by the shoulders,

"Look at me Trace, really look at me,"

Looking into his eyes, slightly unnerved,

"All of this, every last sorry detail, you keep to yourself. Do you hear me? I tell you Trace I will walk out this door now if you even suggest you are going to tell her. No, don't but in just listen. You wanted to know why he didn't stand by her and now you do. You have no idea what Percy's thoughts are on the subject, no baby, you don't."

Trace looked at the floor hurt, Dan's tone softened.

"This is between them. If Percy wants to know she can find out. She is sharp as a tack, but I think right now even she recognizes that there are some things better left unsaid. It's bad enough a bloke who made out he was there for her, showed he had no balls when it counted. The thing is Trace, the good thing? She has a guy now who would walk across flaming coals for her, and that shouldn't be forgotten."

Trace flicked a look at her friend, kicking herself, remembering Dan's words. It just pained her that her friend had been so betrayed, one she threw at her counselor on an almost weekly basis,

"Tracey why is probably the most destructive and useless question in the human vernacular. Perhaps, now, it's time to start asking what can you make of this? Isn't that more empowering?"

Bloody woman had a point. She ground the gears, pulling off the motorway.

"Hey be kind to your little van!"

Percy laughed. Before they knew it Tracey was parking and they fell into silence. They both stood for a moment in the car park, drizzle lightly falling, framing their faces with damp tendrils, matching the darkening mood as they walked towards SellyOaks.

They made their way to the ICU. The Intensive Care Unit where staggering lessons had been learnt in pioneering medical care off the back of seriously injured from Afghanistan. The hush of the ward only pierced by intermittent beeps from life support machines.

79

SLUNG IN A hammock at the rear of the C17, Tom used his leg to rock in sync with the pitch of the aircraft. He was used to the swaying of the bulky plane, often leaving others green with airsickness. Pulling his softie jacket tighter, his eyes flicked to the neon dial of his Sunto, 0215. Not long, maybe a few hours. His stomach heaved with nerves, would that be too late? Not for the first time he castigated himself for not having heard sooner, but God he had tried.

Belize. Posted some six weeks after Sophie had been deployed, Tom and his new Unit were flown by Tristar to support a NATO exercise in Central America. A favourite to test Infantry jungle warfare, Belize had been a hub of training for as long as Tom had been serving. SF, Regular, TA, all ended up in Belize at some point. The trouble was it wasn't exactly an easy place for normal comms. Driving himself to distraction, Tom had pestered the Signals det for any info on how things were in Helmand. Baffled they'd answered Tom's stream of questions every day.

"Nah Tom, you know how it is, if there were casualties, Minimise would have been dropped. What's with you? You know this shit?"

Tom raked a hand over grade one hair, thinning more these days, "I know, it's just...'

He looked away. Just what? There's a girl who may not even remember me? There's a girl who I nearly had something with? What?

He'd been out sweating, batting mozzies for three weeks when he snuck into see the Signals guys again.

"Wondered when you'd come by. There's been an incident. Suicide IED, two female casualties, pretty serious, possibly even Cat 1, no one really knows y'know?"

Blood drained from his face. Time seemed to slow, words slurring. Cat 1? Two females? She was Int, she wouldn't be on the ground, but there was something, he felt it, sick to his stomach.

"Where?"

Barely recognizing his own voice,

"Patrol Base Sanghole. Some young kid snuck in behind a loggie resup, detonated right in the centre of the base…bastard."

Tom nodded, lips pressed, wordless and filed out.

Outside the sun was merciless, blazing heat, dazzling but leaving Tom untouched. He stood eyes closed, face up to the light as if somehow it could burn away this moment and make things ok.

Purgatory. That had been the following months. Tom had tried everything, pleading with his OC, truculence, damn near insubordination but it was no good.

"Tom, I appreciate this is not where you want to be,"

Ramrod straight Tom stared straight ahead in his OC's make shift office. A 6 by 6 heavy canvas tent, some throwback to the 1950s, but it worked, so the Army's logic was why mess with it?

"But this Exercise is where you are needed and will continue to be needed. We've got some SF coming in for a training serial and I need your expertise."

Major Finn smoothed a hand over a bronzed scalp, eyes penetrating but not without sympathy. Built like a tank he didn't need to command presence, his physicality demanded it. So his compassionate side was often came as a surprise. Right now a welcome one, he felt for Tom. He liked this Captain but more than that he respected him and was a little intrigued by him too. He kept a close counsel, tightly reined in, so whatever was eating at him to be like this had to be big, huge. He'd worked hard for him, so payback was only fair, it was right.

"Give me a few months…"

Tom's eyes flicked to Major Finn, grief flickering across his face before his features went blank.

"I will get you back Tom, don't know how, we both know this is a year out here, but I will do my best."

He had taken 4 months, but Major Finn had kept his word and by cover of night, Tom had slipped onto a flight headed back to RAF Linkham, contraband, he was undeclared cargo and everyone on board honoured that.

80

PERCY AND TRACE noticed the difference in the atmosphere almost immediately. Staring through the wide window that gave a bird's eye view of Sophie's room, there were more medical staff than normal gathered around the end of her bed.

Percy and Trace exchanged looks, Percy rubbing her shoulder subconsciously as if soothing a pain. A nurse they recognized caught their eye, excusing herself she seemed to stiffen before ushering the girls to follow her.

"Hey girls, how are you?"

Both nodded, anxiety crippling small talk,

"There is no easy way to say this, but,"

Massaging her hands, the nurse looked at them. Blue eyed, late 30s she had been in this situation more times than she cared to count. Never got any easier. The first had devastated her, cried for days in the staff room when on her breaks, always in private. Now stronger, but not immune, this case, this patient had got to everyone.

"Her parents, they've agreed no resuscitation,"

Trace realized she was gripping Percy's hand.

"And if she doesn't wake from this coma then next week..."

Tracey gasped,

"You are kidding me?? What the...?"

Percy frowned before Tracey finished, leaving her red faced, shaking her head, eyes filling,

"Nurse, I thought the coma was serving her? I thought the doctor had said given the amount of transplants she's had it was her body's way of self- preservation? What's changed?"

The nurse sat down as if weighed by the question itself.

"She's not responding to any medication to wake her Percy. We've tried normal stimulation, you girls have been an amazing incentive for her to wake with your visits, her family have been agonizingly attentive but for some reason…well, it's just not happening."

She looked up, blue eyes full of compassion,

"There is no reason for her not to wake girls, it's just like she doesn't want to?"

81

THE C17 LANDING was slick and Tom was down the ramp and passing through to the car bays, it wasn't like he had baggage to collect. Despite the early hour, the Corporal was all business, paperwork signed, Mod90 checked and Tom was on the road within thirty minutes. After all time was of the essence.

Tom hardly registered the traffic. It was still early so cars were patchy. Grateful for the drive, he prepared himself for what was to come.

The last four months had been hideous. Waking bathed in sweat, his dreams peppered with images of Sophie, always the same; she reaching for him, calling his name, then obliterated before his eyes. It was horrific. It was his every night.

News had dripped through cataloguing the progress of the two females. One had lost an arm, the other more catastrophic internal injuries, both lucky to be alive, both strong female Officers.

After a while Tom had cocooned himself from updates. Sometimes the news was accurate, other times salacious gossip, reveling in the grotesqueness of what had happened, the sheer scale of the devastation. Tom had hoped that somehow Sophie would hang on. That in a way beyond reasoning she would know he was coming, doing everything he could to be there, that nothing could keep him away.

82

EITHER SIDE OF her bed, listening to the metronomic heaving of her ventilator and the steady pips of her heart rate monitor Percy and Tracey gazed at Sophie in silence.

Her skin was clear, hair silky, framing a face that seemed peaceful, just resting, hard to imagine that this sylph like girl had had most of her internal organs replaced, her heart even stopping on the operating table not once but twice during the multitude of procedures.

"So why won't you wake up? After all that why not?"

Percy looked over at her friend, mind so troubled, her face freeze framing sorrow, the impending loss of her friend. She reached over and held Tracey's hand and for a moment, the three of them sat in silence, nothing to be said.

83

PULLING INTO THE car park, the clouds ominous, spattering rain creating a matrix on Tom's windscreen. He looked up at the towering obelisk that was SellyOaks, his heart squeezing that Sophie had been inside for so long without him. Never again, he swore, that is never happening again. Pulling his green softie close, he smoothed on his beret and stepped out of the car.

84

"WHAT DO YOU want to do?"

Percy noticed her voice shook, that the moment had taken a surreal edge to it. She swallowed, her arm ached, everything ached. God she was tired.

Tracey looked up at Percy mournfully. Whilst she could hardly bear to acknowledge it, she had to get back to the Mess, pack, pre-deployment training called and although in this moment it seemed utterly inconsequential, Tracey didn't know what else to do but cling to routine. Yet leaving? Her heart ached, this could not be happening.

"I don't know what to say Perce,"

Eyes flicking to Sophie, so peaceful, oblivious to the emotional tumult around her,

"It seems obscene to leave knowing....well,"

She took a breath to rein in the ocean of grief washing through her,

"I don't know what else to do? There's nothing we can do."

Percy nodded, rising from her chair, she stroked Sophie's hand, her skin warm, normal.

"I think we have to go, it's up to her now."

Flanking their friend, Percy and Tracey bowed heads, each reaching for Sophie's hands, squeezing them, telling her she was loved, always would be. Then in silence, they filed out of the room.

85

TOM HATED HOSPITALS. He'd been CNO and CVO too many times; never good news here. Today however, today he was going to change that.

He didn't notice the admiring glances, the looks of curiosity a soldier attracted. Desert boots, softie jacket, beret expertly shaped. Every inch the professional.

An educated guess saw him head for the ICU. A creeping apprehension slunk up his spine. Would they be bureaucratic? Stop him seeing her? He didn't have much in the way of ID and obviously wasn't family. He set his mouth in a thin line. Didn't matter, nothing was going to stop him. He'd come too far.

Stepping out of the lift two girls, faces white as sheets passed him. One of them looked at him quizzically, her arm slightly distorted. Prosthetic Tom figured, he wondered for a minute as they passed, then his eyes narrowed in on reception and he strode on.

Percy looked after the uniformed stranger. SF maybe? But wasn't that a loggie capbadge? Looked like he'd just stepped off a plane. The lift doors closed, her eyes trained on his back. Something whispered in her mind.

"Sophie Jefferson?"

The receptionist blushed. Eighteen, new to the job, she wasn't used to gorgeous men asking her questions. For a second she forgot her own name. Blushing, flicking through the register, she felt his gaze burning down on her.

"She'll have been here a while, military casualty?"

329

Tom tried to rein in his irritation, glancing up the corridor, gauging where she might be, which room? Could she sense him? Did she know he was here? He almost smiled at his own superstition.

"Ahh yes, Sophie, she's in room 103 half way down on the right. Have you been here before? It's not really a room, so much as cordoned area if you know what I mean? It needs to be easily accessible, there are a lot of machines in there since she's on ventilation still after all her transplants…"

Tom's face tensed, heart aching,

"Transplants?"

The nurse cocked her head, confused,

"Sorry who are you again?"

Sensing her anxiety Tom put on his best game face, charm offensive. She didn't stand a chance.

"I'm a friend, well special friend,"

He couldn't quite bring himself to wink, even for this purpose that would have been crass. Still he needed to put this issue to bed, he didn't want a flying visit.

"I've just flown in from Ops, I'm military…"

He smiled, shrugging to acknowledge the clothes a give away. The nurse relaxed.

"Oh right, no problem. I guess you've come to say goodbye?"

Tom had been on Ops, seen Tours, casualties, lost friends to IEDs, come damn near close himself, but none of it compared to the impact those words had on him that moment. Clutching the side of reception, narrowing his eyes, biting his cheek to check himself,

"Goodbye?'

The nurse might have been young, but she was astute and realized her mistake.

"I'm sorry…?

"Tom, Tom Howing"

"Mr Howing, Sophie has just been put on the do not resuscitate list, which is significant because she's flat lined in surgery twice. I, I'm sorry I thought you would know and…well there's one more thing."

Tom felt the air inside escape as if it couldn't bear to hear anymore.

"Her parents are so distraught that they've asked for her ventilator to be turned off next week. Guess,"

The nurse toyed with a pen, mixed emotions at the decision by people she didn't know. Still how could you?

"Some people can't cope to see a loved one not responding."

"Can I see her?"

Tom's question was so gentle, so quiet the nurse almost didn't hear.

"Course, sorry, yes follow me, do you want to speak to a doctor?"

Tom passed critical patient after critical patient, a spaghetti junction of tubes and machines nestled around each patient. Eerily quiet and then they were there and his heart almost leapt out of his chest.

The nurse left Tom staring through the glass, eventually finding the courage to slide the door open, and stand at the bedside of a girl he'd known for such a short time but had had such a profound impact on him.

Instinctively he pulled off his beret,

"Hey you…"

He reached out, noticed his hand was trembling, took hers.

"Sorry I took so long, s'been a bit tricky getting transport, but excuses excuses eh?"

He reached over, exquisitely gentle, softly pulling a strand of hair back, stroking it down her cheek, religiously tender.

"So guess the lattes around here are rubbish? I missed you Sophie, it's Tom…"

86

TRACEY WAS IN tears, Percy preoccupied. The lift doors slid open, Tracey walking as if a zombie.

"Wait."

Baulking outside the lift, Percy couldn't get the face of the Army bloke out of her head. It was too much of a coincidence. Them being there, then another military guy pitches up? At an ICU? Granted this was SellyOaks but something didn't add up, or it did. God yes it did.

Suddenly Percy's eyes lit up,

"Trace, we need to go back"

"Wha..? No, Perce…it's,"

Tracey, a broken woman shook her head. Bless Percy, she'd clearly lost it. Grief affected people in different ways.

"No seriously,"

Percy grabbed her arm,

"Didn't you see that bloke?"

"What bloke?"

"The Loggie, softie, stepped into the lift as we got out? Didn't Soph say there was some bloke?"

"Some bloke?" Tracey looked at Percy blankly,

"Seriously Perce, I th…wait, a bloke? Yes she did didn't she? Back on PDT? Yes! She went all coy on us. But Perce, so maybe this bloke is visiting Soph? So what? I mean it's lovely, but bless him, it's all a bit late. Poor bloke is gonna be on the receiving end of some pretty shitty news? Should leave him to it shouldn't we? Bit of privacy? What are you suggesting?"

Percy deflated looked out at the pouring rain, visitors pushing past them to get to the lifts. She drifted to a window. God things had been so hard for so long, for all of them. She really thought that they were coming through the worst of it. What with Mackey and her, she smiled to herself. Even Trace seemed to be getting it together and her bloke had been a total rock. It was Soph's turn now and certainly not to bloody die.

Getting a second wind she whipped around to a greyfaced Trace, baffled.

"So the nurse said Sophie wasn't responding?"

"Yes?"

"And that it was really up to her to wake up?"

"I was there too Perce thanks, not a lobotomized monkey y'know."

Percy hugged her friend.

"I think this bloke is the wake up call that Sophie has needed. Right, c'mon let's get back up there."

87

"So tough tour? I thought about you, got posted before you got back, didn't know how to contact you."

Tom looked at her, his eyes welling,

"It's been hard. I missed you. I never thought this would happen. Soph, we'd only just begun..."

He fell silent, rain hammering outside the window, the bleep of the heart monitor counting the seconds down. Until what? Until when? Someone deciding that Sophie had had her allotted time and now it was up?

Tom shook his head. How could anyone decide after what she'd been through that she couldn't take all the time in the world to return? He wasn't sure if he'd have held on so long in her place.

"I'm just gonna sit here for a while if that's ok with you? No hurry, you just take your time, all the time in the world."

Tom unzipped his softie, slid back in the arm chair and watched her. Breathe in, breathe out. Breathe in, breathe out. She was mesmerizing. Always had been.

He felt his eyelids heavy, struggling, felt almost sacrilegious to come all this way and sleep? Still, he was here, finally with her, he could rest now, just rest.

The fluttering of Sophie's fingers was so subtle a normal person might have missed it. Tom wasn't normal. Tom was hyper vigilant and despite being in the latter stages of exhaustion training was training.

Bolt upright he stared at her hand, willing it to move again, barely breathing, hope itself keeping him still. Nothing. Christ had he imagined it? Sleep deprivation mixed with obsession creating a heady cocktail of hallucinations? "Please."

Not realizing he was whispering it aloud. Then, subtle but real, her hand moved again and slowly, achingly slowly, months of stasis making movement awkward, laboured, Sophie turned her head and their eyes locked, a perfect tear rolling down her cheek.

ABOUT THE AUTHOR

LA CLARKE SERVED for 10 years as a Military Intelligence Officer in the British Army, commanding troops in Northern Ireland and Afghanistan as well as serving on the Staff at the Royal Military Academy Sandhurst. She now lives in Gloucestershire working as a consultant in Leadership and Change.

Lightning Source UK Ltd.
Milton Keynes UK
UKHW010612140719
346061UK00001B/49/P